My Little Pony

Friends Forever

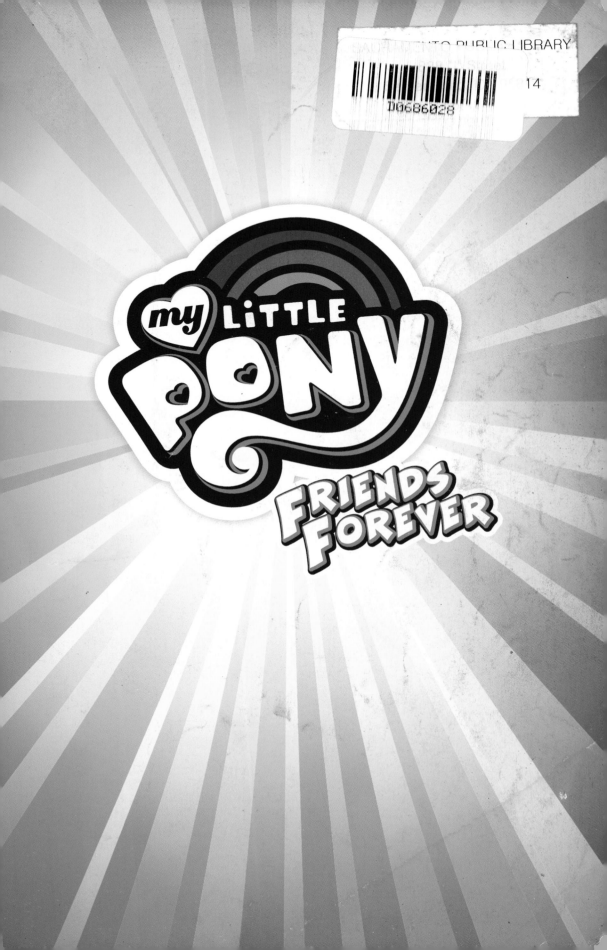

My Little Pony

Friends Forever

Rarity & Maud Pie

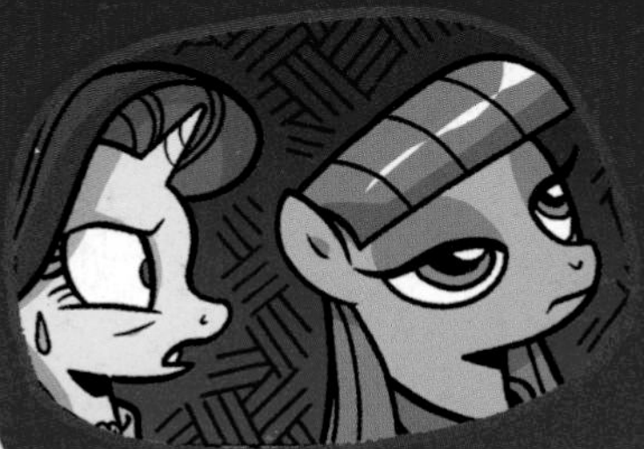

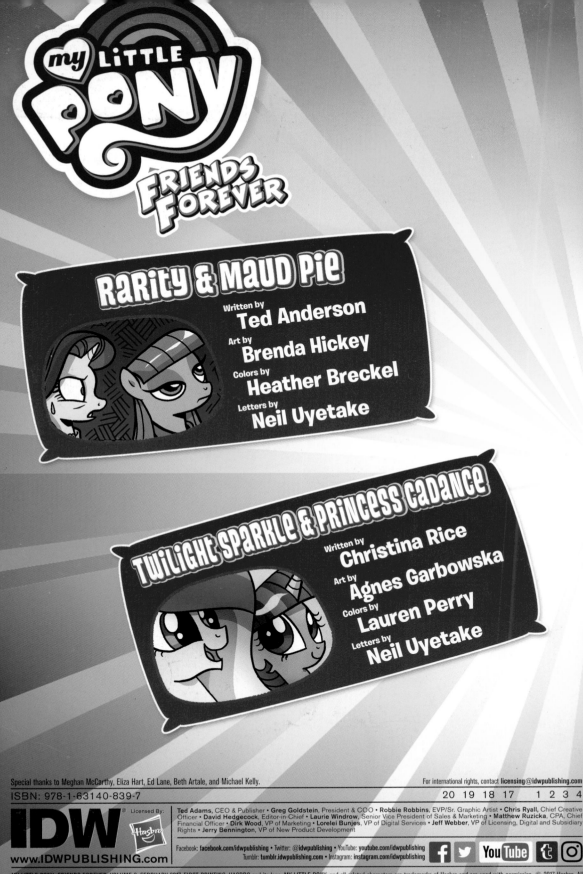

Written by
Ted Anderson
Art by
Brenda Hickey
Colors by
Heather Breckel
Letters by
Neil Uyetake

Twilight Sparkle & Princess Cadance

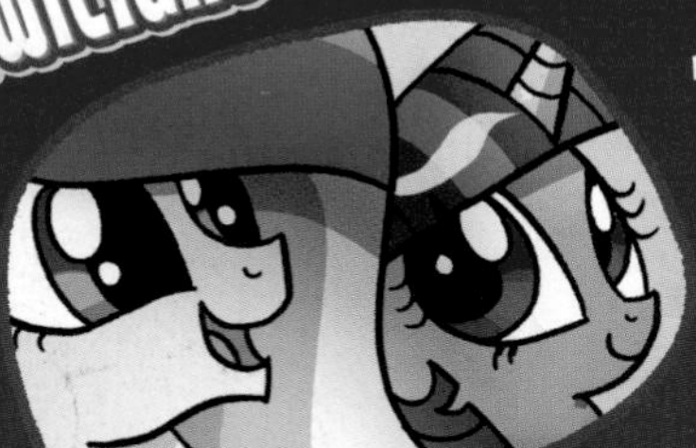

Written by
Christina Rice
Art by
Agnes Garbowska
Colors by
Lauren Perry
Letters by
Neil Uyetake

Special thanks to Meghan McCarthy, Eliza Hart, Ed Lane, Beth Artale, and Michael Kelly.

For international rights, contact **licensing@idwpublishing.com**

ISBN: 978-1-63140-839-7

20 19 18 17 1 2 3 4

IDW® Licensed By: Hasbro

www.IDWPUBLISHING.com

Ted Adams, CEO & Publisher • **Greg Goldstein**, President & COO • **Robbie Robbins**, EVP/Sr. Graphic Artist • **Chris Ryall**, Chief Creative Officer • **David Hedgecock**, Editor-in-Chief • **Laurie Windrow**, Senior Vice President of Sales & Marketing • **Matthew Ruzicka**, CPA, Chief Financial Officer • **Dirk Wood**, VP of Marketing • **Lorelei Bunjes**, VP of Digital Services • **Jeff Webber**, VP of Licensing, Digital and Subsidiary Rights • **Jerry Bennington**, VP of New Product Development

Facebook: **facebook.com/idwpublishing** • Twitter: **@idwpublishing** • YouTube: **youtube.com/idwpublishing**
Tumblr: **tumblr.idwpublishing.com** • Instagram: **instagram.com/idwpublishing**

Originally published as MY LITTLE PONY: FRIENDS FOREVER issues #29–33.

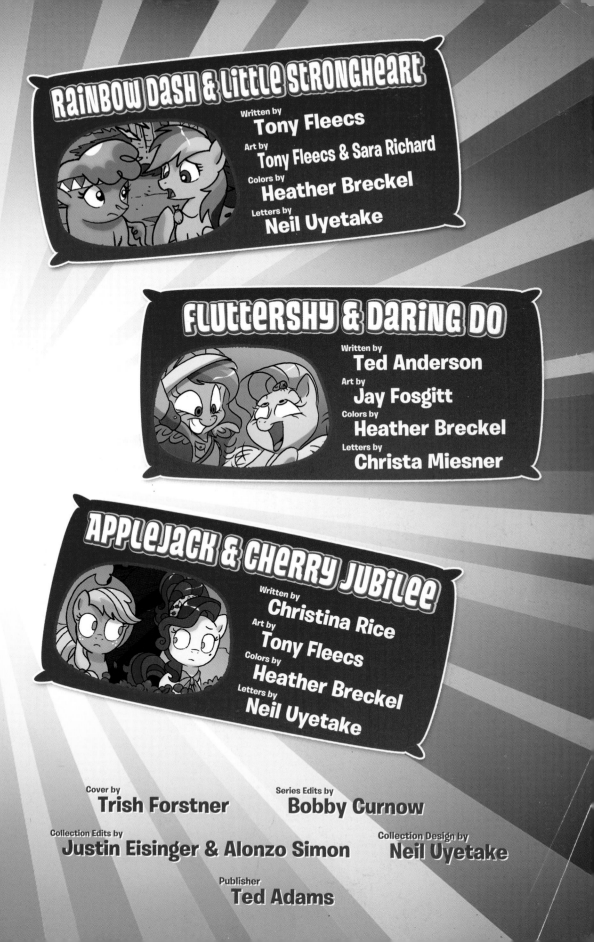

Rainbow Dash & Little Strongheart

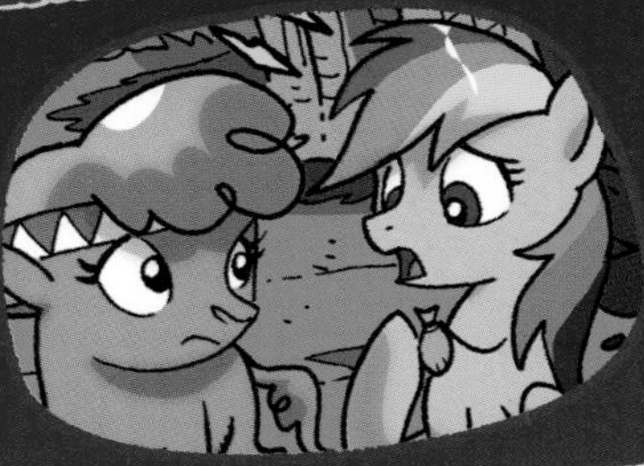

Written by
Tony Fleecs
Art by
Tony Fleecs & Sara Richard
Colors by
Heather Breckel
Letters by
Neil Uyetake

Fluttershy & Daring Do

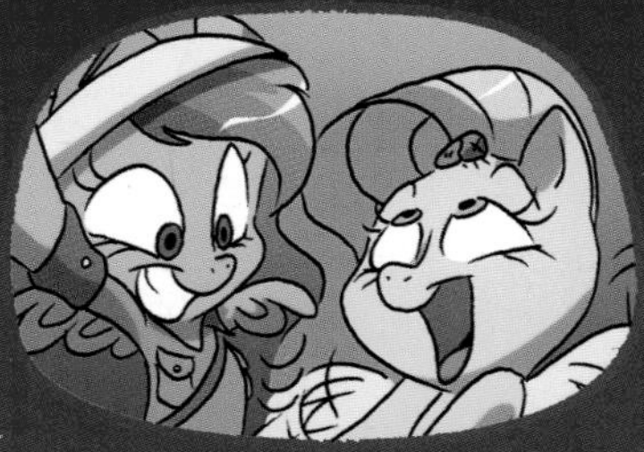

Written by
Ted Anderson
Art by
Jay Fosgitt
Colors by
Heather Breckel
Letters by
Christa Miesner

Applejack & Cherry Jubilee

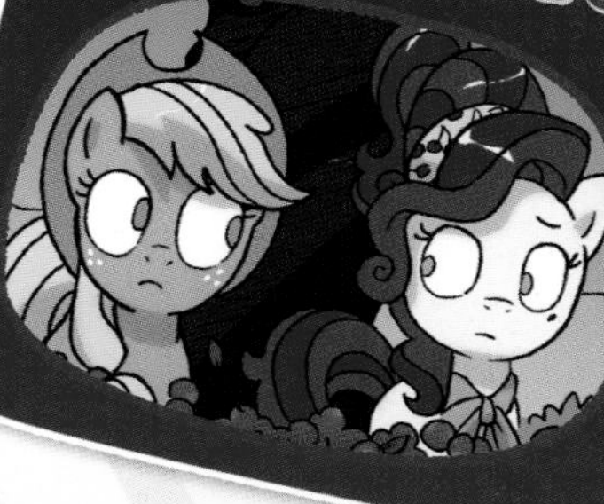

Written by
Christina Rice
Art by
Tony Fleecs
Colors by
Heather Breckel
Letters by
Neil Uyetake

Cover by
Trish Forstner

Series Edits by
Bobby Curnow

Collection Edits by
Justin Eisinger & Alonzo Simon

Collection Design by
Neil Uyetake

Publisher
Ted Adams

Rarity & Maud Pie

art by
Brenda Hickey

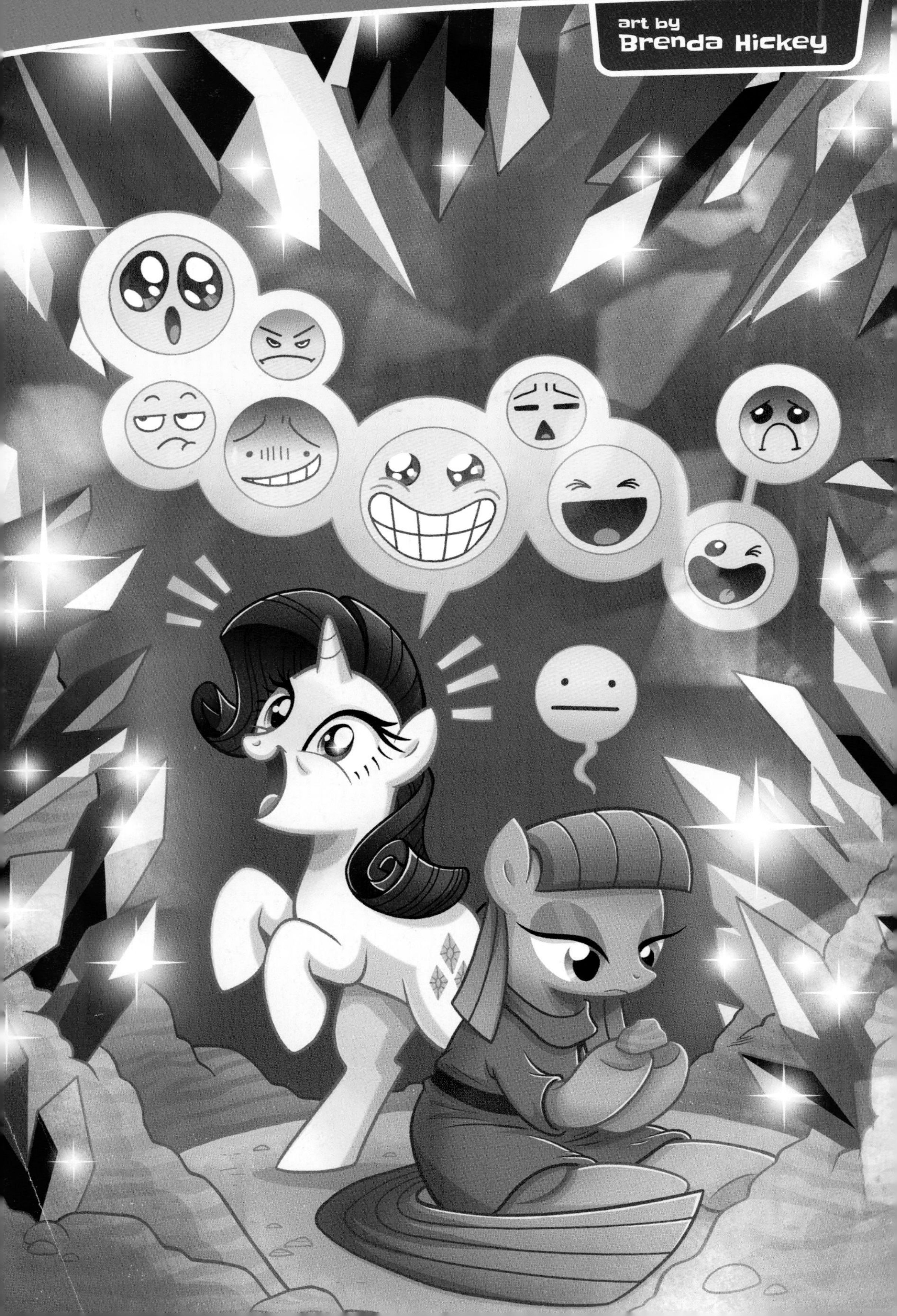

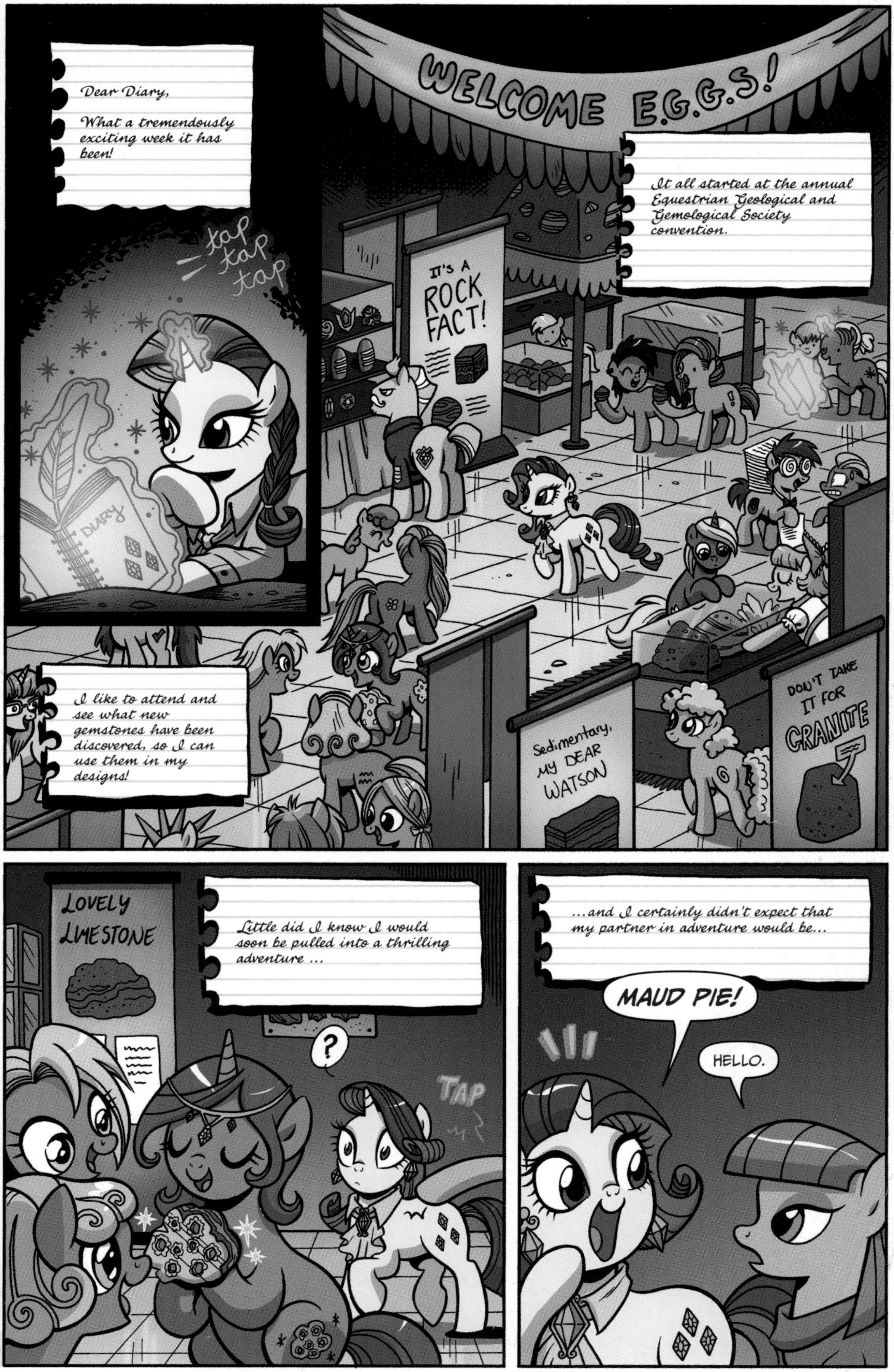
Dear Diary,
What a tremendously exciting week it has been!
tap tap tap
DIARY
WELCOME E.G.G.S!
It all started at the annual Equestrian Geological and Gemological Society convention.
IT'S A ROCK FACT!
I like to attend and see what new gemstones have been discovered, so I can use them in my designs!
Sedimentary, MY DEAR WATSON
DON'T TAKE IT FOR GRANITE
LOVELY LIMESTONE
Little did I know I would soon be pulled into a thrilling adventure ...
?
TAP
...and I certainly didn't expect that my partner in adventure would be...
MAUD PIE!
HELLO.

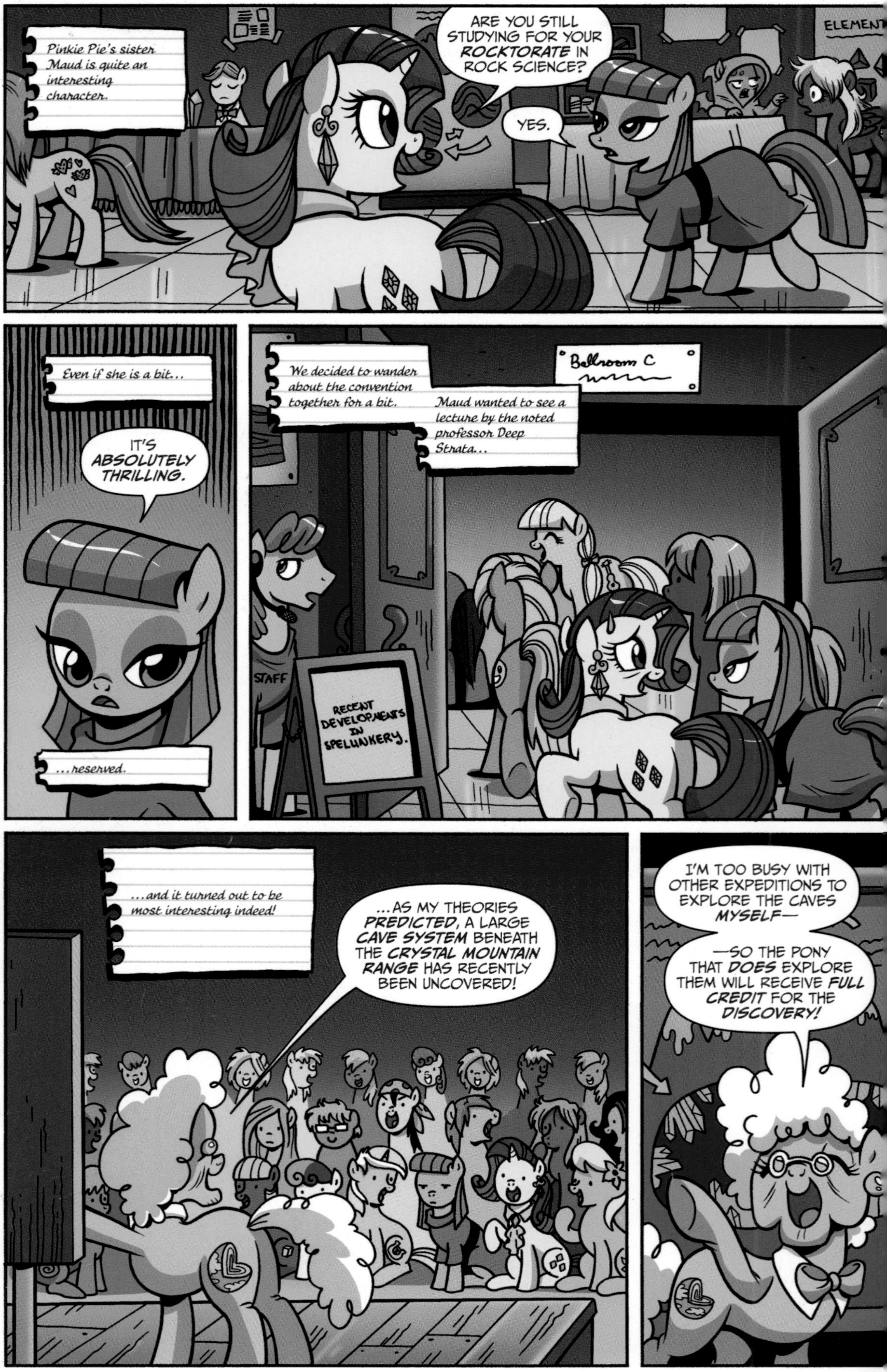

Pinkie Pie's sister Maud is quite an interesting character.
ARE YOU STILL STUDYING FOR YOUR ROCKTORATE IN ROCK SCIENCE?
YES.
ELEMENT
Even if she is a bit...
IT'S ABSOLUTELY THRILLING.
...reserved.
We decided to wander about the convention together for a bit.
Maud wanted to see a lecture by the noted professor Deep Strata...
Ballroom C
STAFF
RECENT DEVELOPMENTS IN SPELUNKERY.
...and it turned out to be most interesting indeed!
...AS MY THEORIES PREDICTED, A LARGE CAVE SYSTEM BENEATH THE CRYSTAL MOUNTAIN RANGE HAS RECENTLY BEEN UNCOVERED!
I'M TOO BUSY WITH OTHER EXPEDITIONS TO EXPLORE THE CAVES MYSELF—
—SO THE PONY THAT DOES EXPLORE THEM WILL RECEIVE FULL CREDIT FOR THE DISCOVERY!

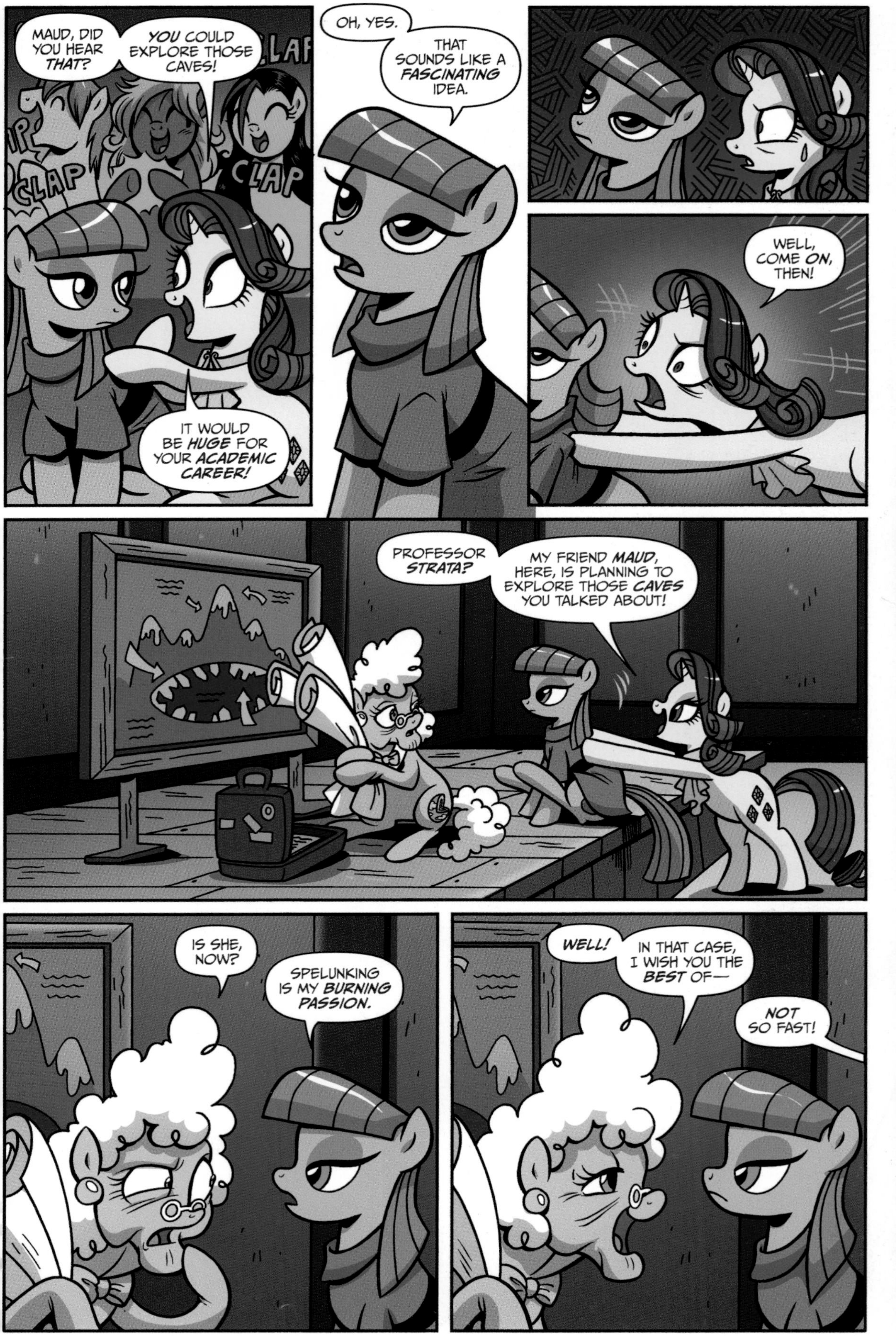
MAUD, DID YOU HEAR THAT?
YOU COULD EXPLORE THOSE CAVES!
CLAP
CLAP
CLAP
IT WOULD BE HUGE FOR YOUR ACADEMIC CAREER!
OH, YES.
THAT SOUNDS LIKE A FASCINATING IDEA.
WELL, COME ON, THEN!
PROFESSOR STRATA?
MY FRIEND MAUD, HERE, IS PLANNING TO EXPLORE THOSE CAVES YOU TALKED ABOUT!
IS SHE, NOW?
SPELUNKING IS MY BURNING PASSION.
WELL!
IN THAT CASE, I WISH YOU THE BEST OF—
NOT SO FAST!

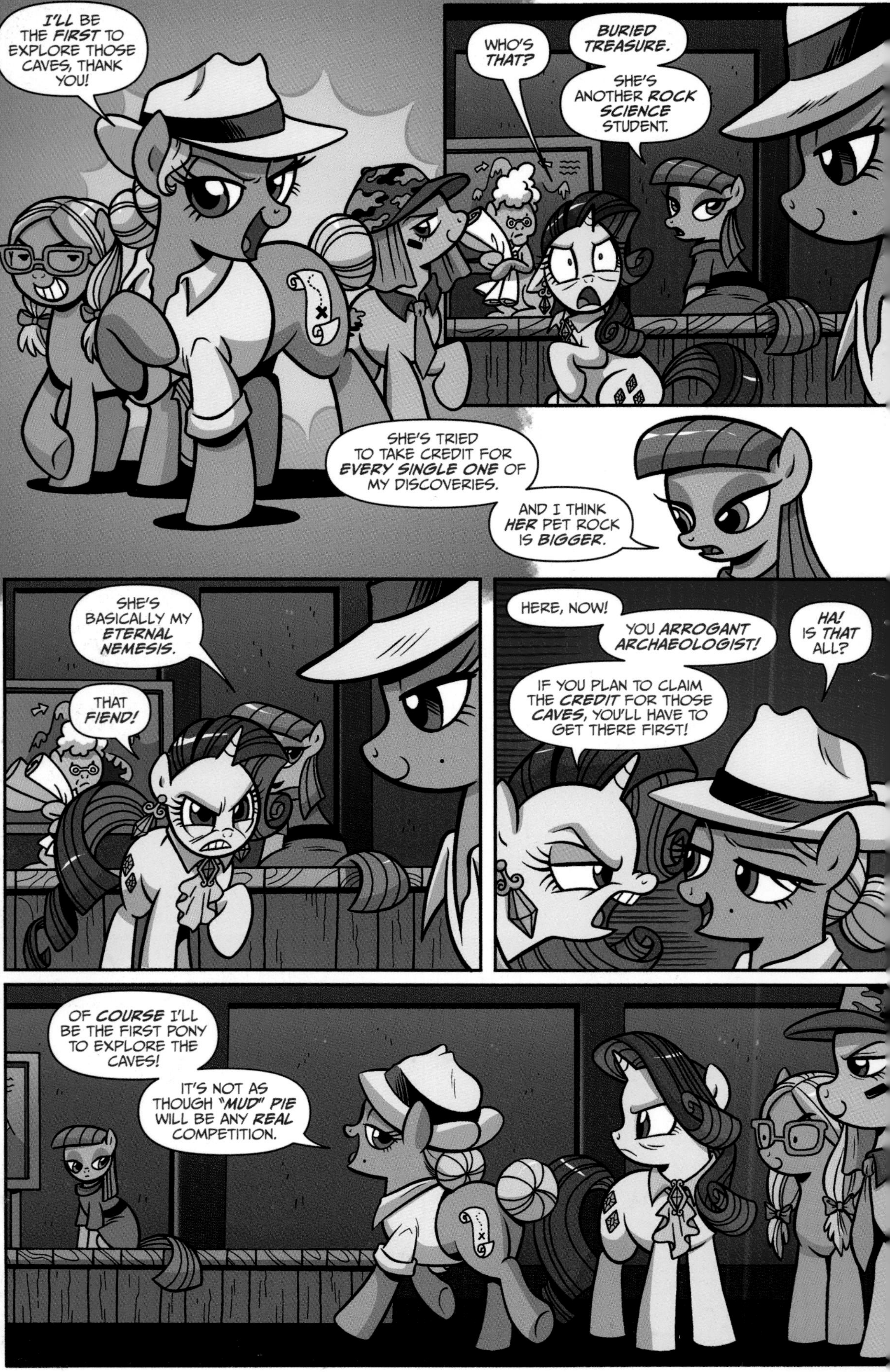
I'LL BE THE FIRST TO EXPLORE THOSE CAVES, THANK YOU!
WHO'S THAT?
BURIED TREASURE.
SHE'S ANOTHER ROCK SCIENCE STUDENT.
SHE'S TRIED TO TAKE CREDIT FOR EVERY SINGLE ONE OF MY DISCOVERIES.
AND I THINK HER PET ROCK IS BIGGER.
SHE'S BASICALLY MY ETERNAL NEMESIS.
THAT FIEND!
HERE, NOW!
YOU ARROGANT ARCHAEOLOGIST!
IF YOU PLAN TO CLAIM THE CREDIT FOR THOSE CAVES, YOU'LL HAVE TO GET THERE FIRST!
HA! IS THAT ALL?
OF COURSE I'LL BE THE FIRST PONY TO EXPLORE THE CAVES!
IT'S NOT AS THOUGH "MUD" PIE WILL BE ANY REAL COMPETITION.

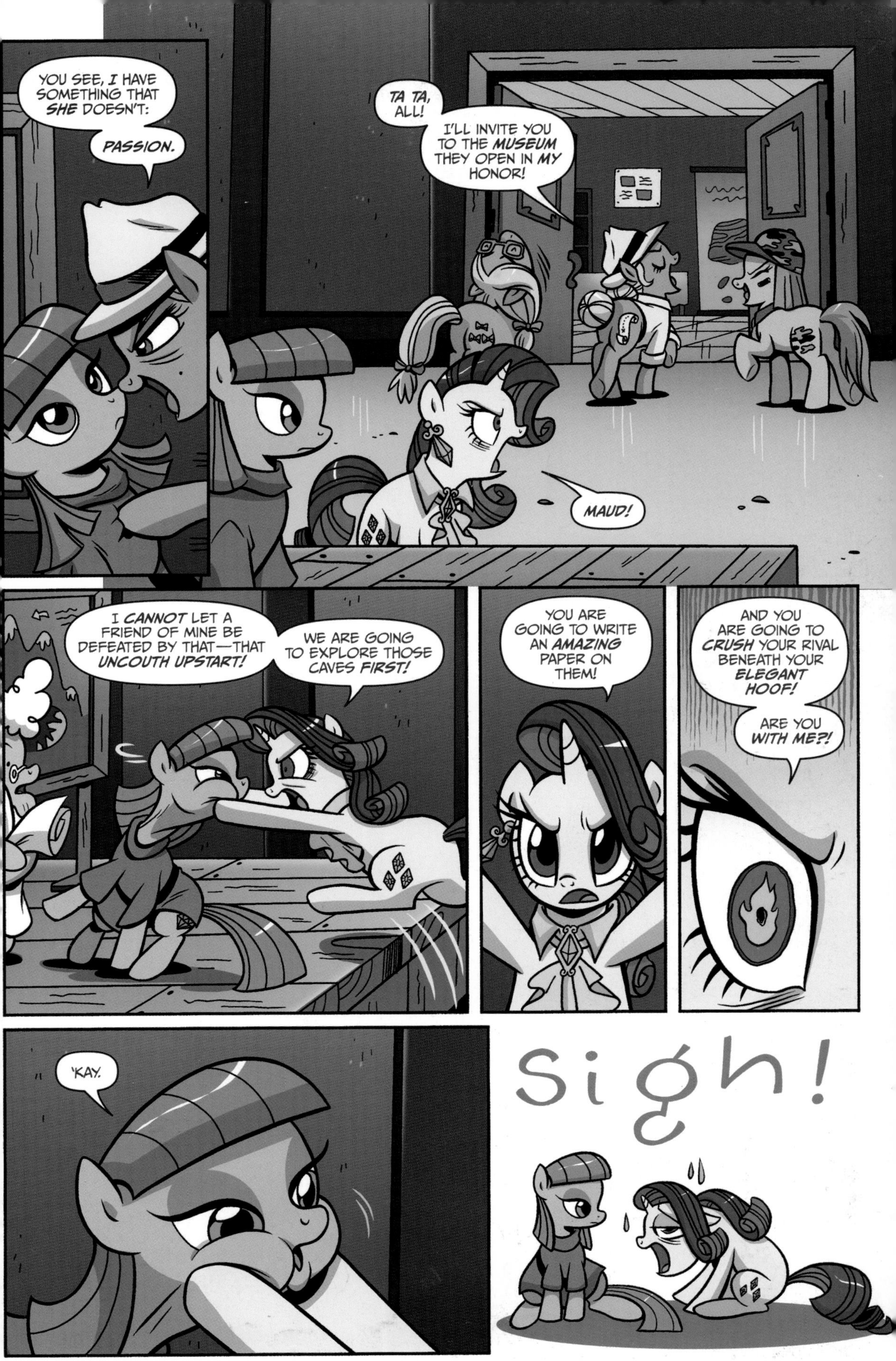
YOU SEE, I HAVE SOMETHING THAT SHE DOESN'T:
PASSION.
TA TA, ALL!
I'LL INVITE YOU TO THE MUSEUM THEY OPEN IN MY HONOR!
MAUD!
I CANNOT LET A FRIEND OF MINE BE DEFEATED BY THAT—THAT UNCOUTH UPSTART!
WE ARE GOING TO EXPLORE THOSE CAVES FIRST!
YOU ARE GOING TO WRITE AN AMAZING PAPER ON THEM!
AND YOU ARE GOING TO CRUSH YOUR RIVAL BENEATH YOUR ELEGANT HOOF!
ARE YOU WITH ME?!
'KAY.
Sigh!

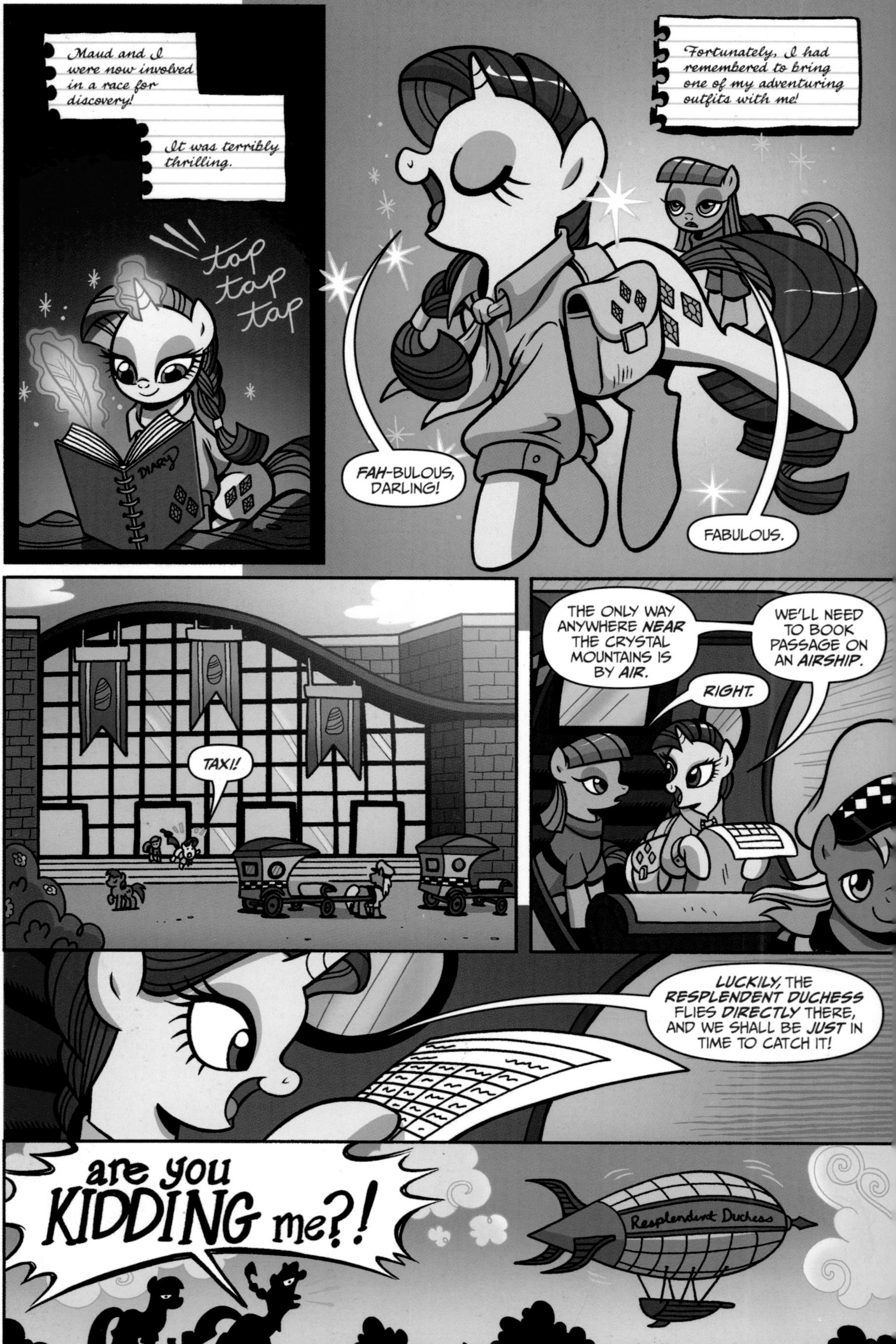
Maud and I were now involved in a race for discovery!
It was terribly thrilling.
tap tap tap
DIARY
Fortunately, I had remembered to bring one of my adventuring outfits with me!
FAH-BULOUS, DARLING!
FABULOUS.
TAXI!
THE ONLY WAY ANYWHERE NEAR THE CRYSTAL MOUNTAINS IS BY AIR.
WE'LL NEED TO BOOK PASSAGE ON AN AIRSHIP.
RIGHT.
LUCKILY, THE RESPLENDENT DUCHESS FLIES DIRECTLY THERE, AND WE SHALL BE JUST IN TIME TO CATCH IT!
are you KIDDING me?!
Resplendent Duchess

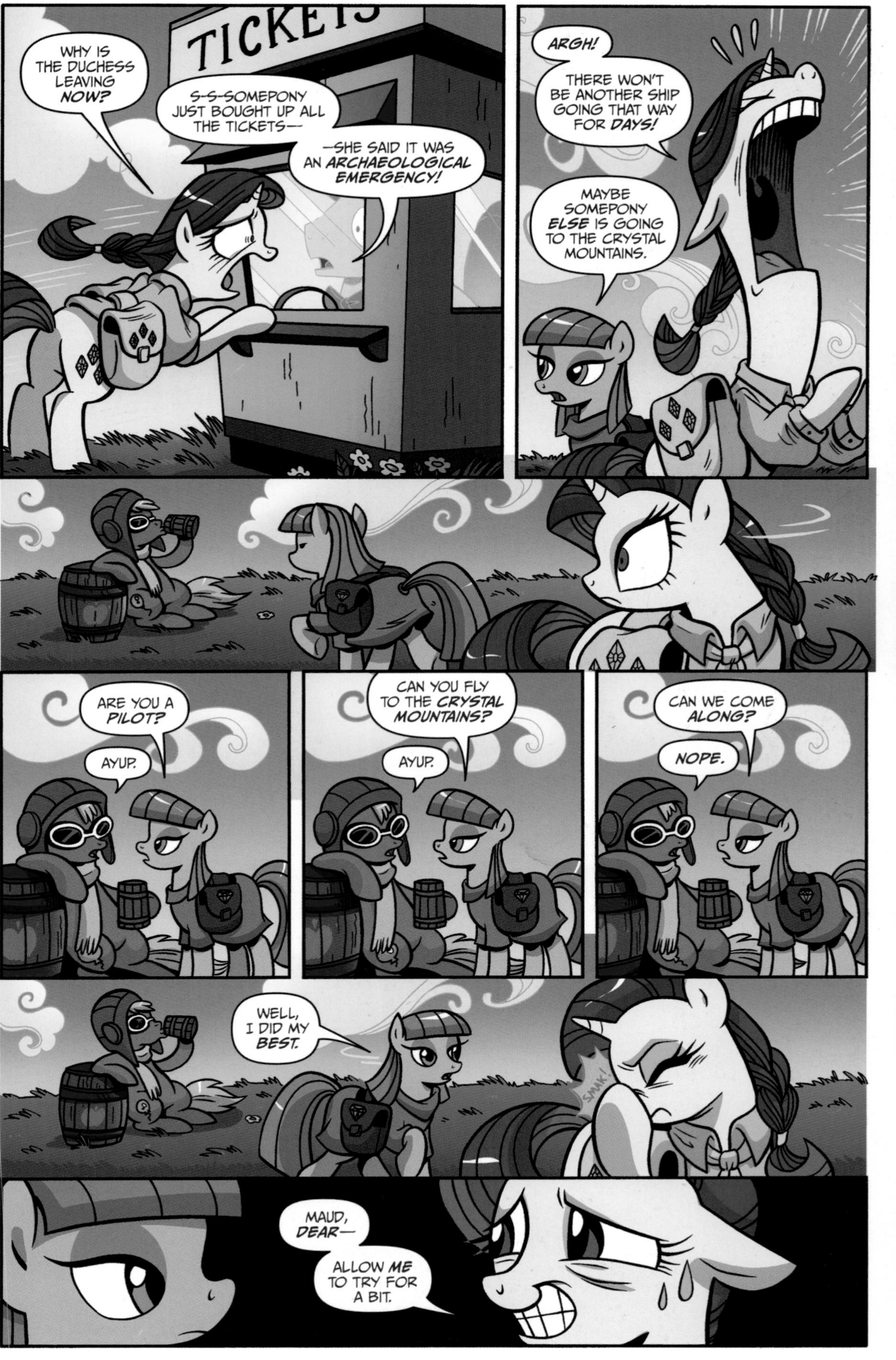

TICKETS
WHY IS THE DUCHESS LEAVING NOW?
S-S-SOMEPONY JUST BOUGHT UP ALL THE TICKETS—
—SHE SAID IT WAS AN ARCHAEOLOGICAL EMERGENCY!
ARGH!
THERE WON'T BE ANOTHER SHIP GOING THAT WAY FOR DAYS!
MAYBE SOMEPONY ELSE IS GOING TO THE CRYSTAL MOUNTAINS.
ARE YOU A PILOT?
AYUP.
CAN YOU FLY TO THE CRYSTAL MOUNTAINS?
AYUP.
CAN WE COME ALONG?
NOPE.
WELL, I DID MY BEST.
SMAK!
MAUD, DEAR—
ALLOW ME TO TRY FOR A BIT.

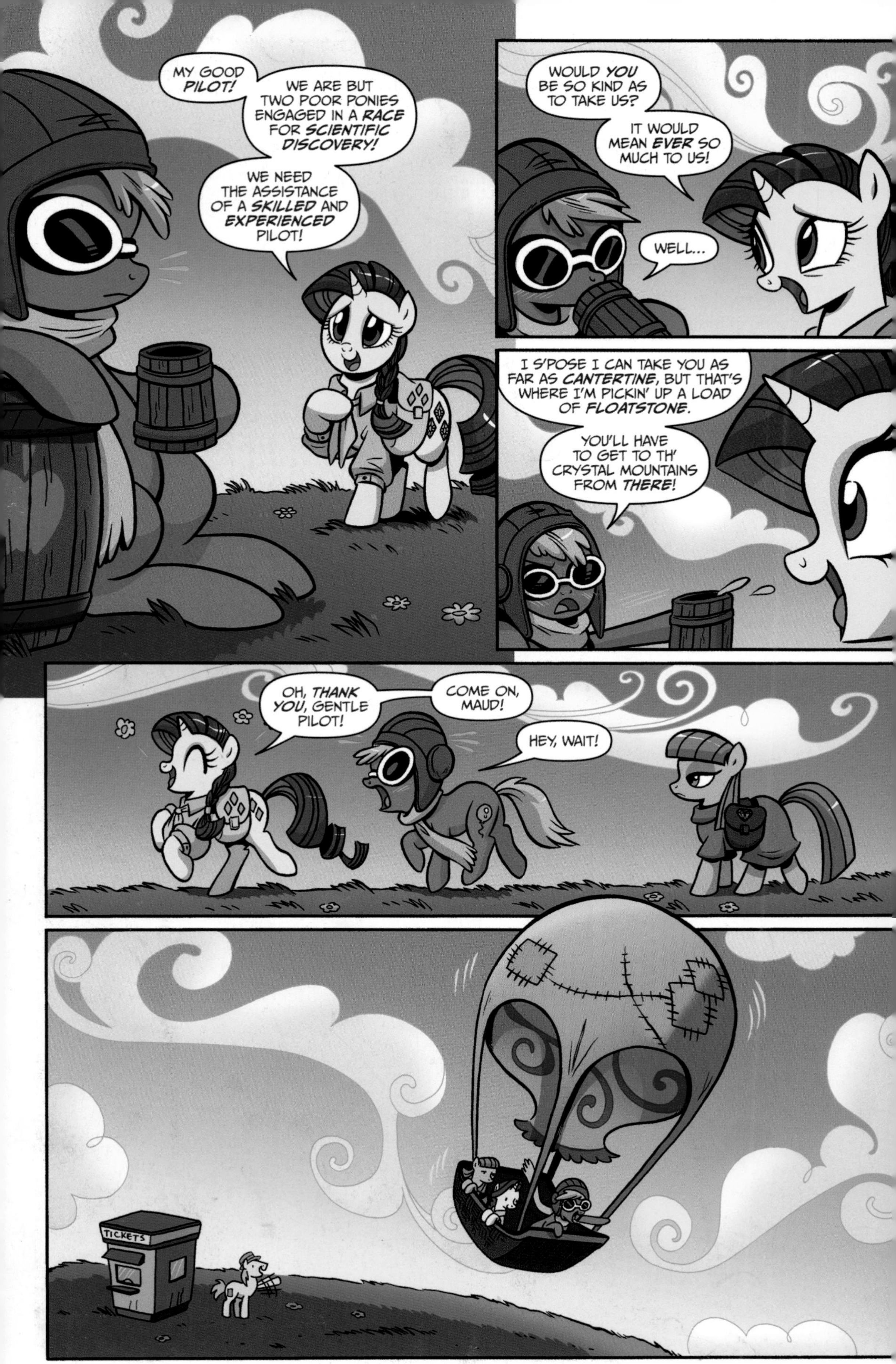

MY GOOD *PILOT!*
WE ARE BUT TWO POOR PONIES ENGAGED IN A *RACE* FOR *SCIENTIFIC DISCOVERY!*
WE NEED THE ASSISTANCE OF A *SKILLED* AND *EXPERIENCED* PILOT!
WOULD *YOU* BE SO KIND AS TO TAKE US?
IT WOULD MEAN *EVER* SO MUCH TO US!
WELL...
I S'POSE I CAN TAKE YOU AS FAR AS *CANTERTINE*, BUT THAT'S WHERE I'M PICKIN' UP A LOAD OF *FLOATSTONE*.
YOU'LL HAVE TO GET TO TH' CRYSTAL MOUNTAINS FROM *THERE!*
OH, *THANK YOU*, GENTLE PILOT!
COME ON, MAUD!
HEY, WAIT!
TICKETS

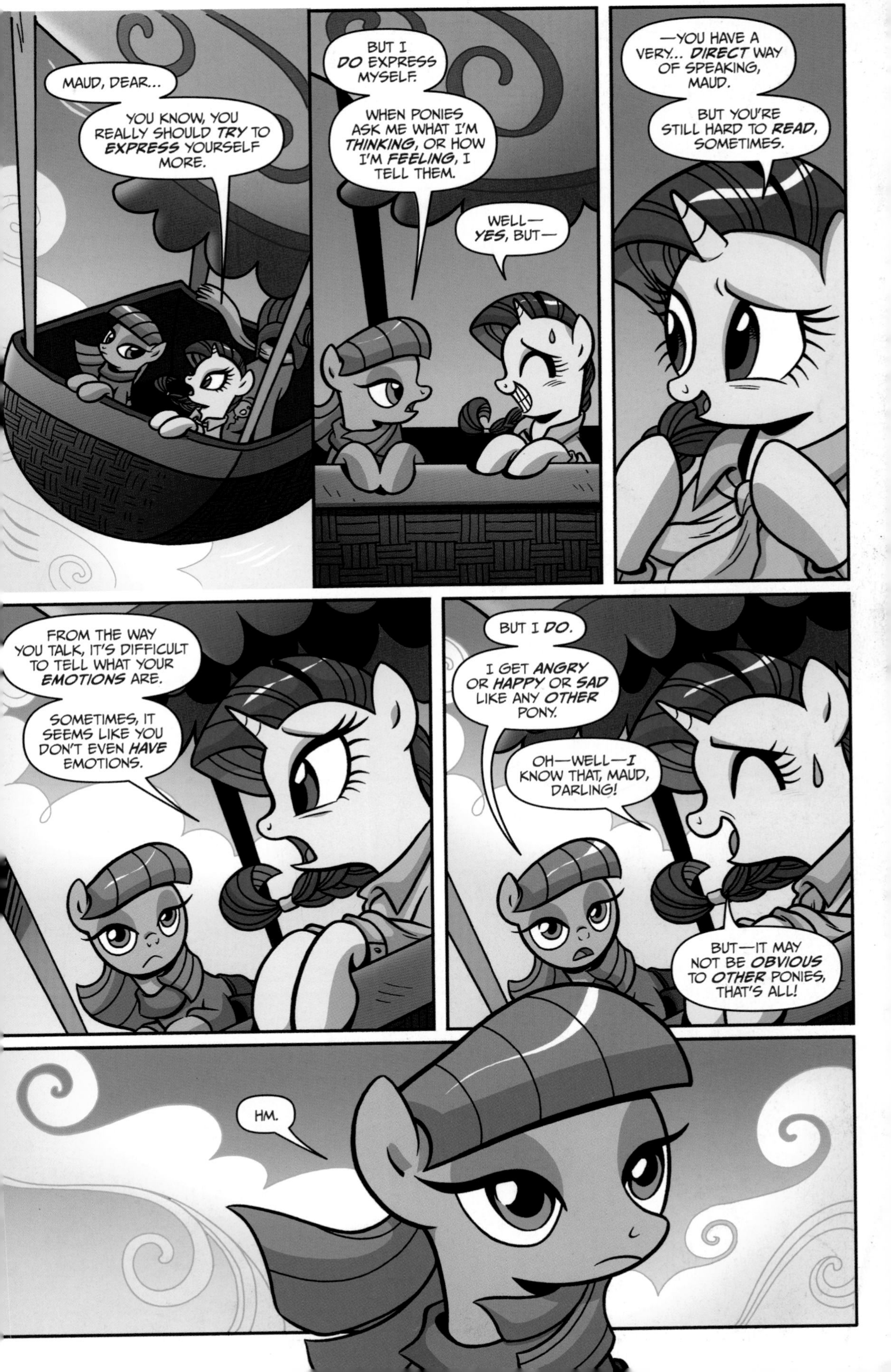
MAUD, DEAR...
YOU KNOW, YOU REALLY SHOULD TRY TO EXPRESS YOURSELF MORE.
BUT I DO EXPRESS MYSELF.
WHEN PONIES ASK ME WHAT I'M THINKING, OR HOW I'M FEELING, I TELL THEM.
WELL— YES, BUT—
—YOU HAVE A VERY... DIRECT WAY OF SPEAKING, MAUD.
BUT YOU'RE STILL HARD TO READ, SOMETIMES.
FROM THE WAY YOU TALK, IT'S DIFFICULT TO TELL WHAT YOUR EMOTIONS ARE.
SOMETIMES, IT SEEMS LIKE YOU DON'T EVEN HAVE EMOTIONS.
BUT I DO.
I GET ANGRY OR HAPPY OR SAD LIKE ANY OTHER PONY.
OH—WELL—I KNOW THAT, MAUD, DARLING!
BUT—IT MAY NOT BE OBVIOUS TO OTHER PONIES, THAT'S ALL!
HM.

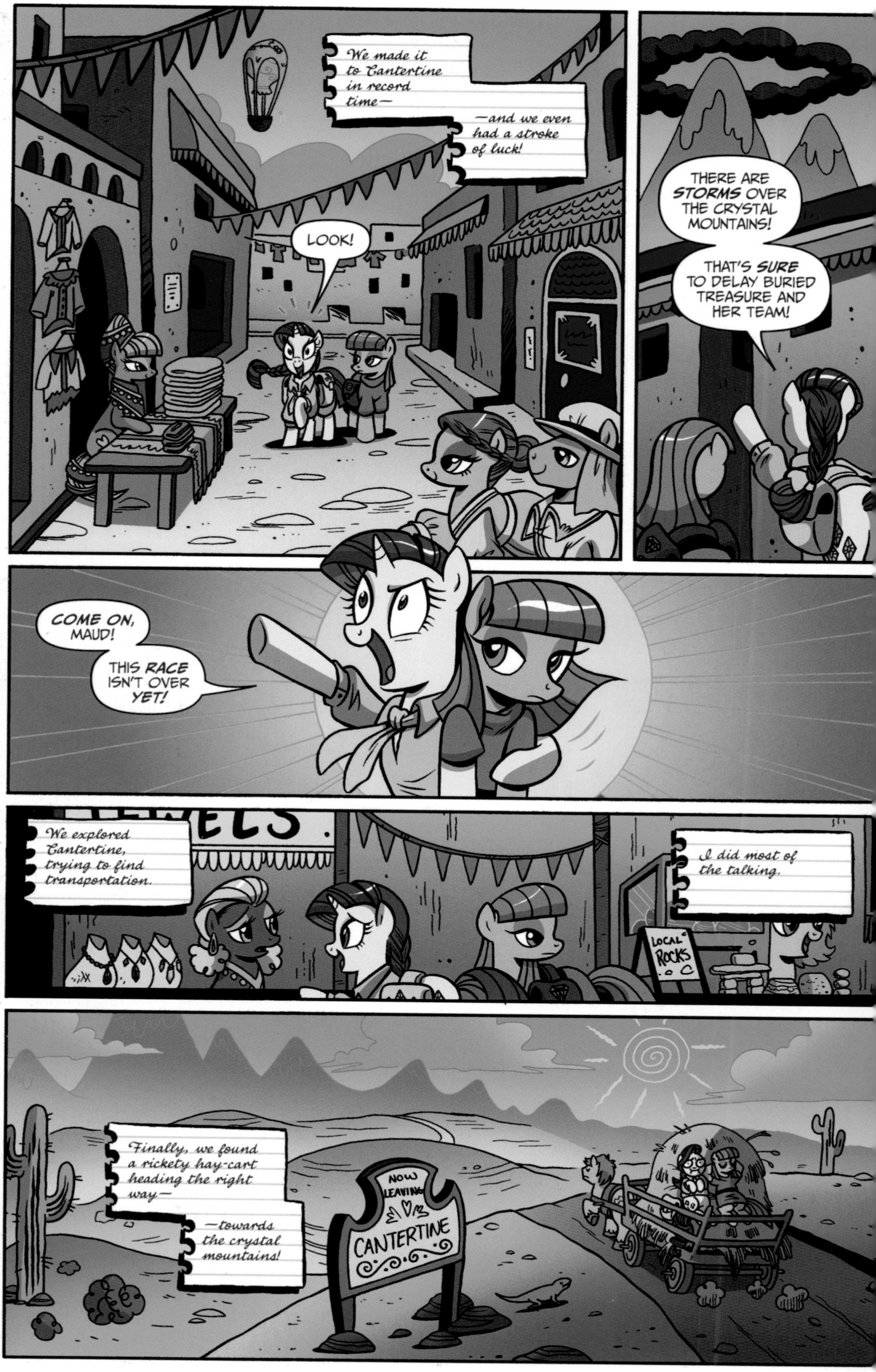
We made it to Cantertine in record time—
—and we even had a stroke of luck!
LOOK!
THERE ARE STORMS OVER THE CRYSTAL MOUNTAINS!
THAT'S SURE TO DELAY BURIED TREASURE AND HER TEAM!
COME ON, MAUD!
THIS RACE ISN'T OVER YET!
We explored Cantertine, trying to find transportation.
I did most of the talking.
LOCAL ROCKS
Finally, we found a rickety hay-cart heading the right way—
—towards the crystal mountains!
NOW LEAVING
CANTERTINE

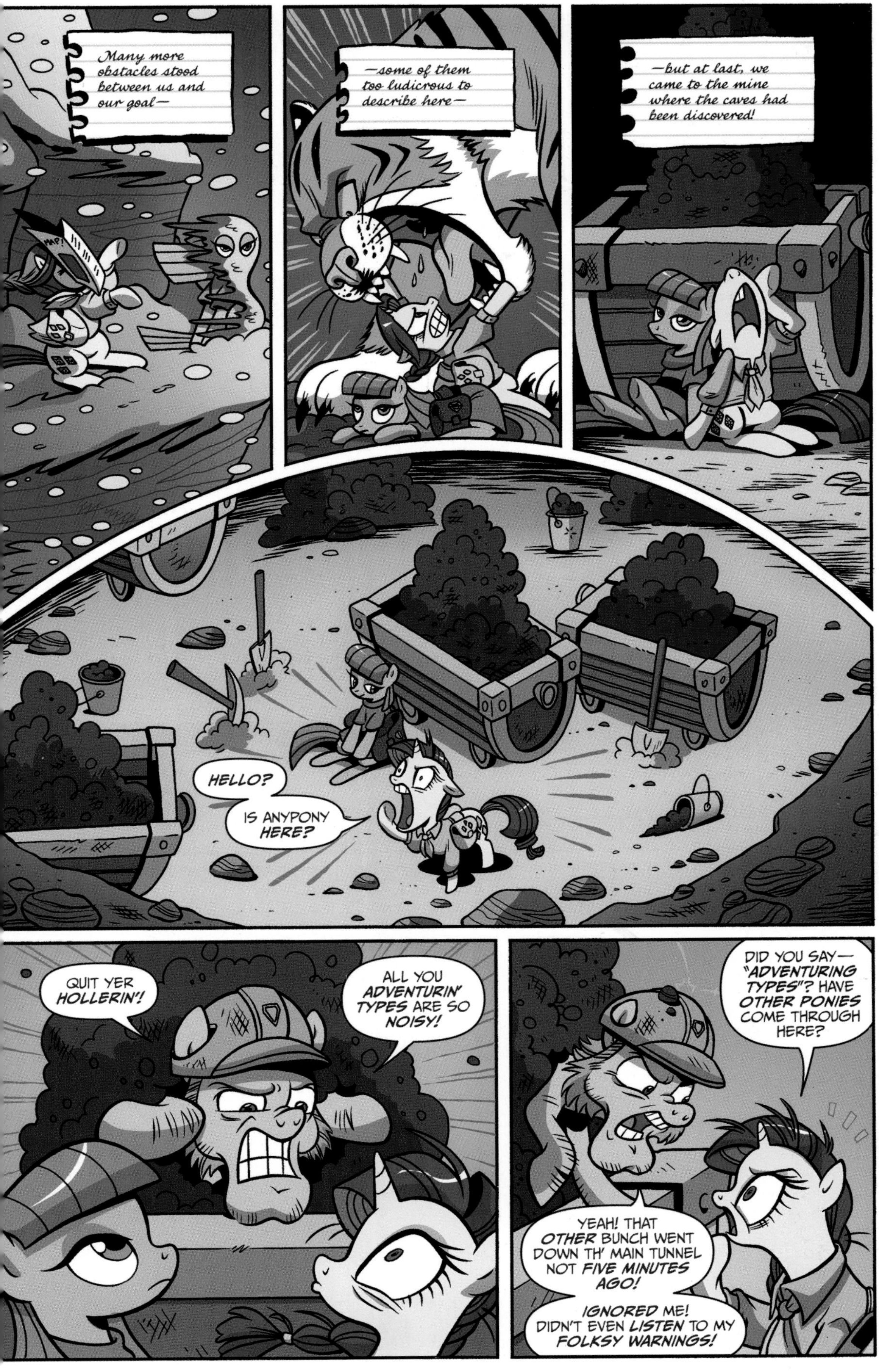
Many more obstacles stood between us and our goal—
MAP!
—some of them too ludicrous to describe here—
—but at last, we came to the mine where the caves had been discovered!
HELLO?
IS ANYPONY HERE?
QUIT YER HOLLERIN'!
ALL YOU ADVENTURIN' TYPES ARE SO NOISY!
DID YOU SAY— "ADVENTURING TYPES"? HAVE OTHER PONIES COME THROUGH HERE?
YEAH! THAT OTHER BUNCH WENT DOWN TH' MAIN TUNNEL NOT FIVE MINUTES AGO!
IGNORED ME! DIDN'T EVEN LISTEN TO MY FOLKSY WARNINGS!

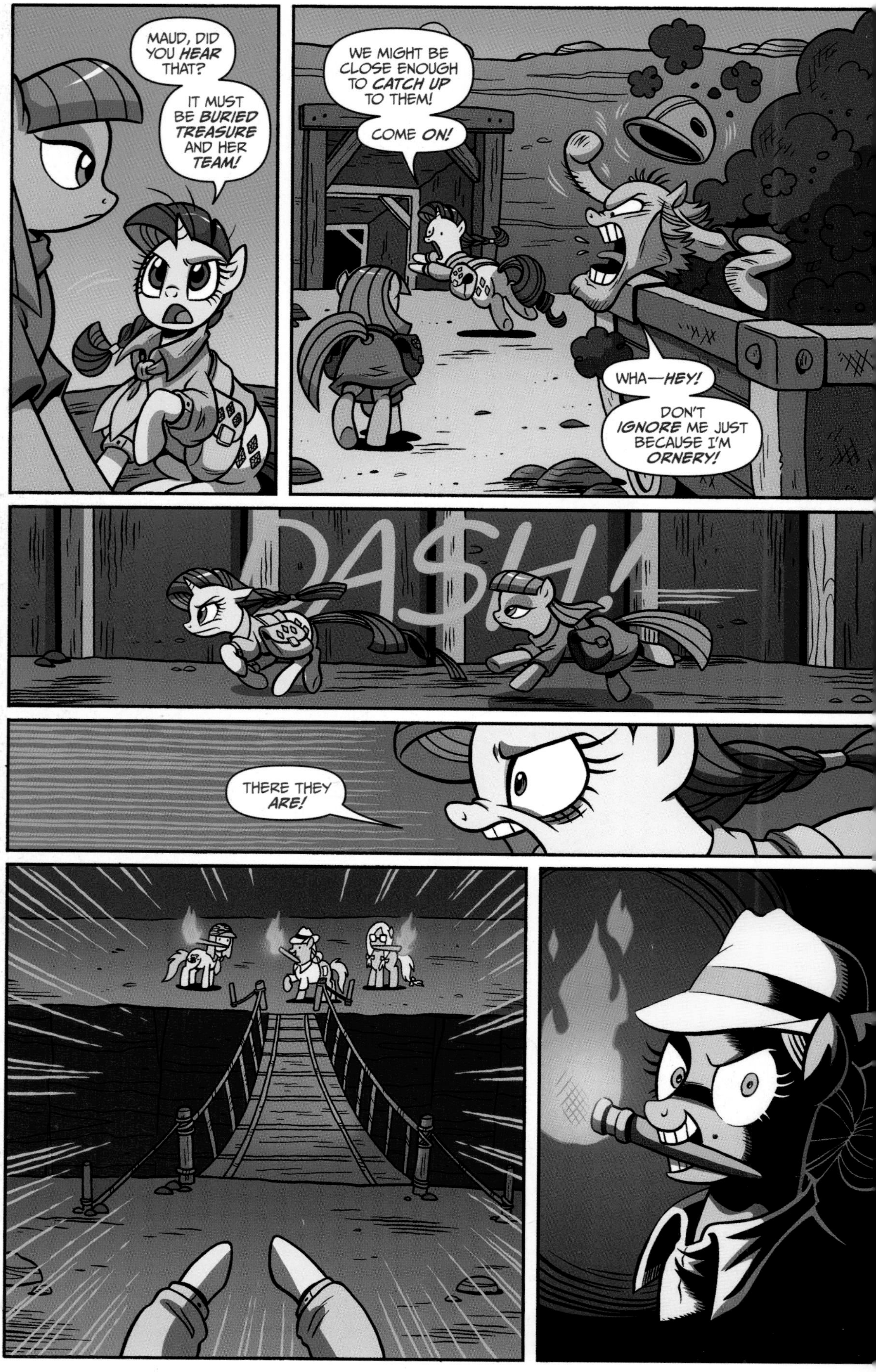
MAUD, DID YOU HEAR THAT?
IT MUST BE BURIED TREASURE AND HER TEAM!
WE MIGHT BE CLOSE ENOUGH TO CATCH UP TO THEM!
COME ON!
WHA—HEY!
DON'T IGNORE ME JUST BECAUSE I'M ORNERY!
DA$H!
THERE THEY ARE!

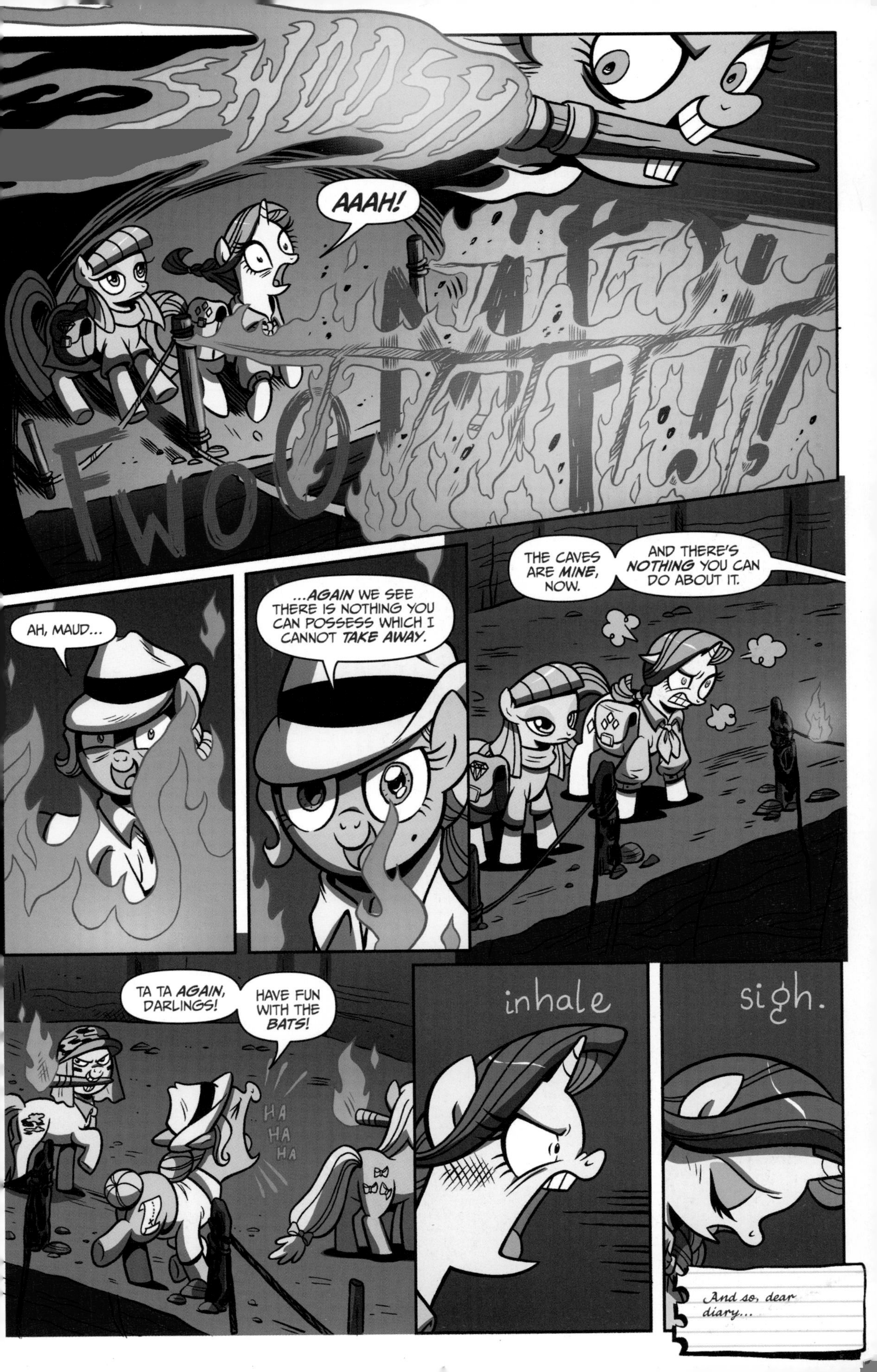
SHWOOSH
AAAH!
AH, MAUD...
...*AGAIN* WE SEE THERE IS NOTHING YOU CAN POSSESS WHICH I CANNOT *TAKE AWAY*.
THE CAVES ARE *MINE*, NOW.
AND THERE'S *NOTHING* YOU CAN DO ABOUT IT.
TA TA *AGAIN*, DARLINGS!
HAVE FUN WITH THE *BATS*!
HA HA HA
inhale
sigh.
And so, dear diary...

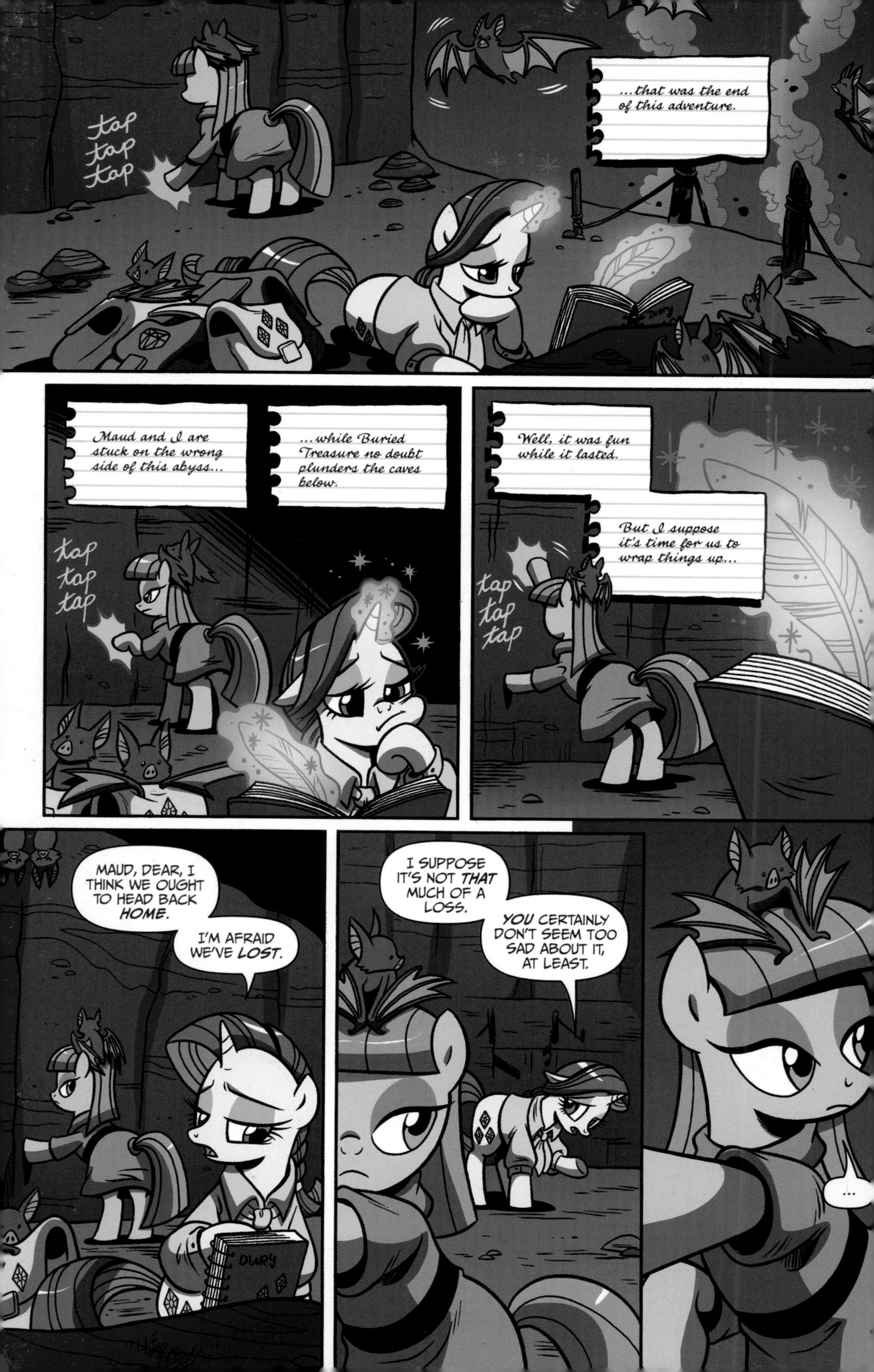
tap tap tap
...that was the end of this adventure.
Maud and I are stuck on the wrong side of this abyss...
...while Buried Treasure no doubt plunders the caves below.
tap tap tap
Well, it was fun while it lasted.
But I suppose it's time for us to wrap things up...
tap tap tap
MAUD, DEAR, I THINK WE OUGHT TO HEAD BACK HOME.
I'M AFRAID WE'VE LOST.
DIARY
I SUPPOSE IT'S NOT THAT MUCH OF A LOSS.
YOU CERTAINLY DON'T SEEM TOO SAD ABOUT IT, AT LEAST.
...

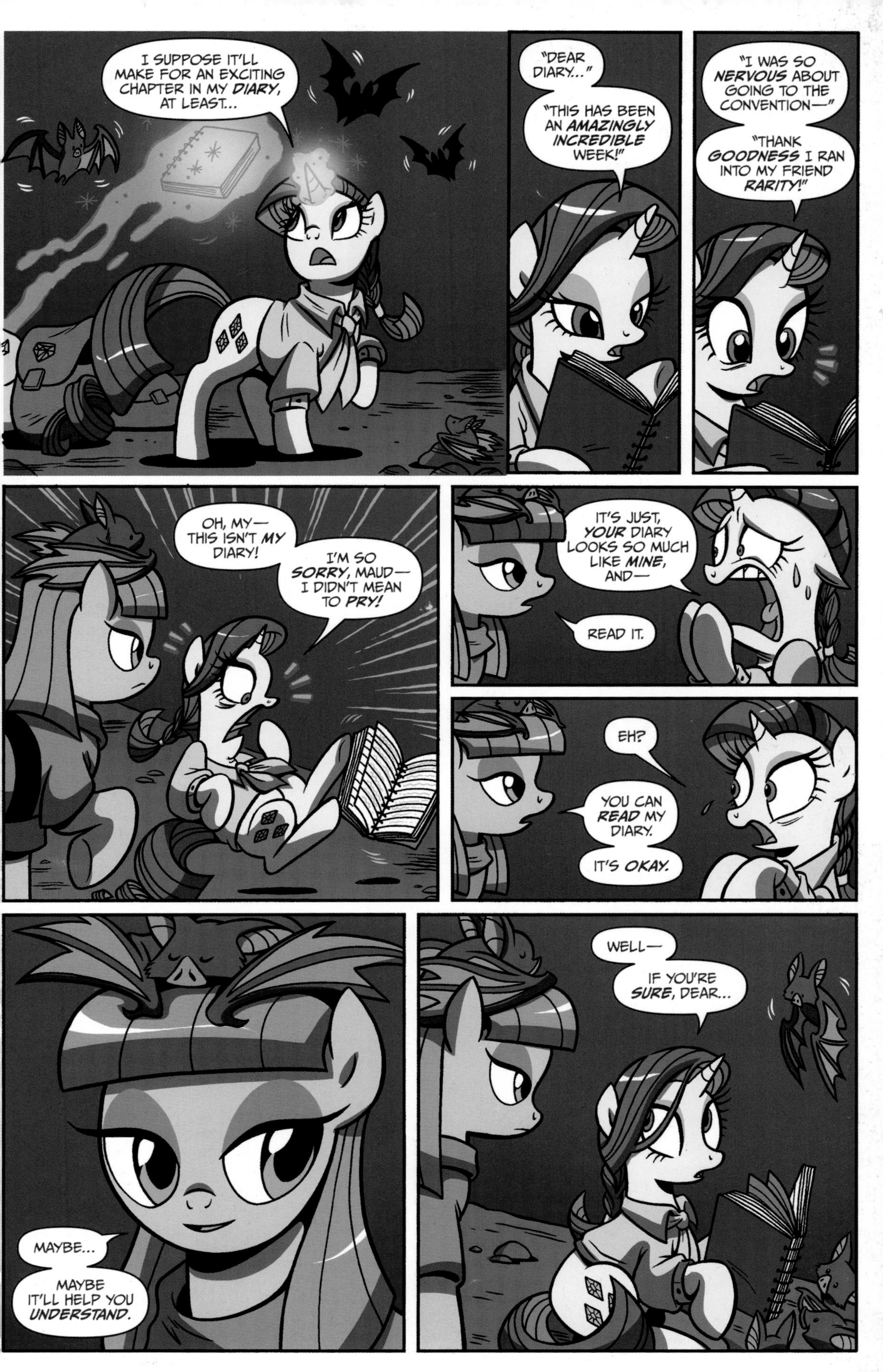
I SUPPOSE IT'LL MAKE FOR AN EXCITING CHAPTER IN MY *DIARY*, AT LEAST...
"DEAR DIARY..."
"THIS HAS BEEN AN *AMAZINGLY INCREDIBLE* WEEK!"
"I WAS SO *NERVOUS* ABOUT GOING TO THE CONVENTION—"
"THANK *GOODNESS* I RAN INTO MY FRIEND *RARITY!*"
OH, MY— THIS ISN'T *MY* DIARY!
I'M SO *SORRY*, MAUD— I DIDN'T MEAN TO *PRY!*
IT'S JUST, *YOUR* DIARY LOOKS SO MUCH LIKE *MINE*, AND—
READ IT.
EH?
YOU CAN *READ* MY DIARY.
IT'S *OKAY.*
MAYBE...
MAYBE IT'LL HELP YOU *UNDERSTAND.*
WELL—
IF YOU'RE *SURE*, DEAR...

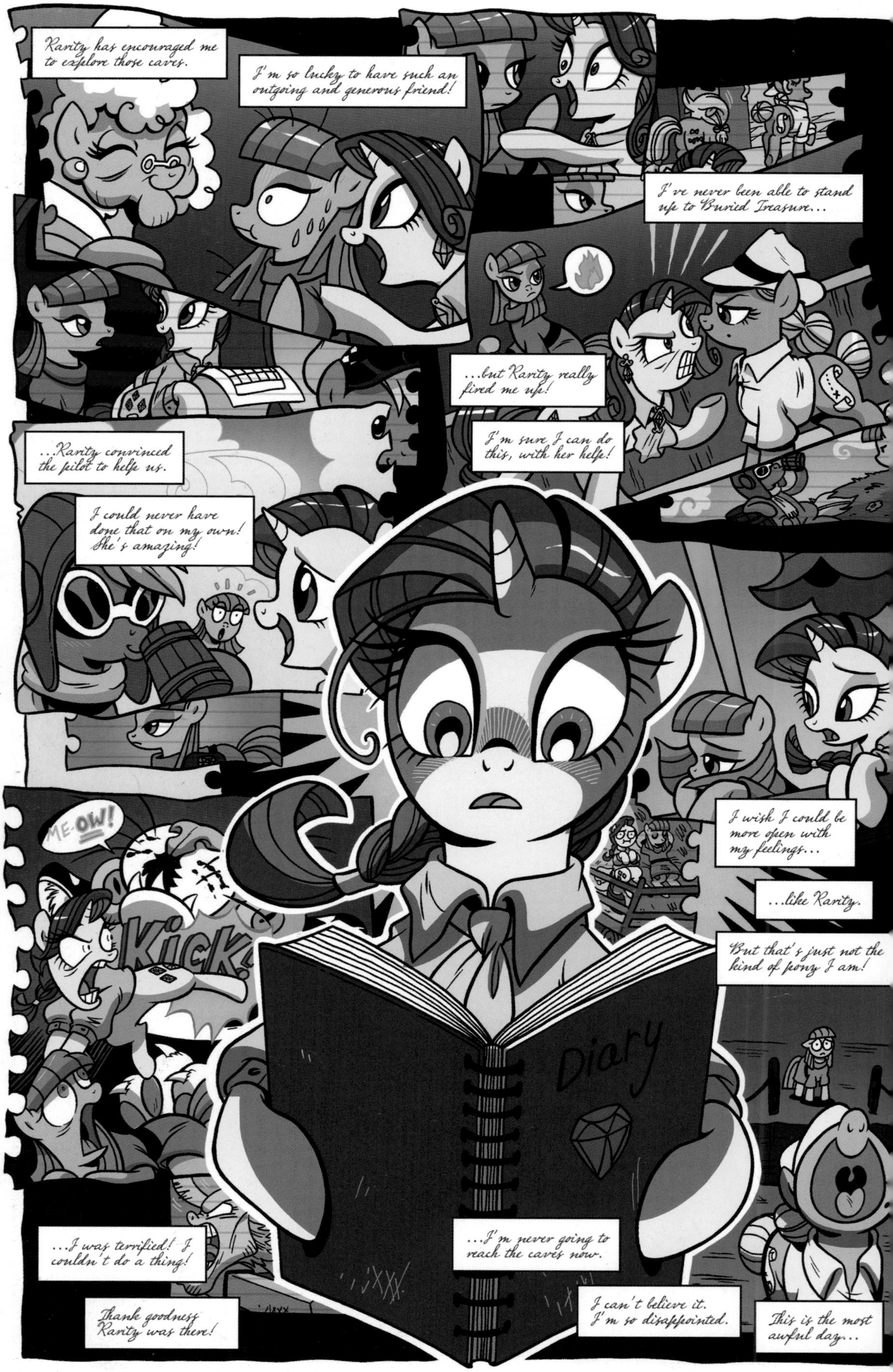

Rarity has encouraged me to explore those caves.
I'm so lucky to have such an outgoing and generous friend!
I've never been able to stand up to Buried Treasure...
...but Rarity really fired me up!
I'm sure I can do this, with her help!
...Rarity convinced the pilot to help us.
I could never have done that on my own! She's amazing!
I wish I could be more open with my feelings...
...like Rarity.
But that's just not the kind of pony I am!
ME-OW!
KICK!
Diary
...I was terrified! I couldn't do a thing!
Thank goodness Rarity was there!
...I'm never going to reach the caves now.
I can't believe it. I'm so disappointed.
This is the most awful day...

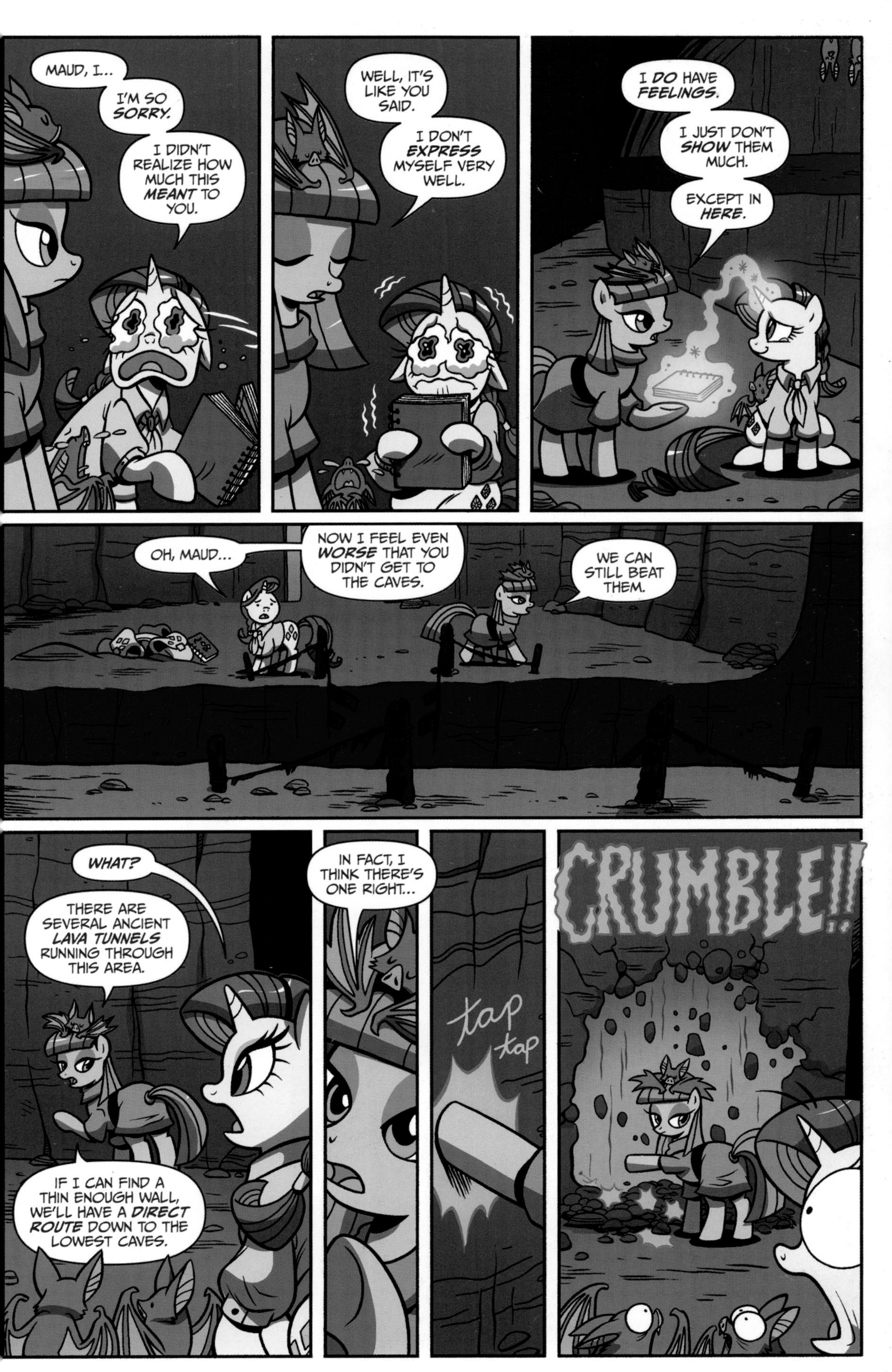
MAUD, I...
I'M SO SORRY.
I DIDN'T REALIZE HOW MUCH THIS MEANT TO YOU.
WELL, IT'S LIKE YOU SAID.
I DON'T EXPRESS MYSELF VERY WELL.
I DO HAVE FEELINGS.
I JUST DON'T SHOW THEM MUCH.
EXCEPT IN HERE.
OH, MAUD...
NOW I FEEL EVEN WORSE THAT YOU DIDN'T GET TO THE CAVES.
WE CAN STILL BEAT THEM.
WHAT?
THERE ARE SEVERAL ANCIENT LAVA TUNNELS RUNNING THROUGH THIS AREA.
IF I CAN FIND A THIN ENOUGH WALL, WE'LL HAVE A DIRECT ROUTE DOWN TO THE LOWEST CAVES.
IN FACT, I THINK THERE'S ONE RIGHT...
tap tap
CRUMBLE!!!

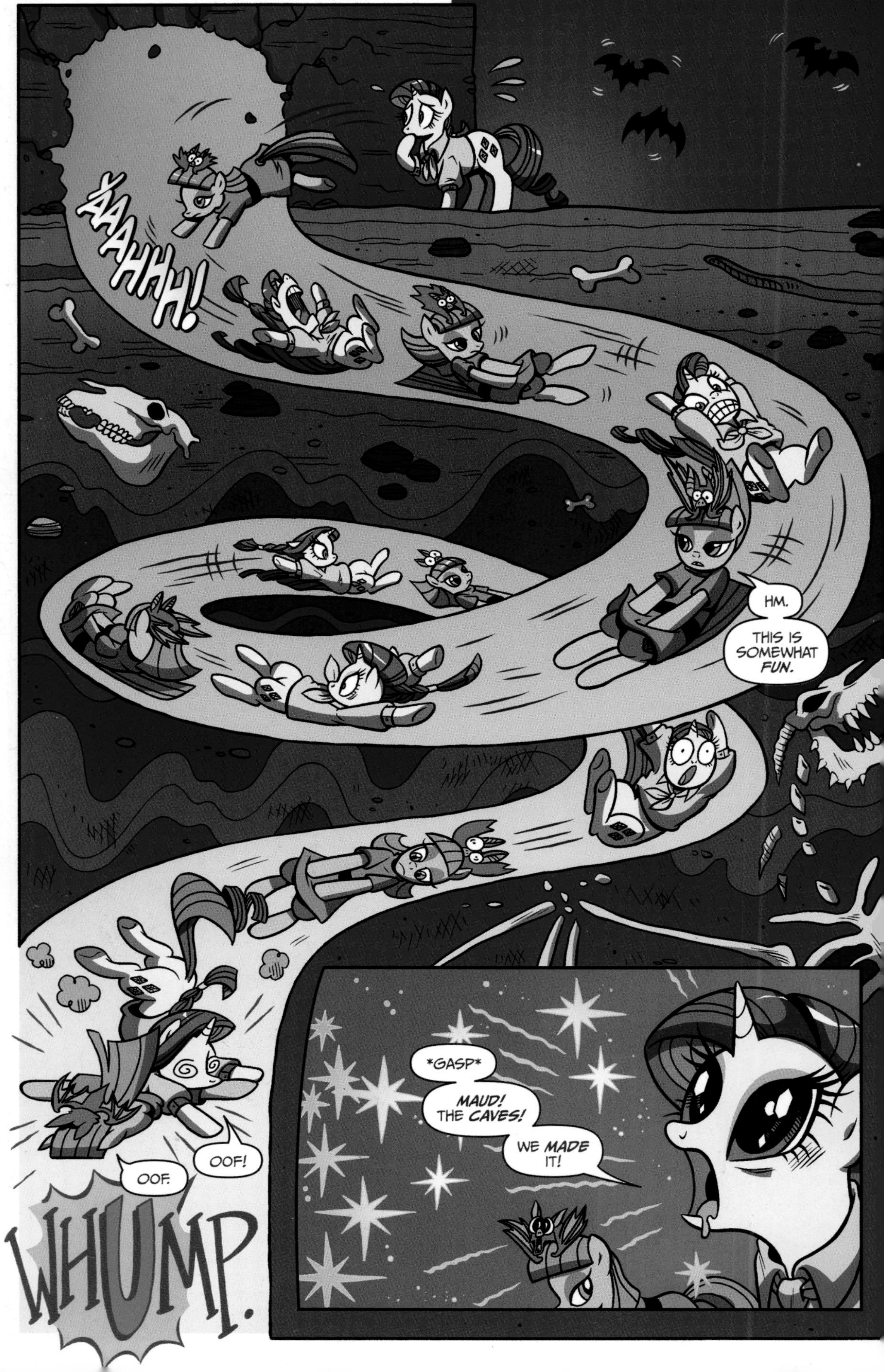
AAAAHHH!
HM.
THIS IS SOMEWHAT FUN.
OOF!
OOF.
WHUMP.
GASP
MAUD! THE CAVES!
WE MADE IT!

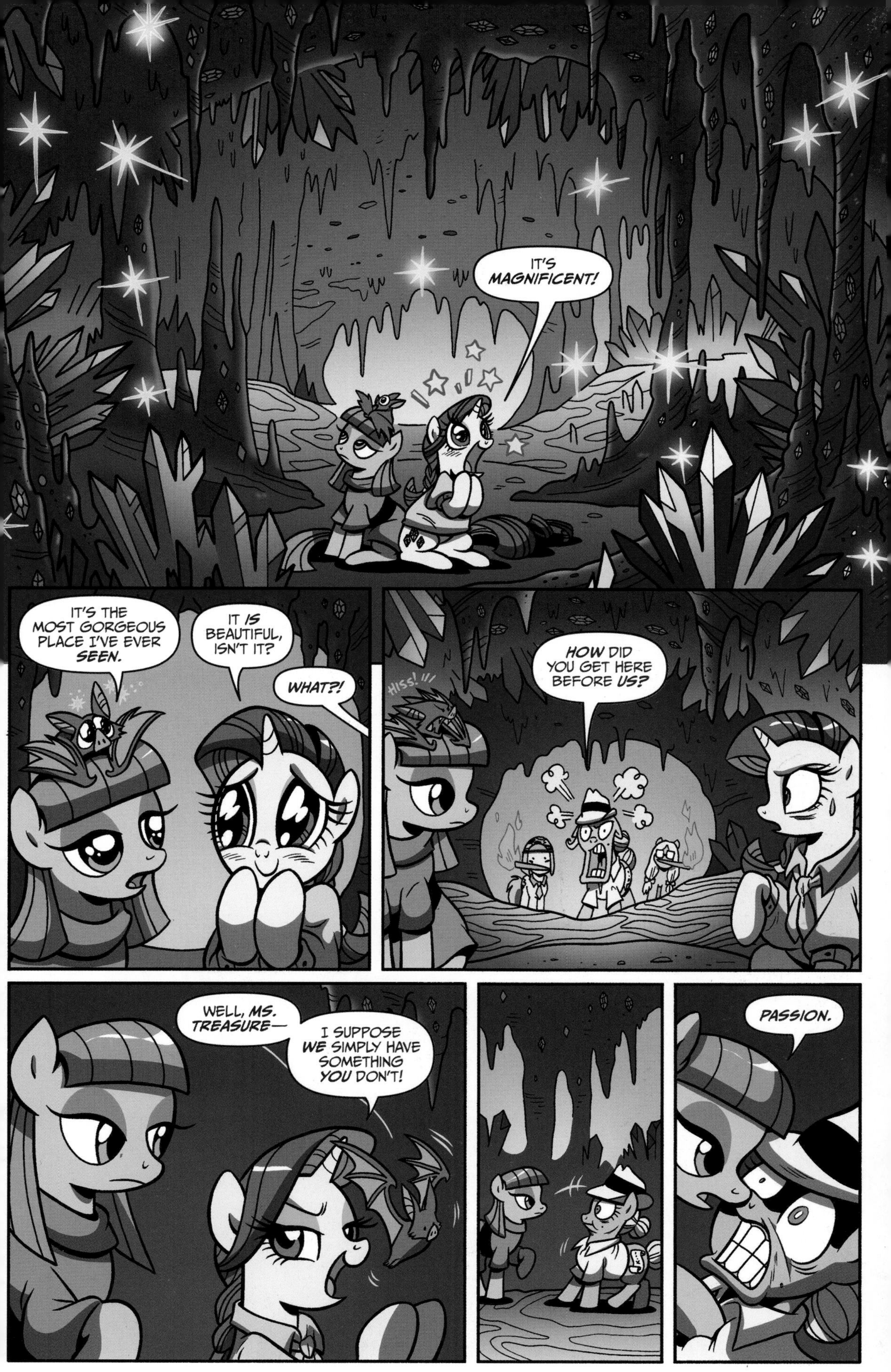
IT'S MAGNIFICENT!
IT'S THE MOST GORGEOUS PLACE I'VE EVER SEEN.
IT IS BEAUTIFUL, ISN'T IT?
WHAT?!
HISS!
HOW DID YOU GET HERE BEFORE US?
WELL, MS. TREASURE—
I SUPPOSE WE SIMPLY HAVE SOMETHING YOU DON'T!
PASSION.

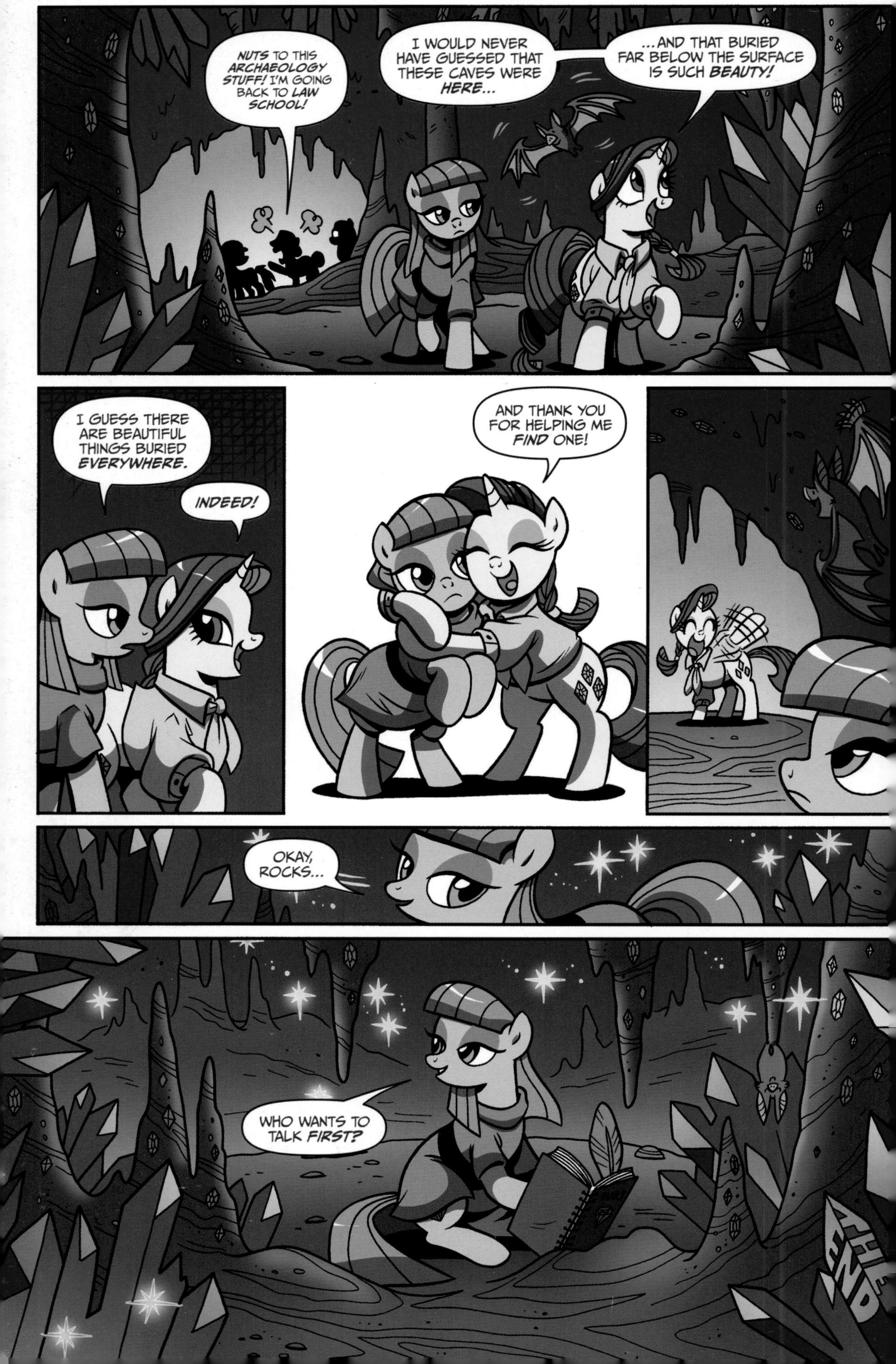
NUTS TO THIS ARCHAEOLOGY STUFF! I'M GOING BACK TO LAW SCHOOL!
I WOULD NEVER HAVE GUESSED THAT THESE CAVES WERE HERE...
...AND THAT BURIED FAR BELOW THE SURFACE IS SUCH BEAUTY!
I GUESS THERE ARE BEAUTIFUL THINGS BURIED EVERYWHERE.
INDEED!
AND THANK YOU FOR HELPING ME FIND ONE!
OKAY, ROCKS...
WHO WANTS TO TALK FIRST?
THE END

My Little Pony

Friends Forever

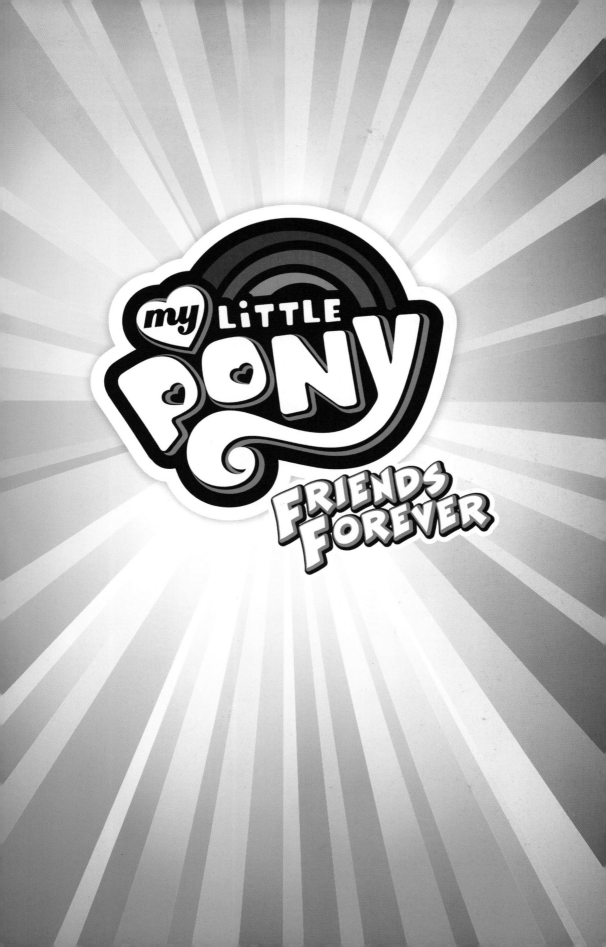

Twilight Sparkle & Princess Cadance

art by
Agnes Garbowska

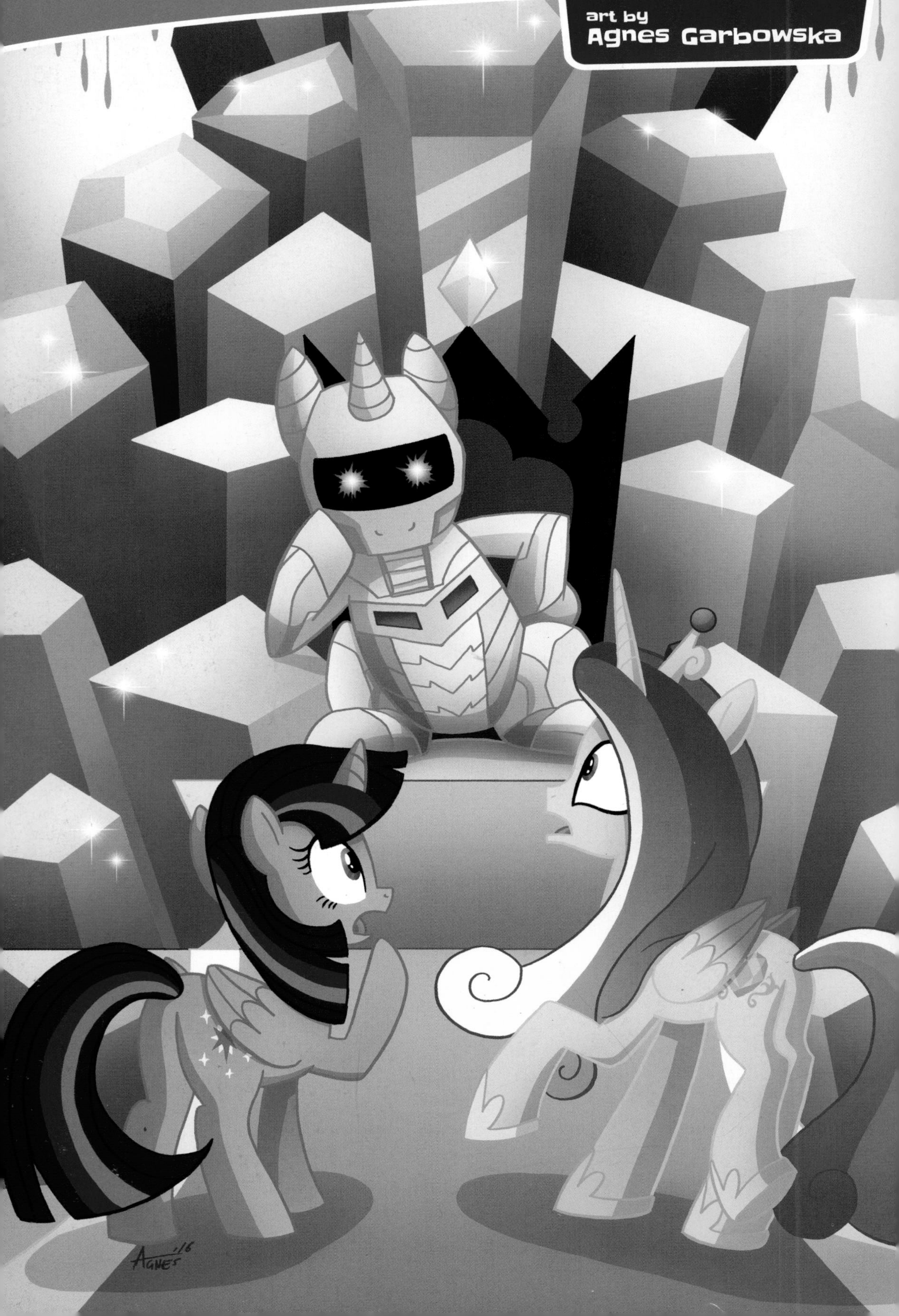
Agnes '16

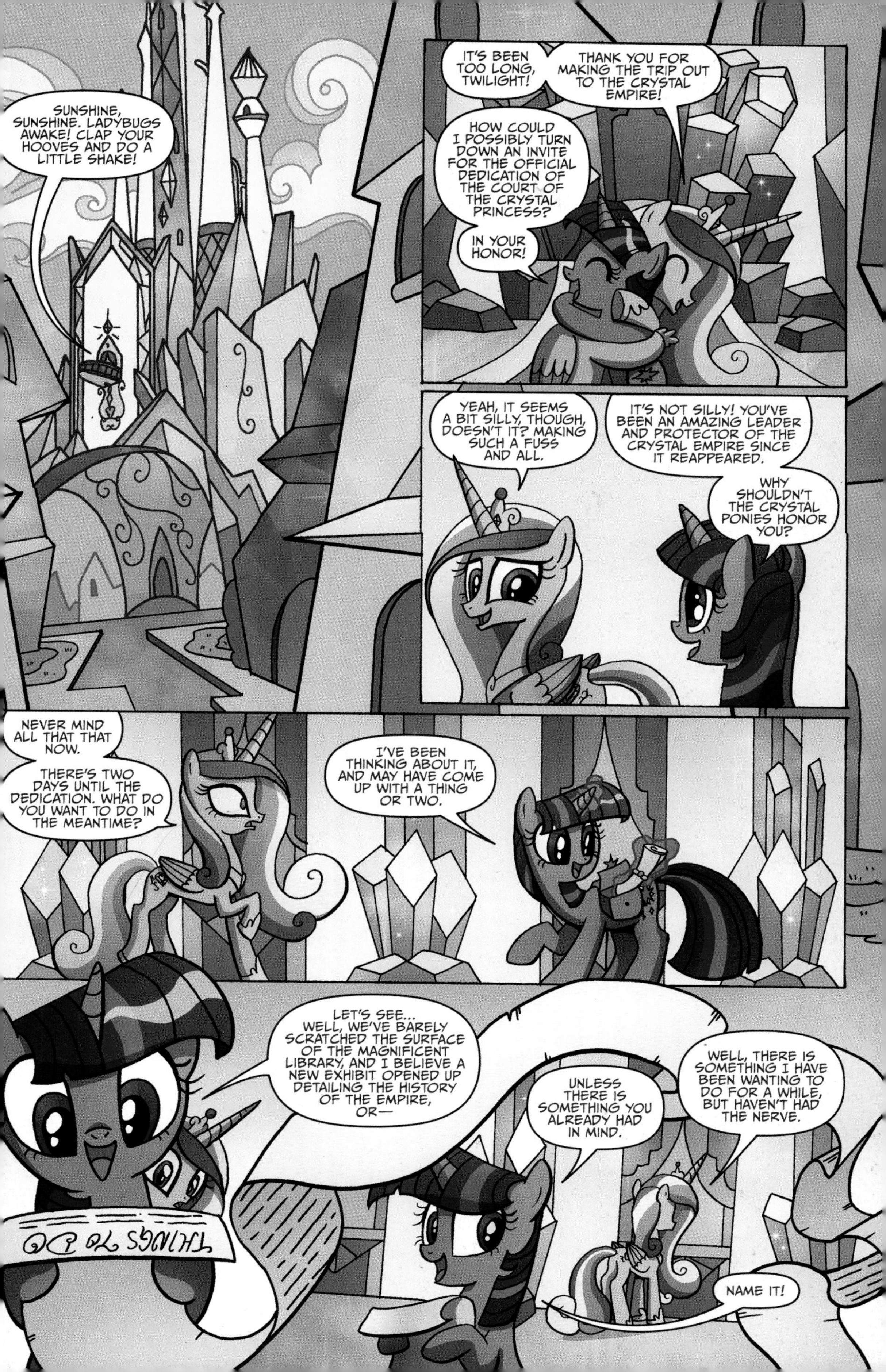

SUNSHINE, SUNSHINE. LADYBUGS AWAKE! CLAP YOUR HOOVES AND DO A LITTLE SHAKE!
IT'S BEEN TOO LONG, TWILIGHT!
THANK YOU FOR MAKING THE TRIP OUT TO THE CRYSTAL EMPIRE!
HOW COULD I POSSIBLY TURN DOWN AN INVITE FOR THE OFFICIAL DEDICATION OF THE COURT OF THE CRYSTAL PRINCESS?
IN YOUR HONOR!
YEAH, IT SEEMS A BIT SILLY, THOUGH, DOESN'T IT? MAKING SUCH A FUSS AND ALL.
IT'S NOT SILLY! YOU'VE BEEN AN AMAZING LEADER AND PROTECTOR OF THE CRYSTAL EMPIRE SINCE IT REAPPEARED.
WHY SHOULDN'T THE CRYSTAL PONIES HONOR YOU?
NEVER MIND ALL THAT THAT NOW.
THERE'S TWO DAYS UNTIL THE DEDICATION. WHAT DO YOU WANT TO DO IN THE MEANTIME?
I'VE BEEN THINKING ABOUT IT, AND MAY HAVE COME UP WITH A THING OR TWO.
THINGS TO DO
LET'S SEE... WELL, WE'VE BARELY SCRATCHED THE SURFACE OF THE MAGNIFICENT LIBRARY, AND I BELIEVE A NEW EXHIBIT OPENED UP DETAILING THE HISTORY OF THE EMPIRE, OR—
UNLESS THERE IS SOMETHING YOU ALREADY HAD IN MIND.
WELL, THERE IS SOMETHING I HAVE BEEN WANTING TO DO FOR A WHILE, BUT HAVEN'T HAD THE NERVE.
NAME IT!

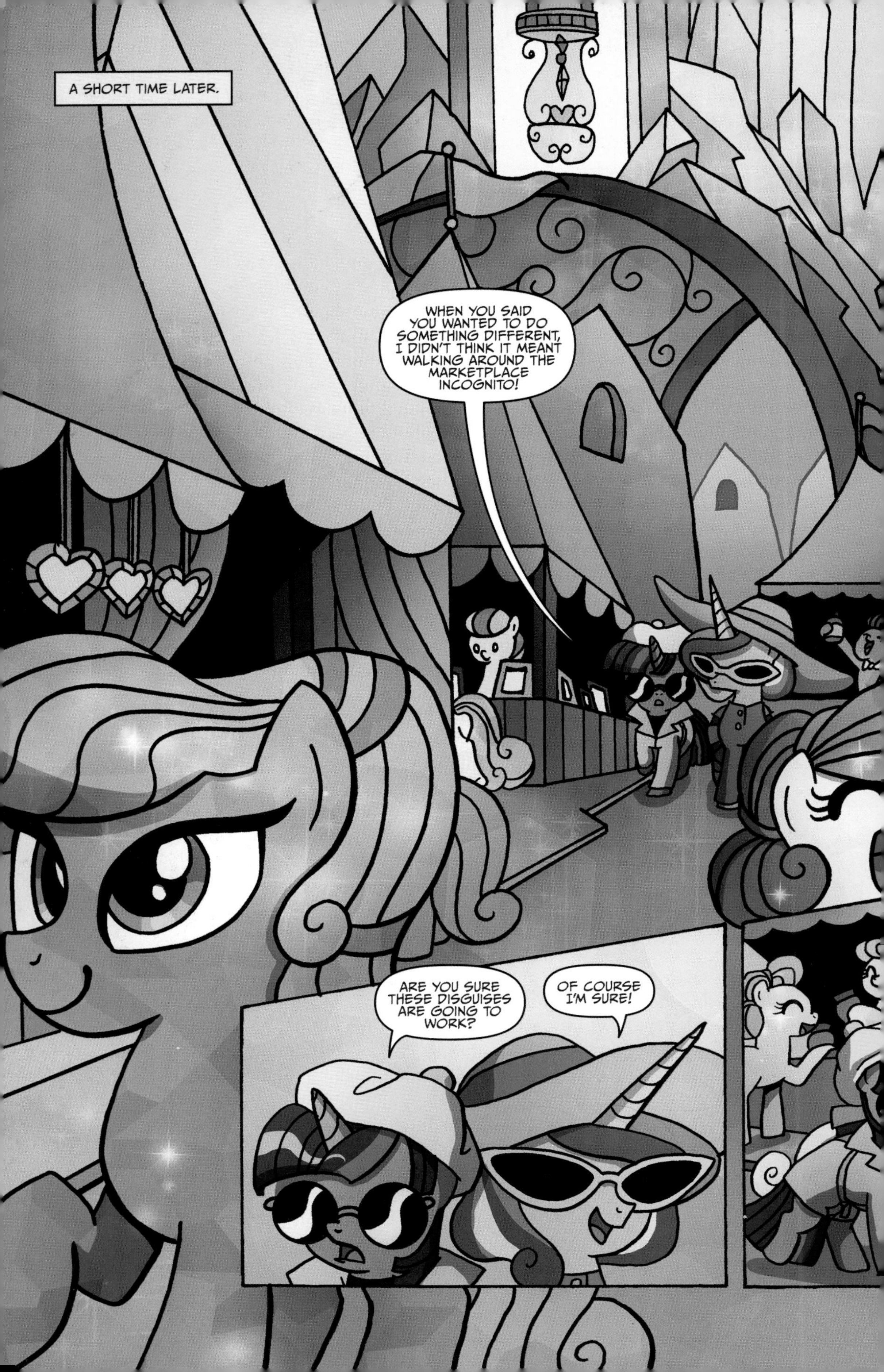
A SHORT TIME LATER.
WHEN YOU SAID YOU WANTED TO DO SOMETHING DIFFERENT, I DIDN'T THINK IT MEANT WALKING AROUND THE MARKETPLACE INCOGNITO!
ARE YOU SURE THESE DISGUISES ARE GOING TO WORK?
OF COURSE I'M SURE!

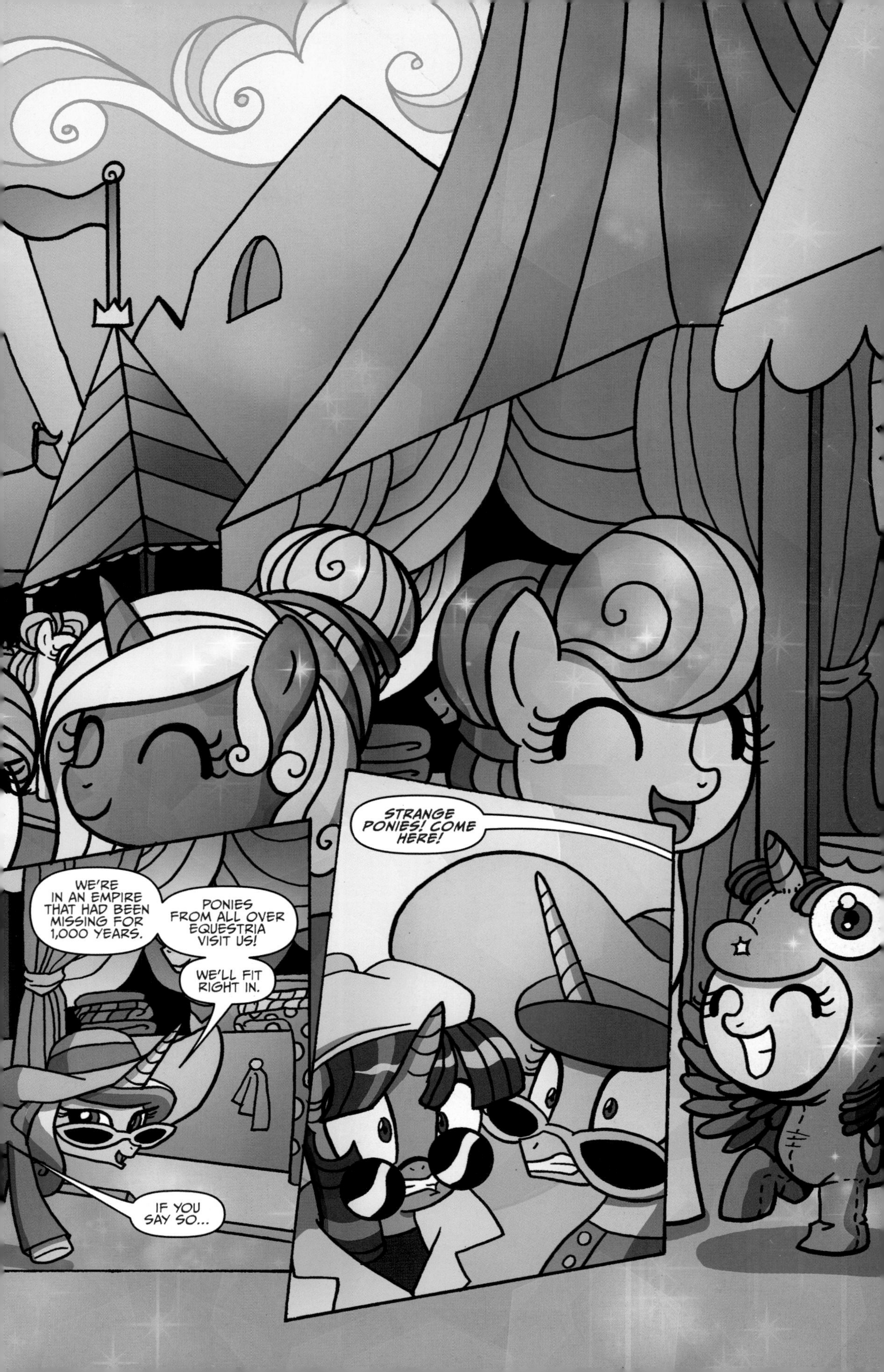
STRANGE PONIES! COME HERE!
WE'RE IN AN EMPIRE THAT HAD BEEN MISSING FOR 1,000 YEARS.
PONIES FROM ALL OVER EQUESTRIA VISIT US!
WE'LL FIT RIGHT IN.
IF YOU SAY SO...

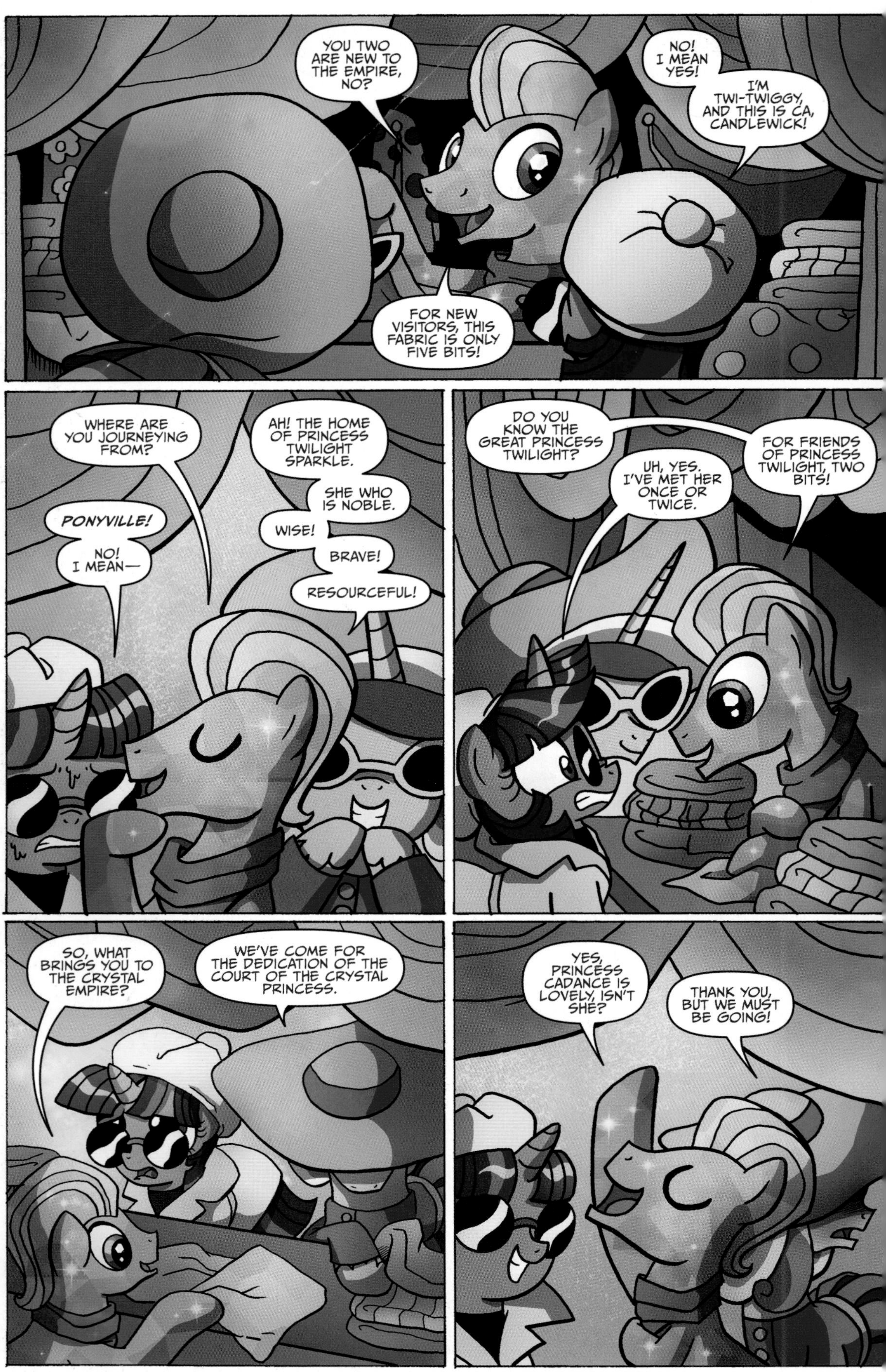
YOU TWO ARE NEW TO THE EMPIRE, NO?
NO! I MEAN YES!
I'M TWI-TWIGGY, AND THIS IS CA, CANDLEWICK!
FOR NEW VISITORS, THIS FABRIC IS ONLY FIVE BITS!
WHERE ARE YOU JOURNEYING FROM?
PONYVILLE!
NO! I MEAN—
AH! THE HOME OF PRINCESS TWILIGHT SPARKLE.
SHE WHO IS NOBLE.
WISE!
BRAVE!
RESOURCEFUL!
DO YOU KNOW THE GREAT PRINCESS TWILIGHT?
UH, YES. I'VE MET HER ONCE OR TWICE.
FOR FRIENDS OF PRINCESS TWILIGHT, TWO BITS!
SO, WHAT BRINGS YOU TO THE CRYSTAL EMPIRE?
WE'VE COME FOR THE DEDICATION OF THE COURT OF THE CRYSTAL PRINCESS.
YES, PRINCESS CADANCE IS LOVELY, ISN'T SHE?
THANK YOU, BUT WE MUST BE GOING!

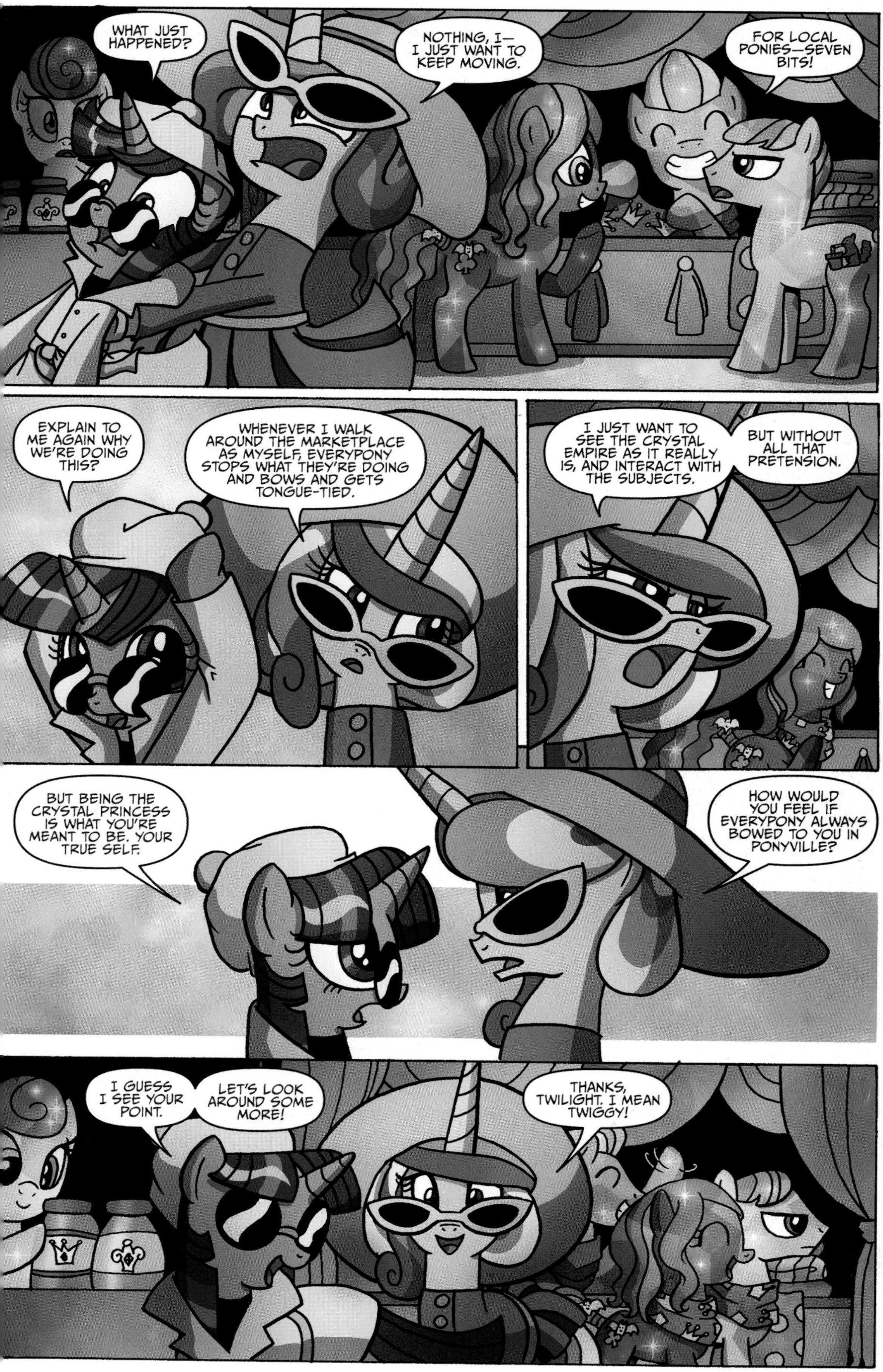

WHAT JUST HAPPENED?
NOTHING, I— I JUST WANT TO KEEP MOVING.
FOR LOCAL PONIES—SEVEN BITS!
EXPLAIN TO ME AGAIN WHY WE'RE DOING THIS?
WHENEVER I WALK AROUND THE MARKETPLACE AS MYSELF, EVERYPONY STOPS WHAT THEY'RE DOING AND BOWS AND GETS TONGUE-TIED.
I JUST WANT TO SEE THE CRYSTAL EMPIRE AS IT REALLY IS, AND INTERACT WITH THE SUBJECTS.
BUT WITHOUT ALL THAT PRETENSION.
BUT BEING THE CRYSTAL PRINCESS IS WHAT YOU'RE MEANT TO BE. YOUR TRUE SELF.
HOW WOULD YOU FEEL IF EVERYPONY ALWAYS BOWED TO YOU IN PONYVILLE?
I GUESS I SEE YOUR POINT.
LET'S LOOK AROUND SOME MORE!
THANKS, TWILIGHT. I MEAN TWIGGY!

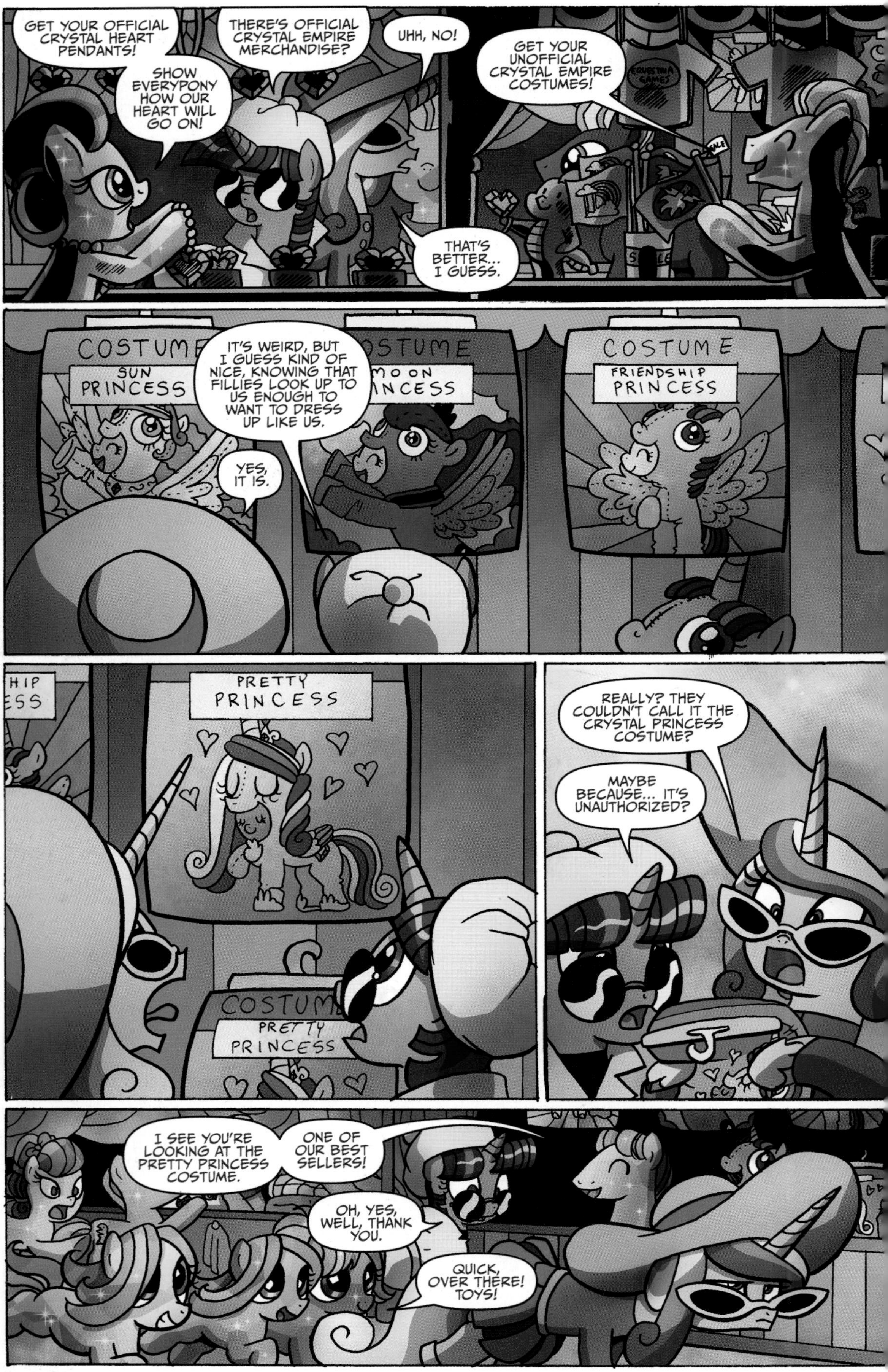
GET YOUR OFFICIAL CRYSTAL HEART PENDANTS!
SHOW EVERYPONY HOW OUR HEART WILL GO ON!
THERE'S OFFICIAL CRYSTAL EMPIRE MERCHANDISE?
UHH, NO!
GET YOUR UNOFFICIAL CRYSTAL EMPIRE COSTUMES!
EQUESTRIA GAMES
THAT'S BETTER... I GUESS.
COSTUME
SUN PRINCESS
COSTUME
MOON PRINCESS
IT'S WEIRD, BUT I GUESS KIND OF NICE, KNOWING THAT FILLIES LOOK UP TO US ENOUGH TO WANT TO DRESS UP LIKE US.
YES, IT IS.
COSTUME
FRIENDSHIP PRINCESS
PRETTY PRINCESS
COSTUME
PRETTY PRINCESS
REALLY? THEY COULDN'T CALL IT THE CRYSTAL PRINCESS COSTUME?
MAYBE BECAUSE... IT'S UNAUTHORIZED?
I SEE YOU'RE LOOKING AT THE PRETTY PRINCESS COSTUME.
ONE OF OUR BEST SELLERS!
OH, YES, WELL, THANK YOU.
QUICK, OVER THERE! TOYS!

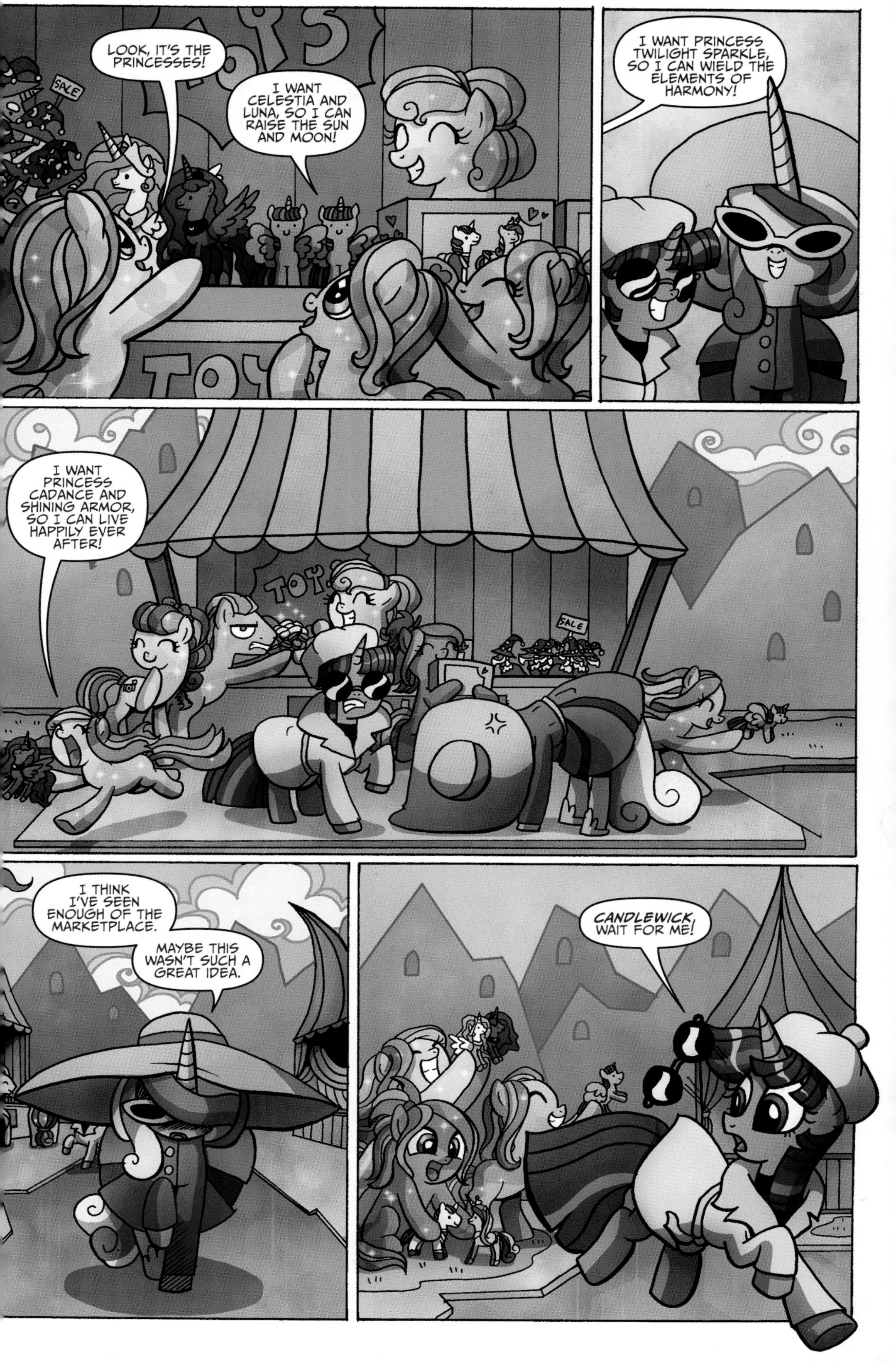
SALE
LOOK, IT'S THE PRINCESSES!
I WANT CELESTIA AND LUNA, SO I CAN RAISE THE SUN AND MOON!
TOYS
TOY
I WANT PRINCESS TWILIGHT SPARKLE, SO I CAN WIELD THE ELEMENTS OF HARMONY!
I WANT PRINCESS CADANCE AND SHINING ARMOR, SO I CAN LIVE HAPPILY EVER AFTER!
TOYS
SALE
I THINK I'VE SEEN ENOUGH OF THE MARKETPLACE.
MAYBE THIS WASN'T SUCH A GREAT IDEA.
CANDLEWICK, WAIT FOR ME!

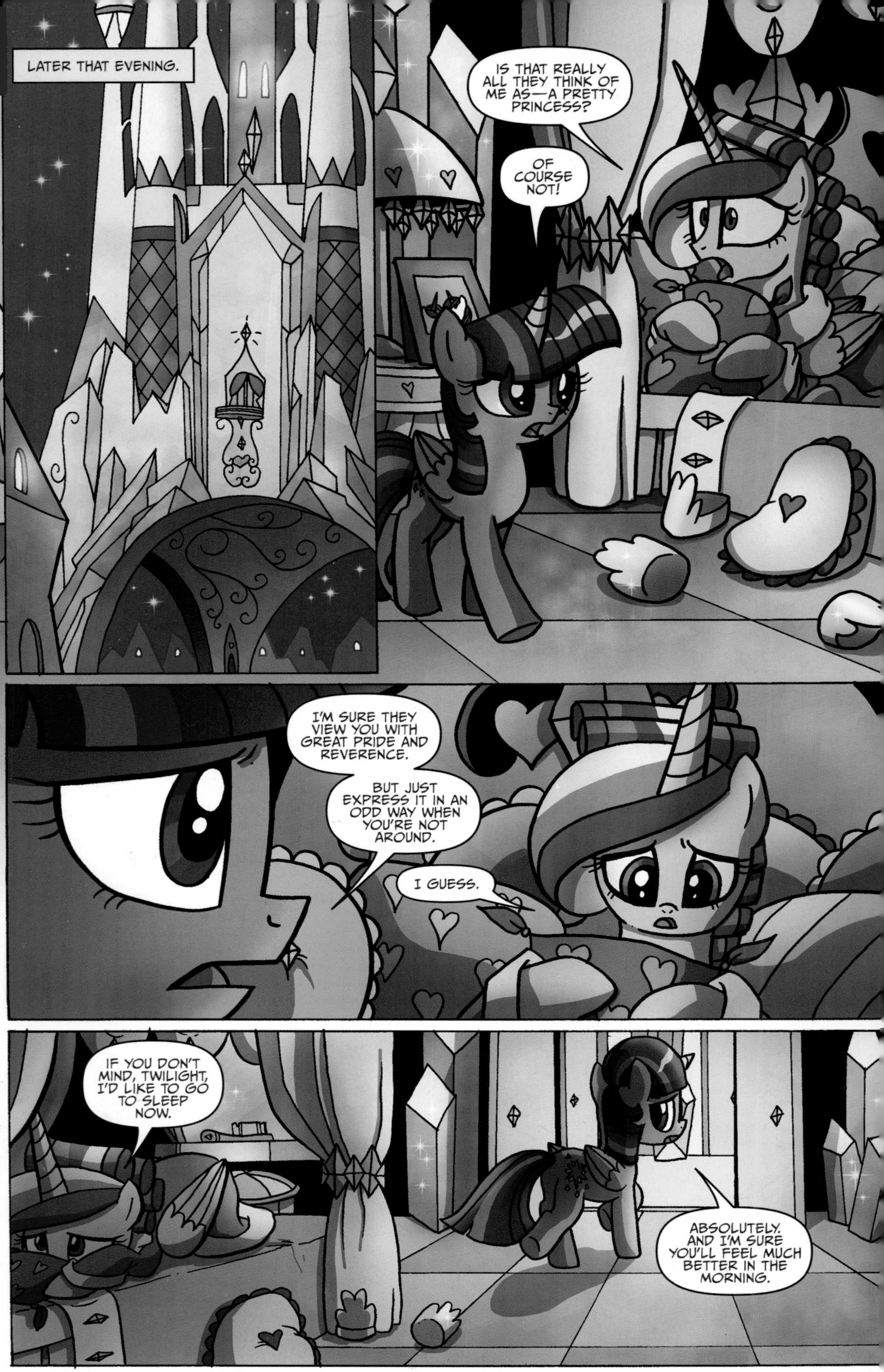
LATER THAT EVENING.
IS THAT REALLY ALL THEY THINK OF ME AS—A PRETTY PRINCESS?
OF COURSE NOT!
I'M SURE THEY VIEW YOU WITH GREAT PRIDE AND REVERENCE.
BUT JUST EXPRESS IT IN AN ODD WAY WHEN YOU'RE NOT AROUND.
I GUESS.
IF YOU DON'T MIND, TWILIGHT, I'D LIKE TO GO TO SLEEP NOW.
ABSOLUTELY. AND I'M SURE YOU'LL FEEL MUCH BETTER IN THE MORNING.

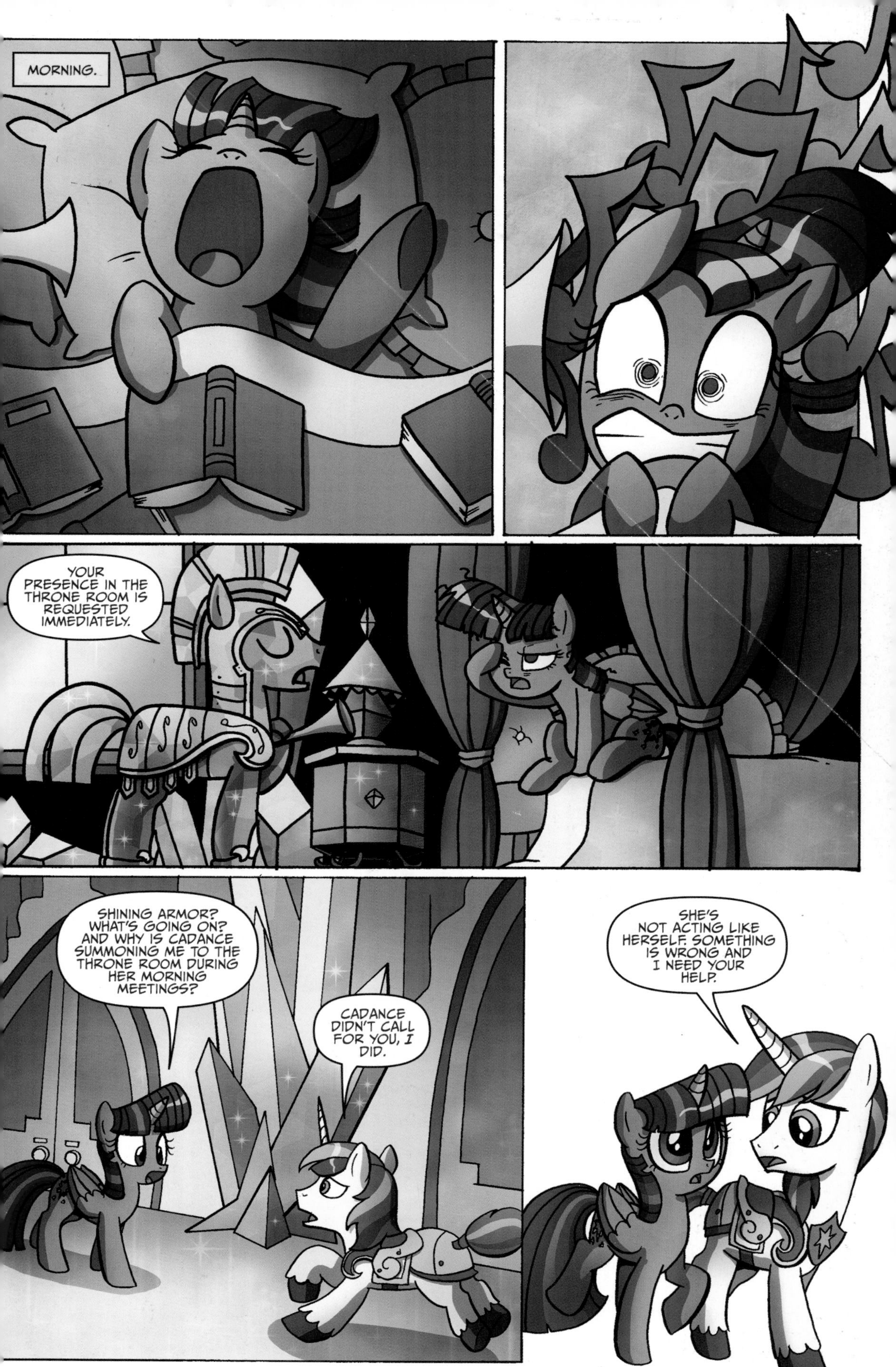
MORNING.
YOUR PRESENCE IN THE THRONE ROOM IS REQUESTED IMMEDIATELY.
SHINING ARMOR? WHAT'S GOING ON? AND WHY IS CADANCE SUMMONING ME TO THE THRONE ROOM DURING HER MORNING MEETINGS?
CADANCE DIDN'T CALL FOR YOU, *I* DID.
SHE'S NOT ACTING LIKE HERSELF. SOMETHING IS WRONG AND I NEED YOUR HELP.

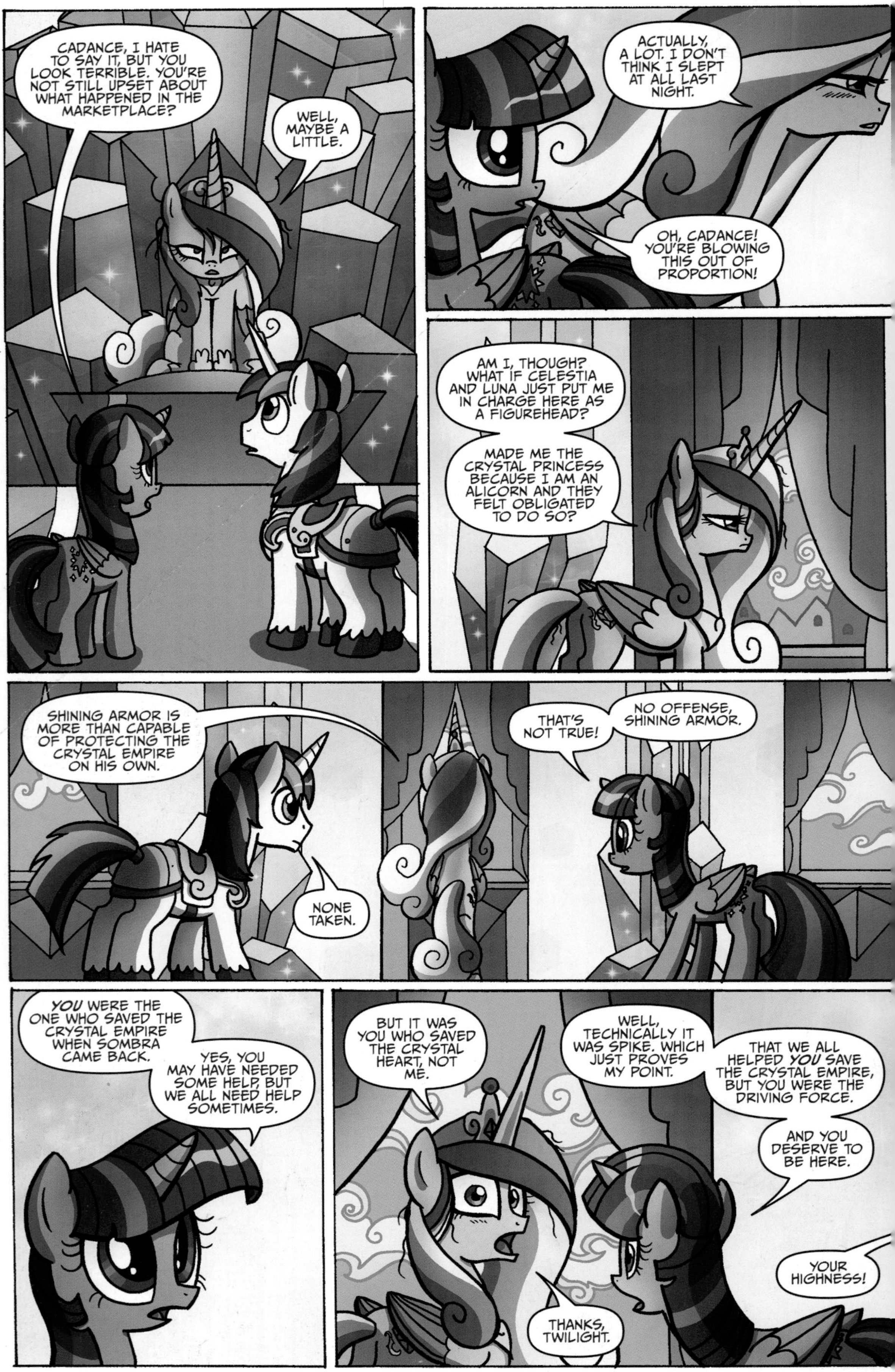
CADANCE, I HATE TO SAY IT, BUT YOU LOOK TERRIBLE. YOU'RE NOT STILL UPSET ABOUT WHAT HAPPENED IN THE MARKETPLACE?
WELL, MAYBE A LITTLE.
ACTUALLY, A LOT. I DON'T THINK I SLEPT AT ALL LAST NIGHT.
OH, CADANCE! YOU'RE BLOWING THIS OUT OF PROPORTION!
AM I, THOUGH? WHAT IF CELESTIA AND LUNA JUST PUT ME IN CHARGE HERE AS A FIGUREHEAD?
MADE ME THE CRYSTAL PRINCESS BECAUSE I AM AN ALICORN AND THEY FELT OBLIGATED TO DO SO?
SHINING ARMOR IS MORE THAN CAPABLE OF PROTECTING THE CRYSTAL EMPIRE ON HIS OWN.
NO OFFENSE, SHINING ARMOR.
NONE TAKEN.
THAT'S NOT TRUE!
YOU WERE THE ONE WHO SAVED THE CRYSTAL EMPIRE WHEN SOMBRA CAME BACK.
YES, YOU MAY HAVE NEEDED SOME HELP, BUT WE ALL NEED HELP SOMETIMES.
BUT IT WAS YOU WHO SAVED THE CRYSTAL HEART, NOT ME.
WELL, TECHNICALLY IT WAS SPIKE. WHICH JUST PROVES MY POINT.
THAT WE ALL HELPED YOU SAVE THE CRYSTAL EMPIRE, BUT YOU WERE THE DRIVING FORCE.
AND YOU DESERVE TO BE HERE.
THANKS, TWILIGHT.
YOUR HIGHNESS!

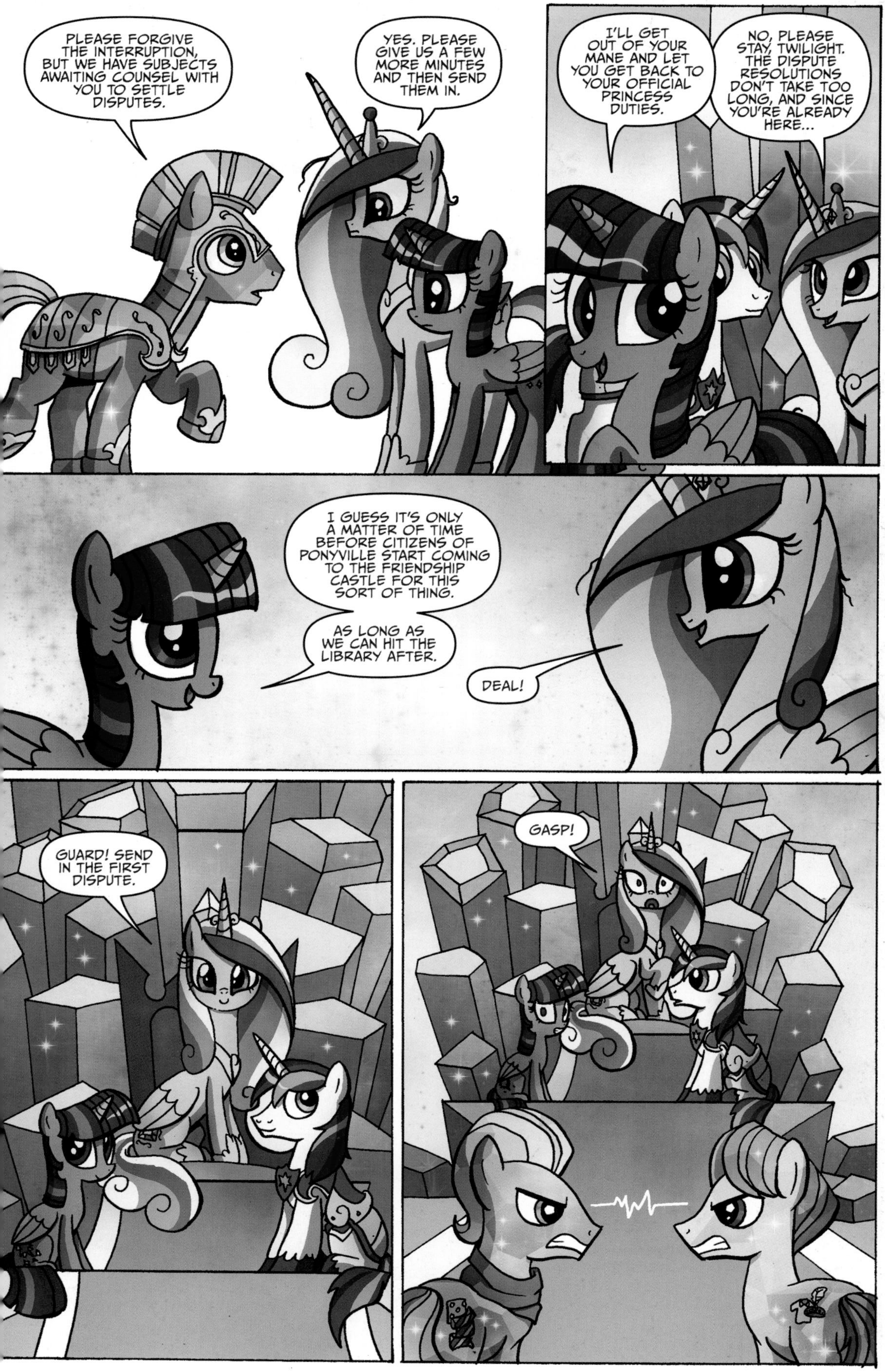
PLEASE FORGIVE THE INTERRUPTION, BUT WE HAVE SUBJECTS AWAITING COUNSEL WITH YOU TO SETTLE DISPUTES.
YES. PLEASE GIVE US A FEW MORE MINUTES AND THEN SEND THEM IN.
I'LL GET OUT OF YOUR MANE AND LET YOU GET BACK TO YOUR OFFICIAL PRINCESS DUTIES.
NO, PLEASE STAY, TWILIGHT. THE DISPUTE RESOLUTIONS DON'T TAKE TOO LONG, AND SINCE YOU'RE ALREADY HERE...
I GUESS IT'S ONLY A MATTER OF TIME BEFORE CITIZENS OF PONYVILLE START COMING TO THE FRIENDSHIP CASTLE FOR THIS SORT OF THING.
AS LONG AS WE CAN HIT THE LIBRARY AFTER.
DEAL!
GUARD! SEND IN THE FIRST DISPUTE.
GASP!

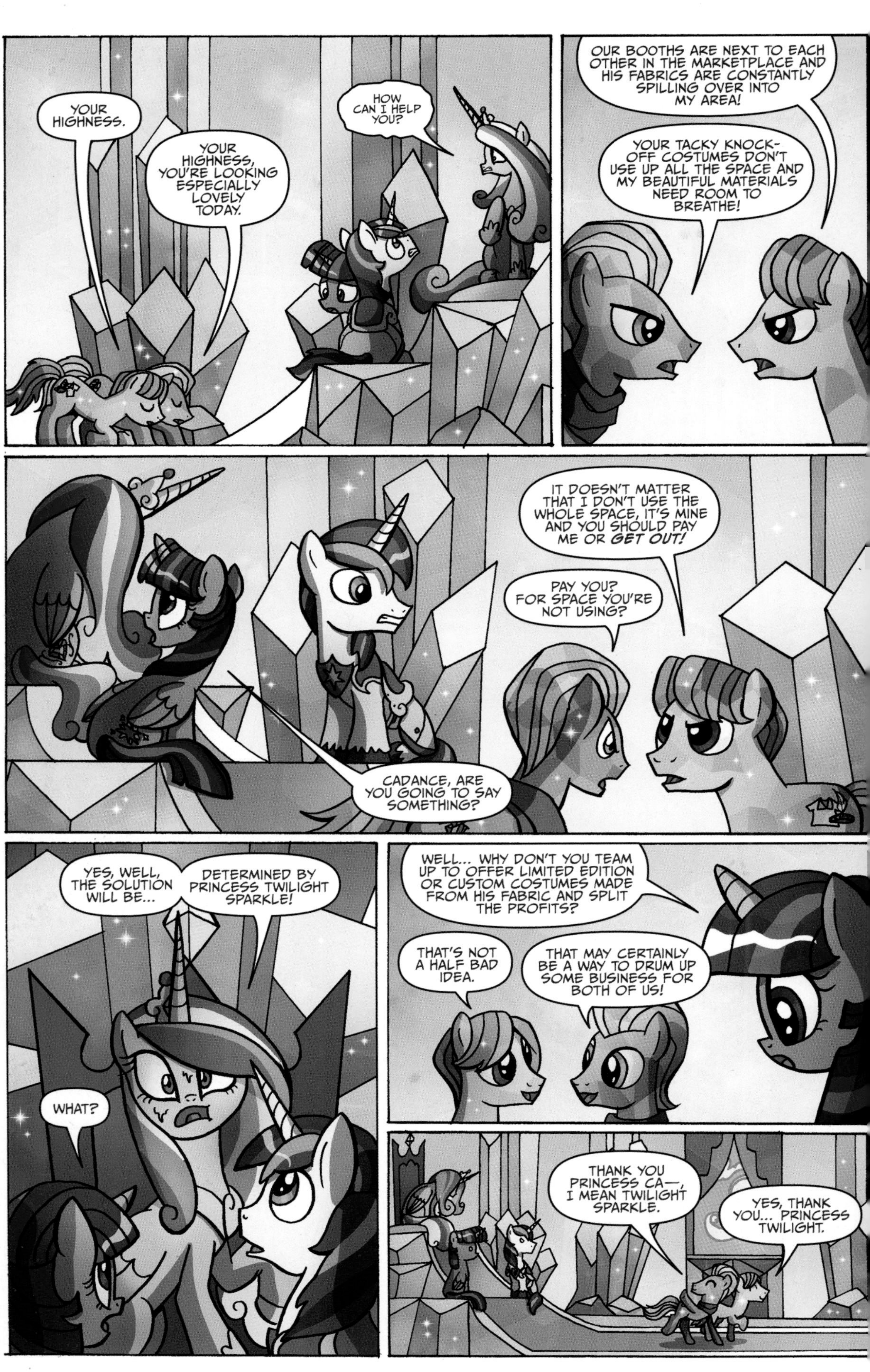
YOUR HIGHNESS.
YOUR HIGHNESS, YOU'RE LOOKING ESPECIALLY LOVELY TODAY.
HOW CAN I HELP YOU?
OUR BOOTHS ARE NEXT TO EACH OTHER IN THE MARKETPLACE AND HIS FABRICS ARE CONSTANTLY SPILLING OVER INTO MY AREA!
YOUR TACKY KNOCK-OFF COSTUMES DON'T USE UP ALL THE SPACE AND MY BEAUTIFUL MATERIALS NEED ROOM TO BREATHE!
IT DOESN'T MATTER THAT I DON'T USE THE WHOLE SPACE, IT'S MINE AND YOU SHOULD PAY ME OR GET OUT!
PAY YOU? FOR SPACE YOU'RE NOT USING?
CADANCE, ARE YOU GOING TO SAY SOMETHING?
YES, WELL, THE SOLUTION WILL BE...
DETERMINED BY PRINCESS TWILIGHT SPARKLE!
WHAT?
WELL... WHY DON'T YOU TEAM UP TO OFFER LIMITED EDITION OR CUSTOM COSTUMES MADE FROM HIS FABRIC AND SPLIT THE PROFITS?
THAT'S NOT A HALF BAD IDEA.
THAT MAY CERTAINLY BE A WAY TO DRUM UP SOME BUSINESS FOR BOTH OF US!
THANK YOU PRINCESS CA—, I MEAN TWILIGHT SPARKLE.
YES, THANK YOU... PRINCESS TWILIGHT.

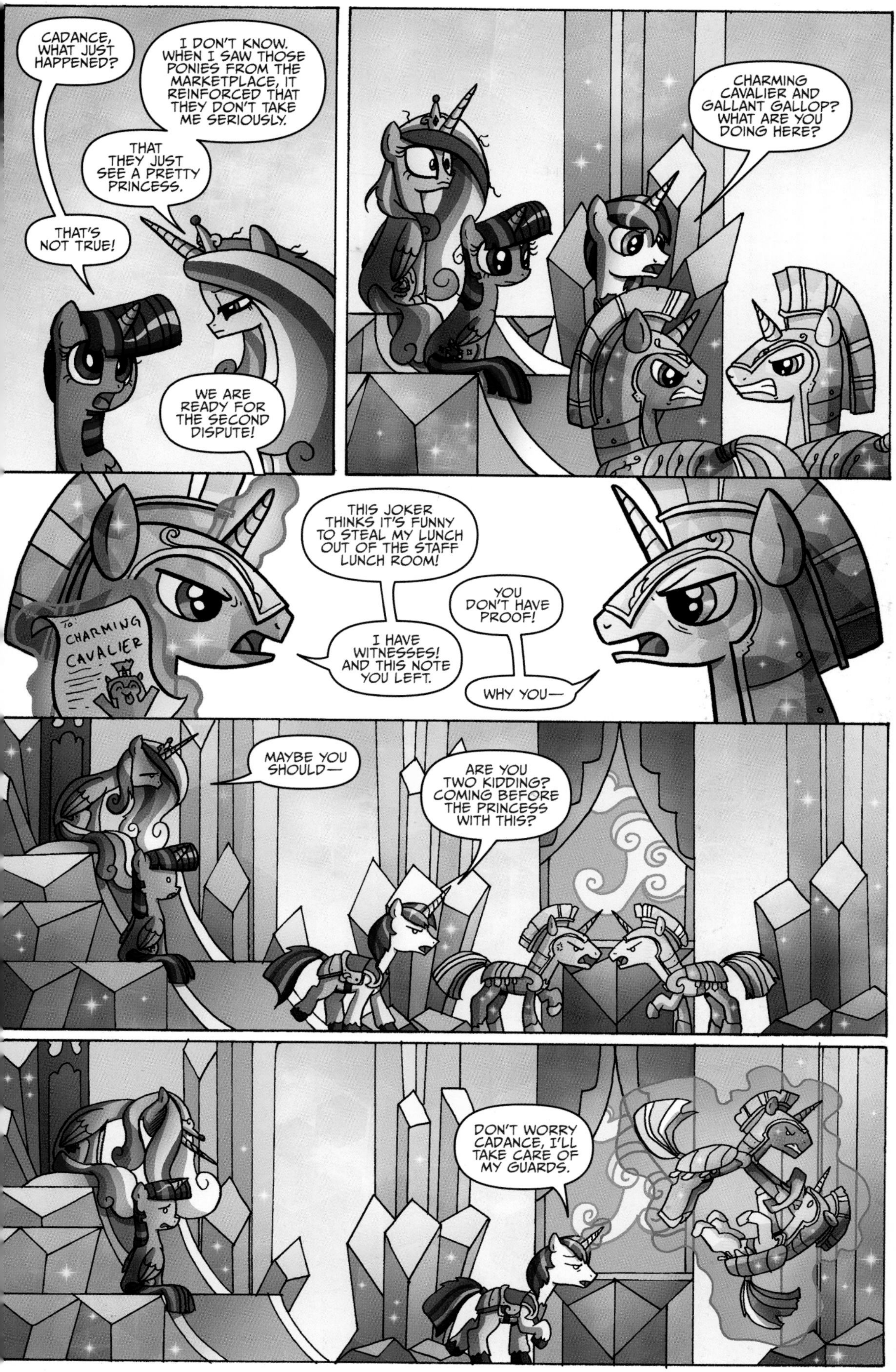
CADANCE, WHAT JUST HAPPENED?
I DON'T KNOW. WHEN I SAW THOSE PONIES FROM THE MARKETPLACE, IT REINFORCED THAT THEY DON'T TAKE ME SERIOUSLY.
THAT THEY JUST SEE A PRETTY PRINCESS.
THAT'S NOT TRUE!
WE ARE READY FOR THE SECOND DISPUTE!
CHARMING CAVALIER AND GALLANT GALLOP? WHAT ARE YOU DOING HERE?
TO: CHARMING CAVALIER
THIS JOKER THINKS IT'S FUNNY TO STEAL MY LUNCH OUT OF THE STAFF LUNCH ROOM!
YOU DON'T HAVE PROOF!
I HAVE WITNESSES! AND THIS NOTE YOU LEFT.
WHY YOU—
MAYBE YOU SHOULD—
ARE YOU TWO KIDDING? COMING BEFORE THE PRINCESS WITH THIS?
DON'T WORRY CADANCE, I'LL TAKE CARE OF MY GUARDS.

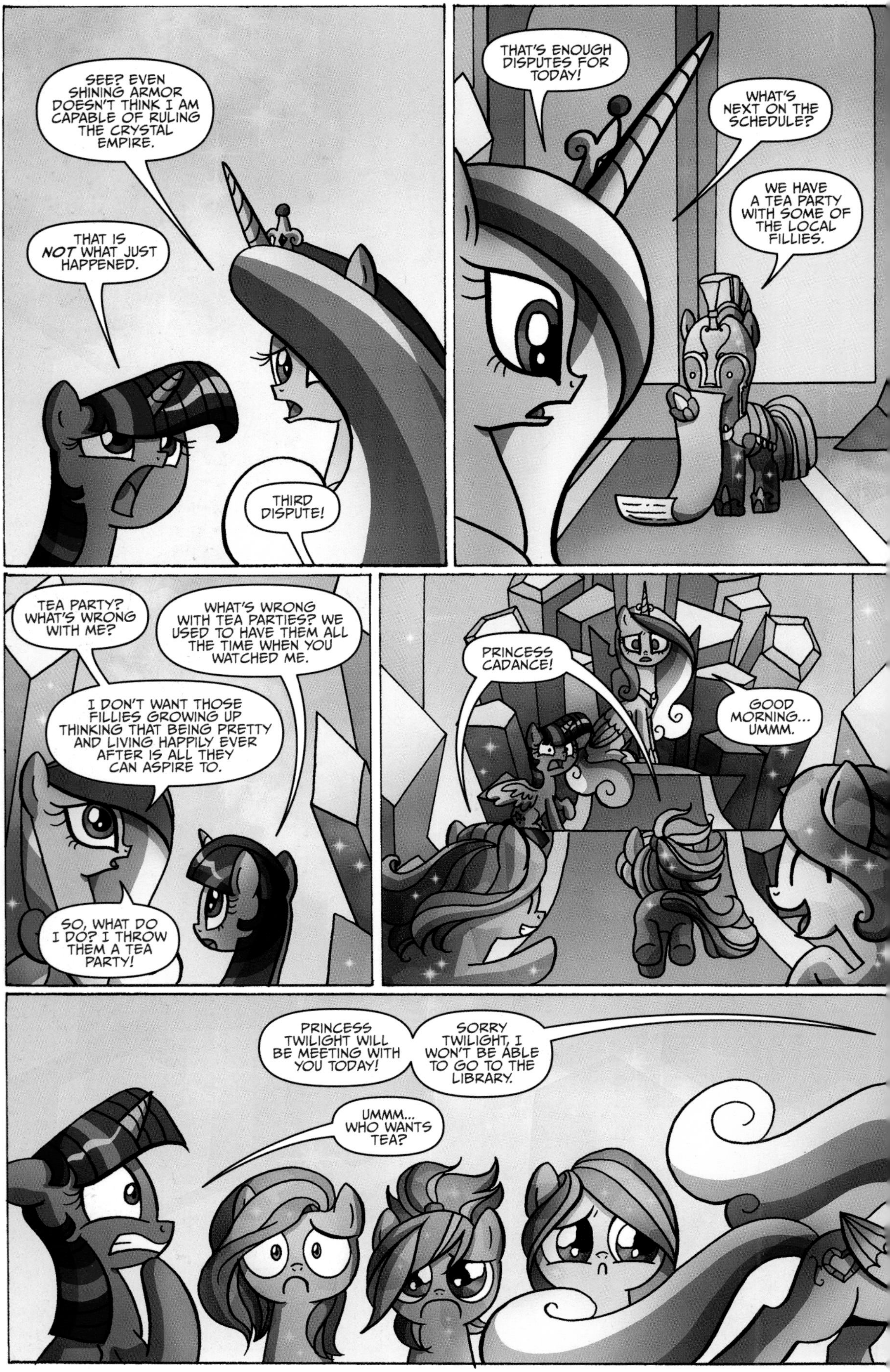
SEE? EVEN SHINING ARMOR DOESN'T THINK I AM CAPABLE OF RULING THE CRYSTAL EMPIRE.
THAT IS *NOT* WHAT JUST HAPPENED.
THIRD DISPUTE!
THAT'S ENOUGH DISPUTES FOR TODAY!
WHAT'S NEXT ON THE SCHEDULE?
WE HAVE A TEA PARTY WITH SOME OF THE LOCAL FILLIES.
TEA PARTY? WHAT'S WRONG WITH ME?
WHAT'S WRONG WITH TEA PARTIES? WE USED TO HAVE THEM ALL THE TIME WHEN YOU WATCHED ME.
I DON'T WANT THOSE FILLIES GROWING UP THINKING THAT BEING PRETTY AND LIVING HAPPILY EVER AFTER IS ALL THEY CAN ASPIRE TO.
SO, WHAT DO I DO? I THROW THEM A TEA PARTY!
PRINCESS CADANCE!
GOOD MORNING... UMMM.
PRINCESS TWILIGHT WILL BE MEETING WITH YOU TODAY!
SORRY TWILIGHT, I WON'T BE ABLE TO GO TO THE LIBRARY.
UMMM... WHO WANTS TEA?

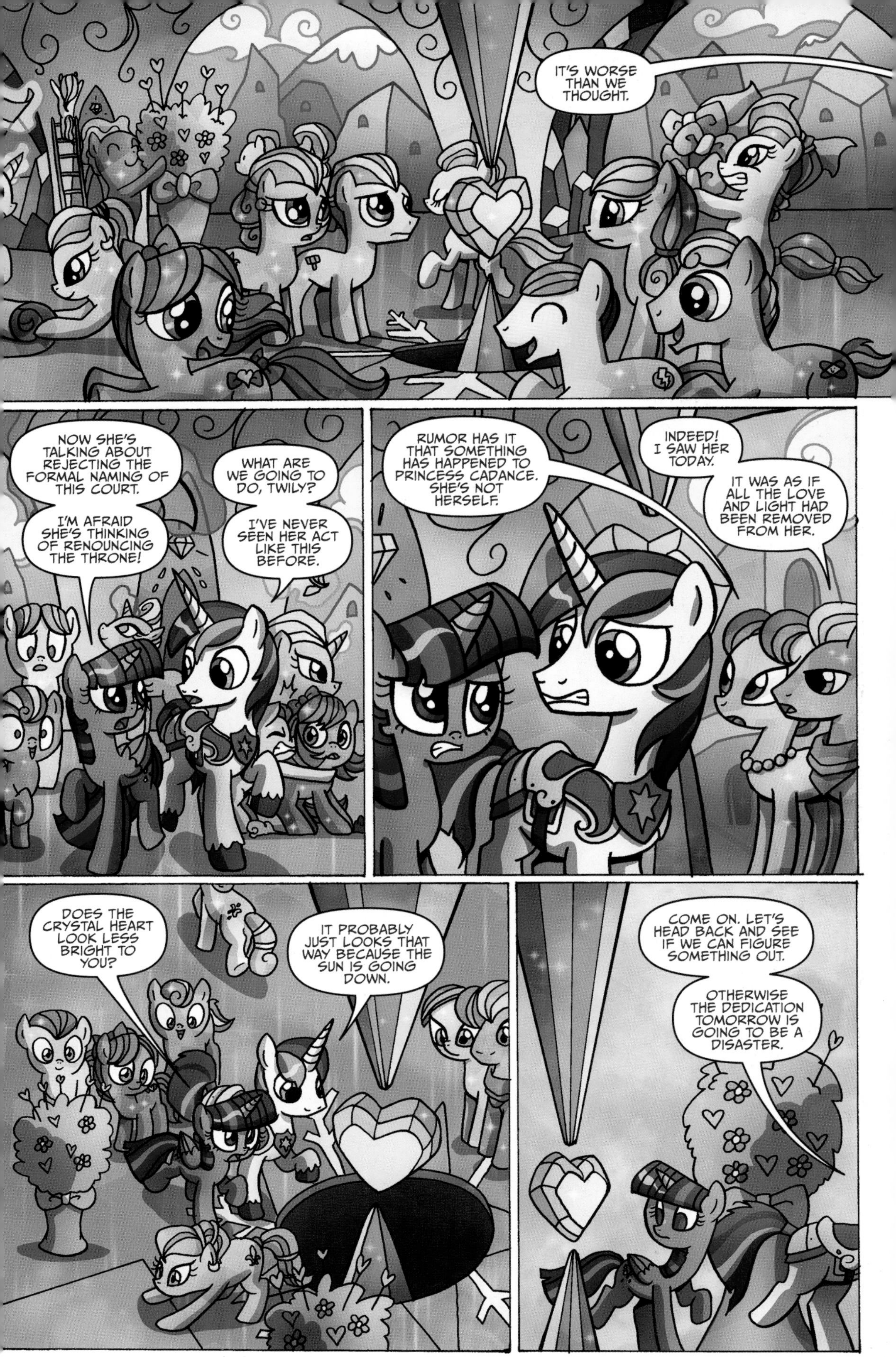

IT'S WORSE THAN WE THOUGHT.
NOW SHE'S TALKING ABOUT REJECTING THE FORMAL NAMING OF THIS COURT.
I'M AFRAID SHE'S THINKING OF RENOUNCING THE THRONE!
WHAT ARE WE GOING TO DO, TWILY?
I'VE NEVER SEEN HER ACT LIKE THIS BEFORE.
RUMOR HAS IT THAT SOMETHING HAS HAPPENED TO PRINCESS CADANCE. SHE'S NOT HERSELF.
INDEED! I SAW HER TODAY.
IT WAS AS IF ALL THE LOVE AND LIGHT HAD BEEN REMOVED FROM HER.
DOES THE CRYSTAL HEART LOOK LESS BRIGHT TO YOU?
IT PROBABLY JUST LOOKS THAT WAY BECAUSE THE SUN IS GOING DOWN.
COME ON. LET'S HEAD BACK AND SEE IF WE CAN FIGURE SOMETHING OUT.
OTHERWISE THE DEDICATION TOMORROW IS GOING TO BE A DISASTER.

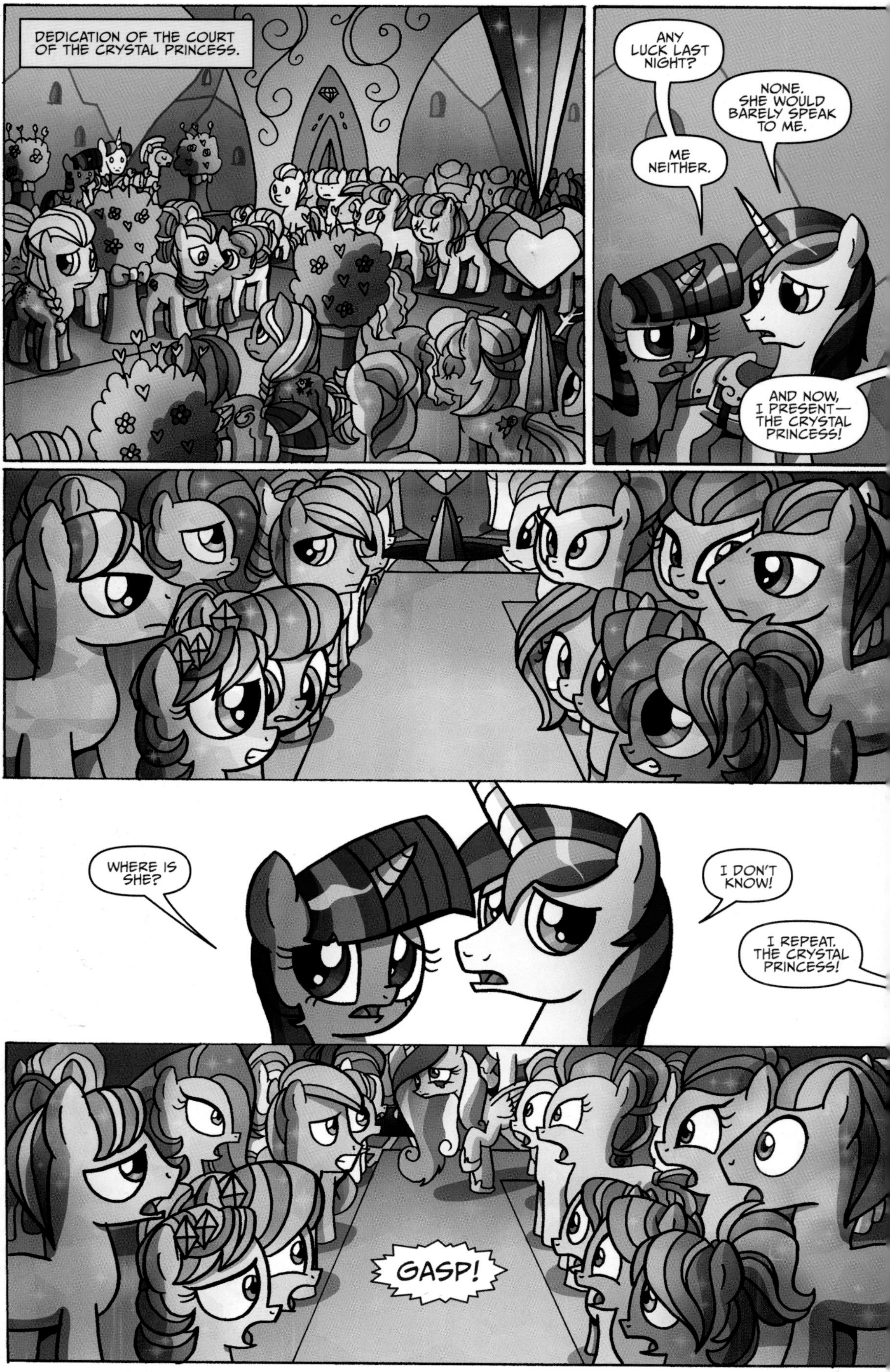
DEDICATION OF THE COURT OF THE CRYSTAL PRINCESS.
ANY LUCK LAST NIGHT?
NONE. SHE WOULD BARELY SPEAK TO ME.
ME NEITHER.
AND NOW, I PRESENT— THE CRYSTAL PRINCESS!
WHERE IS SHE?
I DON'T KNOW!
I REPEAT. THE CRYSTAL PRINCESS!
GASP!

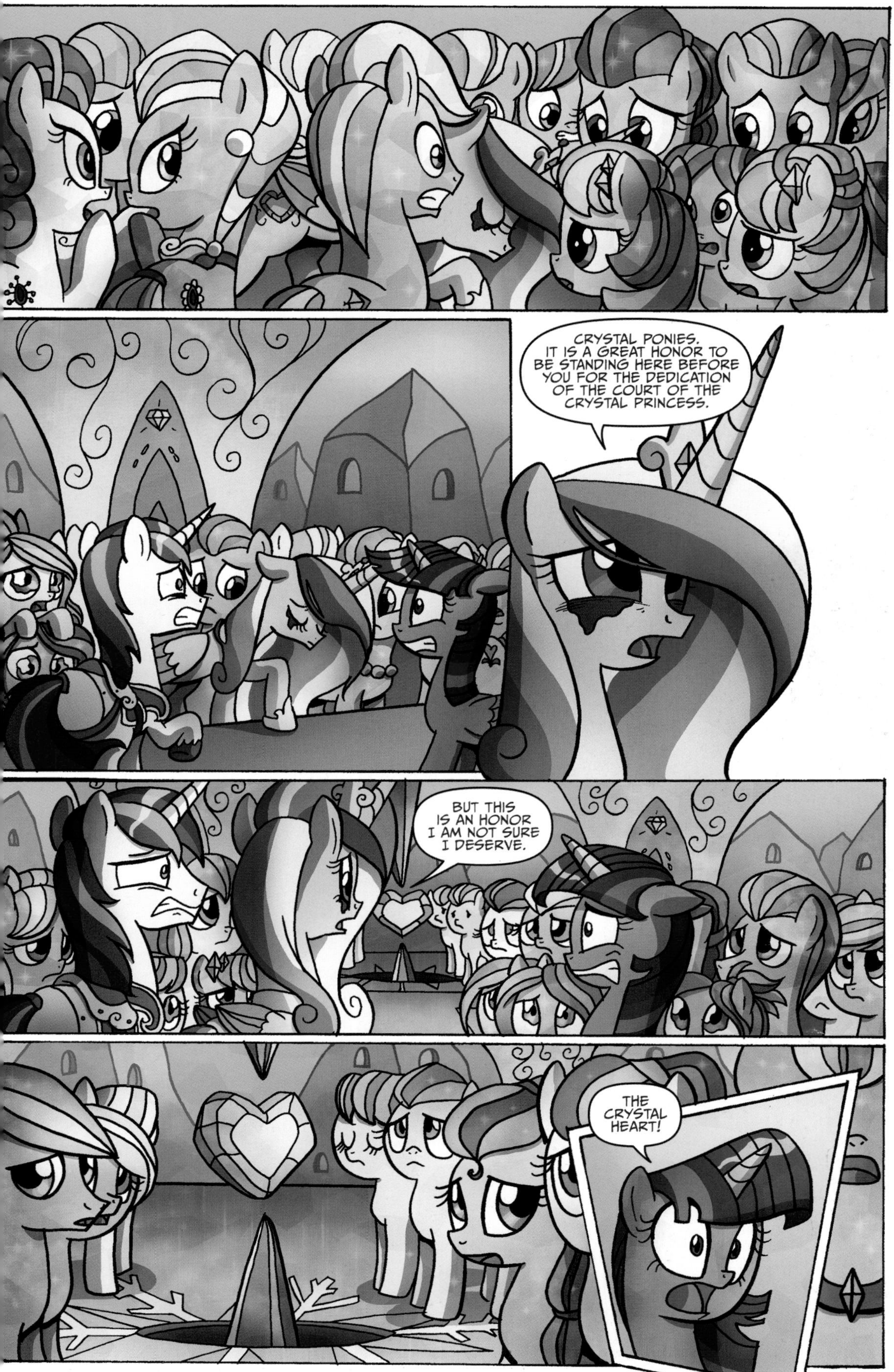
CRYSTAL PONIES. IT IS A GREAT HONOR TO BE STANDING HERE BEFORE YOU FOR THE DEDICATION OF THE COURT OF THE CRYSTAL PRINCESS.
BUT THIS IS AN HONOR I AM NOT SURE I DESERVE.
THE CRYSTAL HEART!

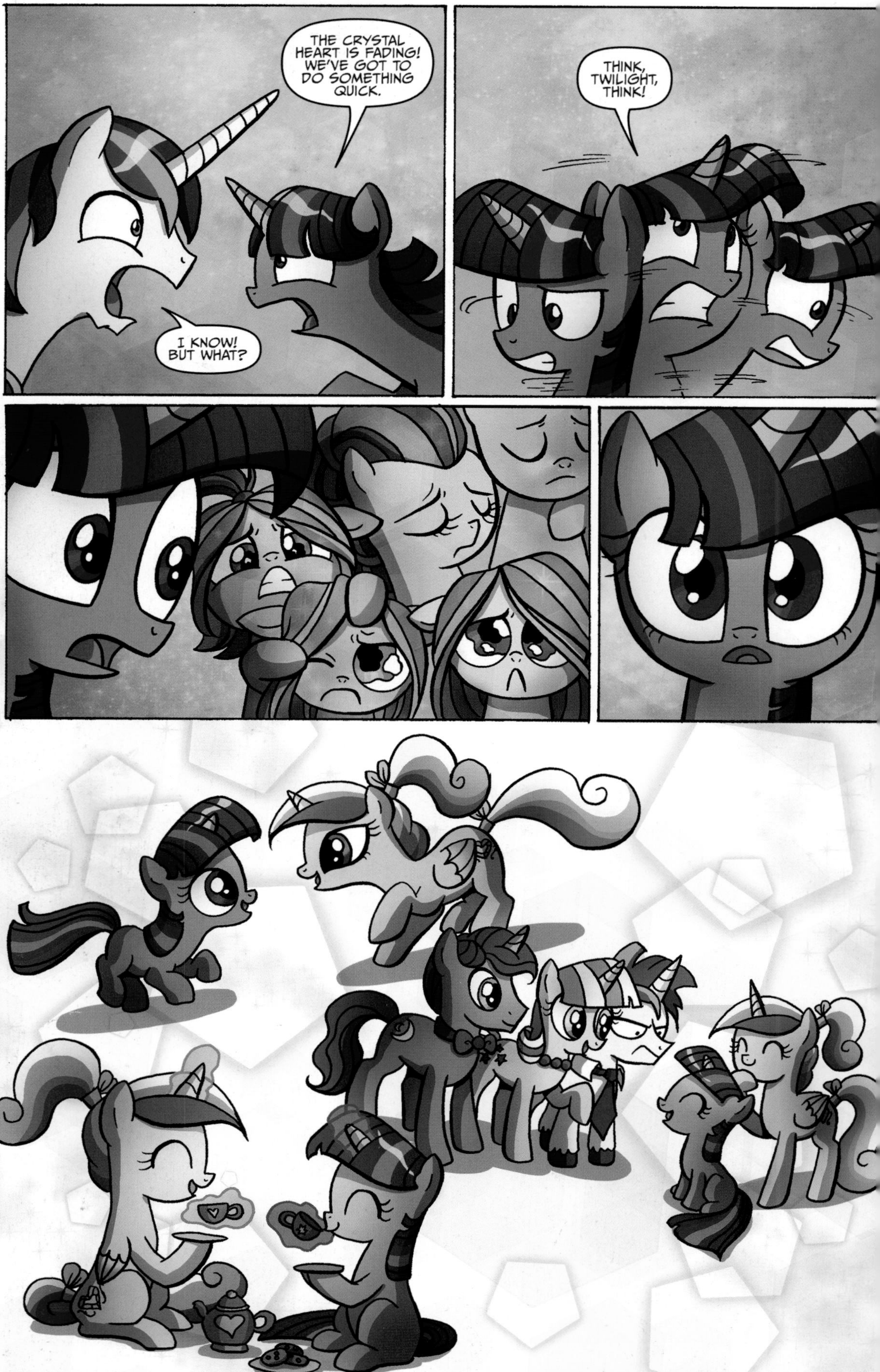
THE CRYSTAL HEART IS FADING! WE'VE GOT TO DO SOMETHING QUICK.
I KNOW! BUT WHAT?
THINK, TWILIGHT, THINK!

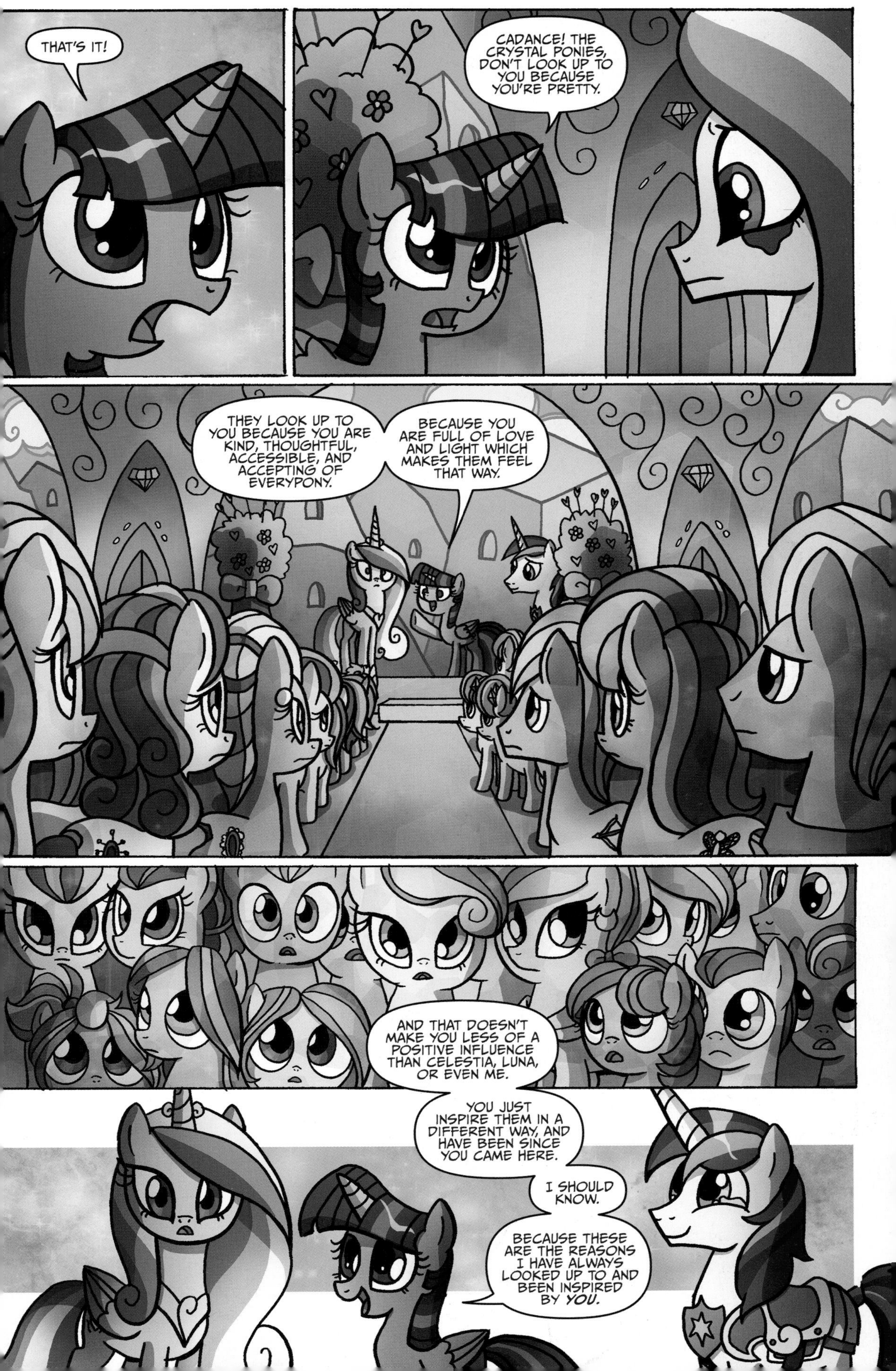
THAT'S IT!
CADANCE! THE CRYSTAL PONIES, DON'T LOOK UP TO YOU BECAUSE YOU'RE PRETTY.
THEY LOOK UP TO YOU BECAUSE YOU ARE KIND, THOUGHTFUL, ACCESSIBLE, AND ACCEPTING OF EVERYPONY.
BECAUSE YOU ARE FULL OF LOVE AND LIGHT WHICH MAKES THEM FEEL THAT WAY.
AND THAT DOESN'T MAKE YOU LESS OF A POSITIVE INFLUENCE THAN CELESTIA, LUNA, OR EVEN ME.
YOU JUST INSPIRE THEM IN A DIFFERENT WAY, AND HAVE BEEN SINCE YOU CAME HERE.
I SHOULD KNOW.
BECAUSE THESE ARE THE REASONS I HAVE ALWAYS LOOKED UP TO AND BEEN INSPIRED BY *YOU*.

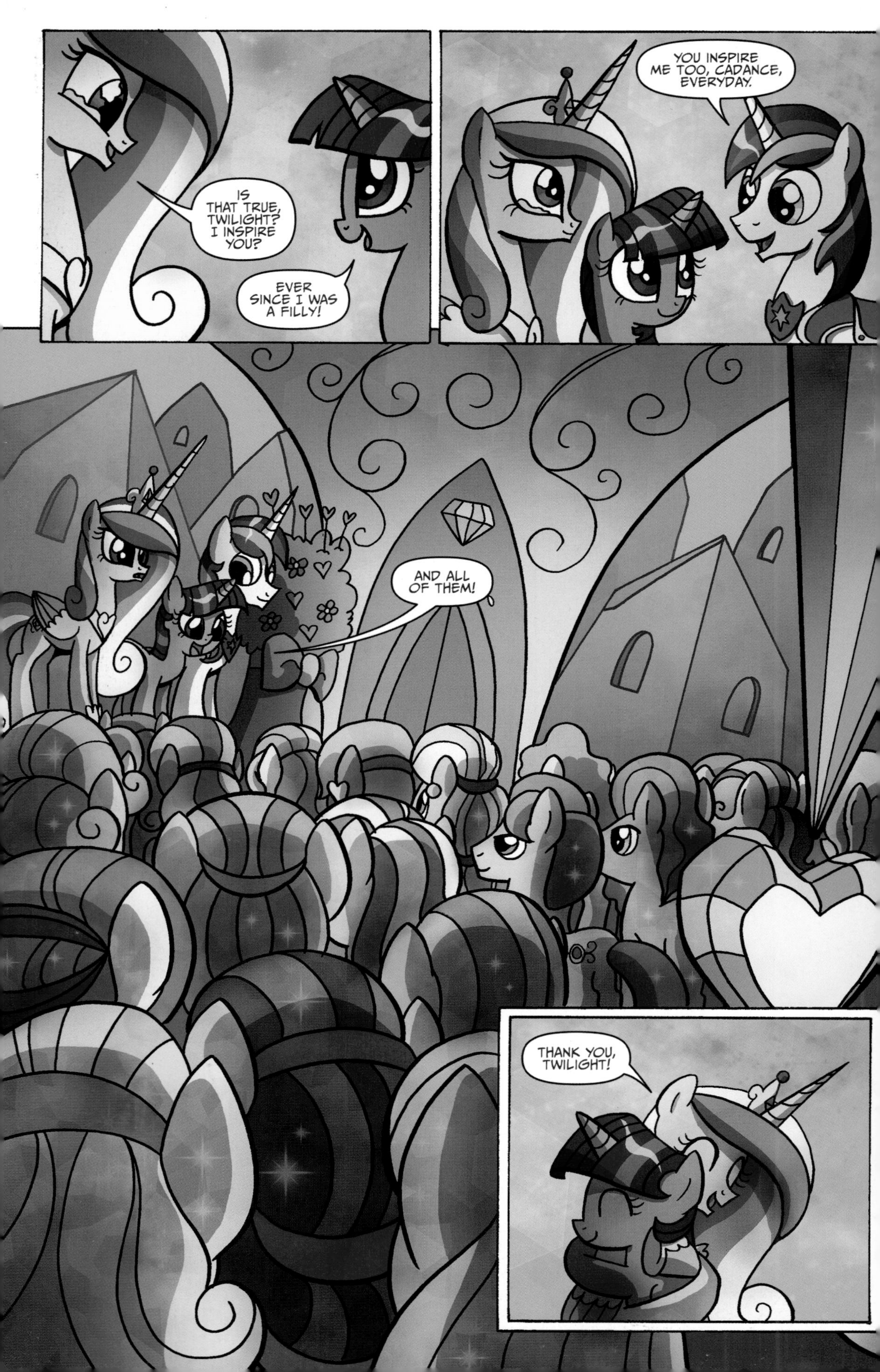

IS THAT TRUE, TWILIGHT? I INSPIRE YOU?
EVER SINCE I WAS A FILLY!
YOU INSPIRE ME TOO, CADANCE, EVERYDAY.
AND ALL OF THEM!
THANK YOU, TWILIGHT!

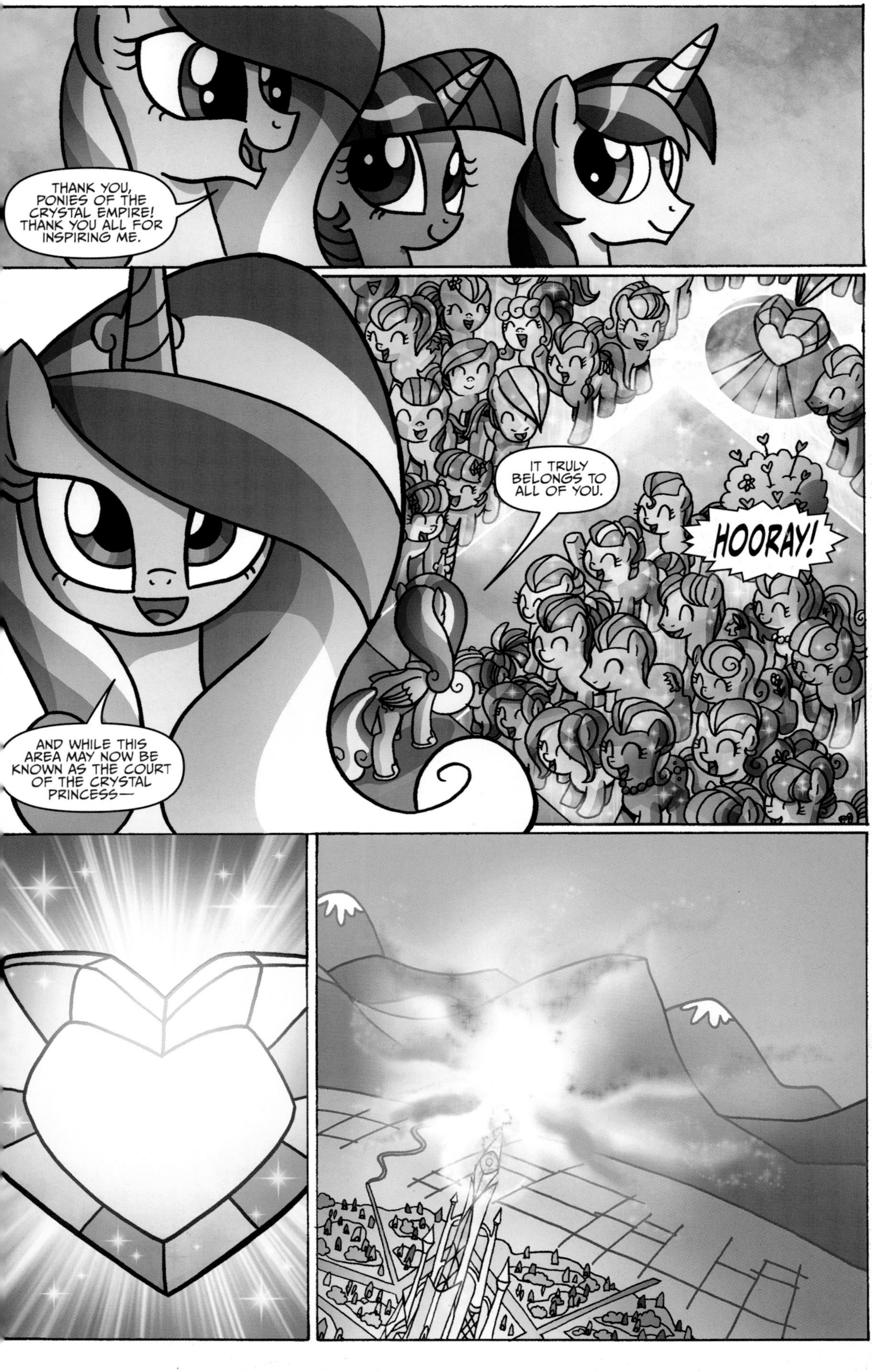
THANK YOU, PONIES OF THE CRYSTAL EMPIRE! THANK YOU ALL FOR INSPIRING ME.
AND WHILE THIS AREA MAY NOW BE KNOWN AS THE COURT OF THE CRYSTAL PRINCESS—
IT TRULY BELONGS TO ALL OF YOU.
HOORAY!

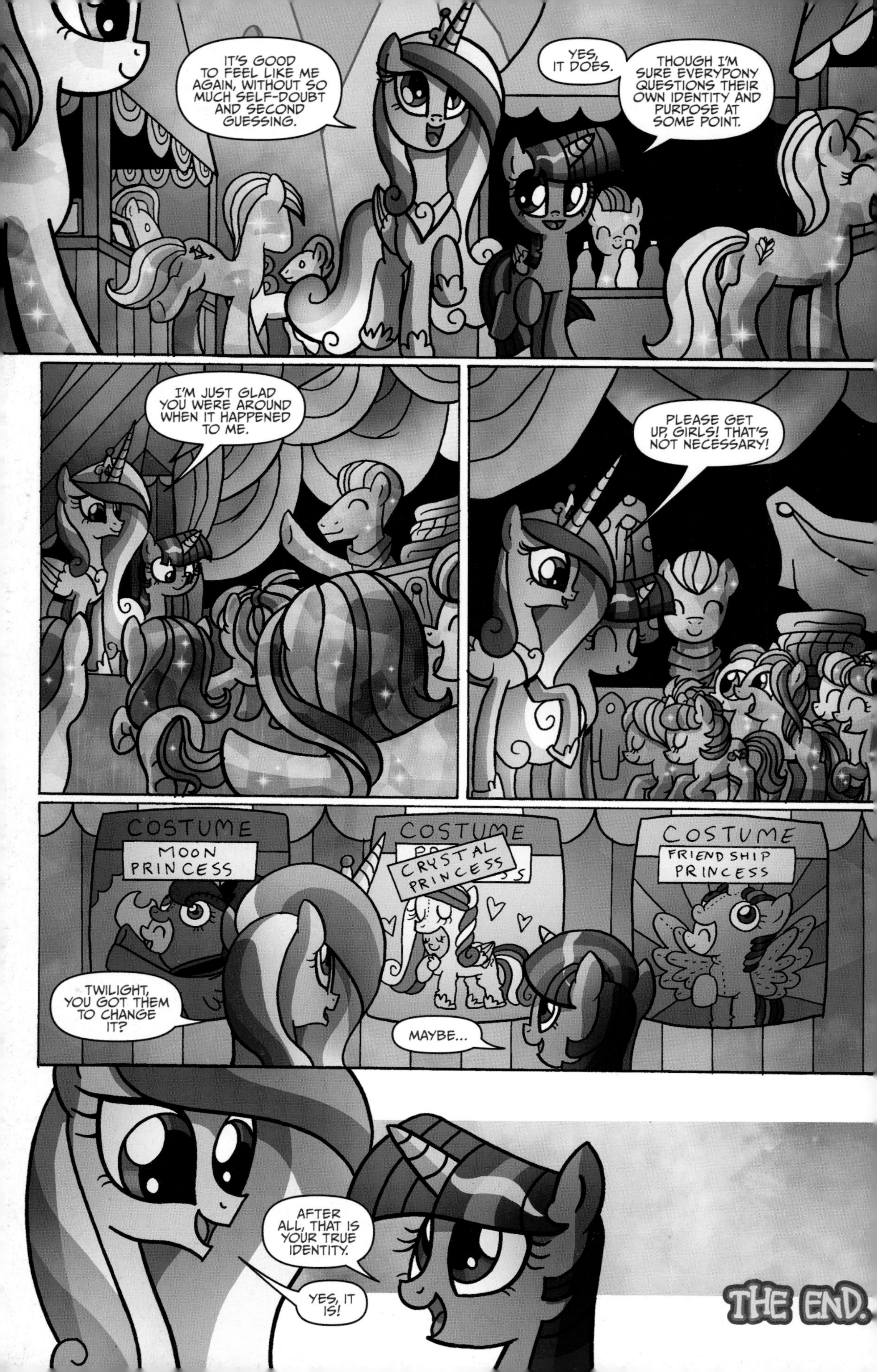
IT'S GOOD TO FEEL LIKE ME AGAIN, WITHOUT SO MUCH SELF-DOUBT AND SECOND GUESSING.
YES, IT DOES.
THOUGH I'M SURE EVERYPONY QUESTIONS THEIR OWN IDENTITY AND PURPOSE AT SOME POINT.
I'M JUST GLAD YOU WERE AROUND WHEN IT HAPPENED TO ME.
PLEASE GET UP, GIRLS! THAT'S NOT NECESSARY!
COSTUME
MOON PRINCESS
COSTUME
CRYSTAL PRINCESS
COSTUME
FRIENDSHIP PRINCESS
TWILIGHT, YOU GOT THEM TO CHANGE IT?
MAYBE...
AFTER ALL, THAT IS YOUR TRUE IDENTITY.
YES, IT IS!
THE END.

my LITTLE PONY

FRIENDS FOREVER

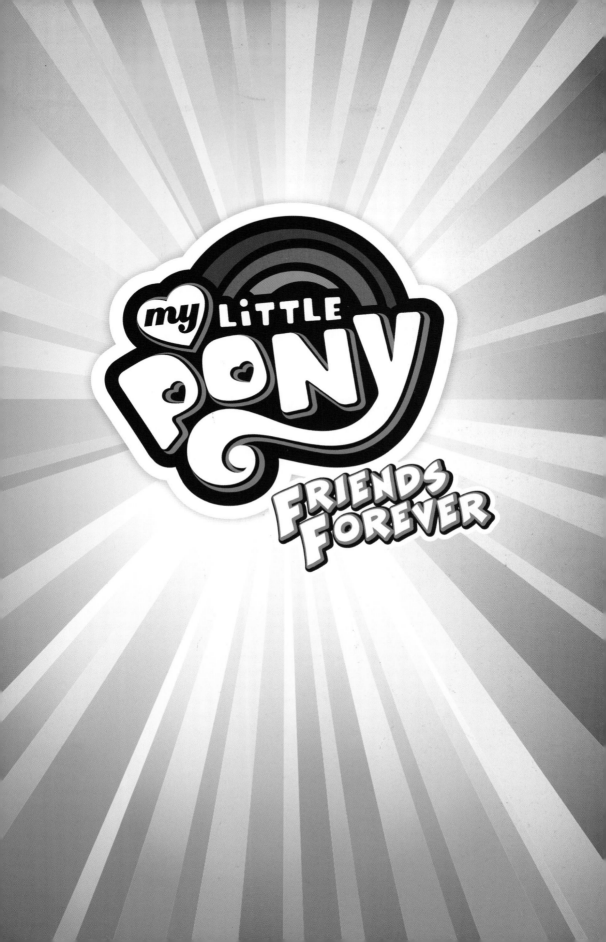

Rainbow Dash & Little StrongHeart

art by
Tony Fleecs

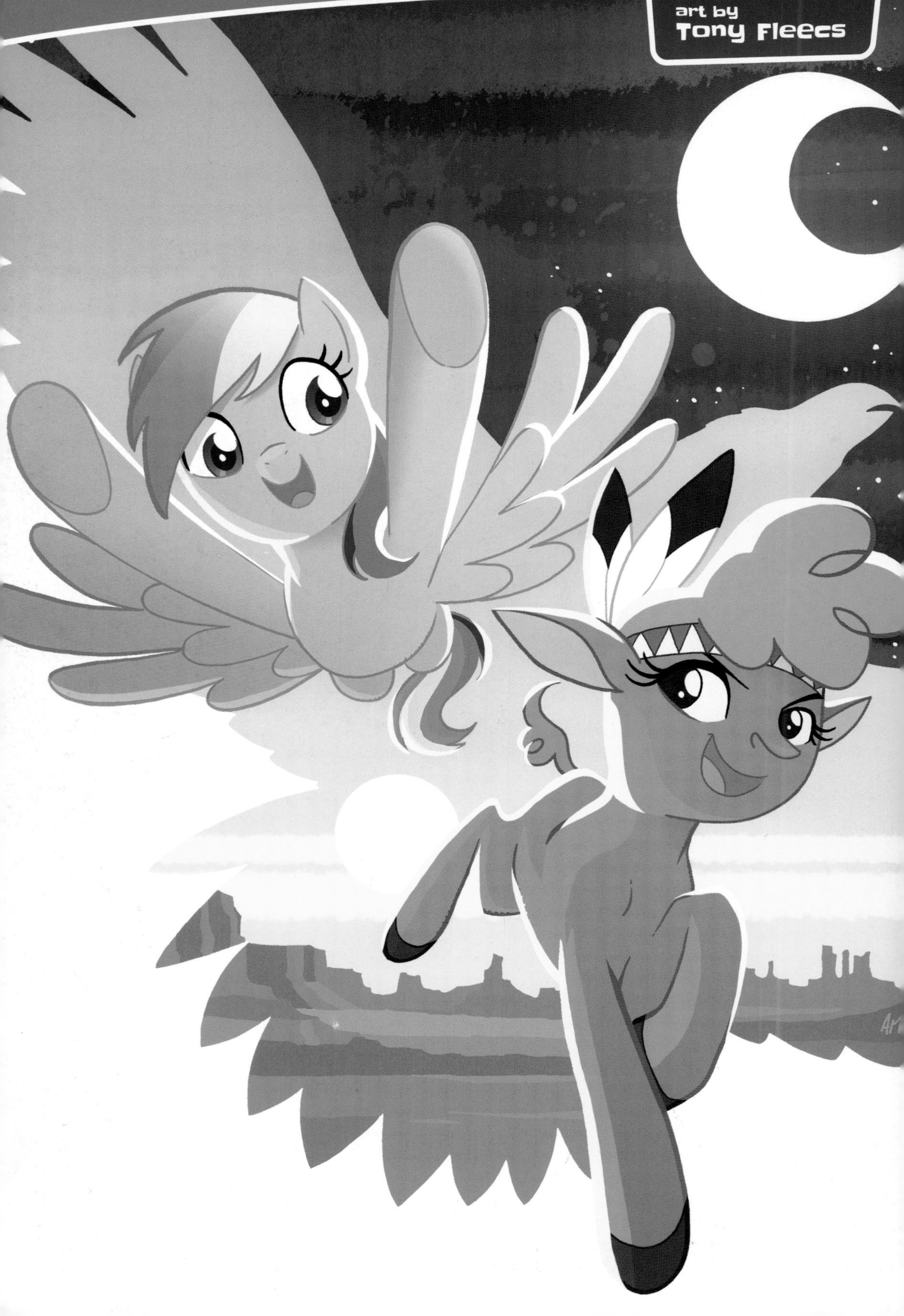

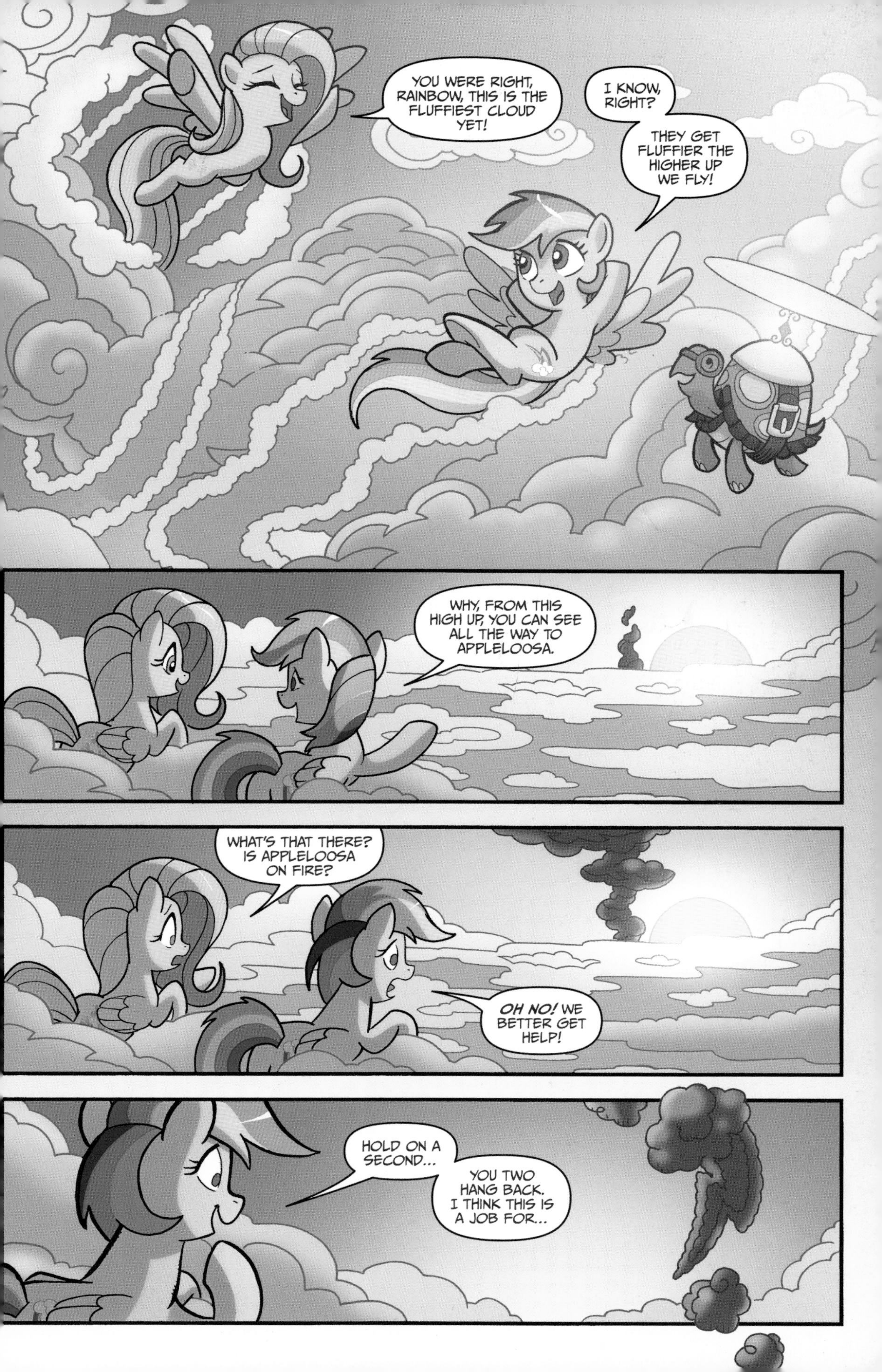
YOU WERE RIGHT, RAINBOW, THIS IS THE FLUFFIEST CLOUD YET!
I KNOW, RIGHT?
THEY GET FLUFFIER THE HIGHER UP WE FLY!
WHY, FROM THIS HIGH UP, YOU CAN SEE ALL THE WAY TO APPLELOOSA.
WHAT'S THAT THERE? IS APPLELOOSA ON FIRE?
OH NO! WE BETTER GET HELP!
HOLD ON A SECOND...
YOU TWO HANG BACK. I THINK THIS IS A JOB FOR...

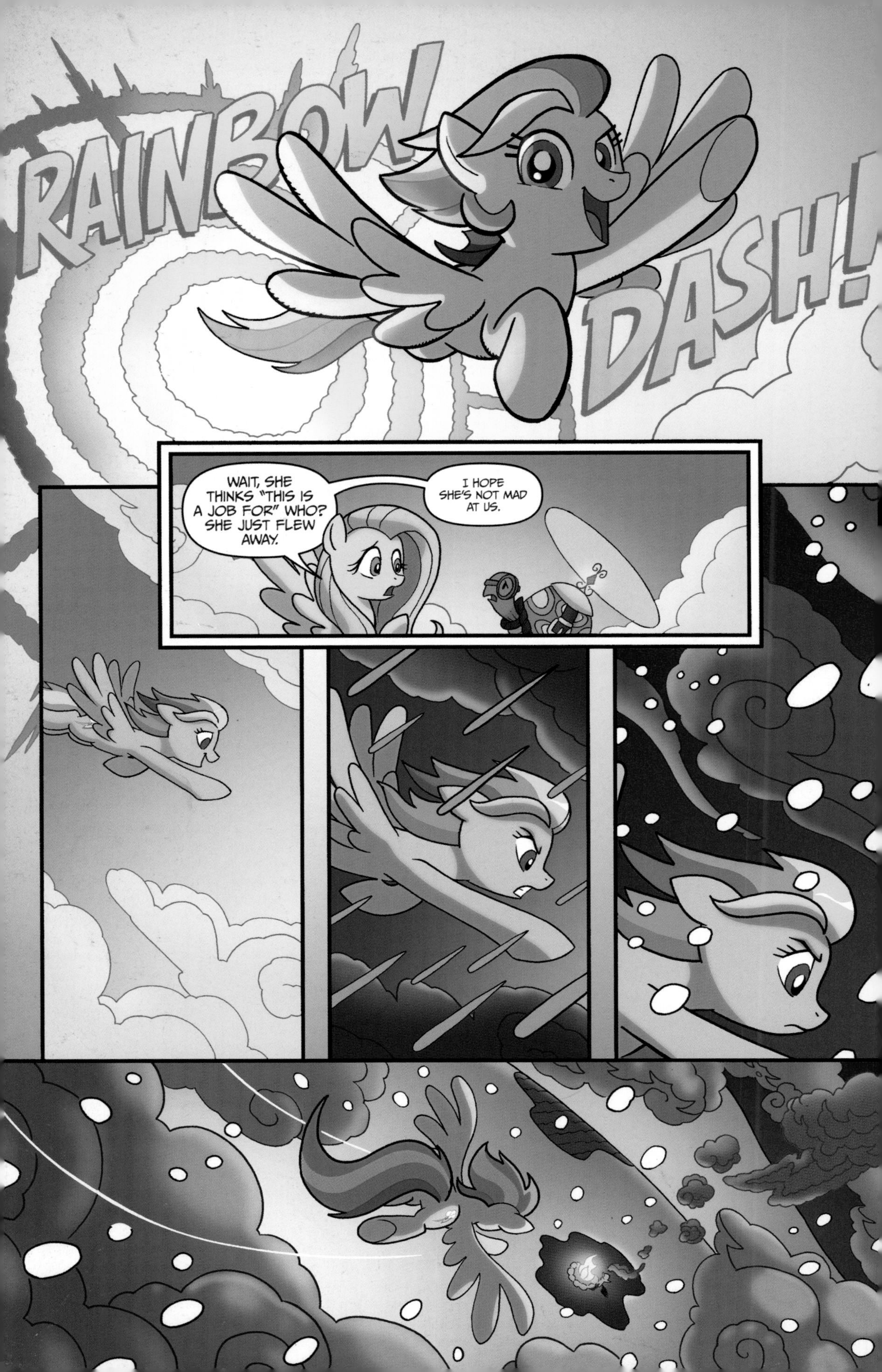
RAINBOW DASH!
WAIT, SHE THINKS "THIS IS A JOB FOR" WHO? SHE JUST FLEW AWAY.
I HOPE SHE'S NOT MAD AT US.

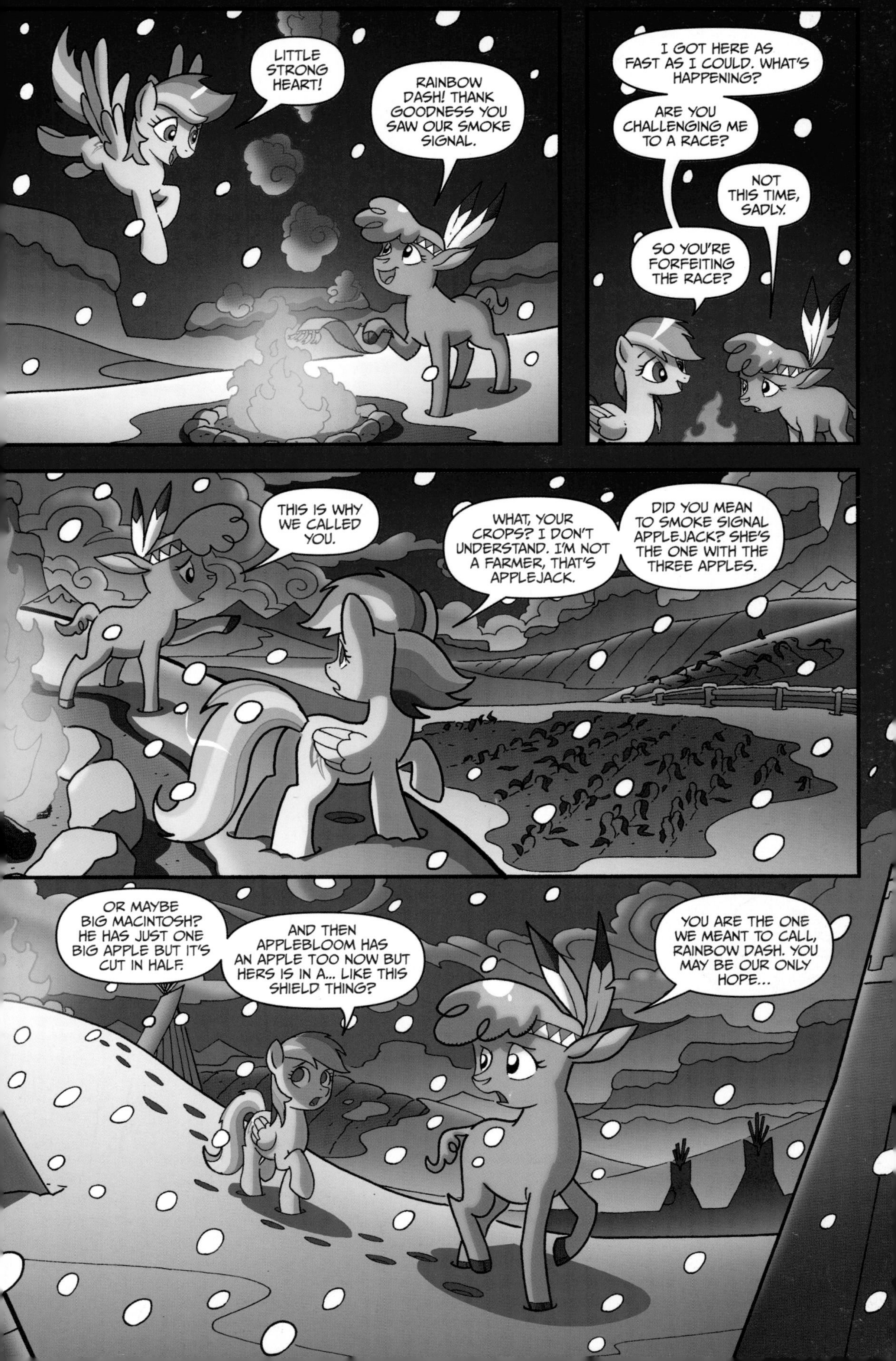
LITTLE STRONG HEART!
RAINBOW DASH! THANK GOODNESS YOU SAW OUR SMOKE SIGNAL.
I GOT HERE AS FAST AS I COULD. WHAT'S HAPPENING?
ARE YOU CHALLENGING ME TO A RACE?
NOT THIS TIME, SADLY.
SO YOU'RE FORFEITING THE RACE?
THIS IS WHY WE CALLED YOU.
WHAT, YOUR CROPS? I DON'T UNDERSTAND. I'M NOT A FARMER, THAT'S APPLEJACK.
DID YOU MEAN TO SMOKE SIGNAL APPLEJACK? SHE'S THE ONE WITH THE THREE APPLES.
OR MAYBE BIG MACINTOSH? HE HAS JUST ONE BIG APPLE BUT IT'S CUT IN HALF.
AND THEN APPLEBLOOM HAS AN APPLE TOO NOW BUT HERS IS IN A... LIKE THIS SHIELD THING?
YOU ARE THE ONE WE MEANT TO CALL, RAINBOW DASH. YOU MAY BE OUR ONLY HOPE...

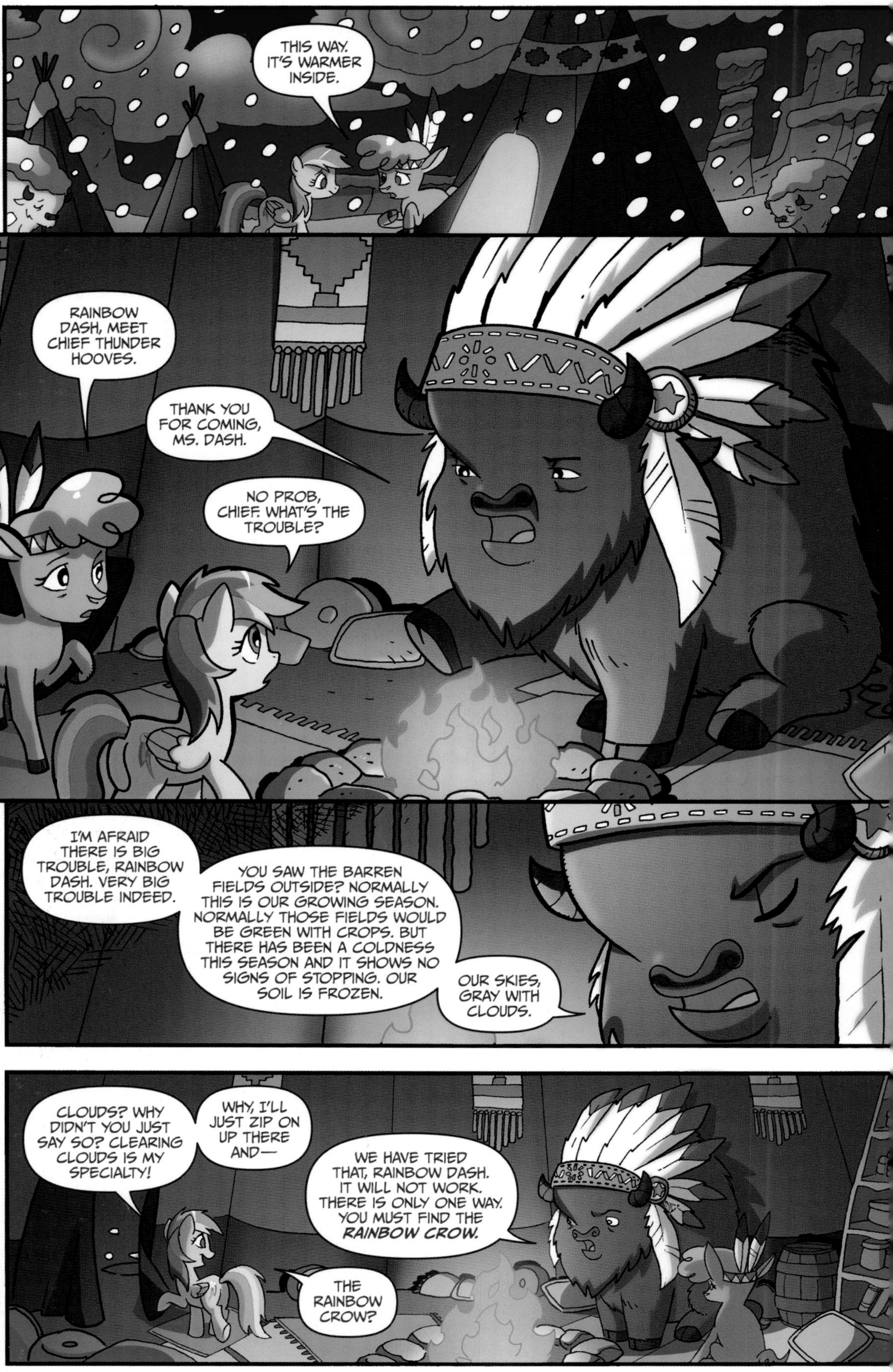
THIS WAY. IT'S WARMER INSIDE.
RAINBOW DASH, MEET CHIEF THUNDER HOOVES.
THANK YOU FOR COMING, MS. DASH.
NO PROB, CHIEF. WHAT'S THE TROUBLE?
I'M AFRAID THERE IS BIG TROUBLE, RAINBOW DASH. VERY BIG TROUBLE INDEED.
YOU SAW THE BARREN FIELDS OUTSIDE? NORMALLY THIS IS OUR GROWING SEASON. NORMALLY THOSE FIELDS WOULD BE GREEN WITH CROPS. BUT THERE HAS BEEN A COLDNESS THIS SEASON AND IT SHOWS NO SIGNS OF STOPPING. OUR SOIL IS FROZEN.
OUR SKIES, GRAY WITH CLOUDS.
CLOUDS? WHY DIDN'T YOU JUST SAY SO? CLEARING CLOUDS IS MY SPECIALTY!
WHY, I'LL JUST ZIP ON UP THERE AND—
WE HAVE TRIED THAT, RAINBOW DASH. IT WILL NOT WORK. THERE IS ONLY ONE WAY. YOU MUST FIND THE ***RAINBOW CROW.***
THE RAINBOW CROW?

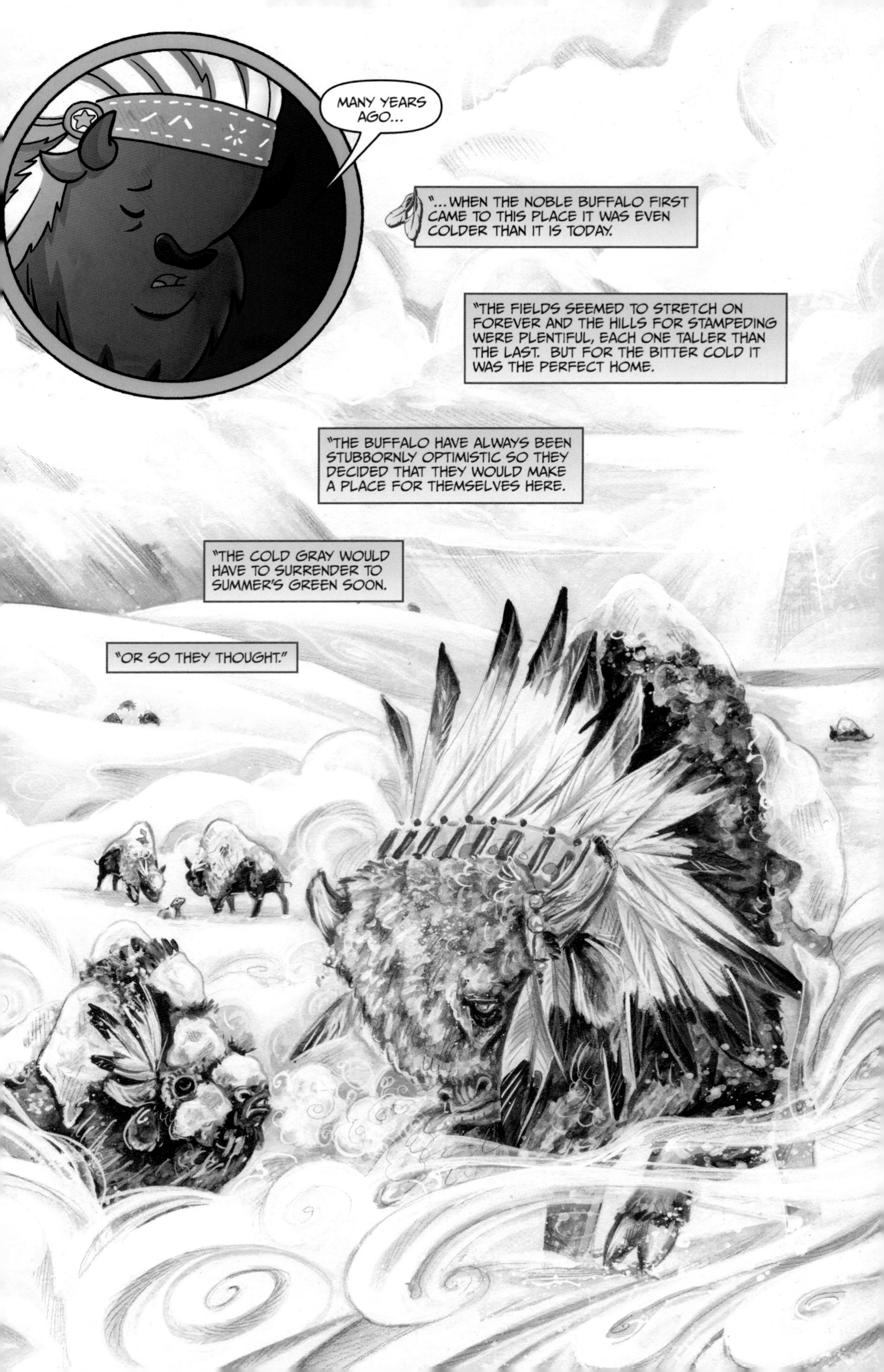
MANY YEARS AGO...
"...WHEN THE NOBLE BUFFALO FIRST CAME TO THIS PLACE IT WAS EVEN COLDER THAN IT IS TODAY.
"THE FIELDS SEEMED TO STRETCH ON FOREVER AND THE HILLS FOR STAMPEDING WERE PLENTIFUL, EACH ONE TALLER THAN THE LAST. BUT FOR THE BITTER COLD IT WAS THE PERFECT HOME.
"THE BUFFALO HAVE ALWAYS BEEN STUBBORNLY OPTIMISTIC SO THEY DECIDED THAT THEY WOULD MAKE A PLACE FOR THEMSELVES HERE.
"THE COLD GRAY WOULD HAVE TO SURRENDER TO SUMMER'S GREEN SOON.
"OR SO THEY THOUGHT."

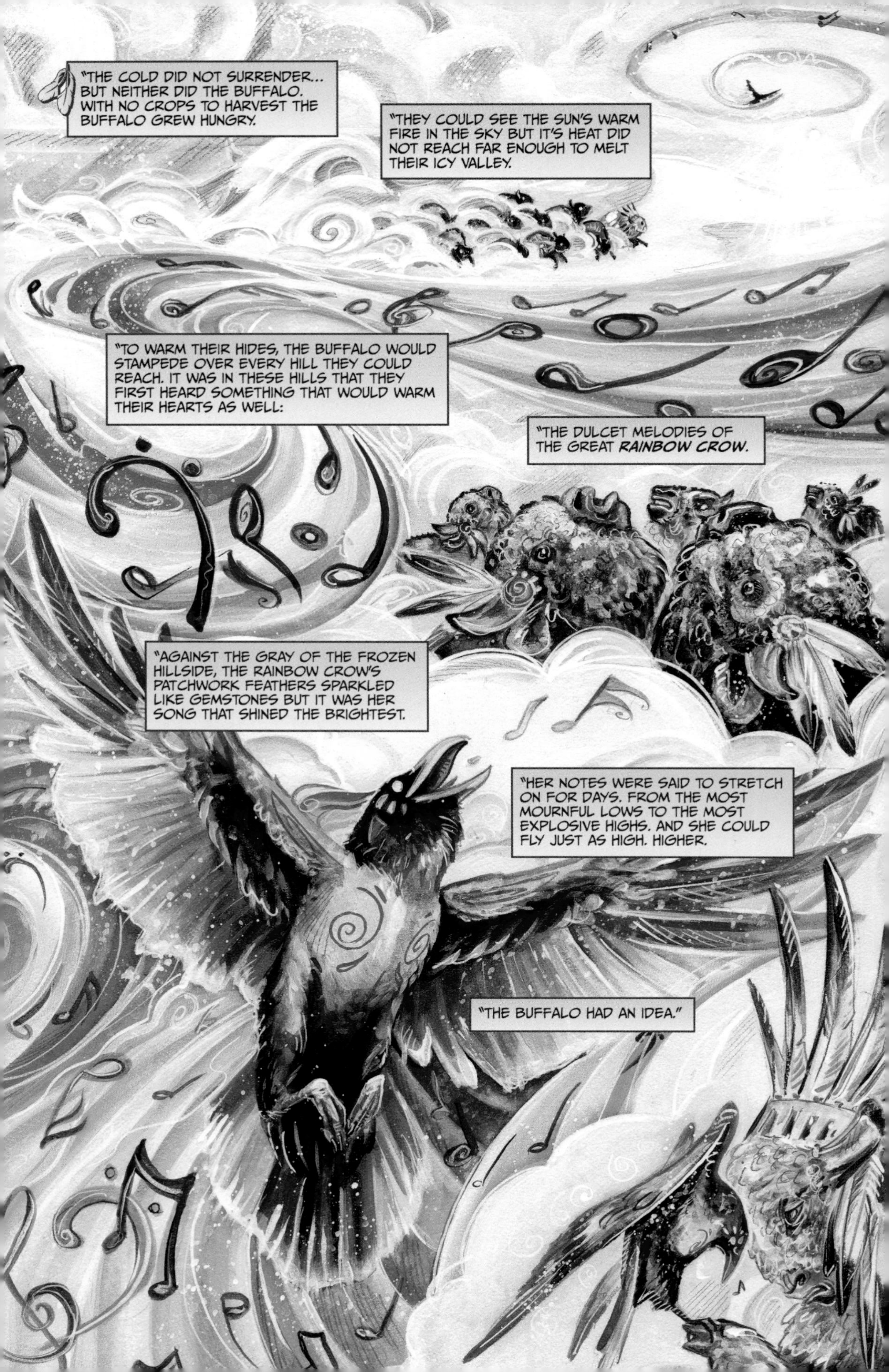
"THE COLD DID NOT SURRENDER... BUT NEITHER DID THE BUFFALO. WITH NO CROPS TO HARVEST THE BUFFALO GREW HUNGRY.
"THEY COULD SEE THE SUN'S WARM FIRE IN THE SKY BUT IT'S HEAT DID NOT REACH FAR ENOUGH TO MELT THEIR ICY VALLEY.
"TO WARM THEIR HIDES, THE BUFFALO WOULD STAMPEDE OVER EVERY HILL THEY COULD REACH. IT WAS IN THESE HILLS THAT THEY FIRST HEARD SOMETHING THAT WOULD WARM THEIR HEARTS AS WELL:
"THE DULCET MELODIES OF THE GREAT *RAINBOW CROW.*
"AGAINST THE GRAY OF THE FROZEN HILLSIDE, THE RAINBOW CROW'S PATCHWORK FEATHERS SPARKLED LIKE GEMSTONES BUT IT WAS HER SONG THAT SHINED THE BRIGHTEST.
"HER NOTES WERE SAID TO STRETCH ON FOR DAYS. FROM THE MOST MOURNFUL LOWS TO THE MOST EXPLOSIVE HIGHS. AND SHE COULD FLY JUST AS HIGH. HIGHER.
"THE BUFFALO HAD AN IDEA."

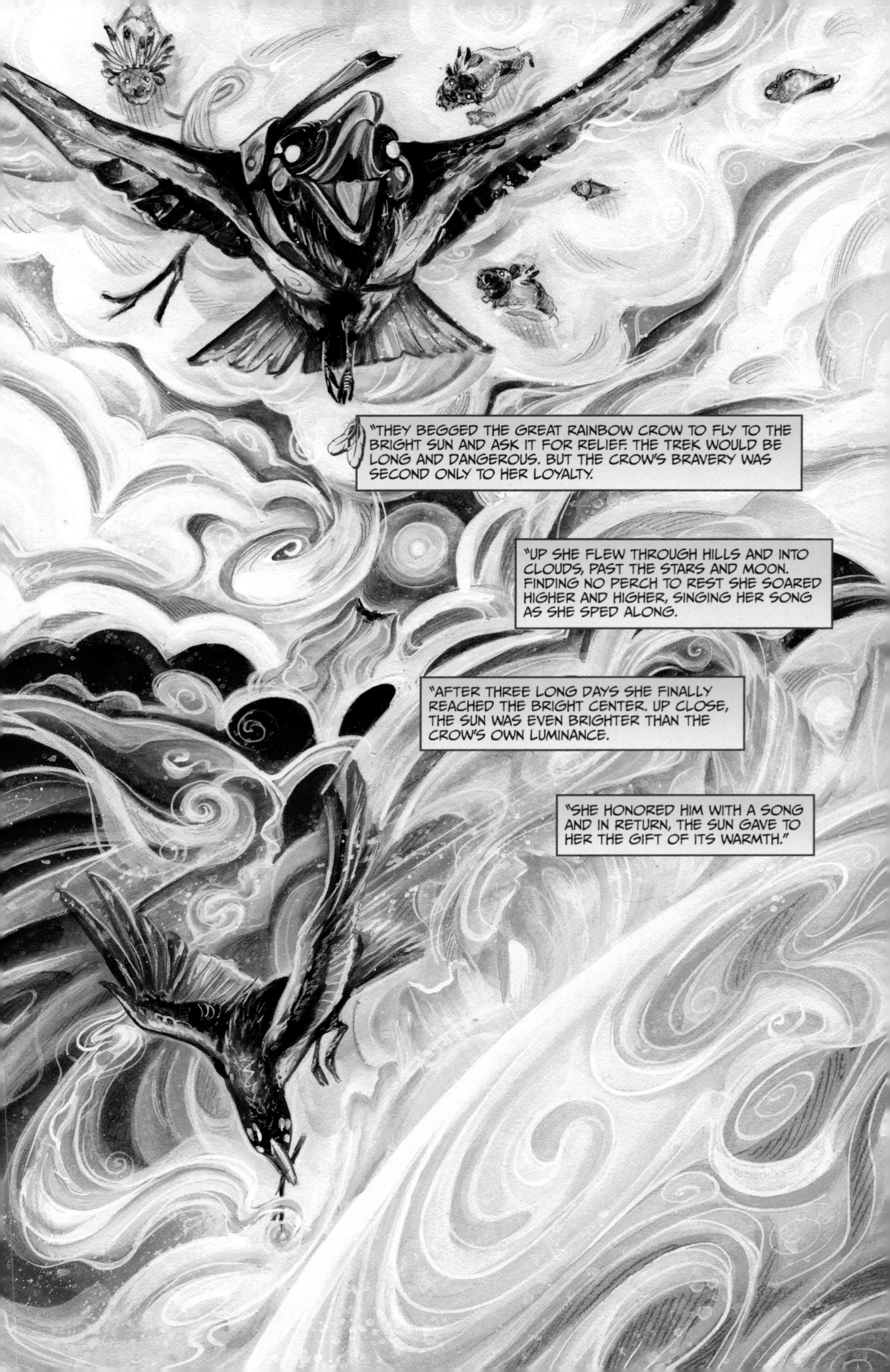
"THEY BEGGED THE GREAT RAINBOW CROW TO FLY TO THE BRIGHT SUN AND ASK IT FOR RELIEF. THE TREK WOULD BE LONG AND DANGEROUS. BUT THE CROW'S BRAVERY WAS SECOND ONLY TO HER LOYALTY.
"UP SHE FLEW THROUGH HILLS AND INTO CLOUDS, PAST THE STARS AND MOON. FINDING NO PERCH TO REST SHE SOARED HIGHER AND HIGHER, SINGING HER SONG AS SHE SPED ALONG.
"AFTER THREE LONG DAYS SHE FINALLY REACHED THE BRIGHT CENTER. UP CLOSE, THE SUN WAS EVEN BRIGHTER THAN THE CROW'S OWN LUMINANCE.
"SHE HONORED HIM WITH A SONG AND IN RETURN, THE SUN GAVE TO HER THE GIFT OF ITS WARMTH."

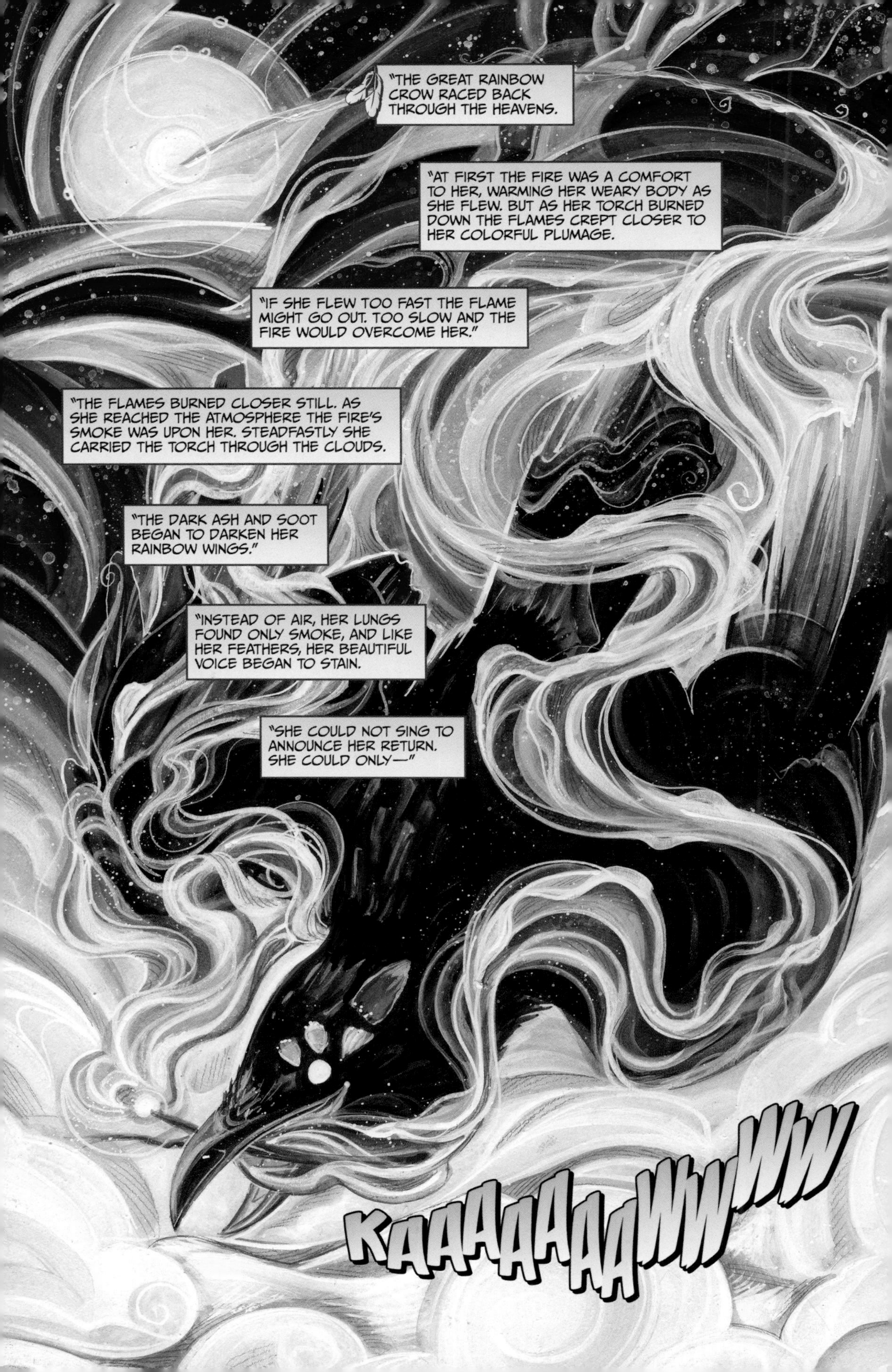
"THE GREAT RAINBOW CROW RACED BACK THROUGH THE HEAVENS.
"AT FIRST THE FIRE WAS A COMFORT TO HER, WARMING HER WEARY BODY AS SHE FLEW. BUT AS HER TORCH BURNED DOWN THE FLAMES CREPT CLOSER TO HER COLORFUL PLUMAGE.
"IF SHE FLEW TOO FAST THE FLAME MIGHT GO OUT. TOO SLOW AND THE FIRE WOULD OVERCOME HER."
"THE FLAMES BURNED CLOSER STILL. AS SHE REACHED THE ATMOSPHERE THE FIRE'S SMOKE WAS UPON HER. STEADFASTLY SHE CARRIED THE TORCH THROUGH THE CLOUDS.
"THE DARK ASH AND SOOT BEGAN TO DARKEN HER RAINBOW WINGS."
"INSTEAD OF AIR, HER LUNGS FOUND ONLY SMOKE, AND LIKE HER FEATHERS, HER BEAUTIFUL VOICE BEGAN TO STAIN.
"SHE COULD NOT SING TO ANNOUNCE HER RETURN. SHE COULD ONLY—"
KAAAAAAAAWWWW

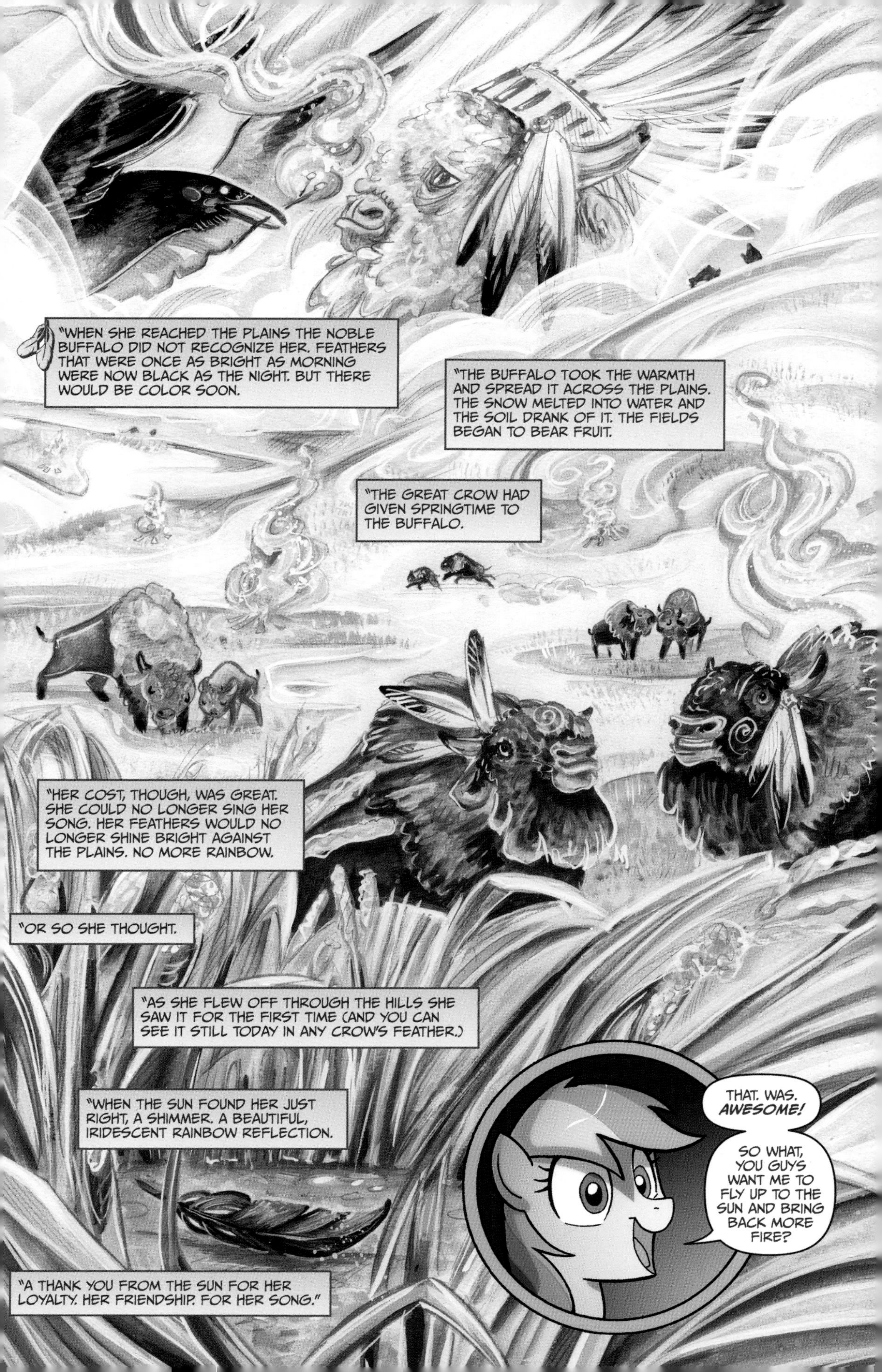
"WHEN SHE REACHED THE PLAINS THE NOBLE BUFFALO DID NOT RECOGNIZE HER. FEATHERS THAT WERE ONCE AS BRIGHT AS MORNING WERE NOW BLACK AS THE NIGHT. BUT THERE WOULD BE COLOR SOON.
"THE BUFFALO TOOK THE WARMTH AND SPREAD IT ACROSS THE PLAINS. THE SNOW MELTED INTO WATER AND THE SOIL DRANK OF IT. THE FIELDS BEGAN TO BEAR FRUIT.
"THE GREAT CROW HAD GIVEN SPRINGTIME TO THE BUFFALO.
"HER COST, THOUGH, WAS GREAT. SHE COULD NO LONGER SING HER SONG. HER FEATHERS WOULD NO LONGER SHINE BRIGHT AGAINST THE PLAINS. NO MORE RAINBOW.
"OR SO SHE THOUGHT.
"AS SHE FLEW OFF THROUGH THE HILLS SHE SAW IT FOR THE FIRST TIME (AND YOU CAN SEE IT STILL TODAY IN ANY CROW'S FEATHER.)
"WHEN THE SUN FOUND HER JUST RIGHT, A SHIMMER. A BEAUTIFUL, IRIDESCENT RAINBOW REFLECTION.
THAT. WAS. ***AWESOME!***
SO WHAT, YOU GUYS WANT ME TO FLY UP TO THE SUN AND BRING BACK MORE FIRE?
"A THANK YOU FROM THE SUN FOR HER LOYALTY. HER FRIENDSHIP. FOR HER SONG."

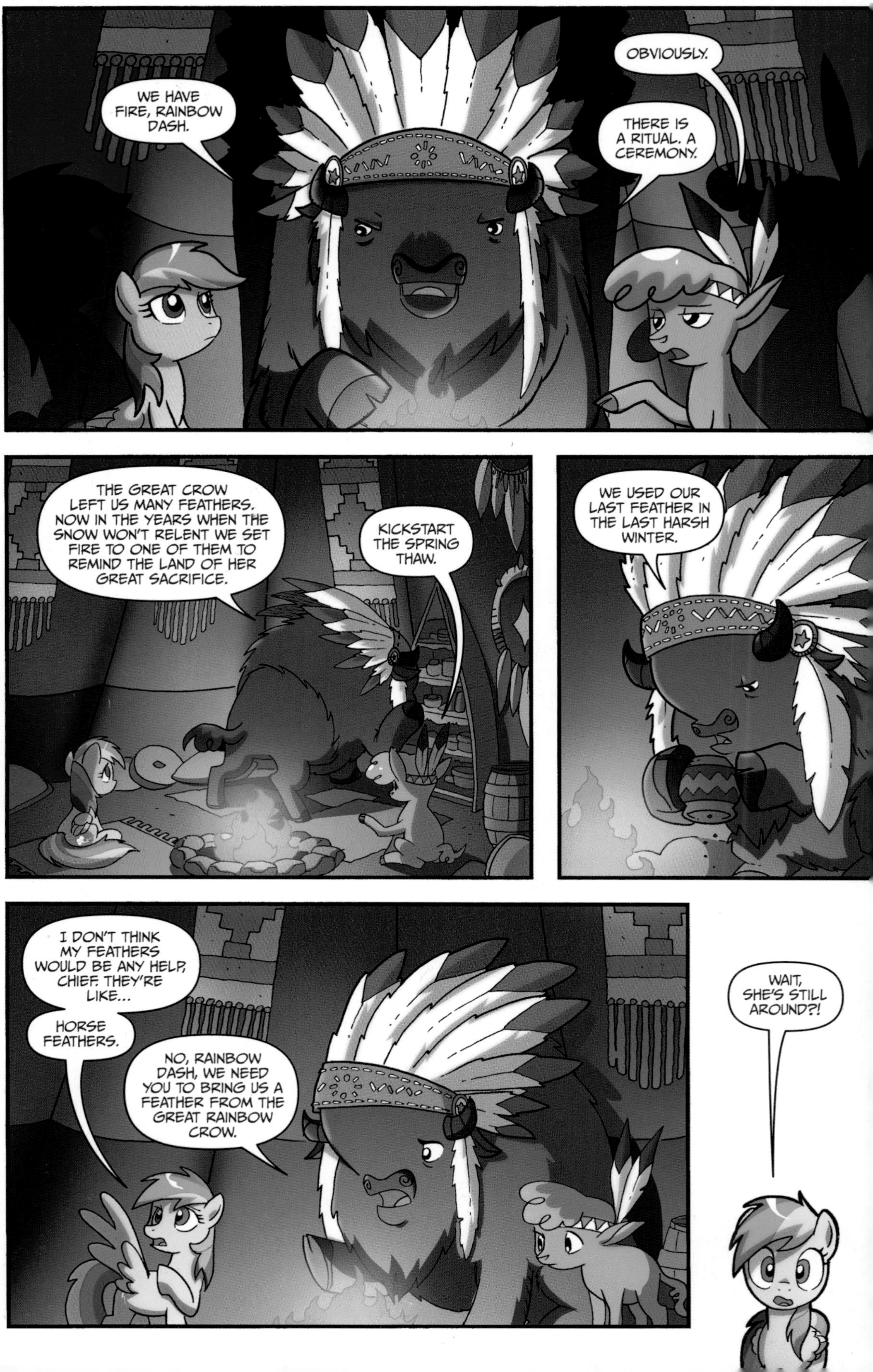
WE HAVE FIRE, RAINBOW DASH.
OBVIOUSLY.
THERE IS A RITUAL. A CEREMONY.
THE GREAT CROW LEFT US MANY FEATHERS. NOW IN THE YEARS WHEN THE SNOW WON'T RELENT WE SET FIRE TO ONE OF THEM TO REMIND THE LAND OF HER GREAT SACRIFICE.
KICKSTART THE SPRING THAW.
WE USED OUR LAST FEATHER IN THE LAST HARSH WINTER.
I DON'T THINK MY FEATHERS WOULD BE ANY HELP, CHIEF. THEY'RE LIKE...
HORSE FEATHERS.
NO, RAINBOW DASH, WE NEED YOU TO BRING US A FEATHER FROM THE GREAT RAINBOW CROW.
WAIT, SHE'S STILL AROUND?!

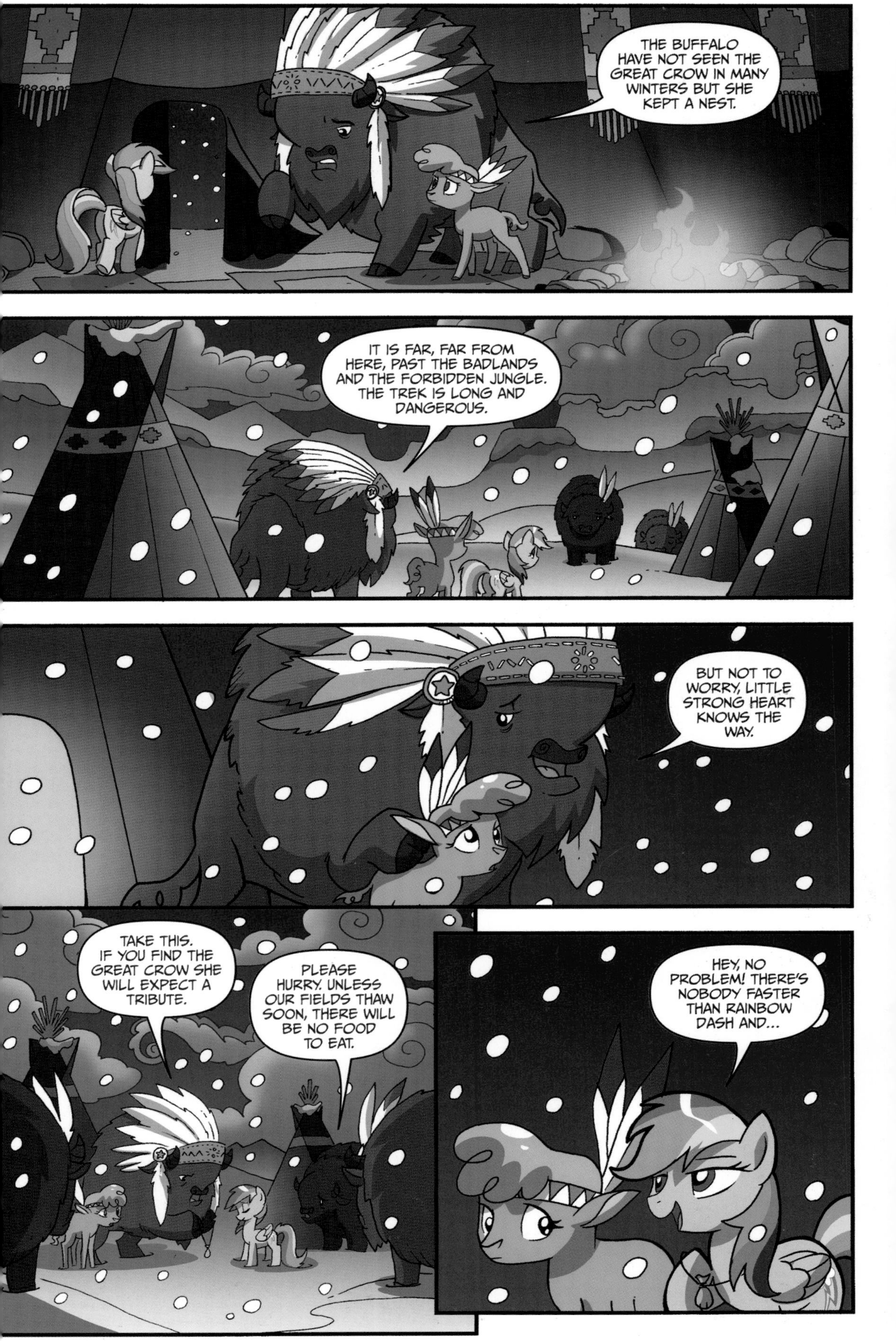
THE BUFFALO HAVE NOT SEEN THE GREAT CROW IN MANY WINTERS BUT SHE KEPT A NEST.
IT IS FAR, FAR FROM HERE, PAST THE BADLANDS AND THE FORBIDDEN JUNGLE. THE TREK IS LONG AND DANGEROUS.
BUT NOT TO WORRY, LITTLE STRONG HEART KNOWS THE WAY.
TAKE THIS. IF YOU FIND THE GREAT CROW SHE WILL EXPECT A TRIBUTE.
PLEASE HURRY. UNLESS OUR FIELDS THAW SOON, THERE WILL BE NO FOOD TO EAT.
HEY, NO PROBLEM! THERE'S NOBODY FASTER THAN RAINBOW DASH AND...

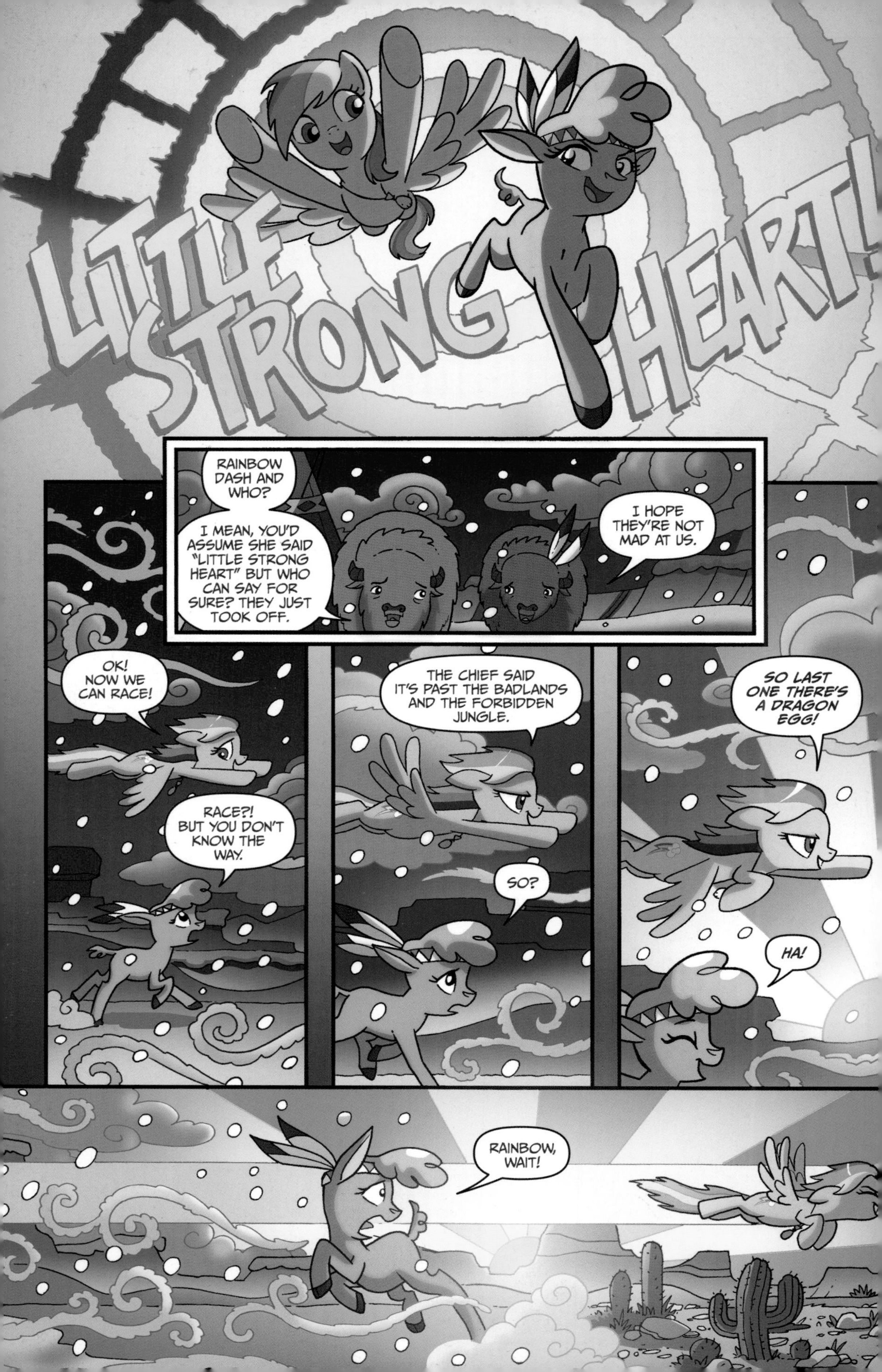
LITTLE STRONG HEART!
RAINBOW DASH AND WHO?
I MEAN, YOU'D ASSUME SHE SAID "LITTLE STRONG HEART" BUT WHO CAN SAY FOR SURE? THEY JUST TOOK OFF.
I HOPE THEY'RE NOT MAD AT US.
OK! NOW WE CAN RACE!
RACE?! BUT YOU DON'T KNOW THE WAY.
THE CHIEF SAID IT'S PAST THE BADLANDS AND THE FORBIDDEN JUNGLE.
SO?
SO LAST ONE THERE'S A DRAGON EGG!
HA!
RAINBOW, WAIT!

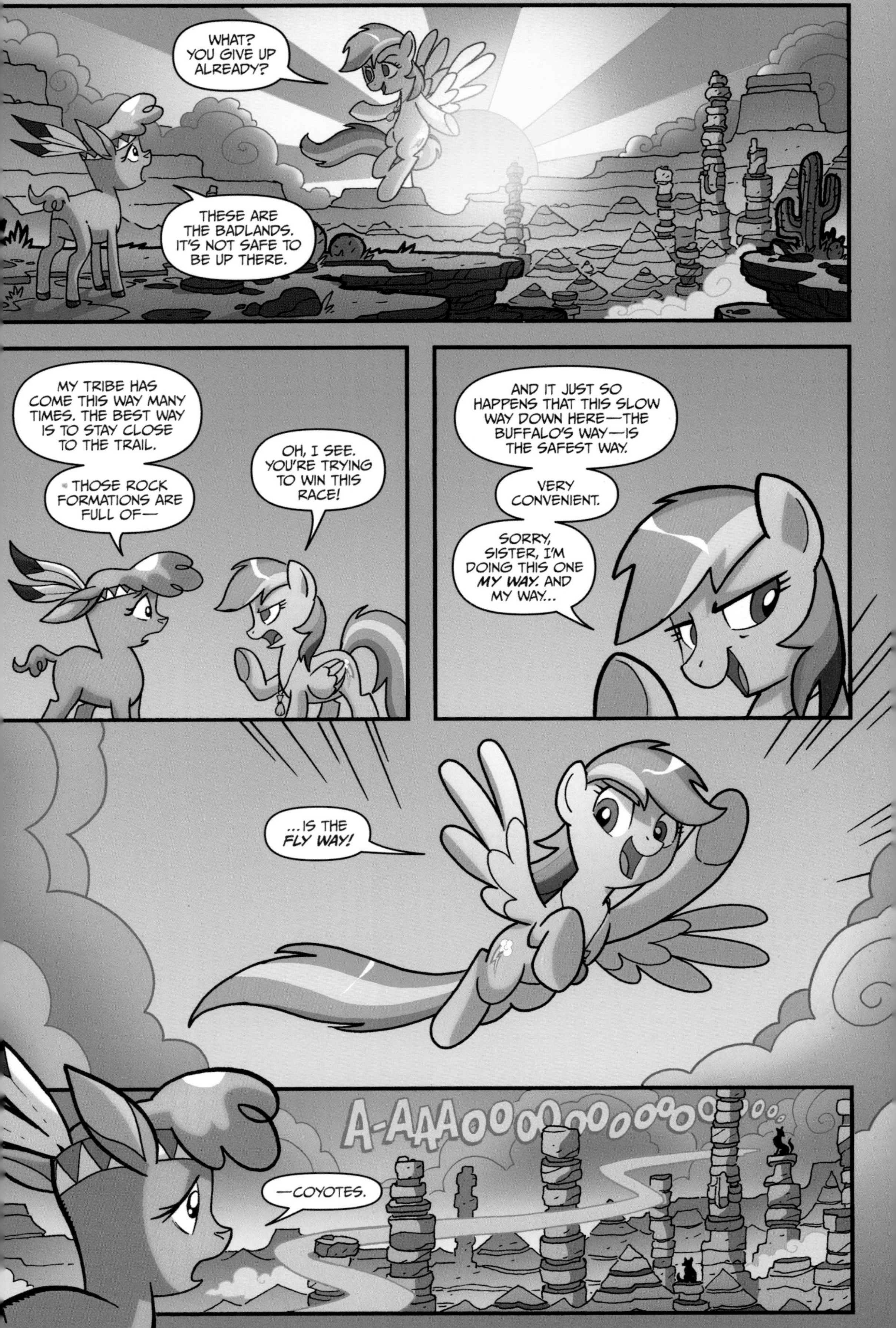
WHAT? YOU GIVE UP ALREADY?
THESE ARE THE BADLANDS. IT'S NOT SAFE TO BE UP THERE.
MY TRIBE HAS COME THIS WAY MANY TIMES. THE BEST WAY IS TO STAY CLOSE TO THE TRAIL.
THOSE ROCK FORMATIONS ARE FULL OF—
OH, I SEE. YOU'RE TRYING TO WIN THIS RACE!
AND IT JUST SO HAPPENS THAT THIS SLOW WAY DOWN HERE—THE BUFFALO'S WAY—IS THE SAFEST WAY.
VERY CONVENIENT.
SORRY, SISTER, I'M DOING THIS ONE *MY WAY.* AND MY WAY...
...IS THE *FLY WAY!*
A-AAAOOOOOOOOOOOooo...
—COYOTES.

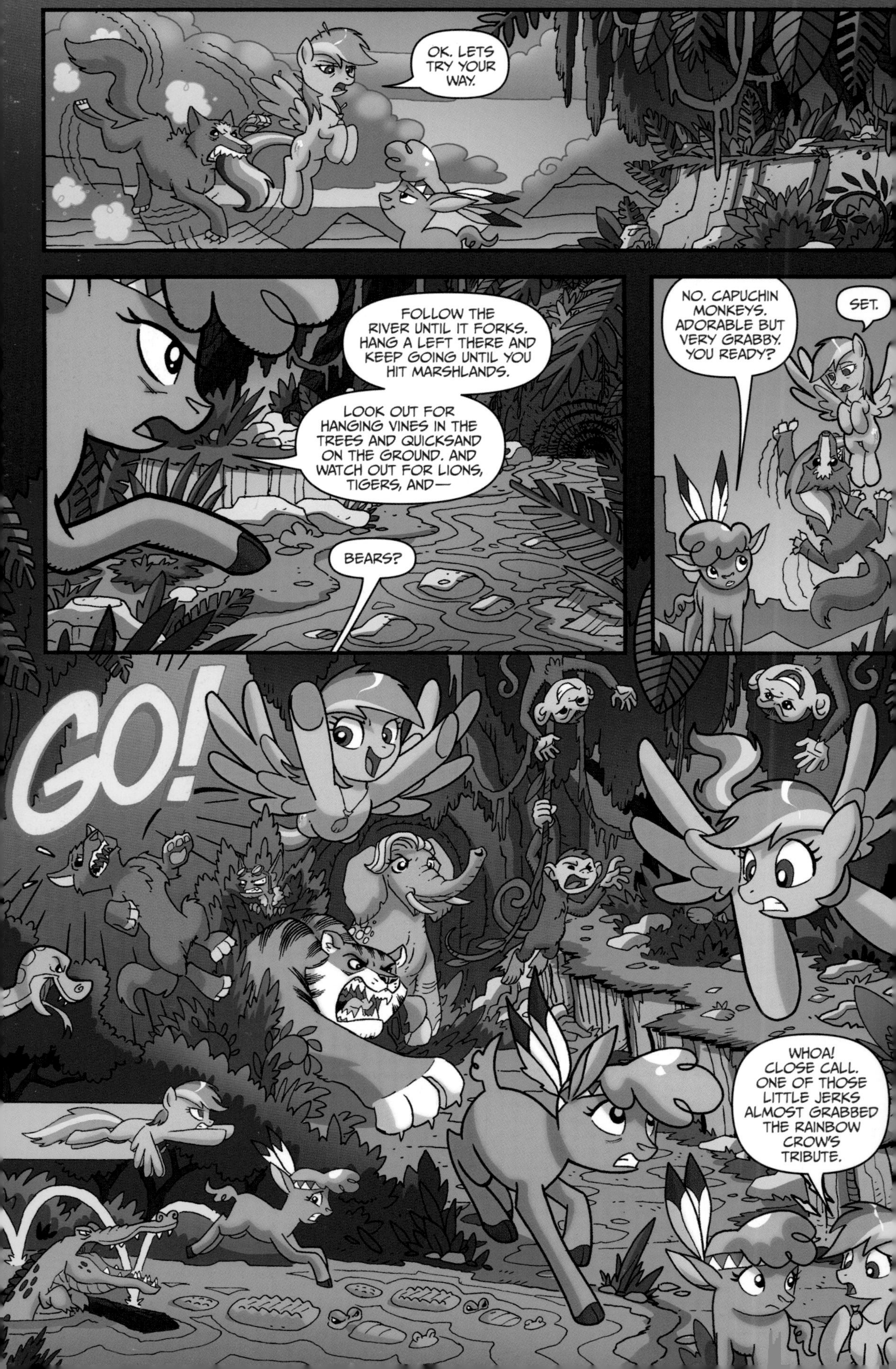
OK. LETS TRY YOUR WAY.
FOLLOW THE RIVER UNTIL IT FORKS. HANG A LEFT THERE AND KEEP GOING UNTIL YOU HIT MARSHLANDS.
LOOK OUT FOR HANGING VINES IN THE TREES AND QUICKSAND ON THE GROUND. AND WATCH OUT FOR LIONS, TIGERS, AND—
BEARS?
NO. CAPUCHIN MONKEYS. ADORABLE BUT VERY GRABBY. YOU READY?
SET.
GO!
WHOA! CLOSE CALL. ONE OF THOSE LITTLE JERKS ALMOST GRABBED THE RAINBOW CROW'S TRIBUTE.

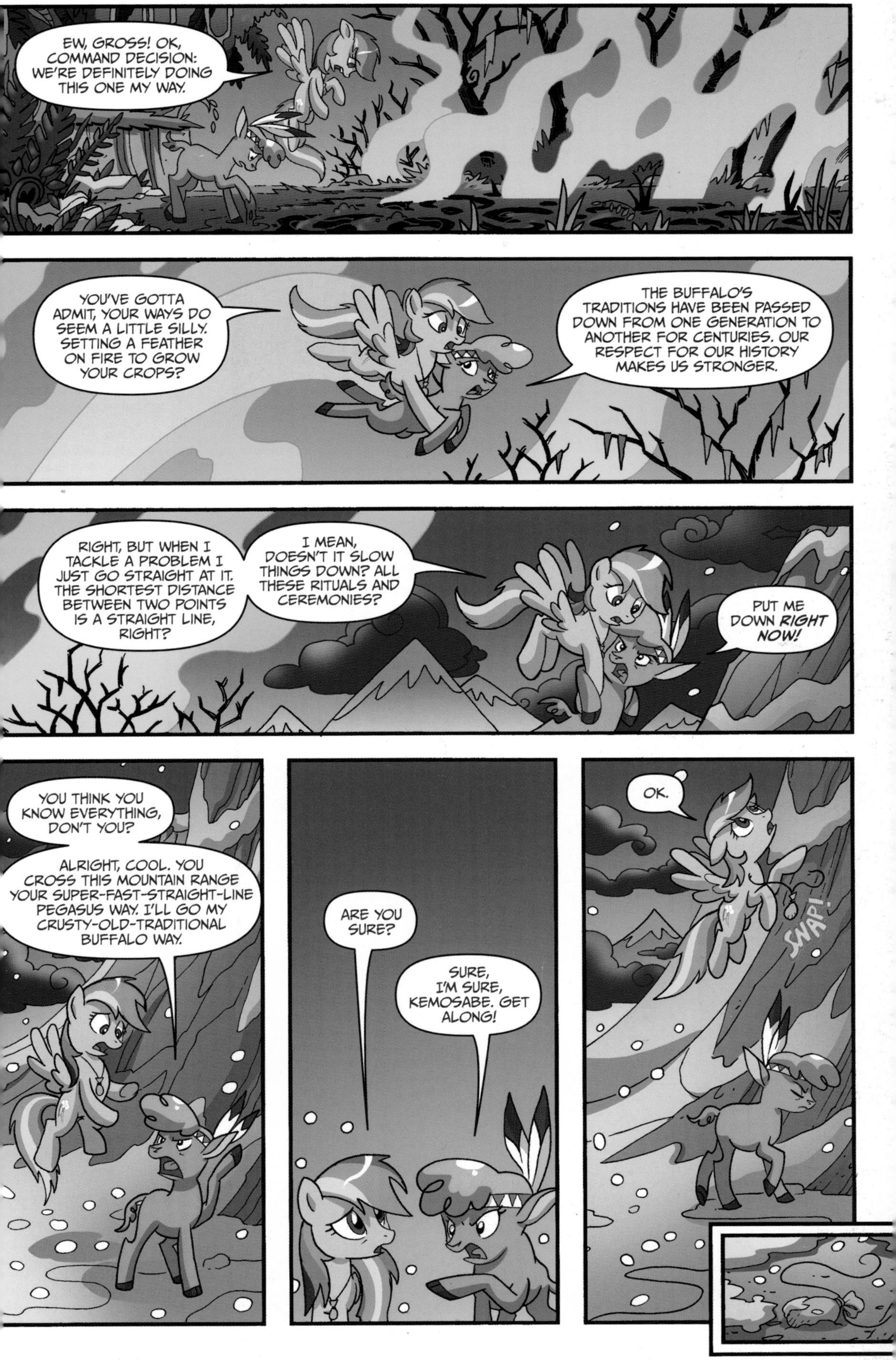
EW, GROSS! OK, COMMAND DECISION: WE'RE DEFINITELY DOING THIS ONE MY WAY.
YOU'VE GOTTA ADMIT, YOUR WAYS DO SEEM A LITTLE SILLY. SETTING A FEATHER ON FIRE TO GROW YOUR CROPS?
THE BUFFALO'S TRADITIONS HAVE BEEN PASSED DOWN FROM ONE GENERATION TO ANOTHER FOR CENTURIES. OUR RESPECT FOR OUR HISTORY MAKES US STRONGER.
RIGHT, BUT WHEN I TACKLE A PROBLEM I JUST GO STRAIGHT AT IT. THE SHORTEST DISTANCE BETWEEN TWO POINTS IS A STRAIGHT LINE, RIGHT?
I MEAN, DOESN'T IT SLOW THINGS DOWN? ALL THESE RITUALS AND CEREMONIES?
PUT ME DOWN *RIGHT NOW!*
YOU THINK YOU KNOW EVERYTHING, DON'T YOU?
ALRIGHT, COOL. YOU CROSS THIS MOUNTAIN RANGE YOUR SUPER-FAST-STRAIGHT-LINE PEGASUS WAY. I'LL GO MY CRUSTY-OLD-TRADITIONAL BUFFALO WAY.
ARE YOU SURE?
SURE, I'M SURE, KEMOSABE. GET ALONG!
OK.
SNAP!

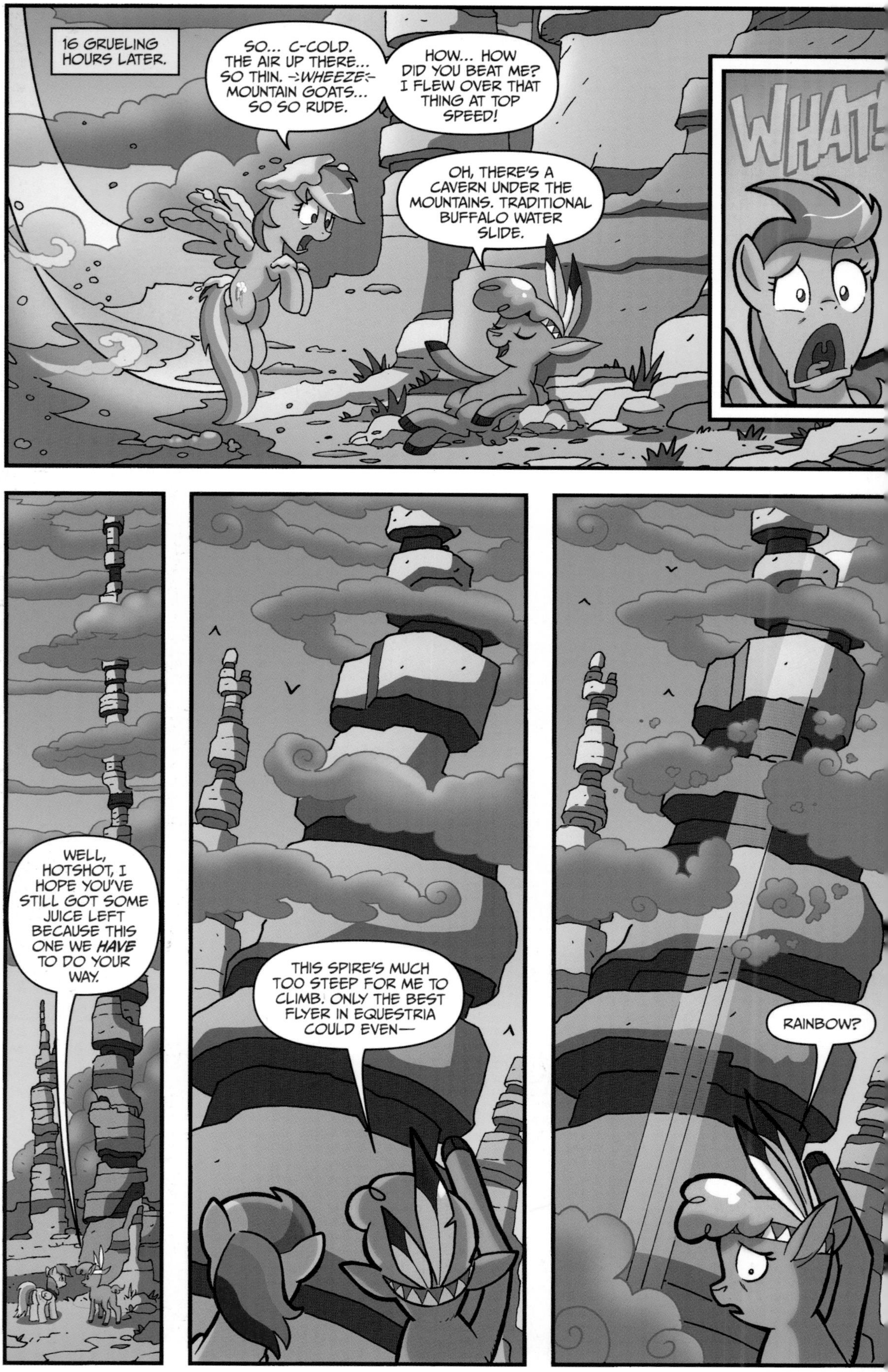
16 GRUELING HOURS LATER.
SO... C-COLD. THE AIR UP THERE... SO THIN. ->WHEEZE<- MOUNTAIN GOATS... SO SO RUDE.
HOW... HOW DID YOU BEAT ME? I FLEW OVER THAT THING AT TOP SPEED!
OH, THERE'S A CAVERN UNDER THE MOUNTAINS. TRADITIONAL BUFFALO WATER SLIDE.
WHAT!
WELL, HOTSHOT, I HOPE YOU'VE STILL GOT SOME JUICE LEFT BECAUSE THIS ONE WE *HAVE* TO DO YOUR WAY.
THIS SPIRE'S MUCH TOO STEEP FOR ME TO CLIMB. ONLY THE BEST FLYER IN EQUESTRIA COULD EVEN—
RAINBOW?

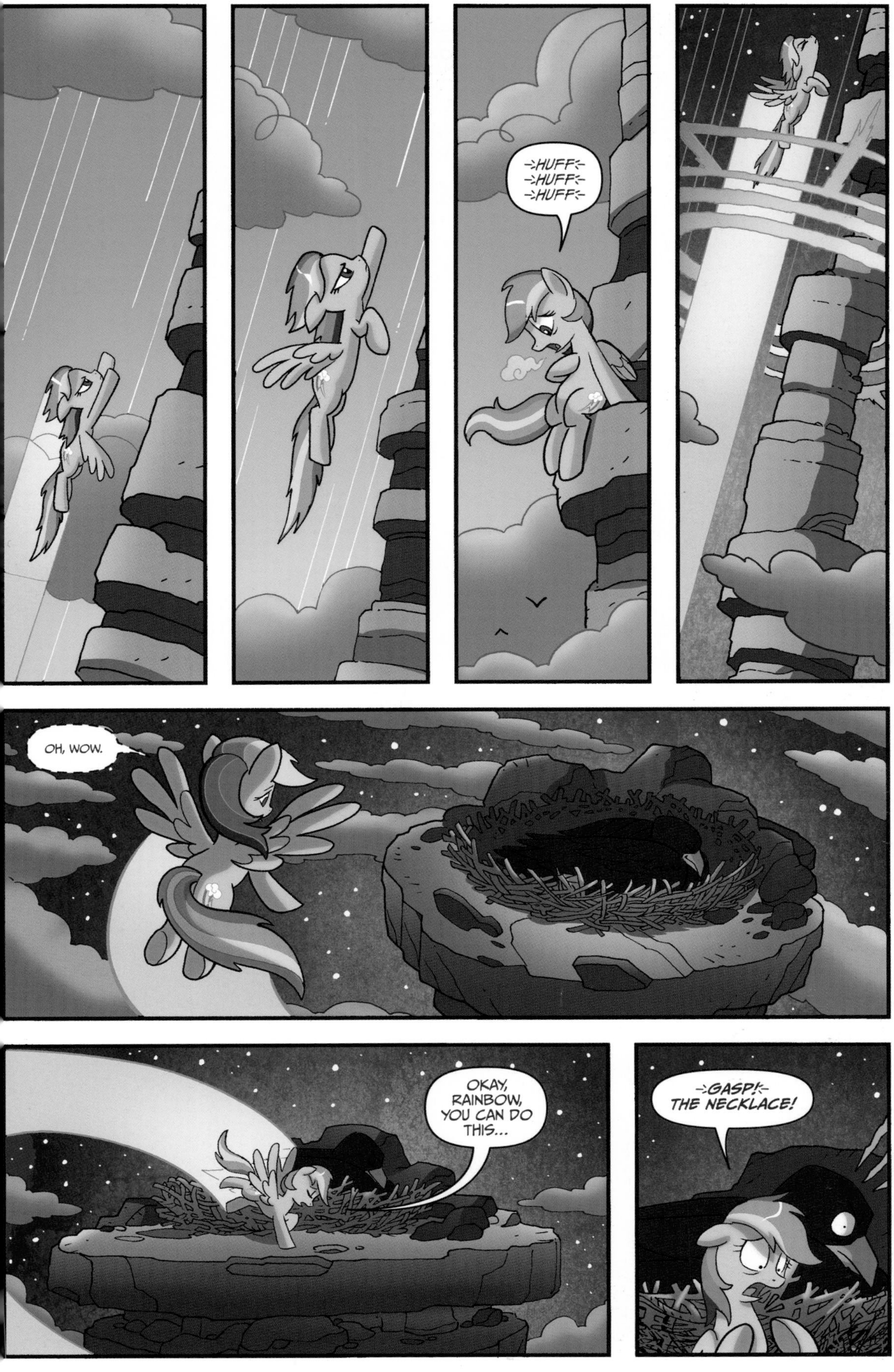
-HUFF-
-HUFF-
-HUFF-
OH, WOW.
OKAY, RAINBOW, YOU CAN DO THIS...
-GASP!- THE NECKLACE!

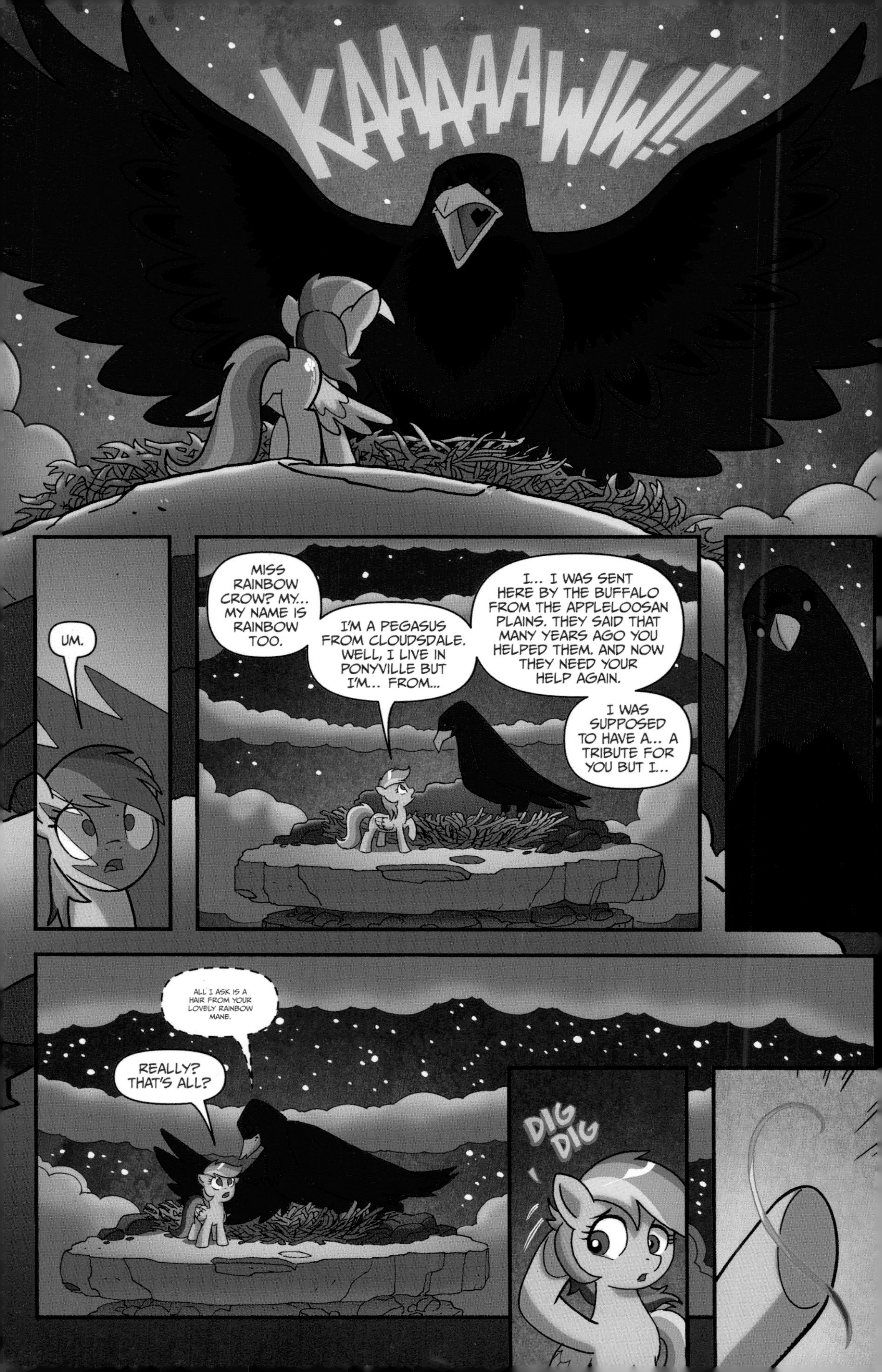
KAAAAAWW!!!
UM.
MISS RAINBOW CROW? MY... MY NAME IS RAINBOW TOO.
I'M A PEGASUS FROM CLOUDSDALE. WELL, I LIVE IN PONYVILLE BUT I'M... FROM...
I... I WAS SENT HERE BY THE BUFFALO FROM THE APPLELOOSAN PLAINS. THEY SAID THAT MANY YEARS AGO YOU HELPED THEM. AND NOW THEY NEED YOUR HELP AGAIN.
I WAS SUPPOSED TO HAVE A... A TRIBUTE FOR YOU BUT I...
ALL I ASK IS A HAIR FROM YOUR LOVELY RAINBOW MANE.
REALLY? THAT'S ALL?
DIG DIG

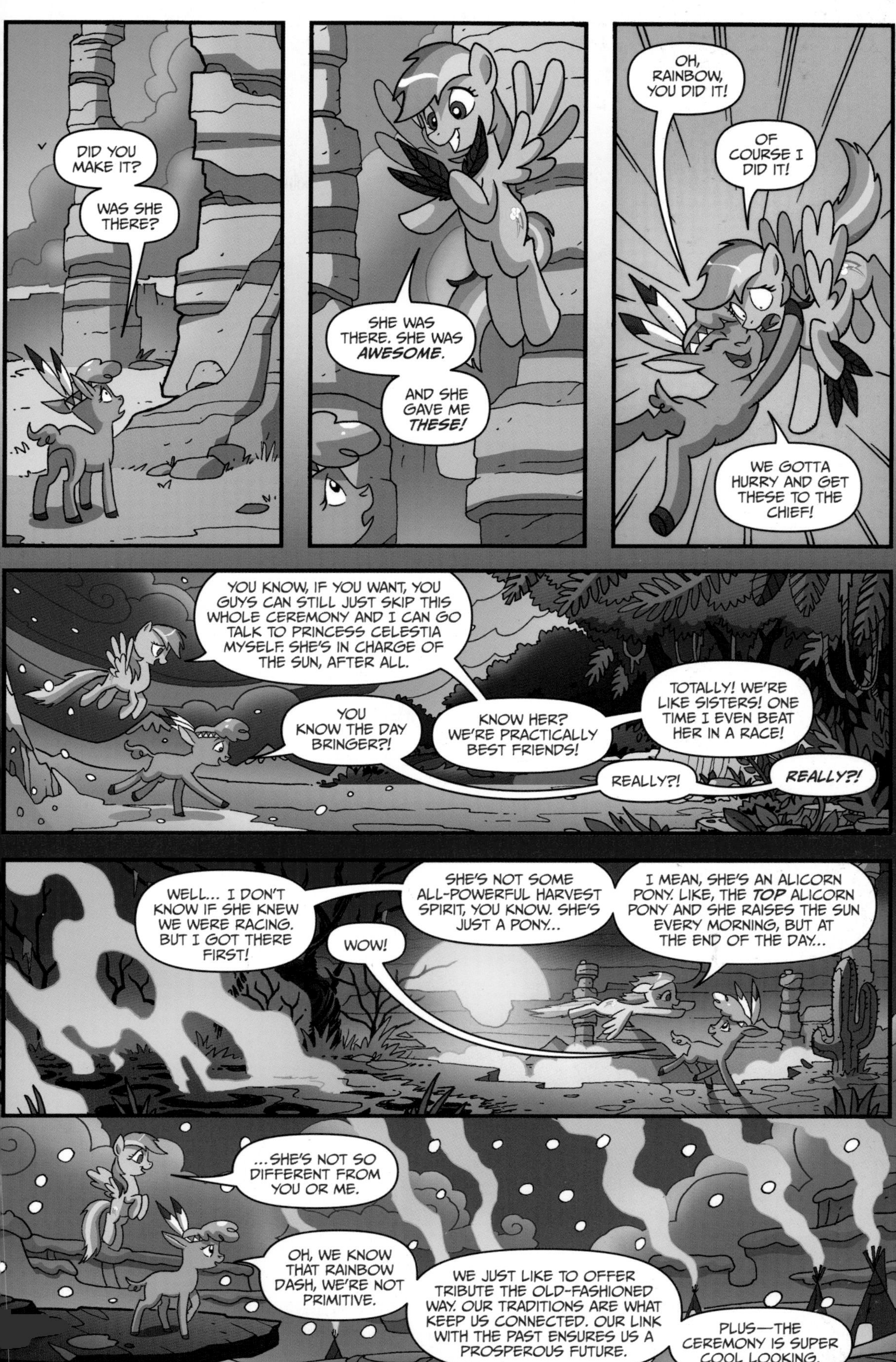

DID YOU MAKE IT?
WAS SHE THERE?
SHE WAS THERE. SHE WAS *AWESOME*.
AND SHE GAVE ME *THESE!*
OH, RAINBOW, YOU DID IT!
OF COURSE I DID IT!
WE GOTTA HURRY AND GET THESE TO THE CHIEF!
YOU KNOW, IF YOU WANT, YOU GUYS CAN STILL JUST SKIP THIS WHOLE CEREMONY AND I CAN GO TALK TO PRINCESS CELESTIA MYSELF. SHE'S IN CHARGE OF THE SUN, AFTER ALL.
YOU KNOW THE DAY BRINGER?!
KNOW HER? WE'RE PRACTICALLY BEST FRIENDS!
TOTALLY! WE'RE LIKE SISTERS! ONE TIME I EVEN BEAT HER IN A RACE!
REALLY?!
REALLY?!
WELL... I DON'T KNOW IF SHE KNEW WE WERE RACING. BUT I GOT THERE FIRST!
WOW!
SHE'S NOT SOME ALL-POWERFUL HARVEST SPIRIT, YOU KNOW. SHE'S JUST A PONY...
I MEAN, SHE'S AN ALICORN PONY. LIKE, THE *TOP* ALICORN PONY AND SHE RAISES THE SUN EVERY MORNING, BUT AT THE END OF THE DAY...
...SHE'S NOT SO DIFFERENT FROM YOU OR ME.
OH, WE KNOW THAT RAINBOW DASH, WE'RE NOT PRIMITIVE.
WE JUST LIKE TO OFFER TRIBUTE THE OLD-FASHIONED WAY. OUR TRADITIONS ARE WHAT KEEP US CONNECTED. OUR LINK WITH THE PAST ENSURES US A PROSPEROUS FUTURE.
PLUS—THE CEREMONY IS SUPER COOL LOOKING.

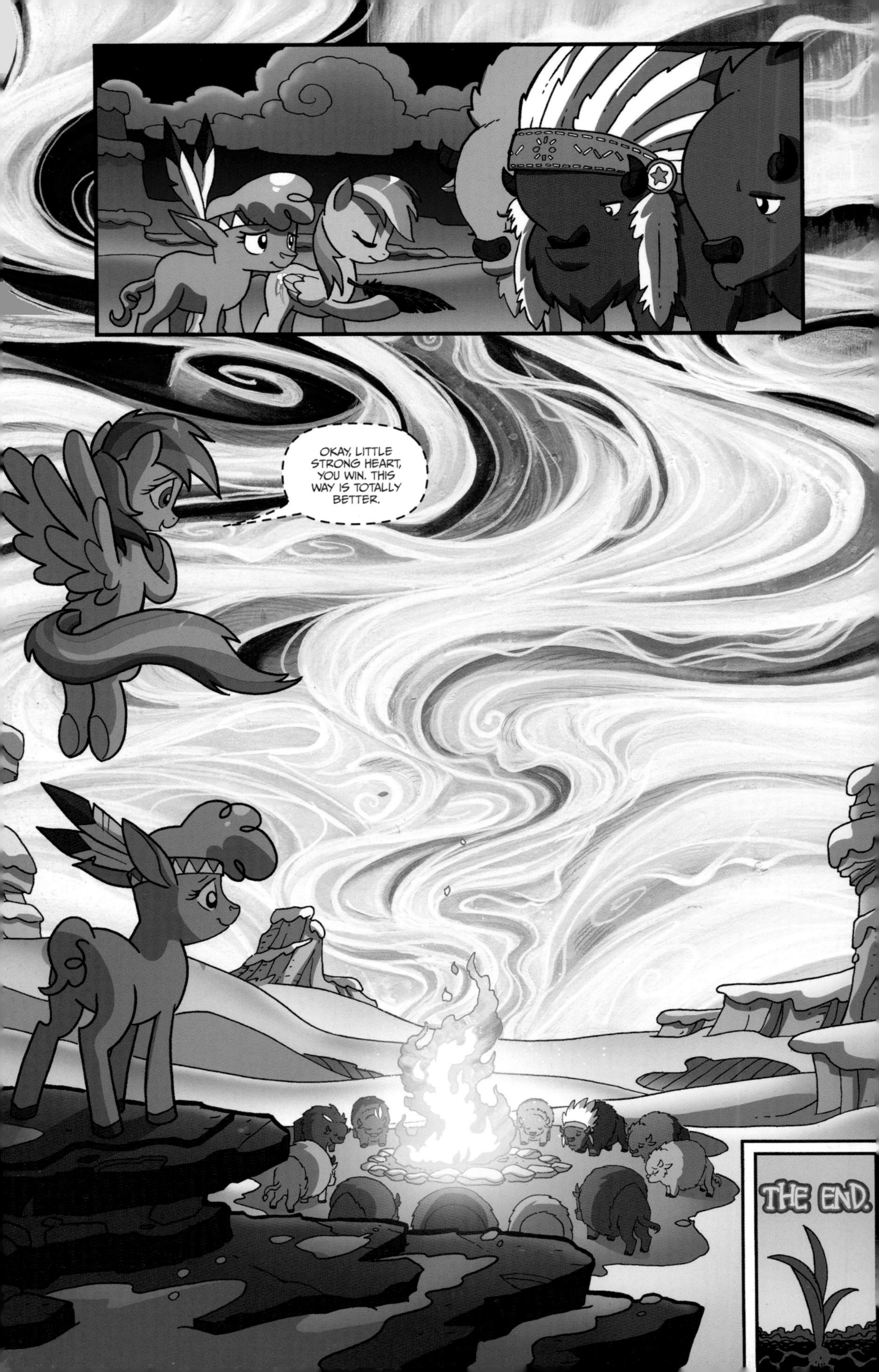
OKAY, LITTLE STRONG HEART, YOU WIN. THIS WAY IS TOTALLY BETTER.
THE END.

My Little Pony

Friends Forever

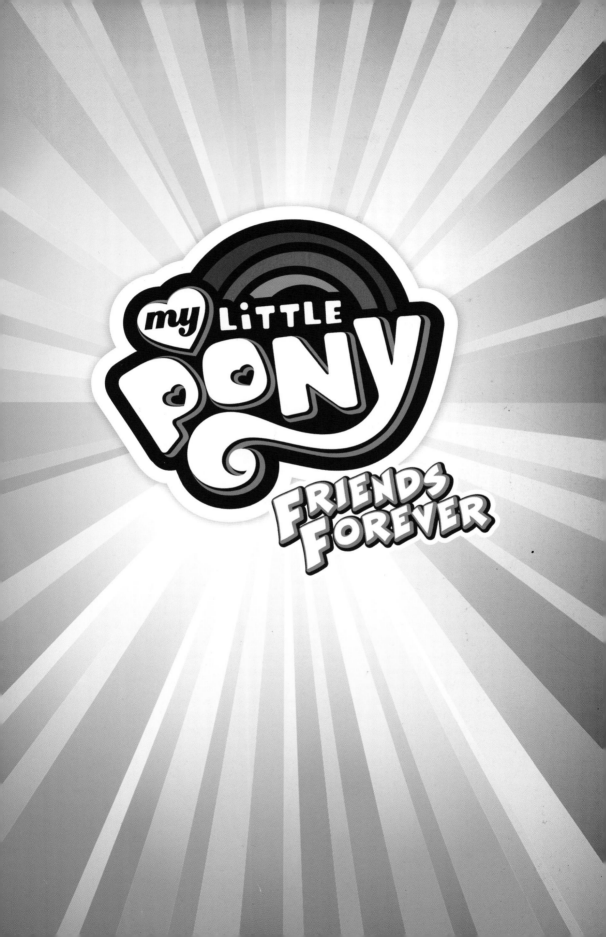

Fluttershy & Daring Do

art by
Jay Fosgitt

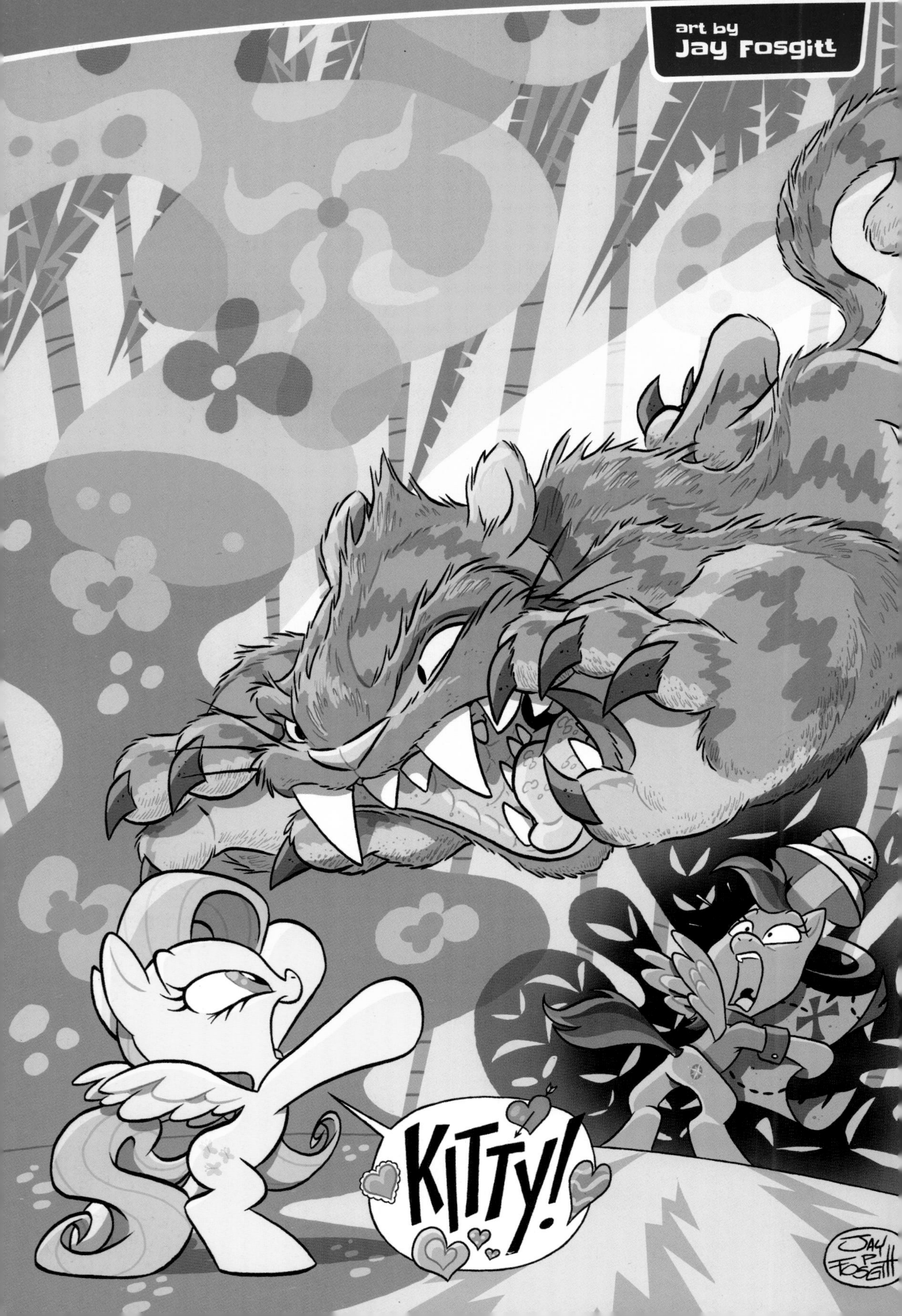
KITTY!

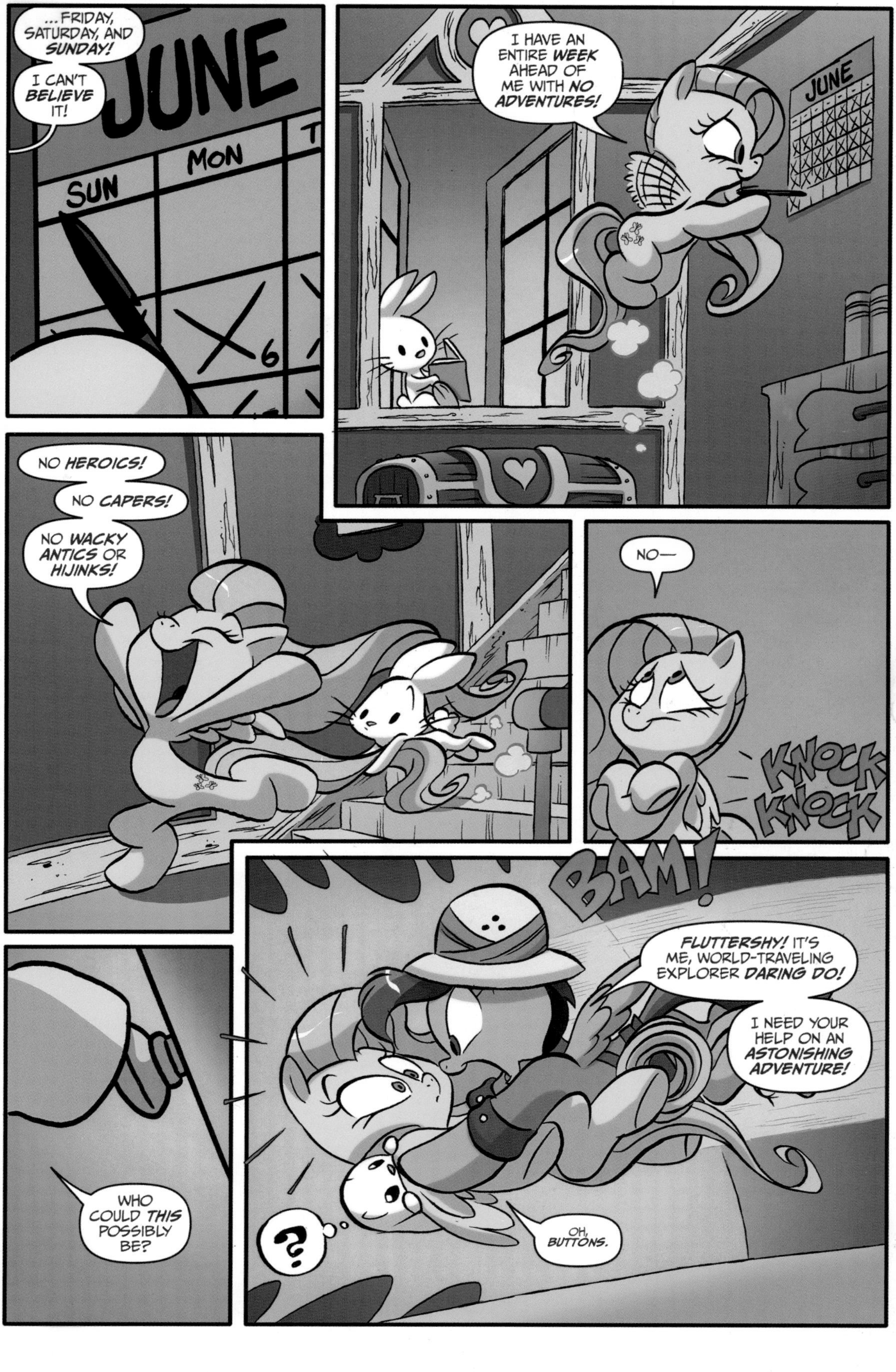

...FRIDAY, SATURDAY, AND SUNDAY!
I CAN'T BELIEVE IT!
JUNE
SUN
MON
I HAVE AN ENTIRE WEEK AHEAD OF ME WITH NO ADVENTURES!
JUNE
NO HEROICS!
NO CAPERS!
NO WACKY ANTICS OR HIJINKS!
NO—
KNOCK KNOCK
WHO COULD THIS POSSIBLY BE?
BAM!
FLUTTERSHY! IT'S ME, WORLD-TRAVELING EXPLORER DARING DO!
I NEED YOUR HELP ON AN ASTONISHING ADVENTURE!
?
OH, BUTTONS.

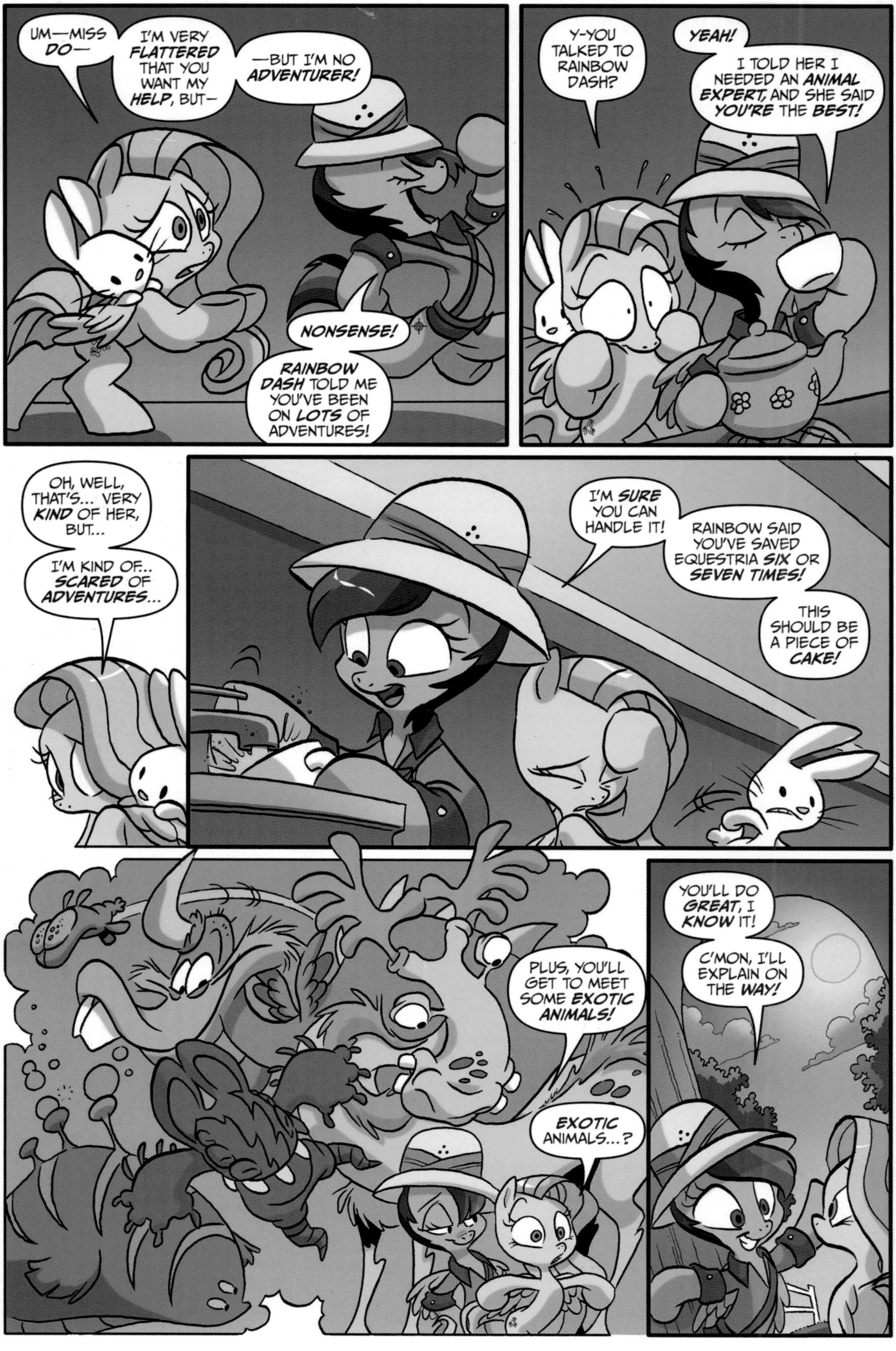
UM—MISS DO—
I'M VERY FLATTERED THAT YOU WANT MY HELP, BUT—
—BUT I'M NO ADVENTURER!
NONSENSE!
RAINBOW DASH TOLD ME YOU'VE BEEN ON LOTS OF ADVENTURES!
Y-YOU TALKED TO RAINBOW DASH?
YEAH!
I TOLD HER I NEEDED AN ANIMAL EXPERT, AND SHE SAID YOU'RE THE BEST!
OH, WELL, THAT'S... VERY KIND OF HER, BUT...
I'M KIND OF... SCARED OF ADVENTURES...
I'M SURE YOU CAN HANDLE IT!
RAINBOW SAID YOU'VE SAVED EQUESTRIA SIX OR SEVEN TIMES!
THIS SHOULD BE A PIECE OF CAKE!
PLUS, YOU'LL GET TO MEET SOME EXOTIC ANIMALS!
EXOTIC ANIMALS...?
YOU'LL DO GREAT, I KNOW IT!
C'MON, I'LL EXPLAIN ON THE WAY!

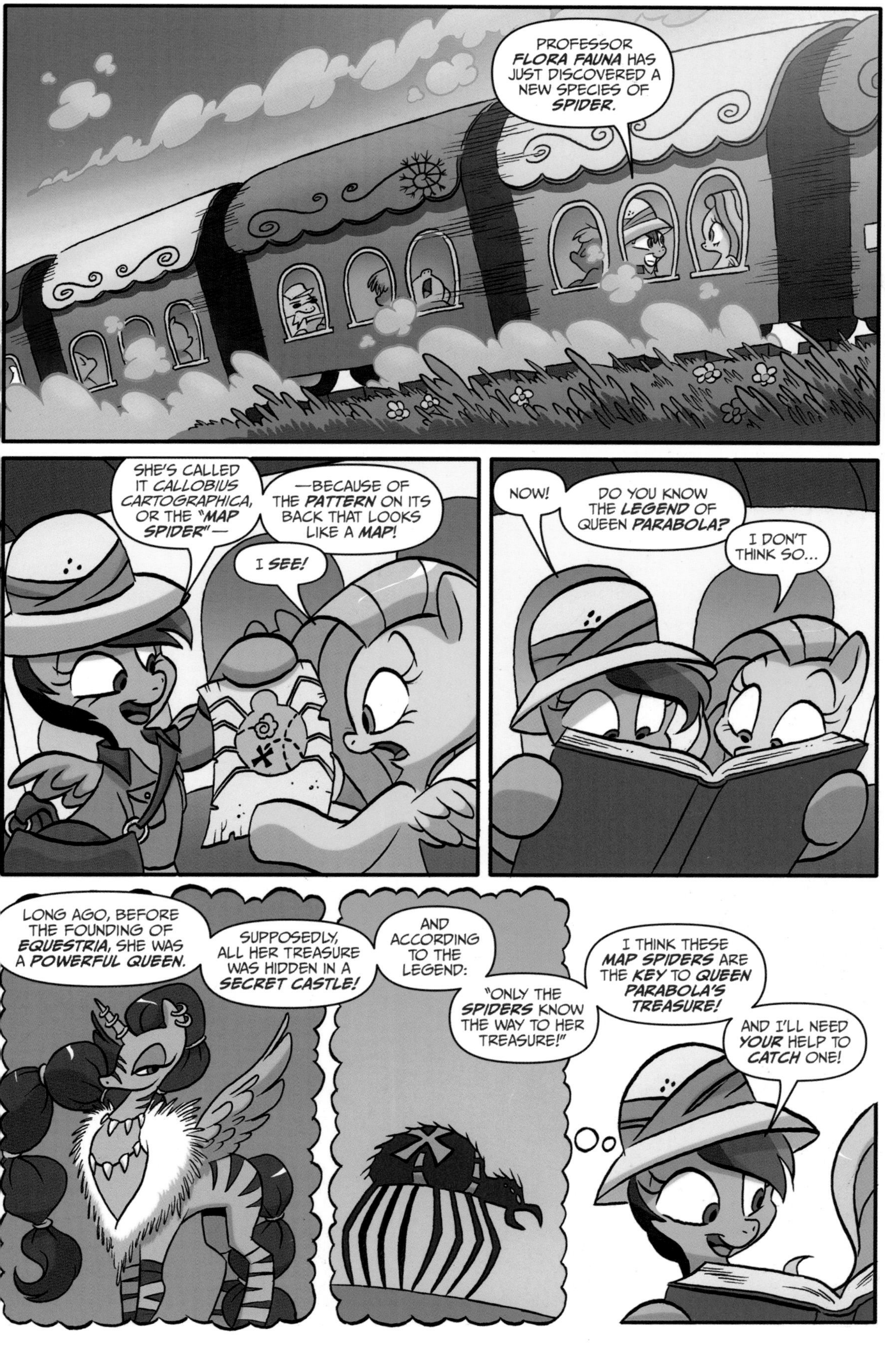
PROFESSOR FLORA FAUNA HAS JUST DISCOVERED A NEW SPECIES OF SPIDER.
SHE'S CALLED IT CALLOBIUS CARTOGRAPHICA, OR THE "MAP SPIDER"—
—BECAUSE OF THE PATTERN ON ITS BACK THAT LOOKS LIKE A MAP!
I SEE!
NOW!
DO YOU KNOW THE LEGEND OF QUEEN PARABOLA?
I DON'T THINK SO...
LONG AGO, BEFORE THE FOUNDING OF EQUESTRIA, SHE WAS A POWERFUL QUEEN.
SUPPOSEDLY, ALL HER TREASURE WAS HIDDEN IN A SECRET CASTLE!
AND ACCORDING TO THE LEGEND:
"ONLY THE SPIDERS KNOW THE WAY TO HER TREASURE!"
I THINK THESE MAP SPIDERS ARE THE KEY TO QUEEN PARABOLA'S TREASURE!
AND I'LL NEED YOUR HELP TO CATCH ONE!

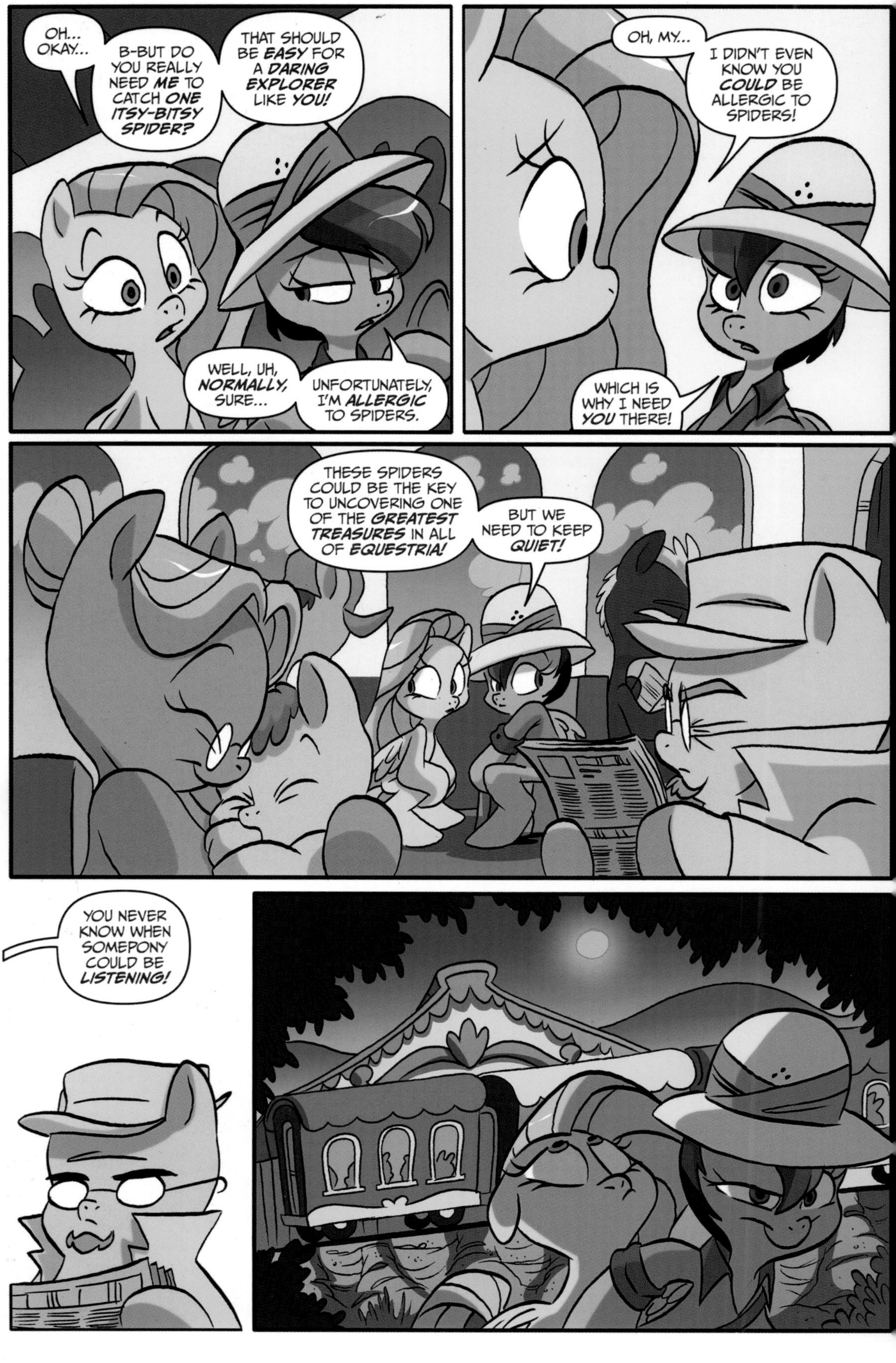
OH... OKAY...
B-BUT DO YOU REALLY NEED ME TO CATCH ONE ITSY-BITSY SPIDER?
THAT SHOULD BE EASY FOR A DARING EXPLORER LIKE YOU!
WELL, UH, NORMALLY, SURE...
UNFORTUNATELY, I'M ALLERGIC TO SPIDERS.
OH, MY...
I DIDN'T EVEN KNOW YOU COULD BE ALLERGIC TO SPIDERS!
WHICH IS WHY I NEED YOU THERE!
THESE SPIDERS COULD BE THE KEY TO UNCOVERING ONE OF THE GREATEST TREASURES IN ALL OF EQUESTRIA!
BUT WE NEED TO KEEP QUIET!
YOU NEVER KNOW WHEN SOMEPONY COULD BE LISTENING!

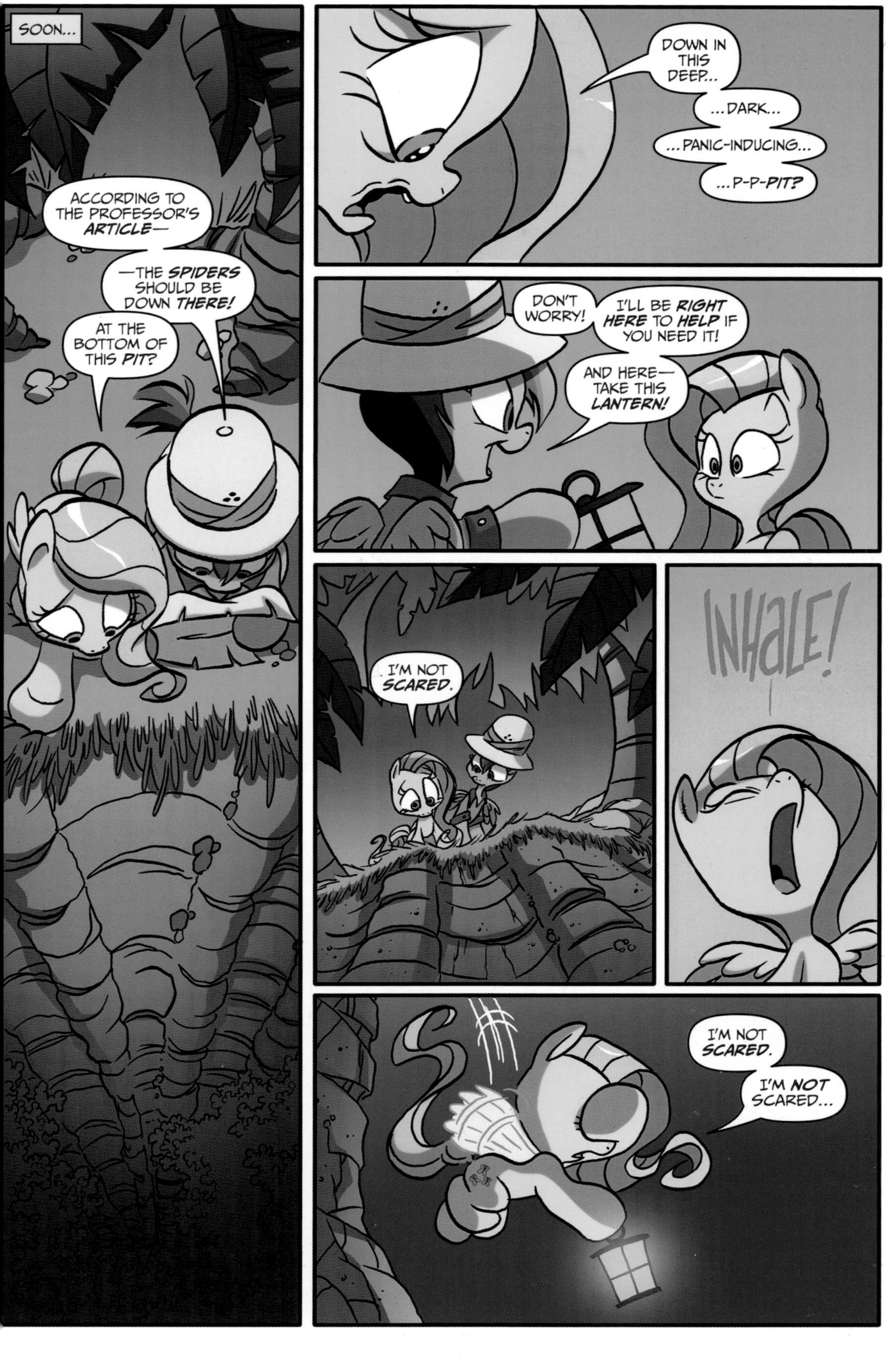
SOON...
ACCORDING TO THE PROFESSOR'S ARTICLE—
—THE SPIDERS SHOULD BE DOWN THERE!
AT THE BOTTOM OF THIS PIT?
DOWN IN THIS DEEP...
...DARK...
...PANIC-INDUCING...
...P-P-PIT?
DON'T WORRY!
I'LL BE RIGHT HERE TO HELP IF YOU NEED IT!
AND HERE— TAKE THIS LANTERN!
I'M NOT SCARED.
INHALE!
I'M NOT SCARED.
I'M NOT SCARED...

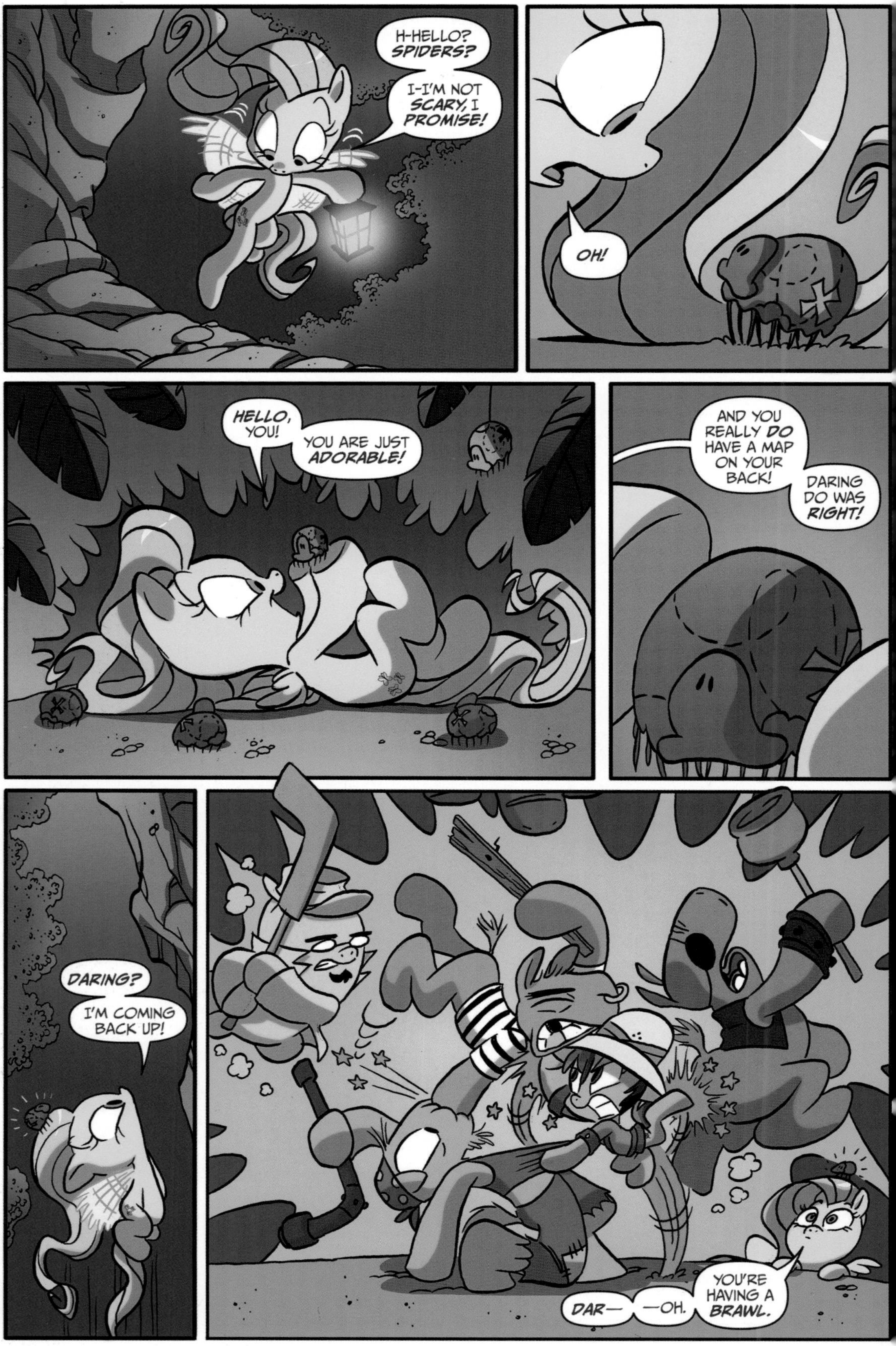
H-HELLO? SPIDERS?
I-I'M NOT SCARY, I PROMISE!
OH!
HELLO, YOU!
YOU ARE JUST ADORABLE!
AND YOU REALLY DO HAVE A MAP ON YOUR BACK!
DARING DO WAS RIGHT!
DARING?
I'M COMING BACK UP!
DAR—
—OH.
YOU'RE HAVING A BRAWL.

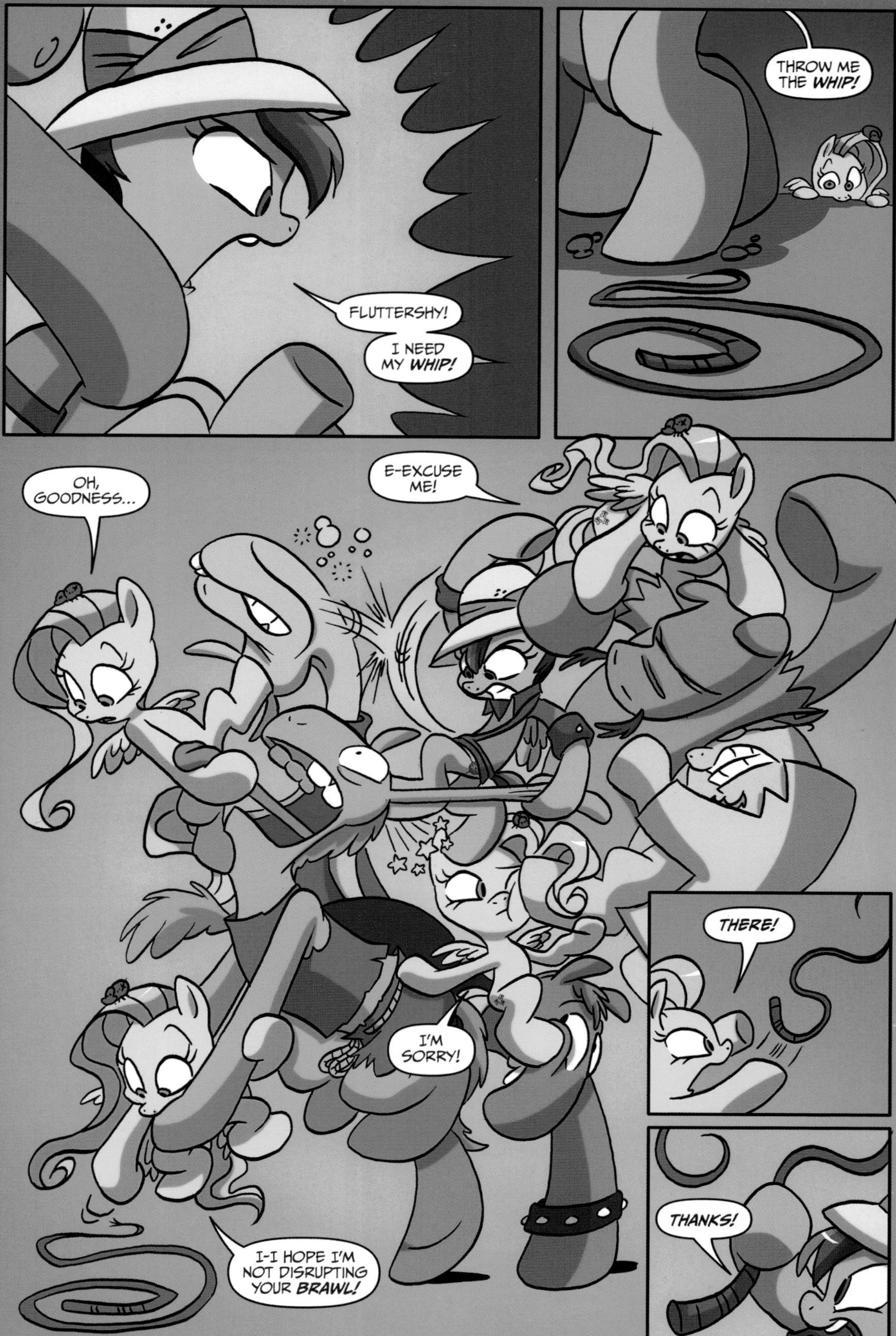
FLUTTERSHY!
I NEED MY WHIP!
THROW ME THE WHIP!
OH, GOODNESS...
E-EXCUSE ME!
I'M SORRY!
I-I HOPE I'M NOT DISRUPTING YOUR BRAWL!
THERE!
THANKS!

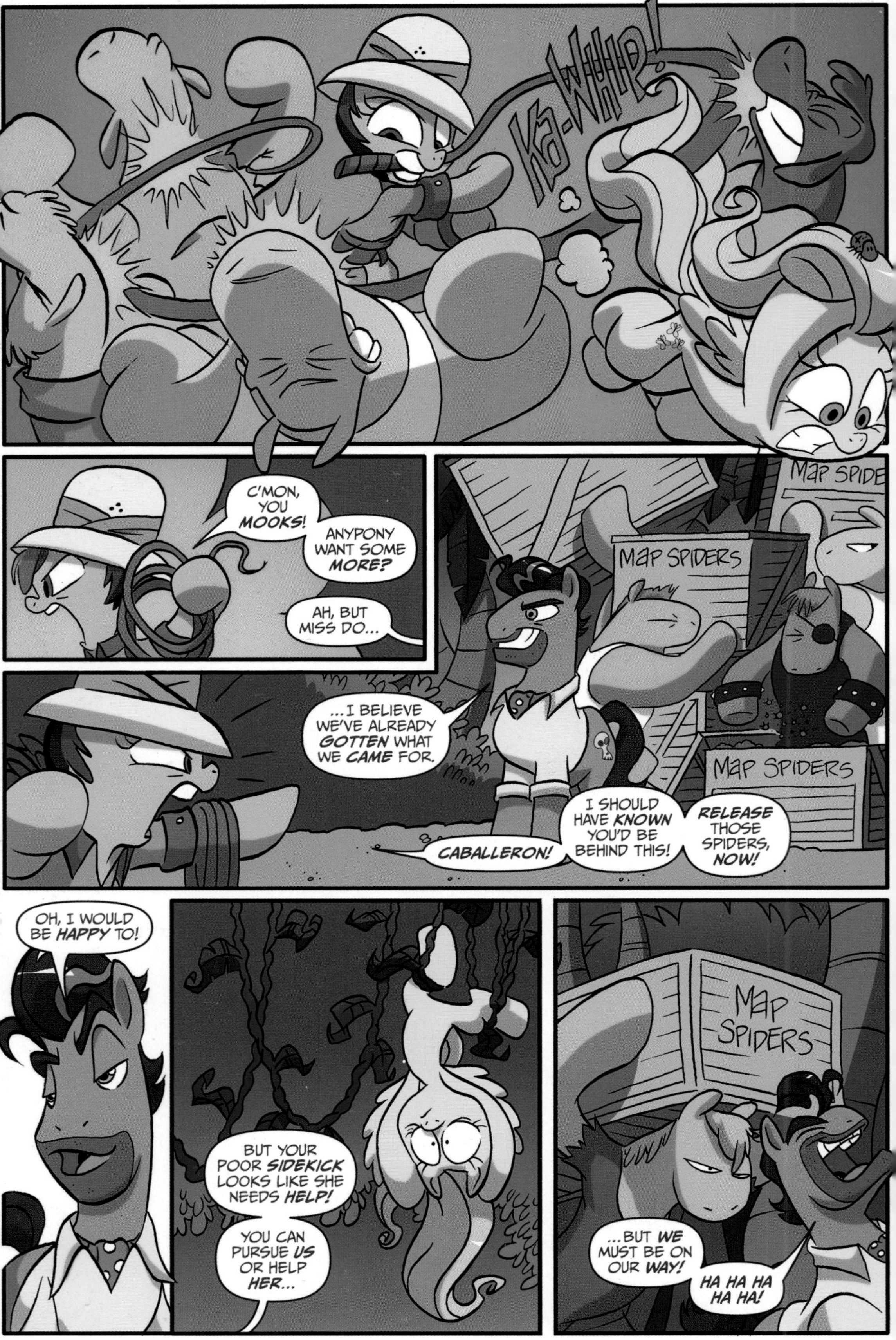
KA-WHIIIP!
C'MON, YOU MOOKS!
ANYPONY WANT SOME MORE?
AH, BUT MISS DO...
MAP SPIDERS
MAP SPIDERS
...I BELIEVE WE'VE ALREADY GOTTEN WHAT WE CAME FOR.
MAP SPIDERS
CABALLERON!
I SHOULD HAVE KNOWN YOU'D BE BEHIND THIS!
RELEASE THOSE SPIDERS, NOW!
OH, I WOULD BE HAPPY TO!
BUT YOUR POOR SIDEKICK LOOKS LIKE SHE NEEDS HELP!
YOU CAN PURSUE US OR HELP HER...
MAP SPIDERS
...BUT WE MUST BE ON OUR WAY!
HA HA HA HA HA!

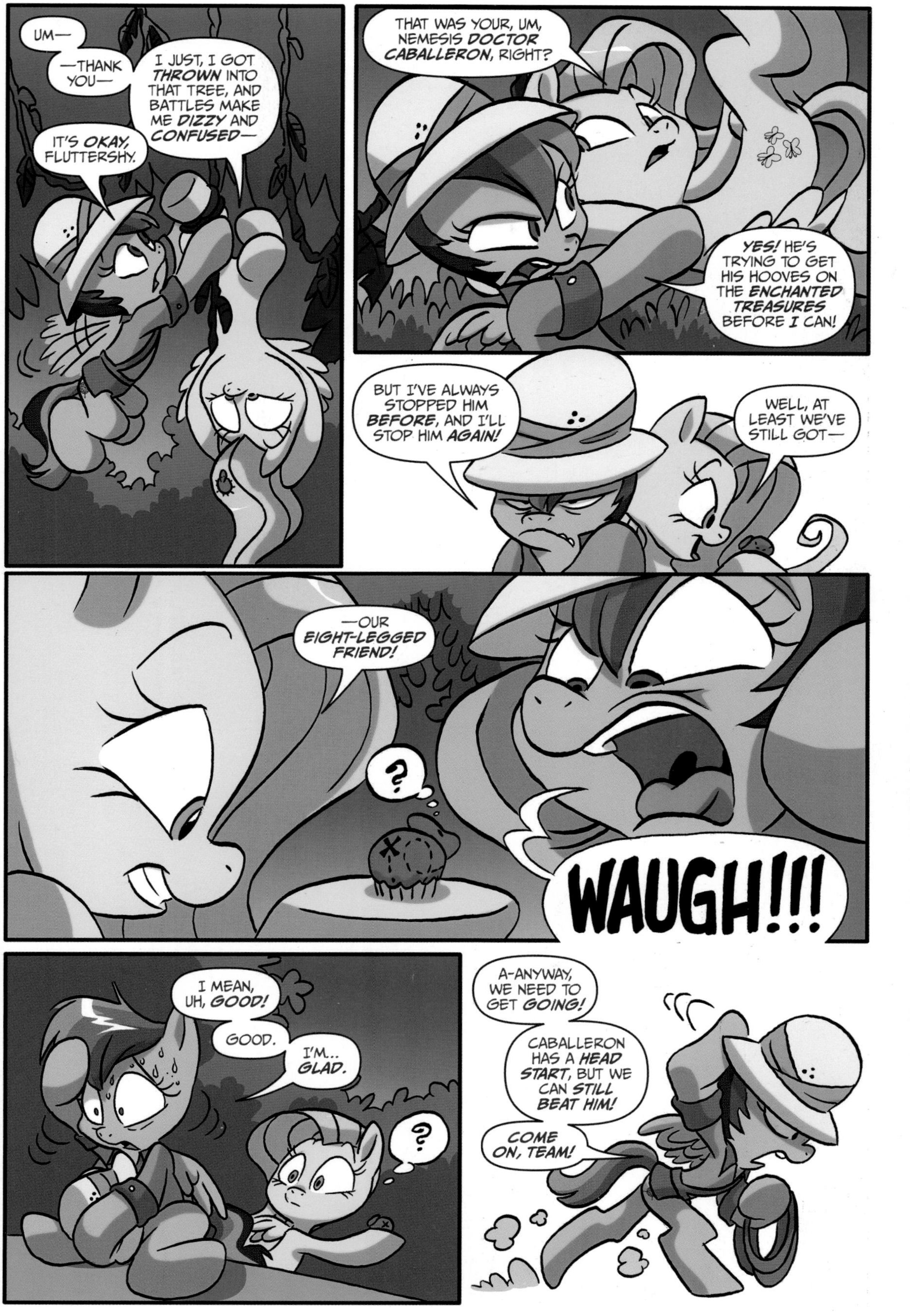
UM—
—THANK YOU—
I JUST, I GOT THROWN INTO THAT TREE, AND BATTLES MAKE ME DIZZY AND CONFUSED—
IT'S OKAY, FLUTTERSHY.
THAT WAS YOUR, UM, NEMESIS DOCTOR CABALLERON, RIGHT?
YES! HE'S TRYING TO GET HIS HOOVES ON THE ENCHANTED TREASURES BEFORE I CAN!
BUT I'VE ALWAYS STOPPED HIM BEFORE, AND I'LL STOP HIM AGAIN!
WELL, AT LEAST WE'VE STILL GOT—
—OUR EIGHT-LEGGED FRIEND!
?
WAUGH!!!
I MEAN, UH, GOOD!
GOOD.
I'M... GLAD.
?
A-ANYWAY, WE NEED TO GET GOING!
CABALLERON HAS A HEAD START, BUT WE CAN STILL BEAT HIM!
COME ON, TEAM!

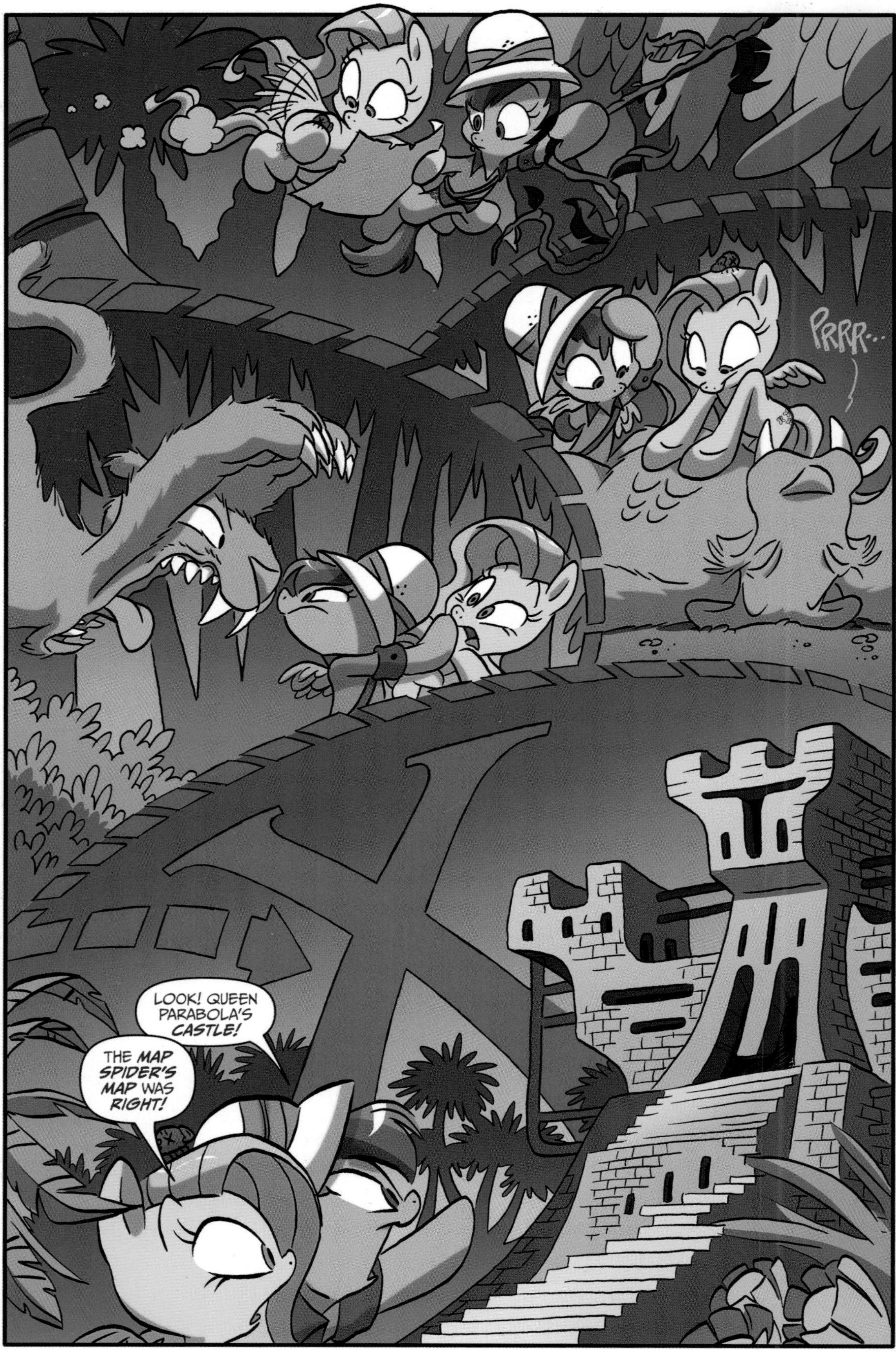
PRRRR...
LOOK! QUEEN PARABOLA'S CASTLE!
THE MAP SPIDER'S MAP WAS RIGHT!

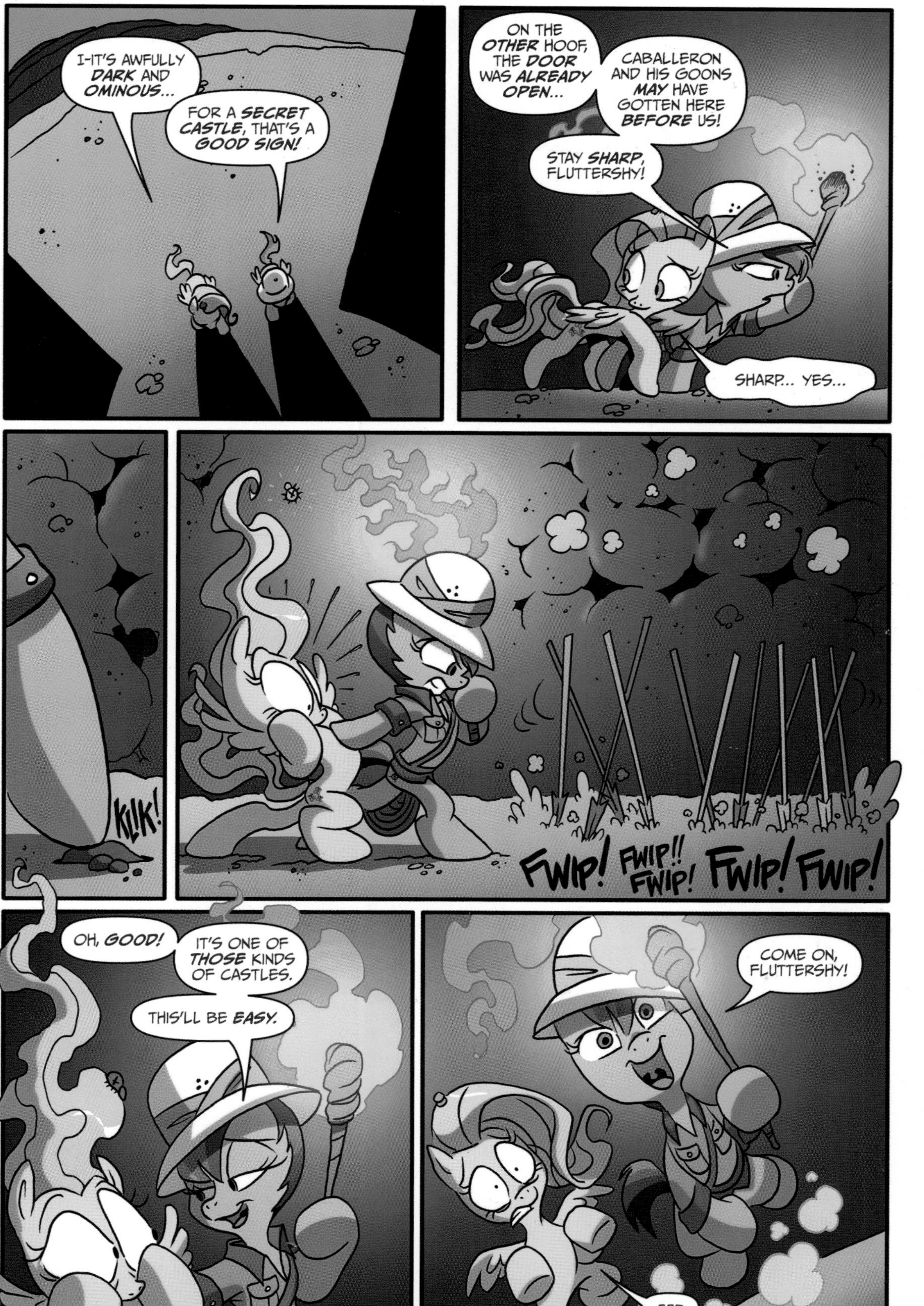
I-IT'S AWFULLY **DARK** AND **OMINOUS**...
FOR A **SECRET CASTLE**, THAT'S A **GOOD SIGN!**
ON THE **OTHER** HOOF, THE **DOOR** WAS **ALREADY OPEN**...
CABALLERON AND HIS GOONS **MAY** HAVE GOTTEN HERE **BEFORE** US!
STAY **SHARP**, FLUTTERSHY!
SHARP... YES...
KLIK!
FWIP! FWIP!! FWIP! FWIP! FWIP!
OH, **GOOD!**
IT'S ONE OF **THOSE** KINDS OF CASTLES.
THIS'LL BE **EASY.**
COME ON, FLUTTERSHY!
EEP.

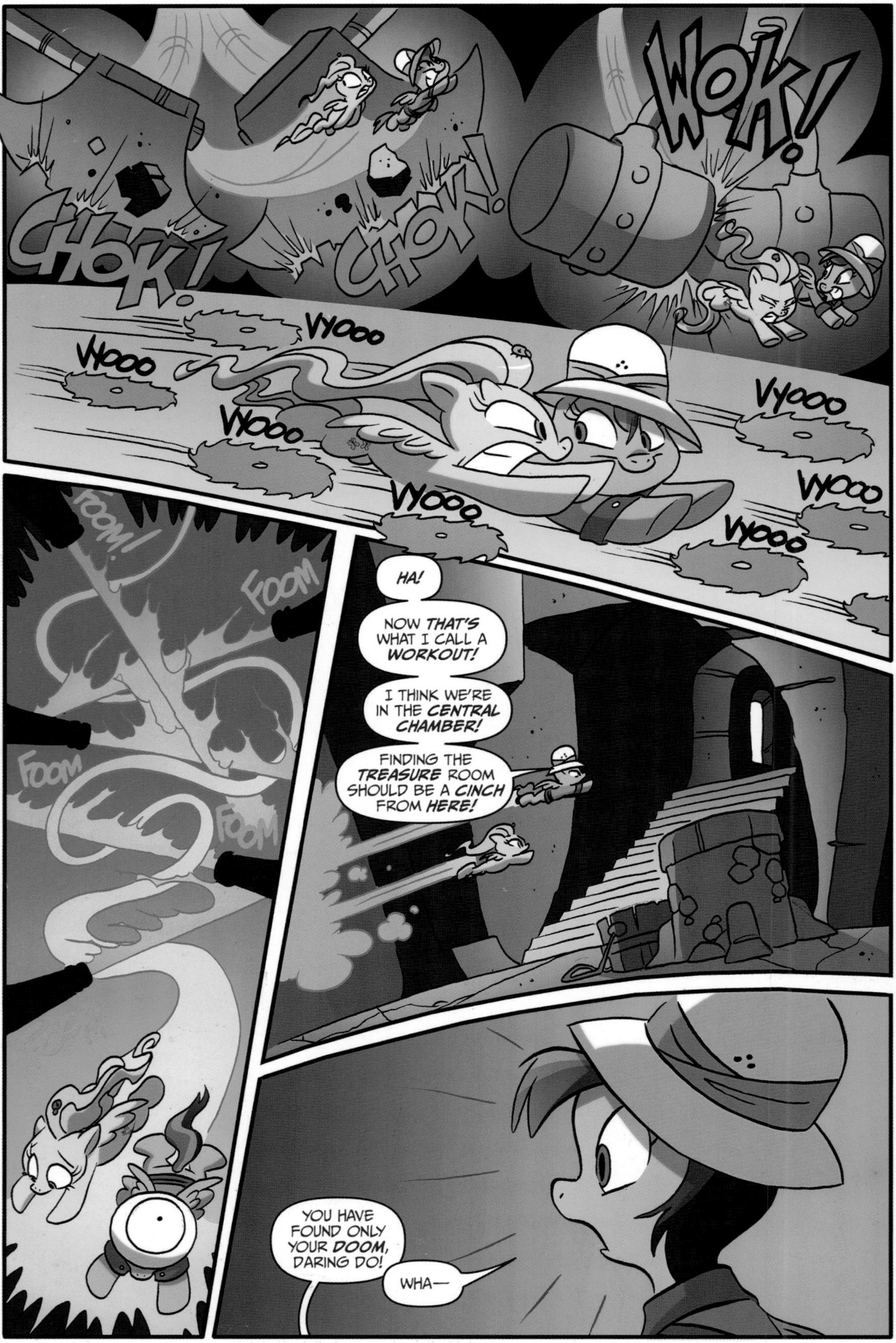
CHOK!
CHOK!
WOK!
VYOOO
VYOOO
VYOOO
VYOOO
VYOOO
VYOOO
VYOOO
FOOM!
FOOM
FOOM
FOOM
HA!
NOW THAT'S WHAT I CALL A WORKOUT!
I THINK WE'RE IN THE CENTRAL CHAMBER!
FINDING THE TREASURE ROOM SHOULD BE A CINCH FROM HERE!
YOU HAVE FOUND ONLY YOUR DOOM, DARING DO!
WHA—

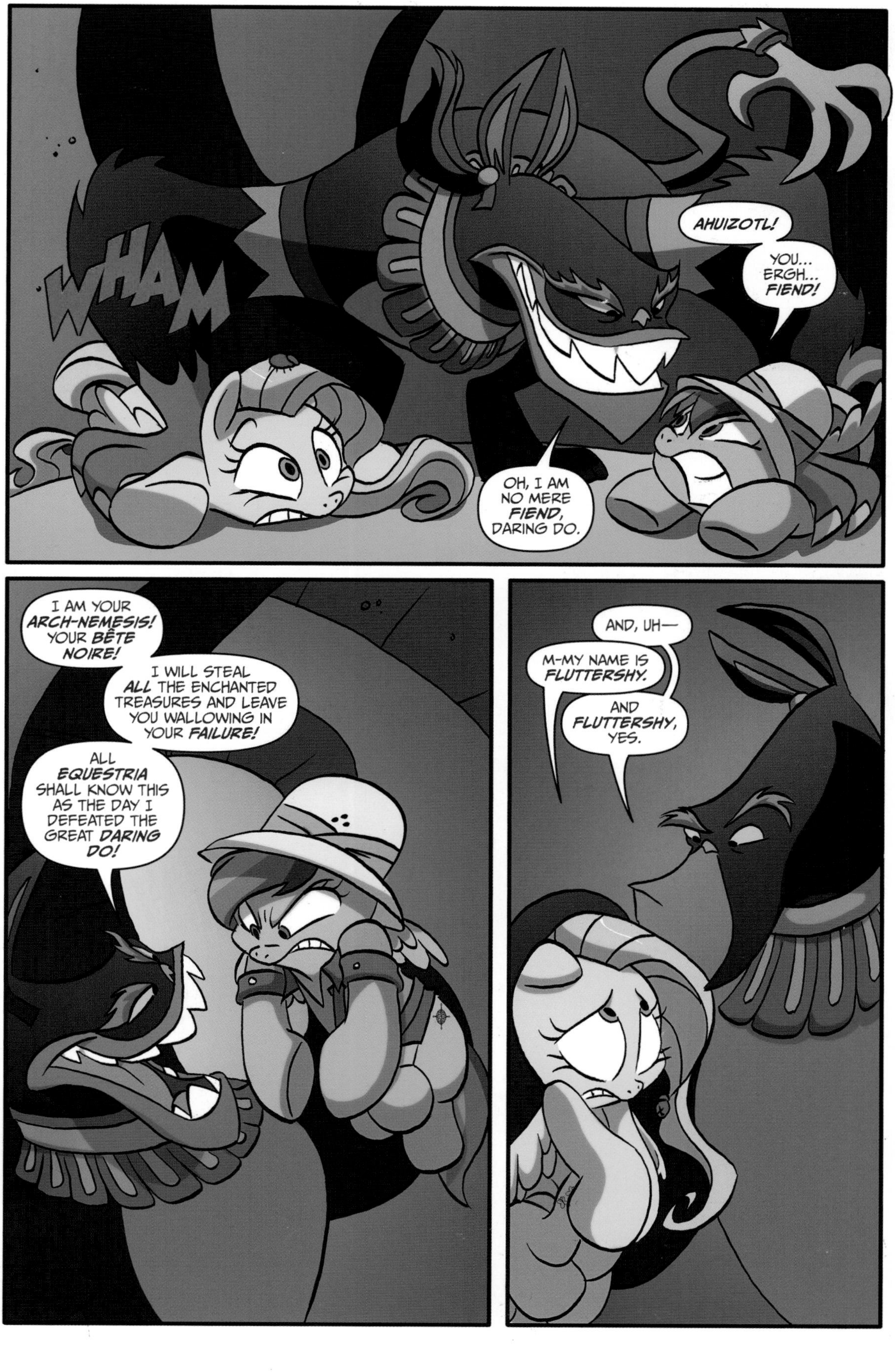
WHAM
AHUIZOTL!
YOU... ERGH... FIEND!
OH, I AM NO MERE FIEND, DARING DO.
I AM YOUR ARCH-NEMESIS! YOUR BÊTE NOIRE!
I WILL STEAL ALL THE ENCHANTED TREASURES AND LEAVE YOU WALLOWING IN YOUR FAILURE!
ALL EQUESTRIA SHALL KNOW THIS AS THE DAY I DEFEATED THE GREAT DARING DO!
M-MY NAME IS FLUTTERSHY.
AND, UH—
AND FLUTTERSHY, YES.

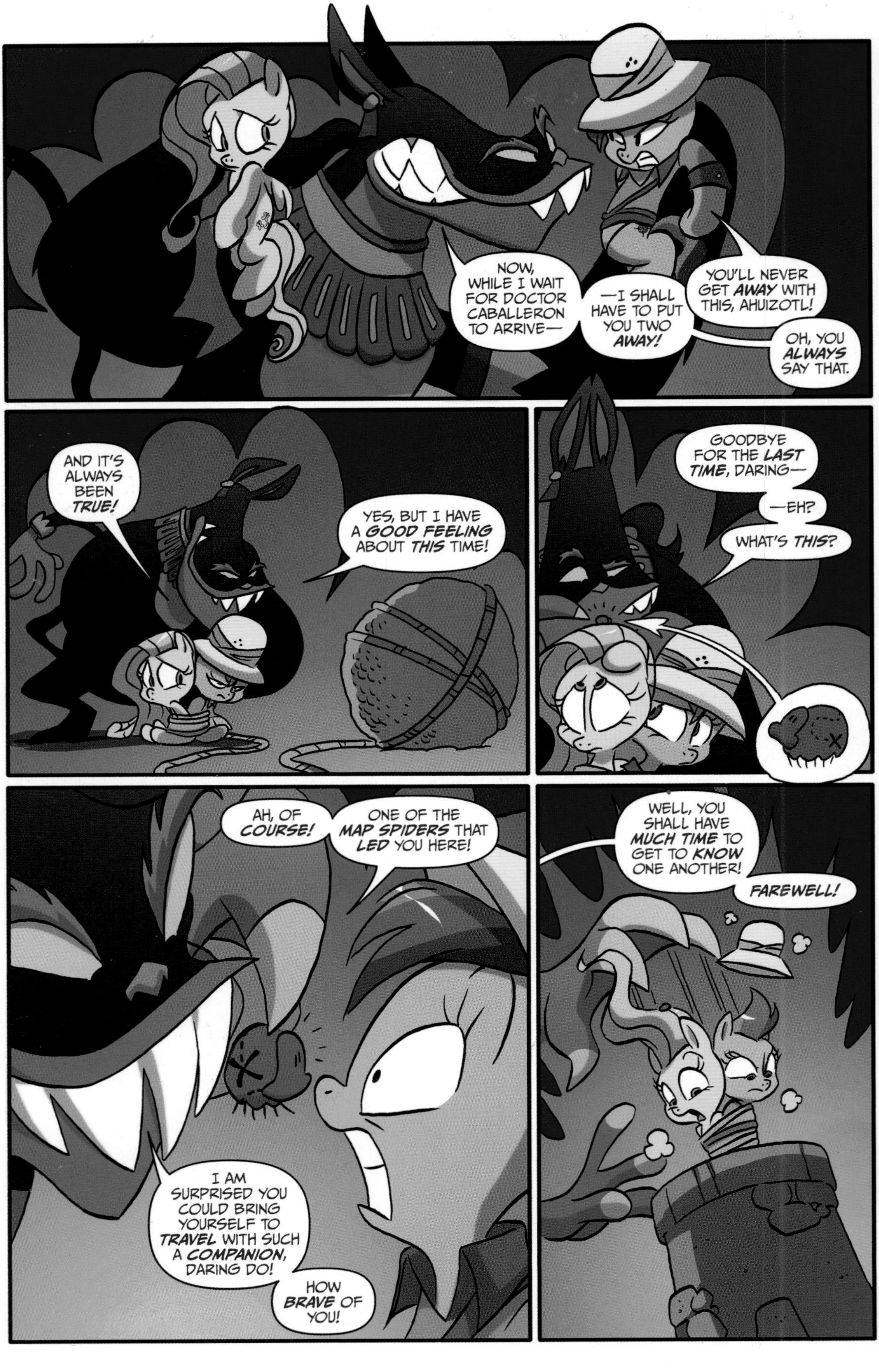
NOW, WHILE I WAIT FOR DOCTOR CABALLERON TO ARRIVE—
—I SHALL HAVE TO PUT YOU TWO AWAY!
YOU'LL NEVER GET AWAY WITH THIS, AHUIZOTL!
OH, YOU ALWAYS SAY THAT.
AND IT'S ALWAYS BEEN TRUE!
YES, BUT I HAVE A GOOD FEELING ABOUT THIS TIME!
GOODBYE FOR THE LAST TIME, DARING—
—EH?
WHAT'S THIS?
AH, OF COURSE!
ONE OF THE MAP SPIDERS THAT LED YOU HERE!
I AM SURPRISED YOU COULD BRING YOURSELF TO TRAVEL WITH SUCH A COMPANION, DARING DO!
HOW BRAVE OF YOU!
WELL, YOU SHALL HAVE MUCH TIME TO GET TO KNOW ONE ANOTHER!
FAREWELL!

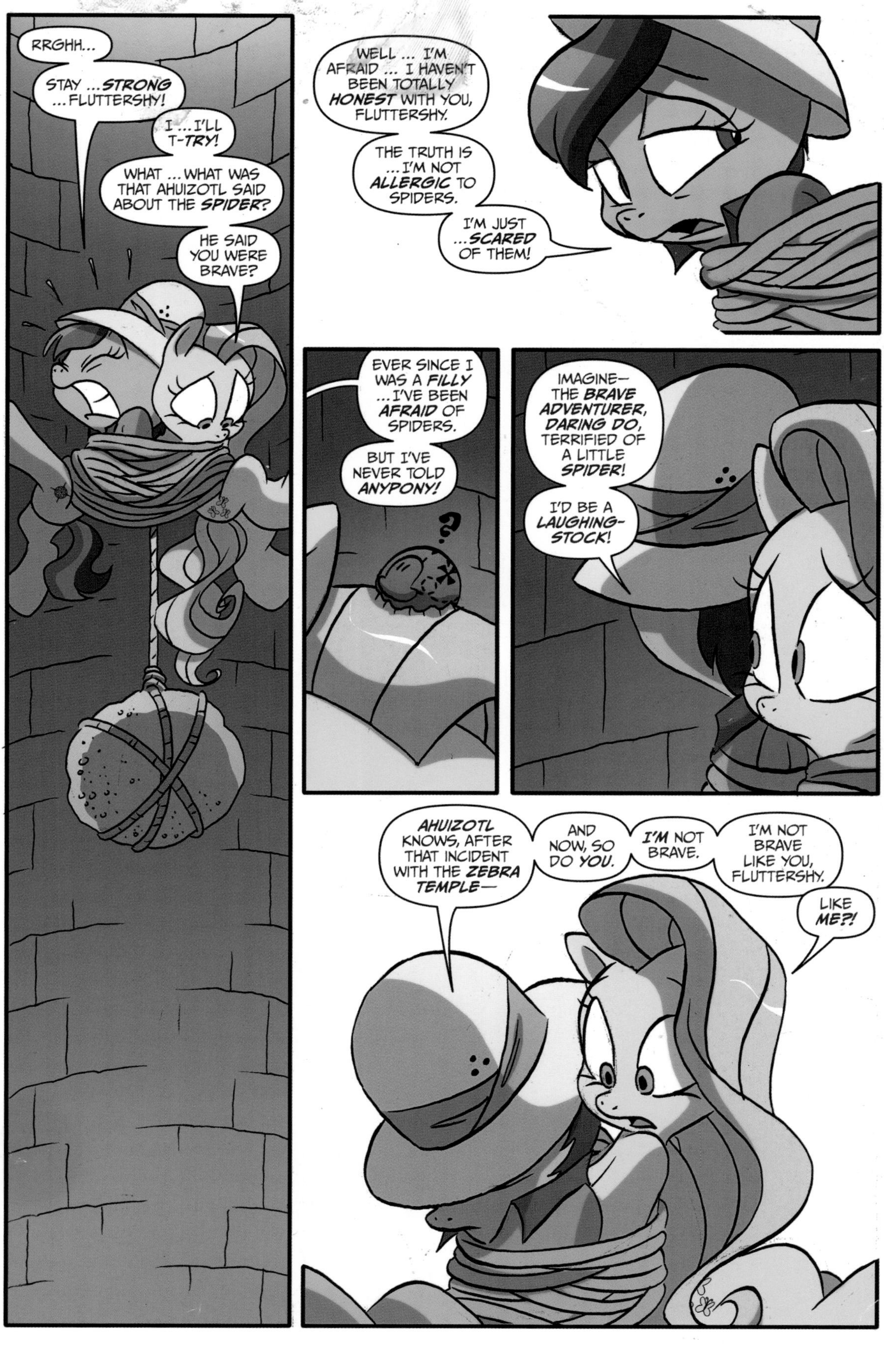
RRGHH...
STAY ...STRONG ...FLUTTERSHY!
I ...I'LL T-TRY!
WHAT ...WHAT WAS THAT AHUIZOTL SAID ABOUT THE SPIDER?
HE SAID YOU WERE BRAVE?
WELL ... I'M AFRAID ... I HAVEN'T BEEN TOTALLY HONEST WITH YOU, FLUTTERSHY.
THE TRUTH IS ...I'M NOT ALLERGIC TO SPIDERS.
I'M JUST ...SCARED OF THEM!
EVER SINCE I WAS A FILLY ...I'VE BEEN AFRAID OF SPIDERS.
BUT I'VE NEVER TOLD ANYPONY!
?
IMAGINE— THE BRAVE ADVENTURER, DARING DO, TERRIFIED OF A LITTLE SPIDER!
I'D BE A LAUGHING-STOCK!
AHUIZOTL KNOWS, AFTER THAT INCIDENT WITH THE ZEBRA TEMPLE—
AND NOW, SO DO YOU.
I'M NOT BRAVE.
I'M NOT BRAVE LIKE YOU, FLUTTERSHY.
LIKE ME?!

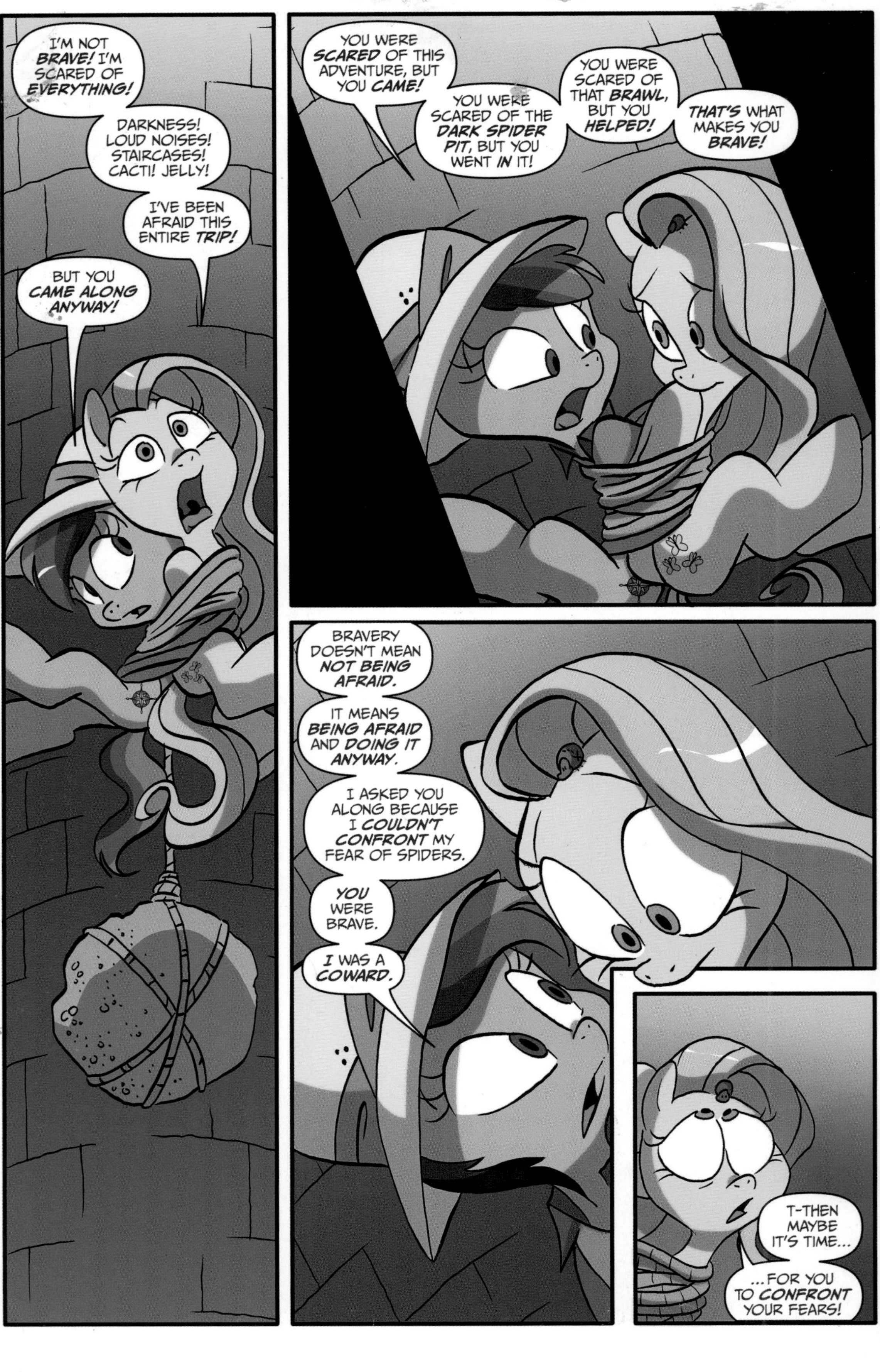
I'M NOT BRAVE! I'M SCARED OF EVERYTHING!
DARKNESS! LOUD NOISES! STAIRCASES! CACTI! JELLY!
I'VE BEEN AFRAID THIS ENTIRE TRIP!
BUT YOU CAME ALONG ANYWAY!
YOU WERE SCARED OF THIS ADVENTURE, BUT YOU CAME!
YOU WERE SCARED OF THE DARK SPIDER PIT, BUT YOU WENT IN IT!
YOU WERE SCARED OF THAT BRAWL, BUT YOU HELPED!
THAT'S WHAT MAKES YOU BRAVE!
BRAVERY DOESN'T MEAN NOT BEING AFRAID.
IT MEANS BEING AFRAID AND DOING IT ANYWAY.
I ASKED YOU ALONG BECAUSE I COULDN'T CONFRONT MY FEAR OF SPIDERS.
YOU WERE BRAVE.
I WAS A COWARD.
T-THEN MAYBE IT'S TIME...
...FOR YOU TO CONFRONT YOUR FEARS!

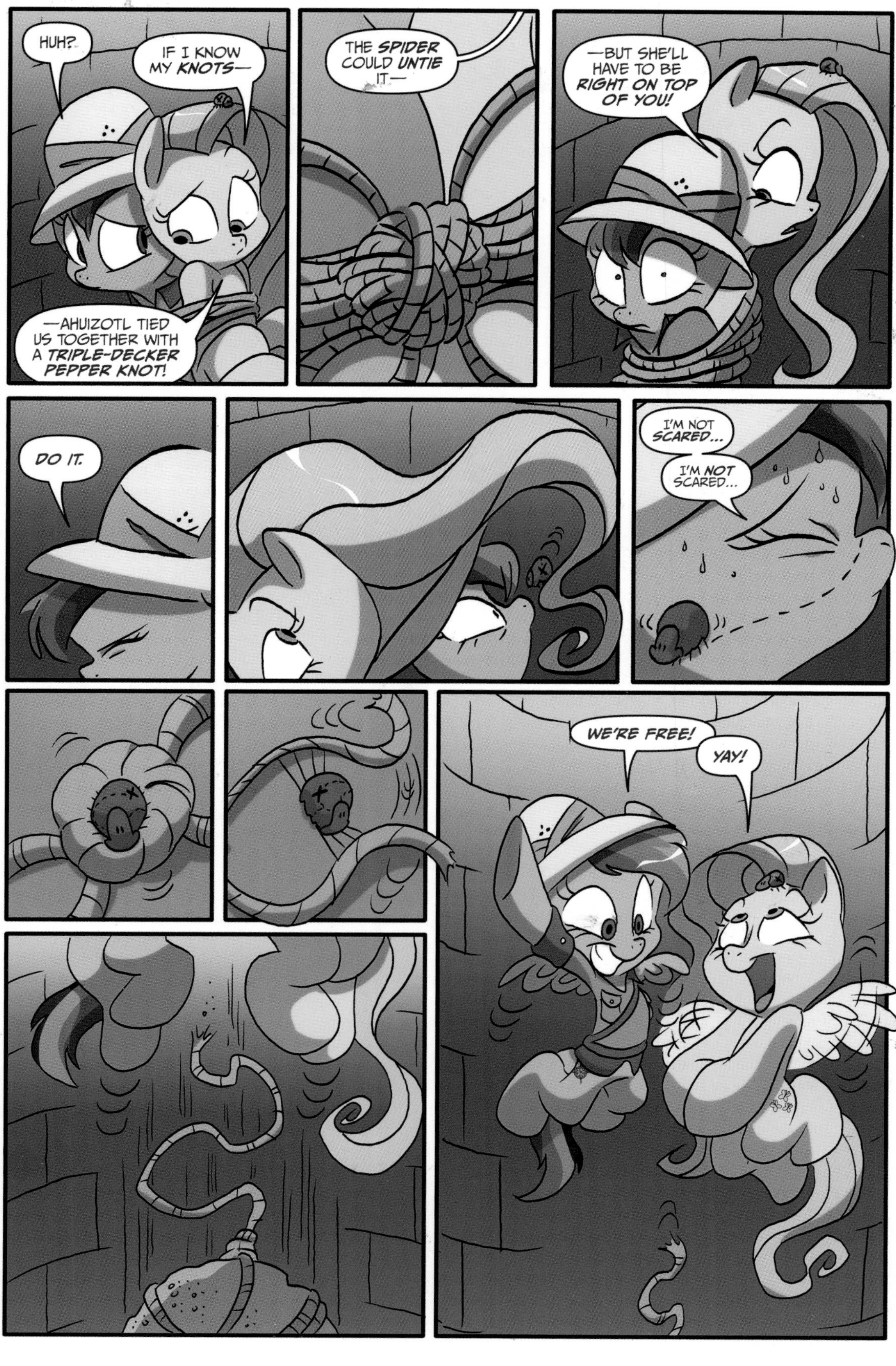
HUH?
IF I KNOW MY KNOTS—
—AHUIZOTL TIED US TOGETHER WITH A TRIPLE-DECKER PEPPER KNOT!
THE SPIDER COULD UNTIE IT—
—BUT SHE'LL HAVE TO BE RIGHT ON TOP OF YOU!
DO IT.
I'M NOT SCARED...
I'M NOT SCARED...
WE'RE FREE!
YAY!

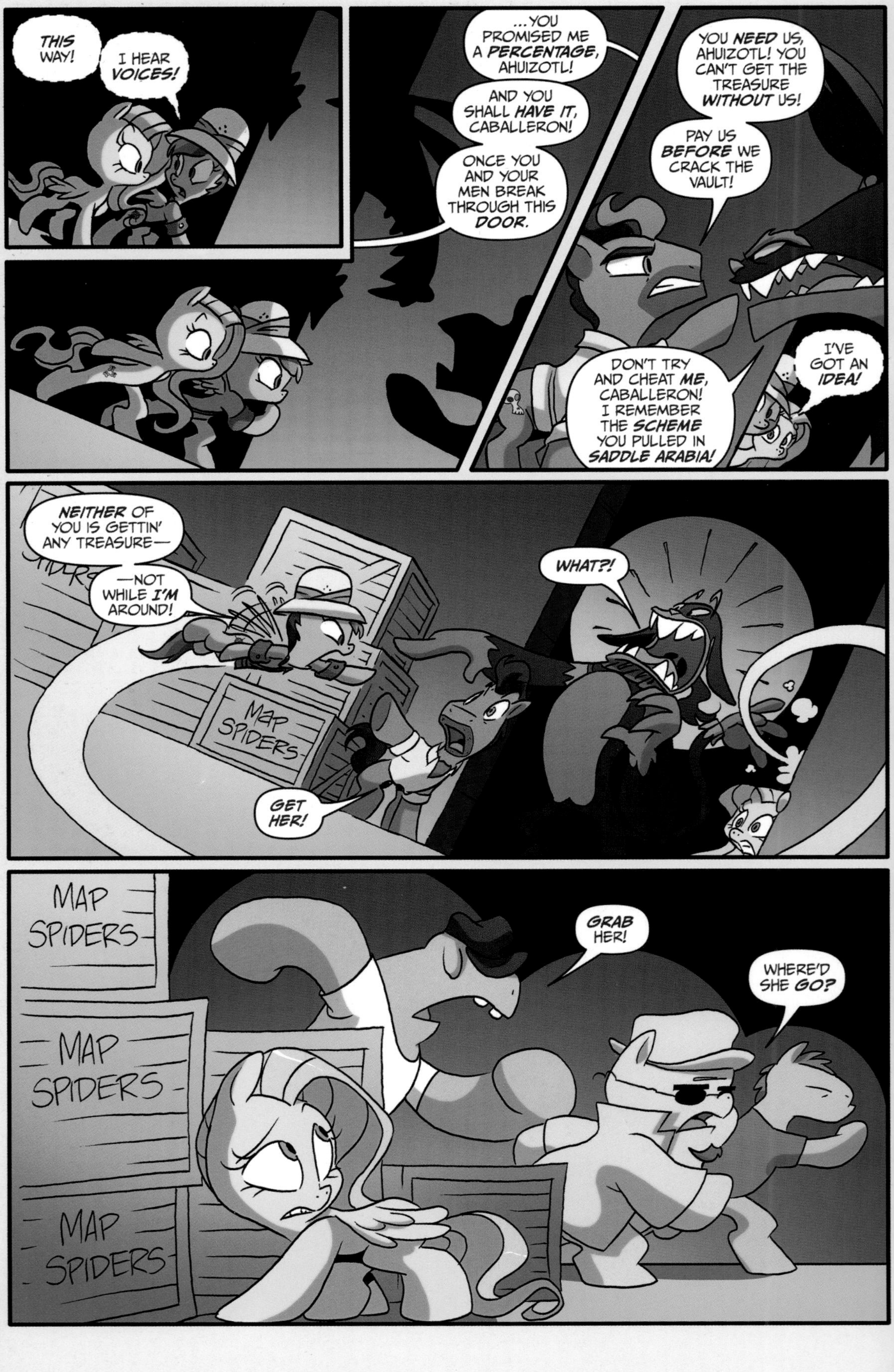
THIS WAY!
I HEAR VOICES!
...YOU PROMISED ME A PERCENTAGE, AHUIZOTL!
AND YOU SHALL HAVE IT, CABALLERON!
ONCE YOU AND YOUR MEN BREAK THROUGH THIS DOOR.
YOU NEED US, AHUIZOTL! YOU CAN'T GET THE TREASURE WITHOUT US!
PAY US BEFORE WE CRACK THE VAULT!
DON'T TRY AND CHEAT ME, CABALLERON! I REMEMBER THE SCHEME YOU PULLED IN SADDLE ARABIA!
I'VE GOT AN IDEA!
NEITHER OF YOU IS GETTIN' ANY TREASURE—
—NOT WHILE I'M AROUND!
WHAT?!
MAP SPIDERS
GET HER!
MAP SPIDERS
MAP SPIDERS
MAP SPIDERS
GRAB HER!
WHERE'D SHE GO?

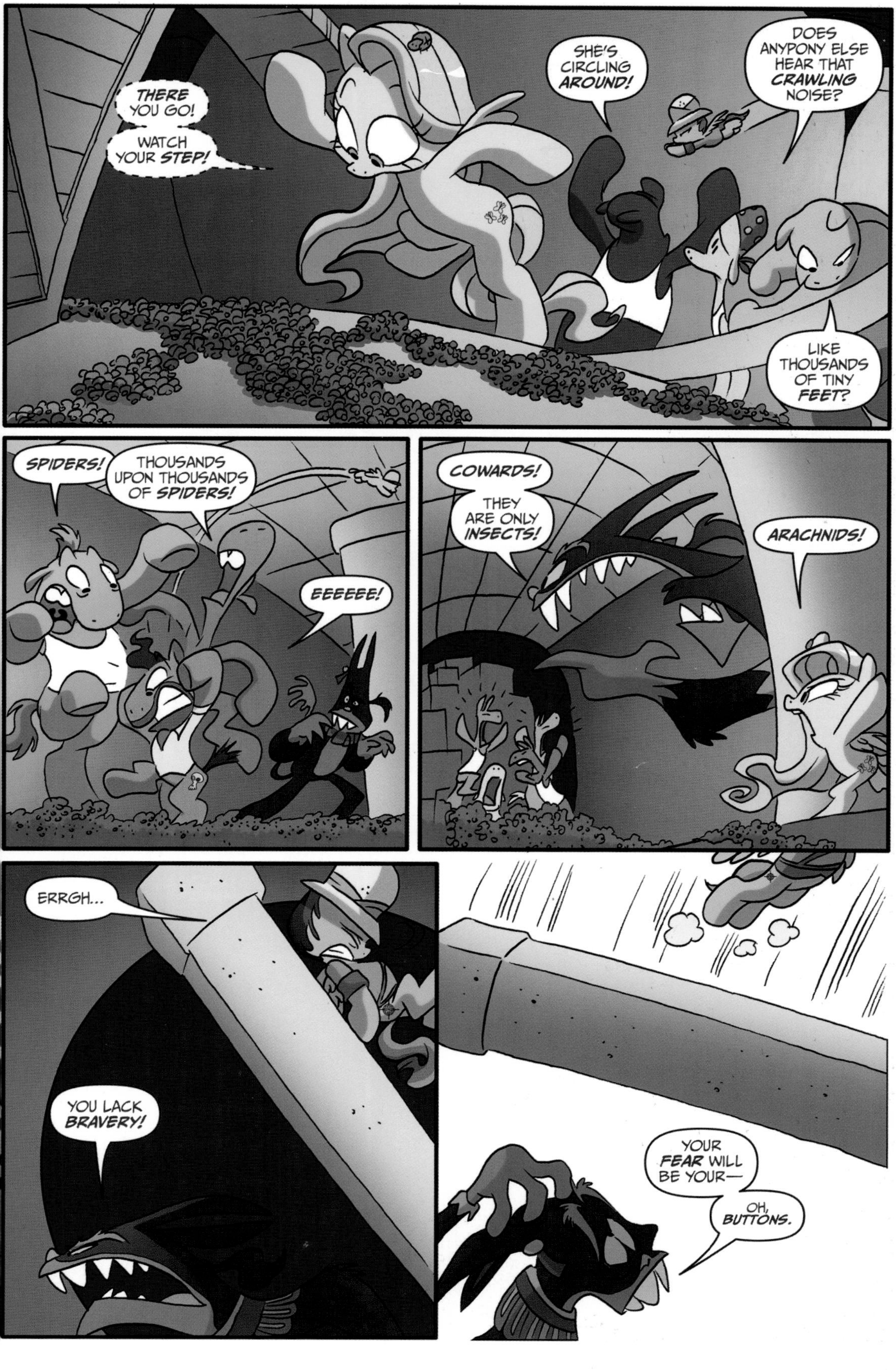
THERE YOU GO!
WATCH YOUR STEP!
SHE'S CIRCLING AROUND!
DOES ANYPONY ELSE HEAR THAT CRAWLING NOISE?
LIKE THOUSANDS OF TINY FEET?
SPIDERS!
THOUSANDS UPON THOUSANDS OF SPIDERS!
EEEEEE!
COWARDS!
THEY ARE ONLY INSECTS!
ARACHNIDS!
ERRGH...
YOU LACK BRAVERY!
YOUR FEAR WILL BE YOUR—
OH, BUTTONS.

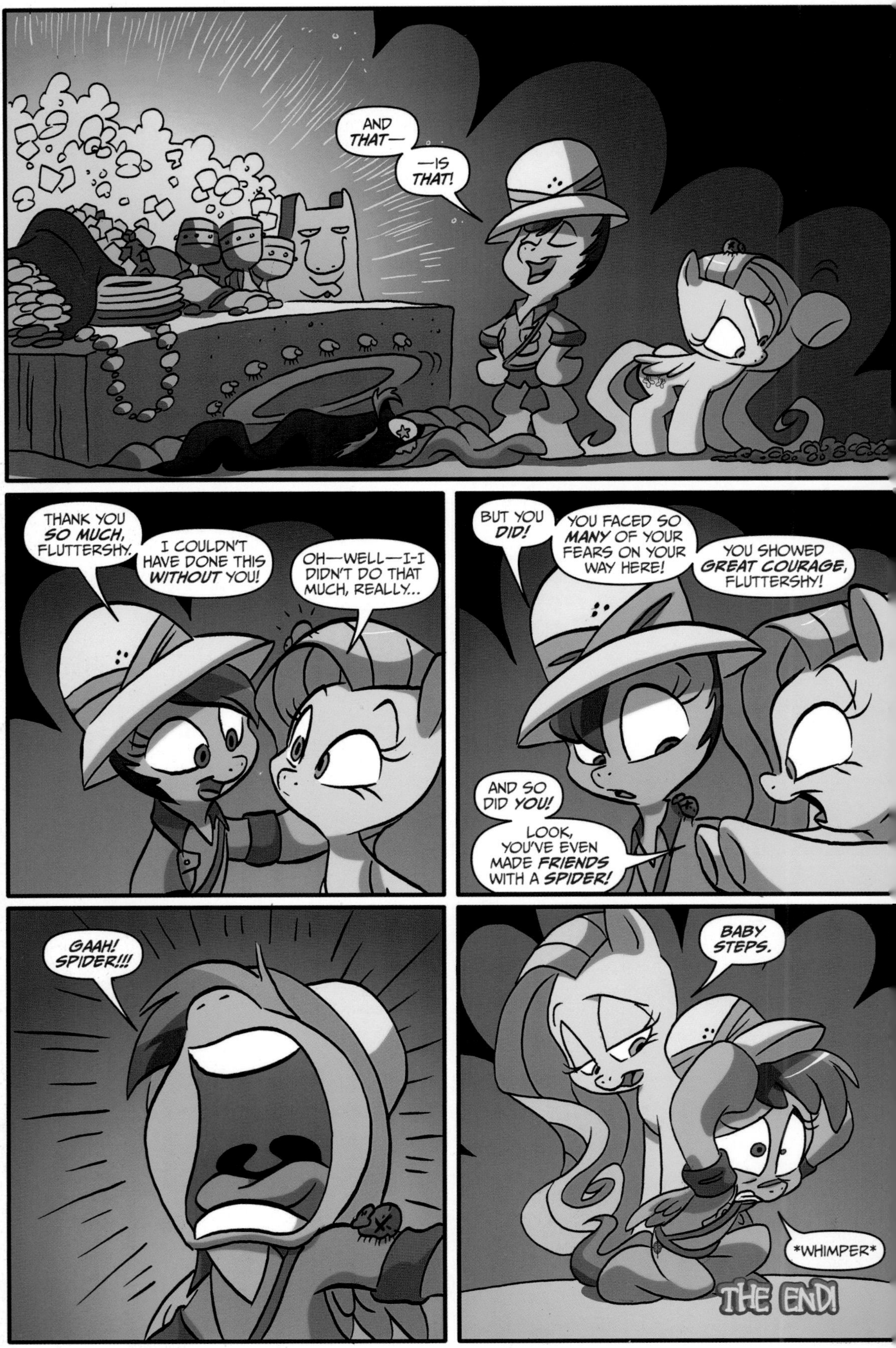
AND THAT—
—IS THAT!
THANK YOU SO MUCH, FLUTTERSHY.
I COULDN'T HAVE DONE THIS WITHOUT YOU!
OH—WELL—I-I DIDN'T DO THAT MUCH, REALLY...
BUT YOU DID!
YOU FACED SO MANY OF YOUR FEARS ON YOUR WAY HERE!
YOU SHOWED GREAT COURAGE, FLUTTERSHY!
AND SO DID YOU!
LOOK, YOU'VE EVEN MADE FRIENDS WITH A SPIDER!
GAAH! SPIDER!!!
BABY STEPS.
WHIMPER
THE END!

my LITTLE PONY

FRIENDS FOREVER

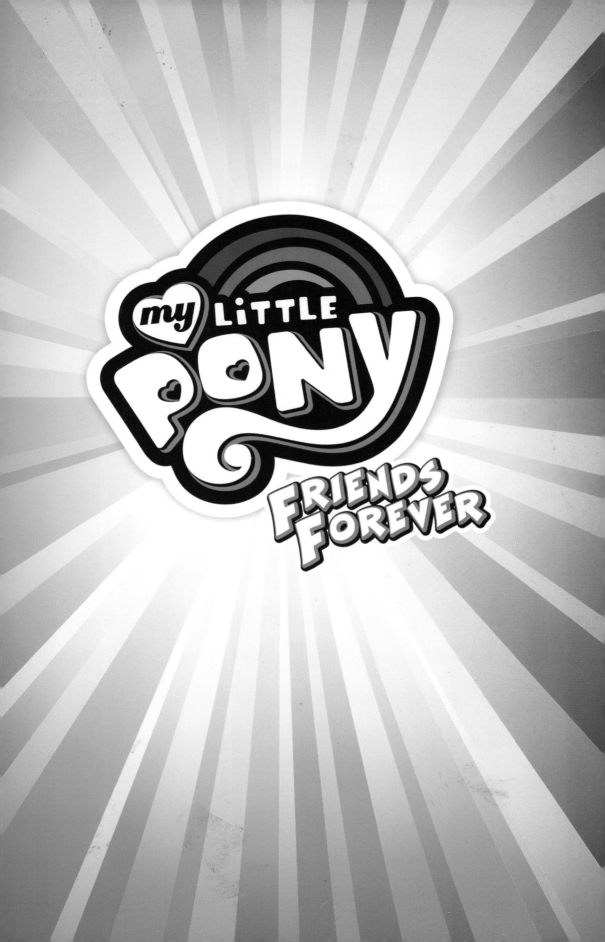

Applejack & Cherry Jubilee

art by
Tony Fleecs

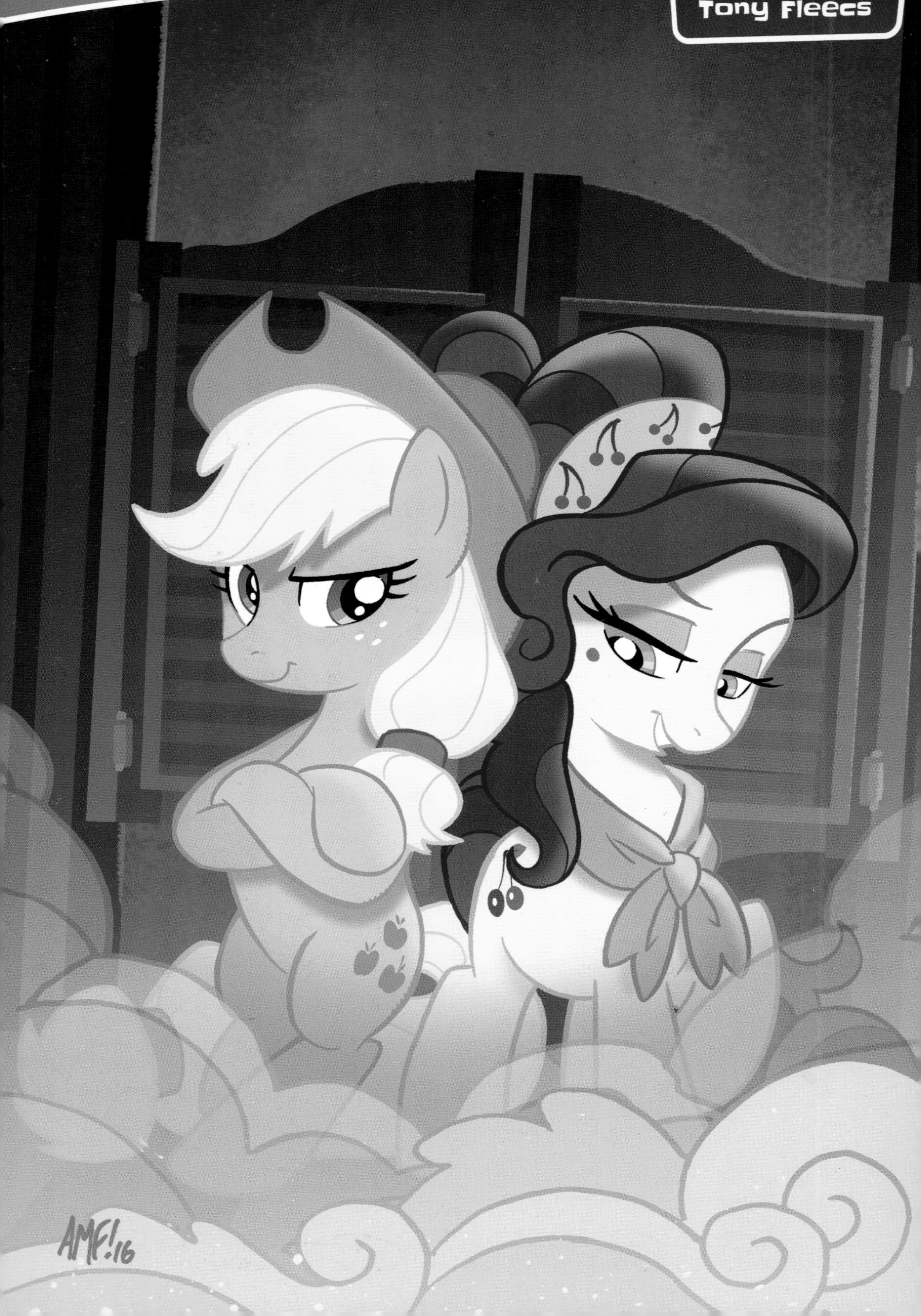
AMF! '16

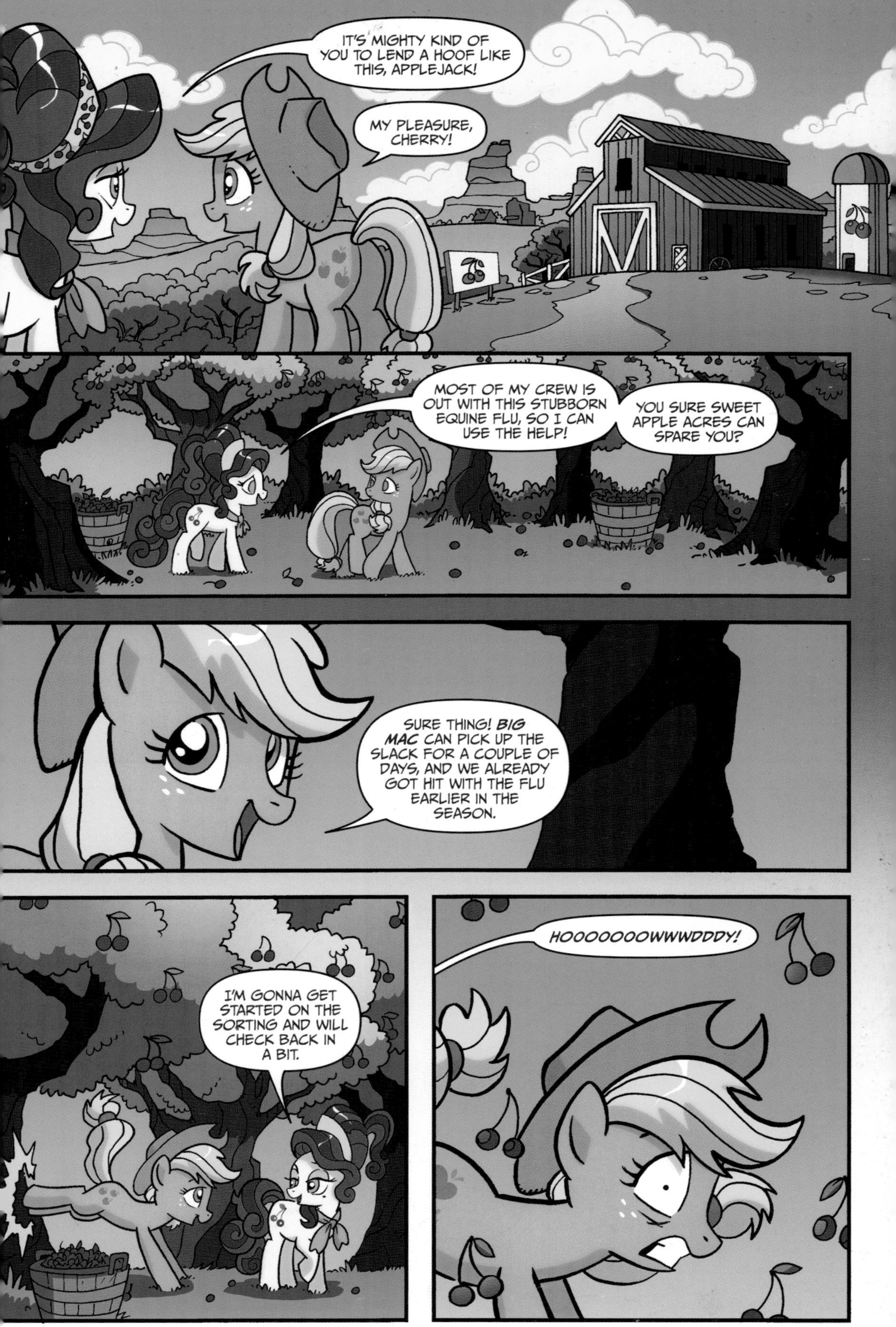
IT'S MIGHTY KIND OF YOU TO LEND A HOOF LIKE THIS, APPLEJACK!
MY PLEASURE, CHERRY!
MOST OF MY CREW IS OUT WITH THIS STUBBORN EQUINE FLU, SO I CAN USE THE HELP!
YOU SURE SWEET APPLE ACRES CAN SPARE YOU?
SURE THING! BIG MAC CAN PICK UP THE SLACK FOR A COUPLE OF DAYS, AND WE ALREADY GOT HIT WITH THE FLU EARLIER IN THE SEASON.
I'M GONNA GET STARTED ON THE SORTING AND WILL CHECK BACK IN A BIT.
HOOOOOOOWWWDDDY!

CAN I HELP YOU?

I CERTAINLY HOPE SO!

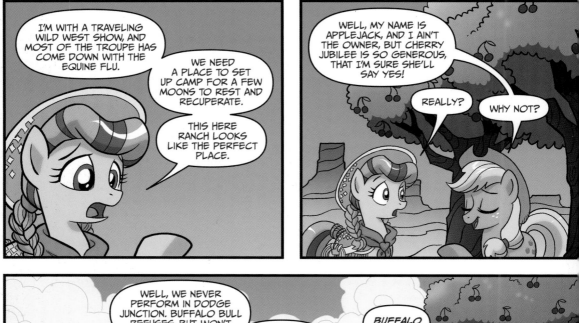

I'M WITH A TRAVELING WILD WEST SHOW, AND MOST OF THE TROUPE HAS COME DOWN WITH THE EQUINE FLU.

WE NEED A PLACE TO SET UP CAMP FOR A FEW MOONS TO REST AND RECUPERATE.

THIS HERE RANCH LOOKS LIKE THE PERFECT PLACE.

WELL, MY NAME IS APPLEJACK, AND I AIN'T THE OWNER, BUT CHERRY JUBILEE IS SO GENEROUS, THAT I'M SURE SHE'LL SAY YES!

REALLY?

WHY NOT?

WELL, WE NEVER PERFORM IN DODGE JUNCTION. BUFFALO BULL REFUSES, BUT WON'T SAY WHY.

I WASN'T SURE IF WE WEREN'T WELCOME OR SOMETHING.

BUFFALO BULL?

BUFFALO BULL'S ☆ AMAZING ☆ WILD WEST SHOW

THEN THAT MUST MAKE YOU CALAMITY MANE!

THE ONE AND ONLY!

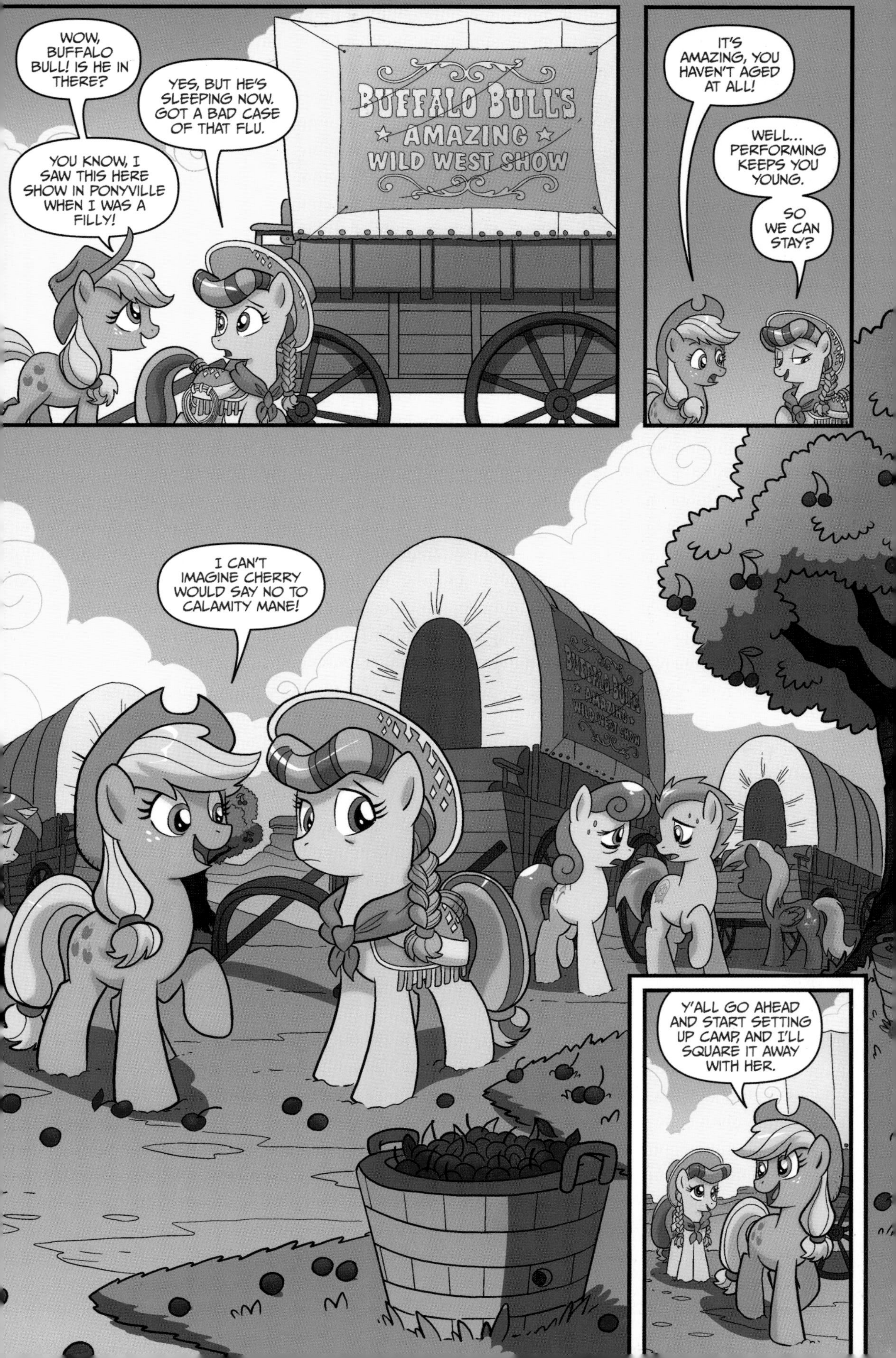
WOW, BUFFALO BULL! IS HE IN THERE?
YES, BUT HE'S SLEEPING NOW. GOT A BAD CASE OF THAT FLU.
BUFFALO BULL'S AMAZING WILD WEST SHOW
YOU KNOW, I SAW THIS HERE SHOW IN PONYVILLE WHEN I WAS A FILLY!
IT'S AMAZING, YOU HAVEN'T AGED AT ALL!
WELL... PERFORMING KEEPS YOU YOUNG.
SO WE CAN STAY?
I CAN'T IMAGINE CHERRY WOULD SAY NO TO CALAMITY MANE!
BUFFALO BULL'S AMAZING WILD WEST SHOW
Y'ALL GO AHEAD AND START SETTING UP CAMP, AND I'LL SQUARE IT AWAY WITH HER.

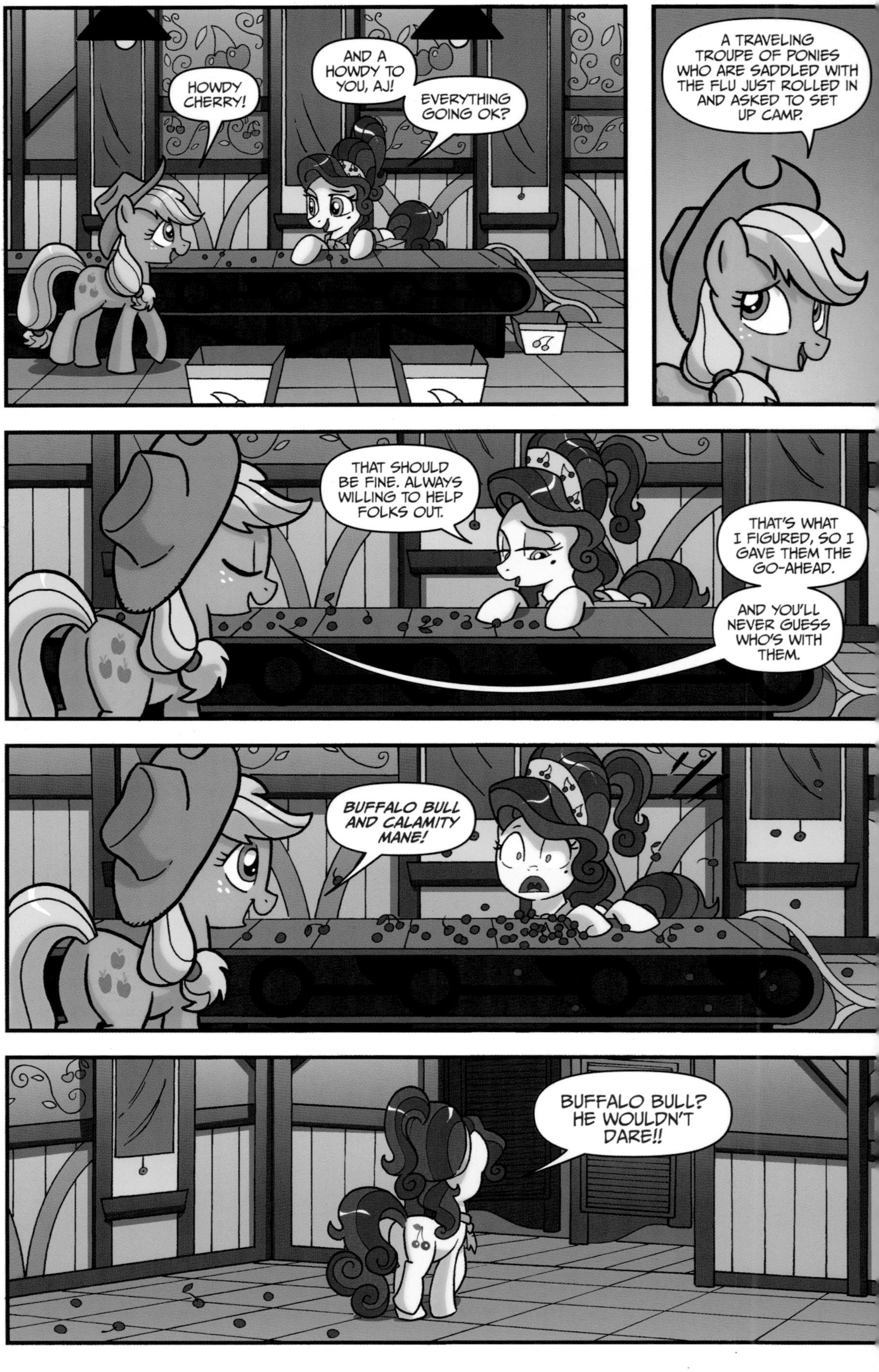
HOWDY CHERRY!
AND A HOWDY TO YOU, AJ!
EVERYTHING GOING OK?
A TRAVELING TROUPE OF PONIES WHO ARE SADDLED WITH THE FLU JUST ROLLED IN AND ASKED TO SET UP CAMP.
THAT SHOULD BE FINE. ALWAYS WILLING TO HELP FOLKS OUT.
THAT'S WHAT I FIGURED, SO I GAVE THEM THE GO-AHEAD.
AND YOU'LL NEVER GUESS WHO'S WITH THEM.
BUFFALO BULL AND CALAMITY MANE!
BUFFALO BULL? HE WOULDN'T DARE!!

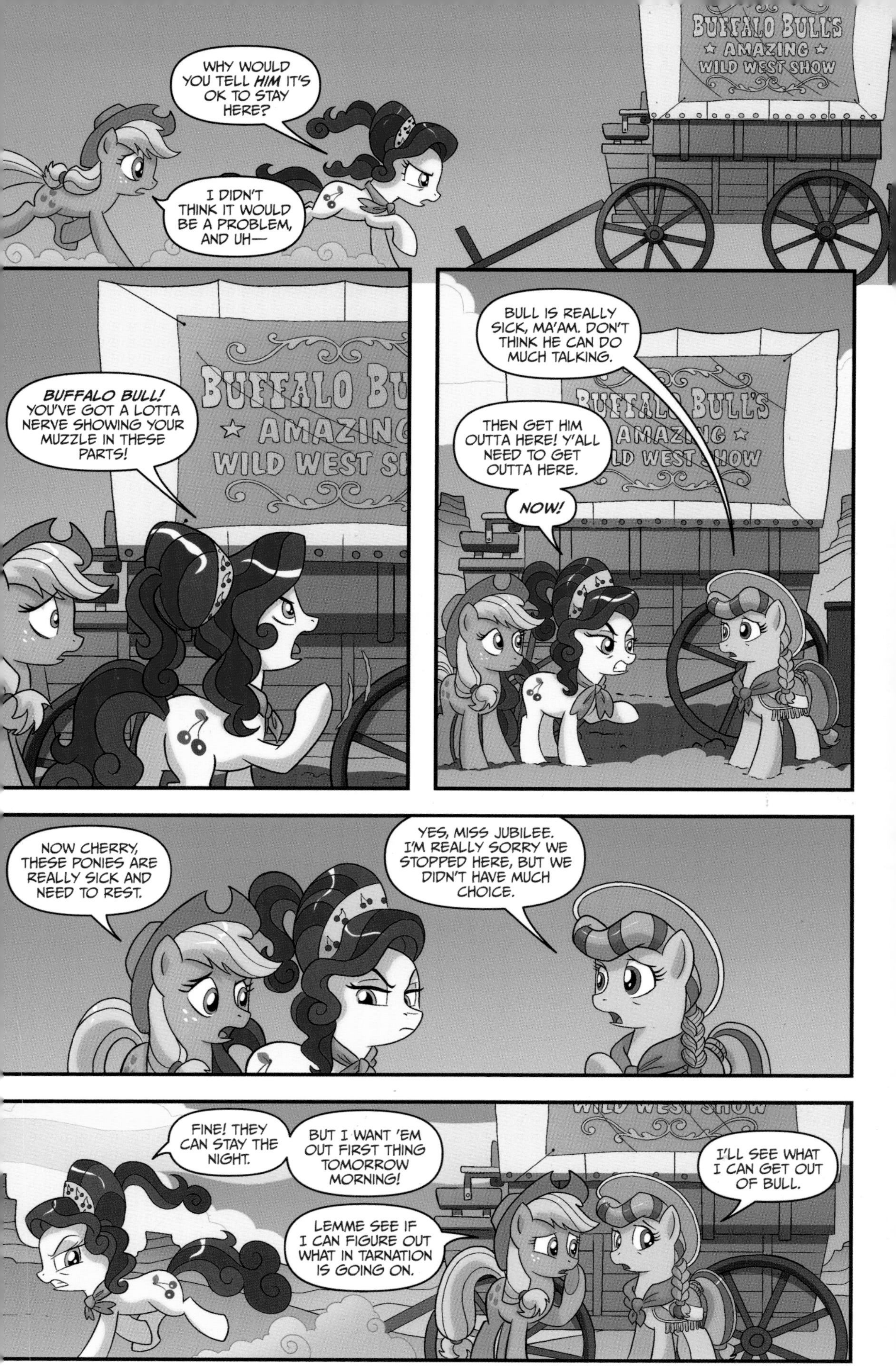
BUFFALO BULL'S AMAZING WILD WEST SHOW
WHY WOULD YOU TELL *HIM* IT'S OK TO STAY HERE?
I DIDN'T THINK IT WOULD BE A PROBLEM, AND UH—
BUFFALO BULL! YOU'VE GOT A LOTTA NERVE SHOWING YOUR MUZZLE IN THESE PARTS!
BUFFALO BU
AMAZING
WILD WEST SH
BULL IS REALLY SICK, MA'AM. DON'T THINK HE CAN DO MUCH TALKING.
THEN GET HIM OUTTA HERE! Y'ALL NEED TO GET OUTTA HERE.
NOW!
BUFFALO BULL'S
AMAZING
LD WEST SHOW
NOW CHERRY, THESE PONIES ARE REALLY SICK AND NEED TO REST.
YES, MISS JUBILEE. I'M REALLY SORRY WE STOPPED HERE, BUT WE DIDN'T HAVE MUCH CHOICE.
WILD WEST SHOW
FINE! THEY CAN STAY THE NIGHT.
BUT I WANT 'EM OUT FIRST THING TOMORROW MORNING!
I'LL SEE WHAT I CAN GET OUT OF BULL.
LEMME SEE IF I CAN FIGURE OUT WHAT IN TARNATION IS GOING ON.

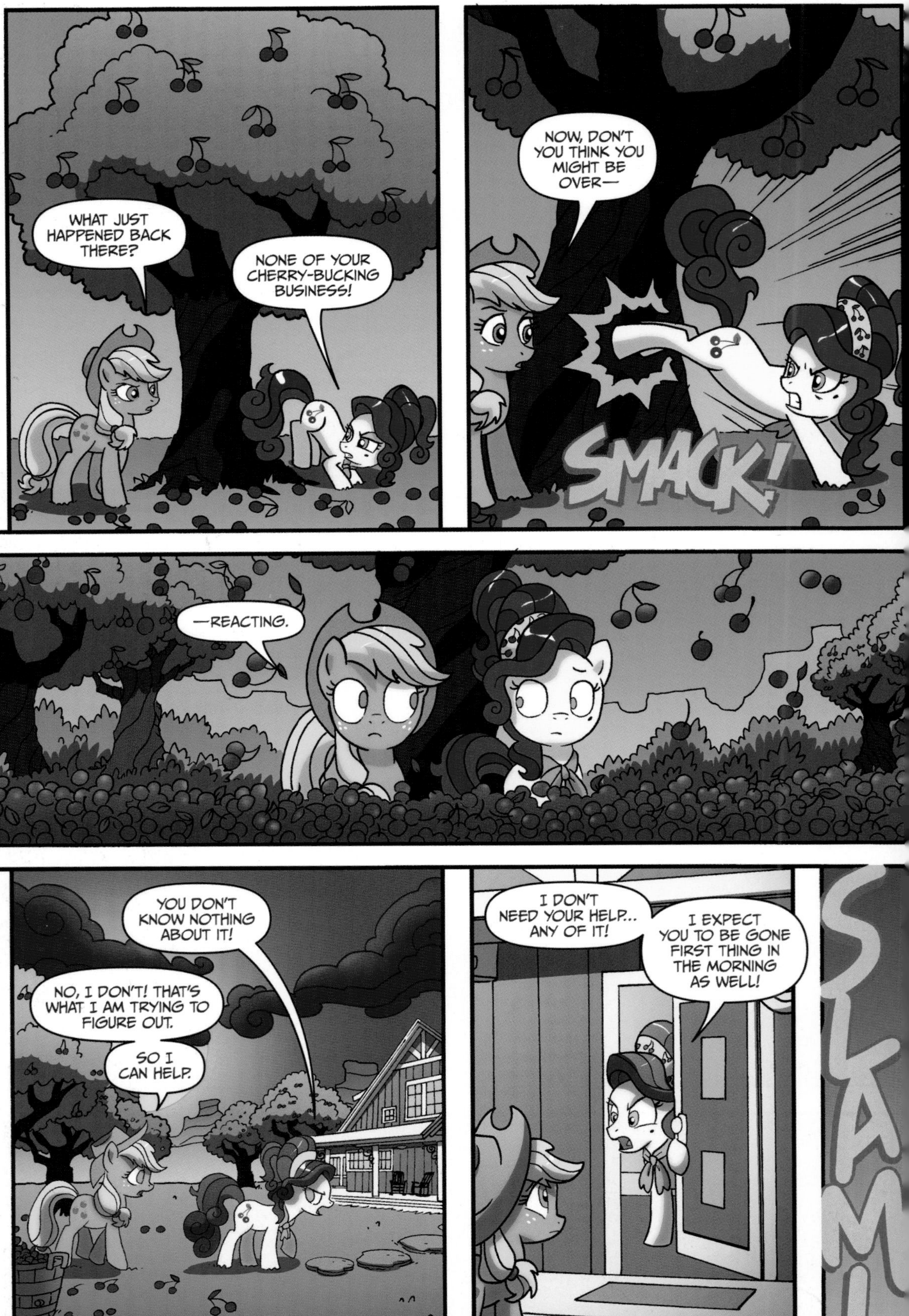
WHAT JUST HAPPENED BACK THERE?
NONE OF YOUR CHERRY-BUCKING BUSINESS!
NOW, DON'T YOU THINK YOU MIGHT BE OVER—
SMACK!
—REACTING.
YOU DON'T KNOW NOTHING ABOUT IT!
NO, I DON'T! THAT'S WHAT I AM TRYING TO FIGURE OUT.
SO I CAN HELP.
I DON'T NEED YOUR HELP... ANY OF IT!
I EXPECT YOU TO BE GONE FIRST THING IN THE MORNING AS WELL!
SLAM!

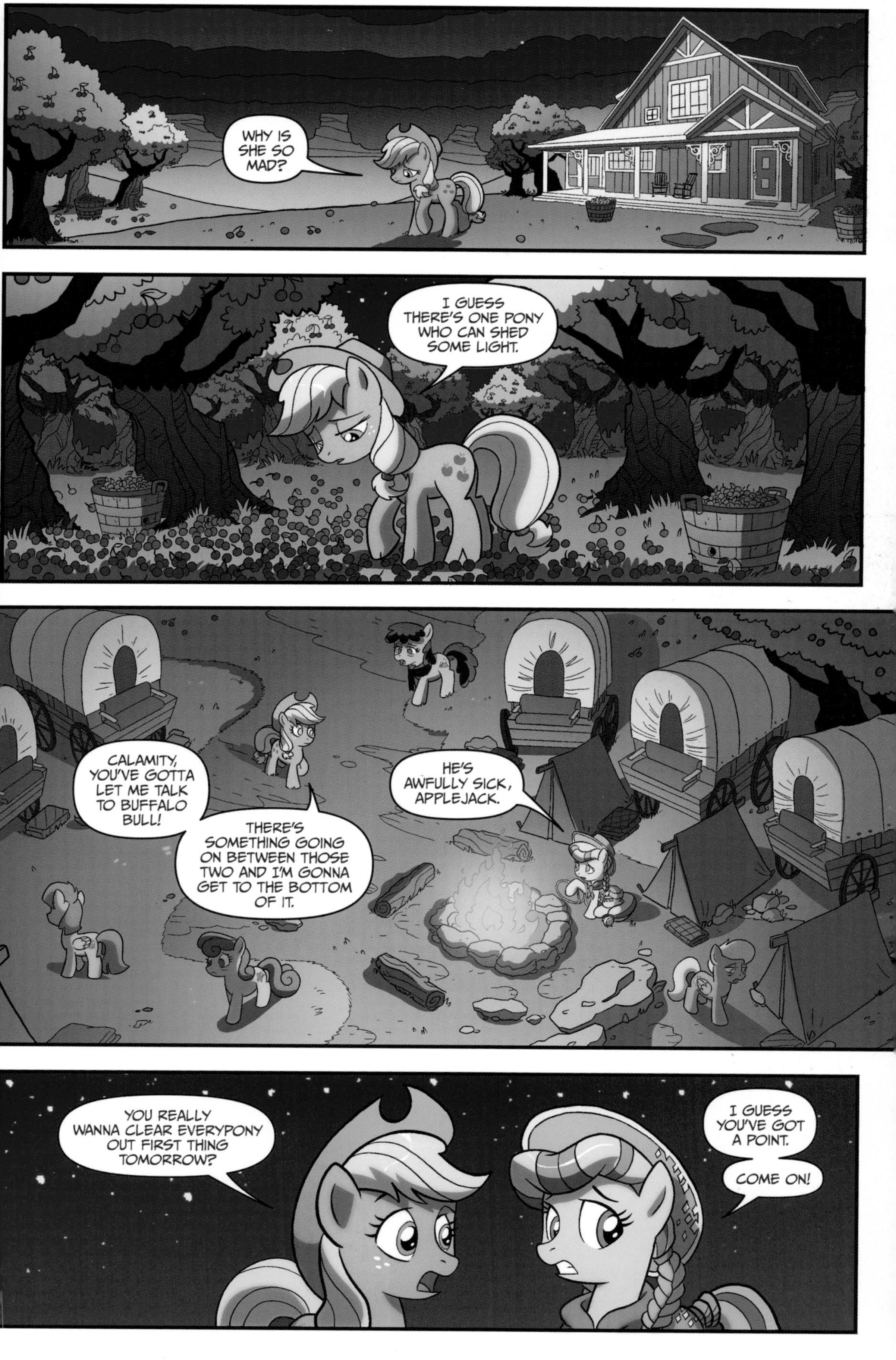
WHY IS SHE SO MAD?
I GUESS THERE'S ONE PONY WHO CAN SHED SOME LIGHT.
CALAMITY, YOU'VE GOTTA LET ME TALK TO BUFFALO BULL!
THERE'S SOMETHING GOING ON BETWEEN THOSE TWO AND I'M GONNA GET TO THE BOTTOM OF IT.
HE'S AWFULLY SICK, APPLEJACK.
YOU REALLY WANNA CLEAR EVERYPONY OUT FIRST THING TOMORROW?
I GUESS YOU'VE GOT A POINT.
COME ON!

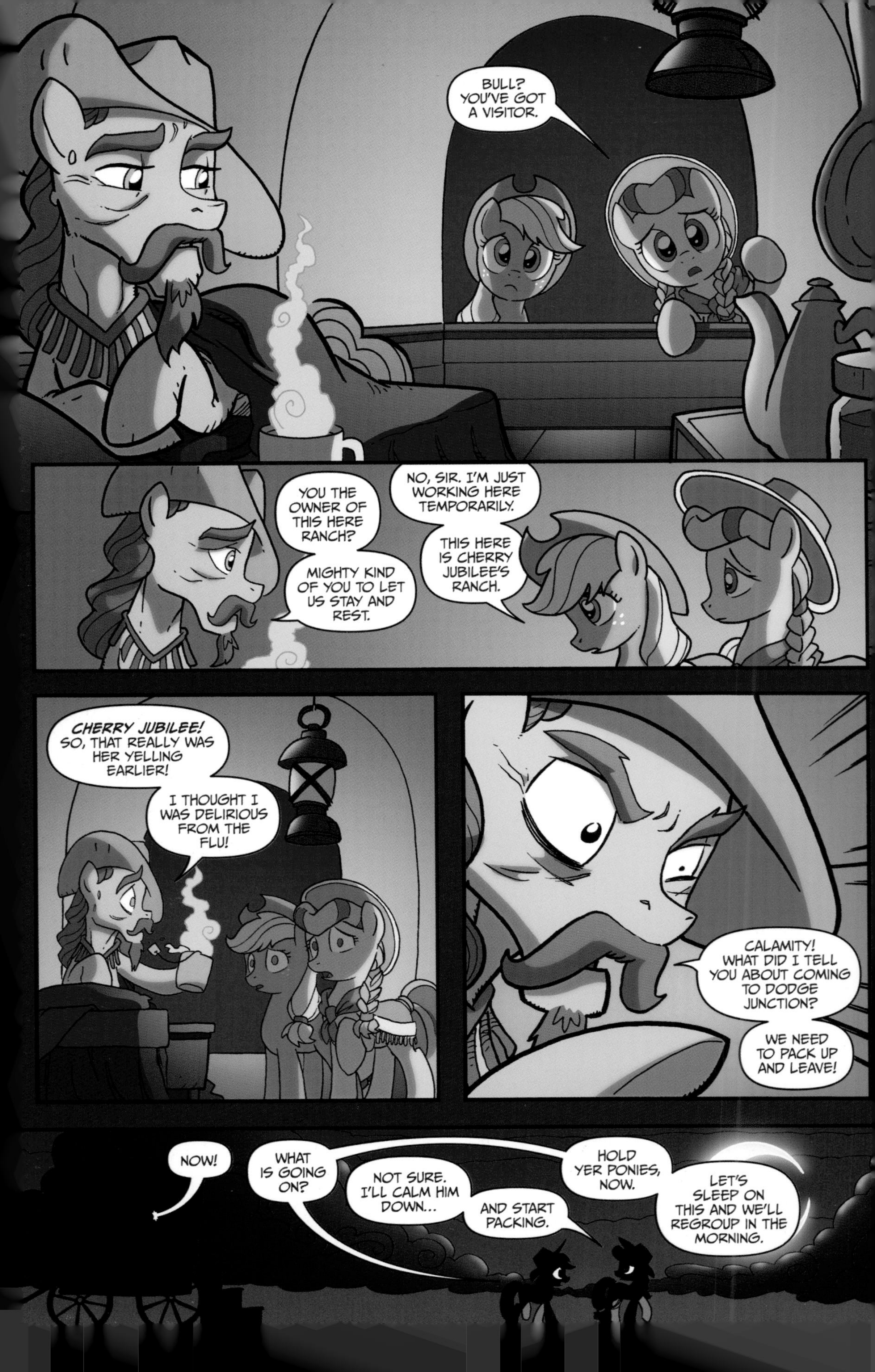
BULL? YOU'VE GOT A VISITOR.
YOU THE OWNER OF THIS HERE RANCH?
MIGHTY KIND OF YOU TO LET US STAY AND REST.
NO, SIR. I'M JUST WORKING HERE TEMPORARILY.
THIS HERE IS CHERRY JUBILEE'S RANCH.
CHERRY JUBILEE! SO, THAT REALLY WAS HER YELLING EARLIER!
I THOUGHT I WAS DELIRIOUS FROM THE FLU!
CALAMITY! WHAT DID I TELL YOU ABOUT COMING TO DODGE JUNCTION?
WE NEED TO PACK UP AND LEAVE!
NOW!
WHAT IS GOING ON?
NOT SURE. I'LL CALM HIM DOWN...
AND START PACKING.
HOLD YER PONIES, NOW.
LET'S SLEEP ON THIS AND WE'LL REGROUP IN THE MORNING.

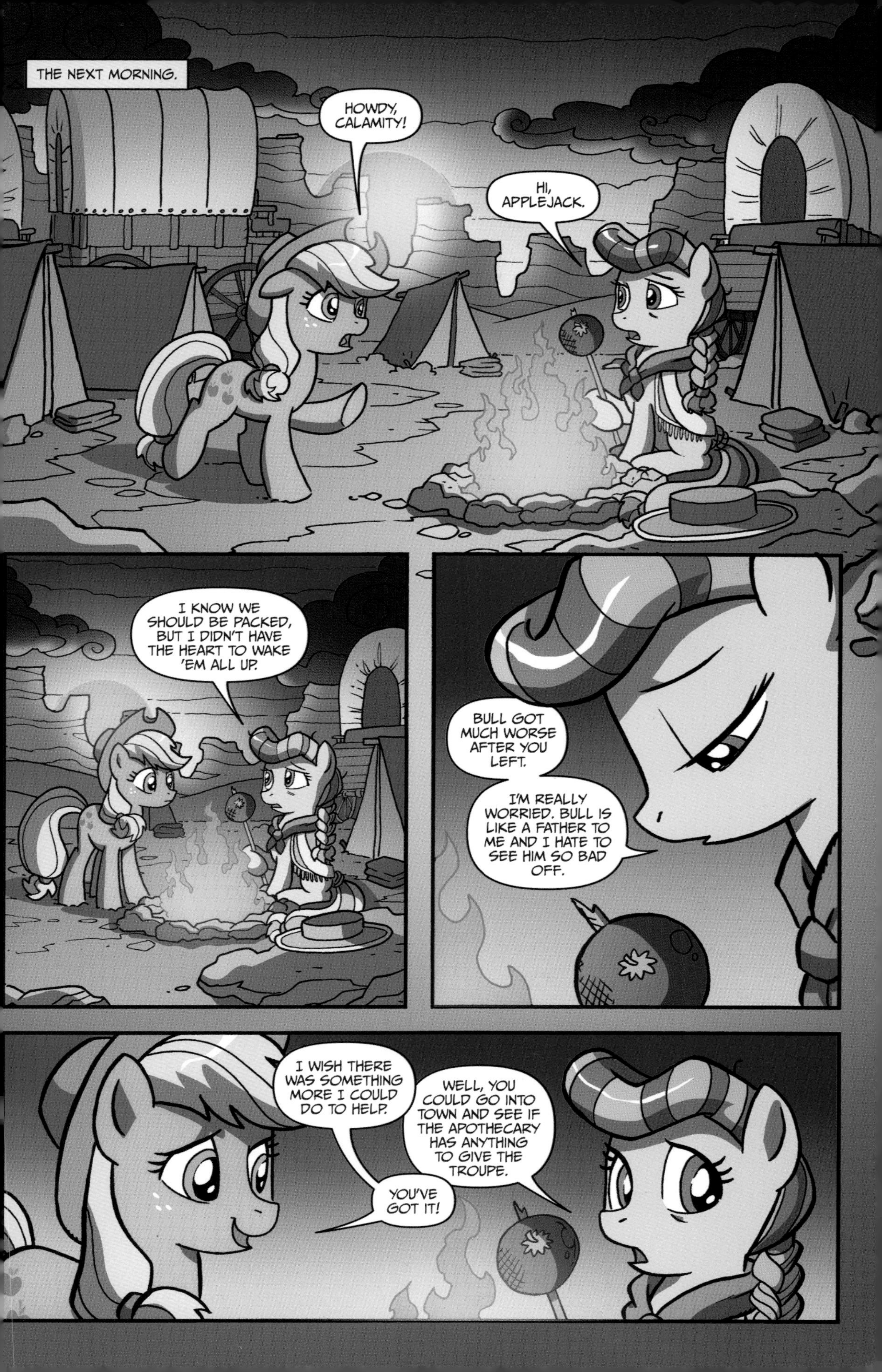
THE NEXT MORNING.
HOWDY, CALAMITY!
HI, APPLEJACK.
I KNOW WE SHOULD BE PACKED, BUT I DIDN'T HAVE THE HEART TO WAKE 'EM ALL UP.
BULL GOT MUCH WORSE AFTER YOU LEFT.
I'M REALLY WORRIED. BULL IS LIKE A FATHER TO ME AND I HATE TO SEE HIM SO BAD OFF.
I WISH THERE WAS SOMETHING MORE I COULD DO TO HELP.
WELL, YOU COULD GO INTO TOWN AND SEE IF THE APOTHECARY HAS ANYTHING TO GIVE THE TROUPE.
YOU'VE GOT IT!

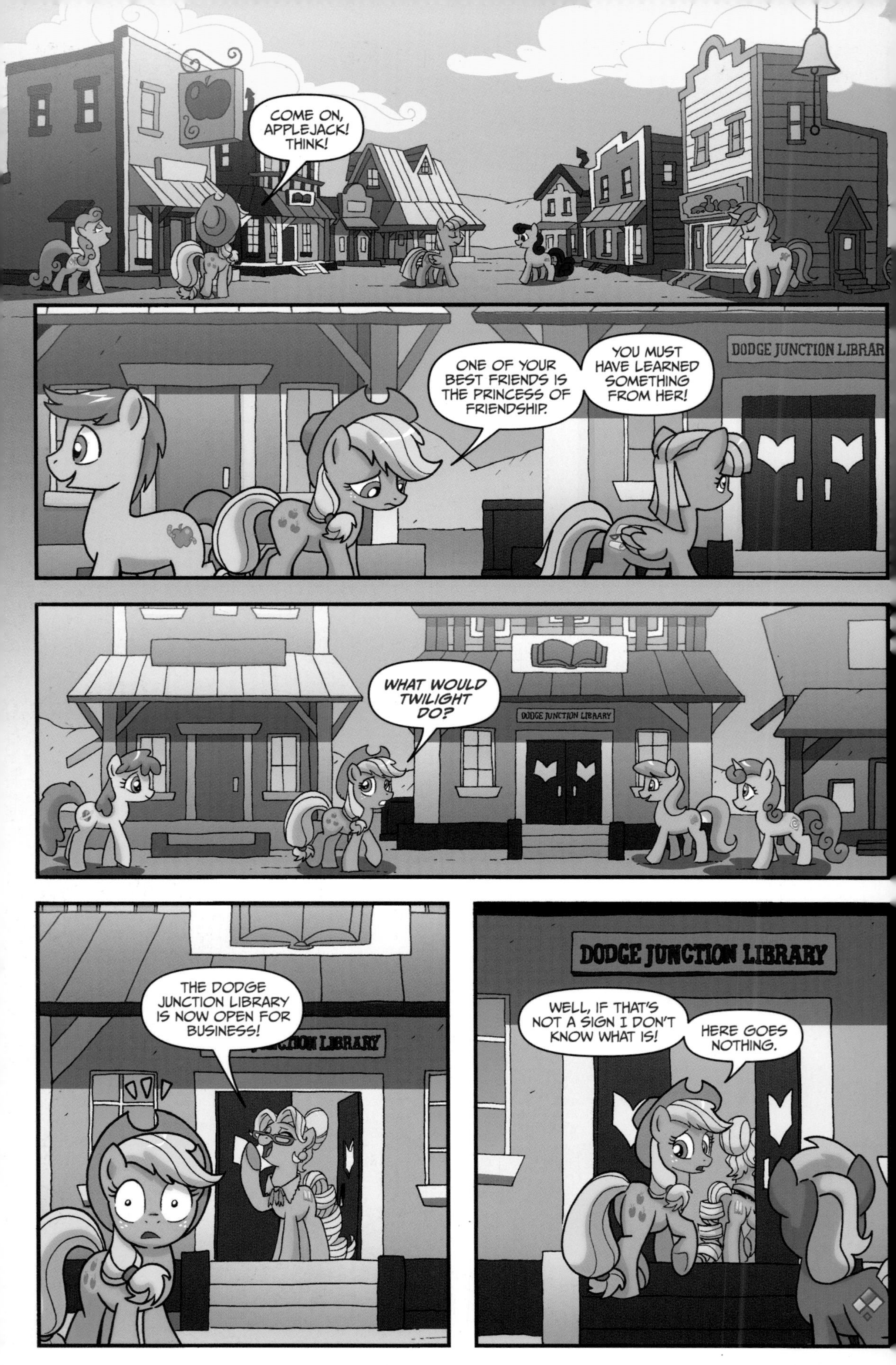
COME ON, APPLEJACK! THINK!
ONE OF YOUR BEST FRIENDS IS THE PRINCESS OF FRIENDSHIP.
YOU MUST HAVE LEARNED SOMETHING FROM HER!
DODGE JUNCTION LIBRARY
WHAT WOULD TWILIGHT DO?
DODGE JUNCTION LIBRARY
THE DODGE JUNCTION LIBRARY IS NOW OPEN FOR BUSINESS!
DODGE JUNCTION LIBRARY
WELL, IF THAT'S NOT A SIGN I DON'T KNOW WHAT IS!
HERE GOES NOTHING.

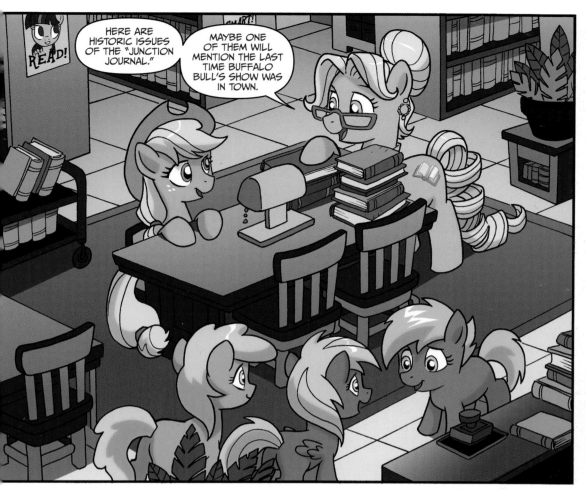

HERE ARE HISTORIC ISSUES OF THE "JUNCTION JOURNAL."

MAYBE ONE OF THEM WILL MENTION THE LAST TIME BUFFALO BULL'S SHOW WAS IN TOWN.

20 MINUTES LATER.

2 HOURS LATER.

BIG MAC! WE GOTTA SPEED UP THE HARVEST!

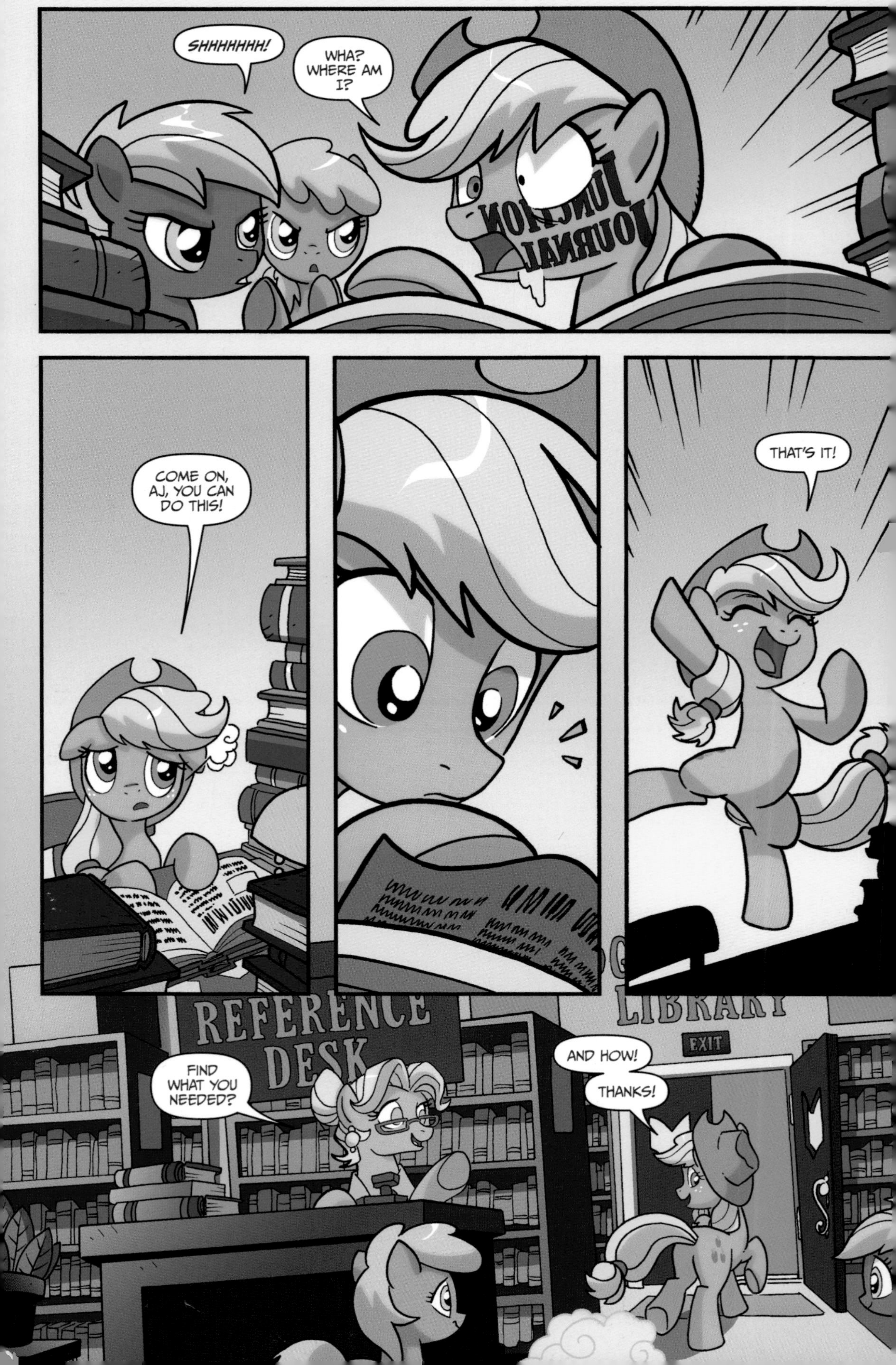
SHHHHHHH!
WHA? WHERE AM I?
JUNCTION JOURNAL
COME ON, AJ, YOU CAN DO THIS!
THAT'S IT!
REFERENCE DESK
LIBRARY
EXIT
FIND WHAT YOU NEEDED?
AND HOW!
THANKS!

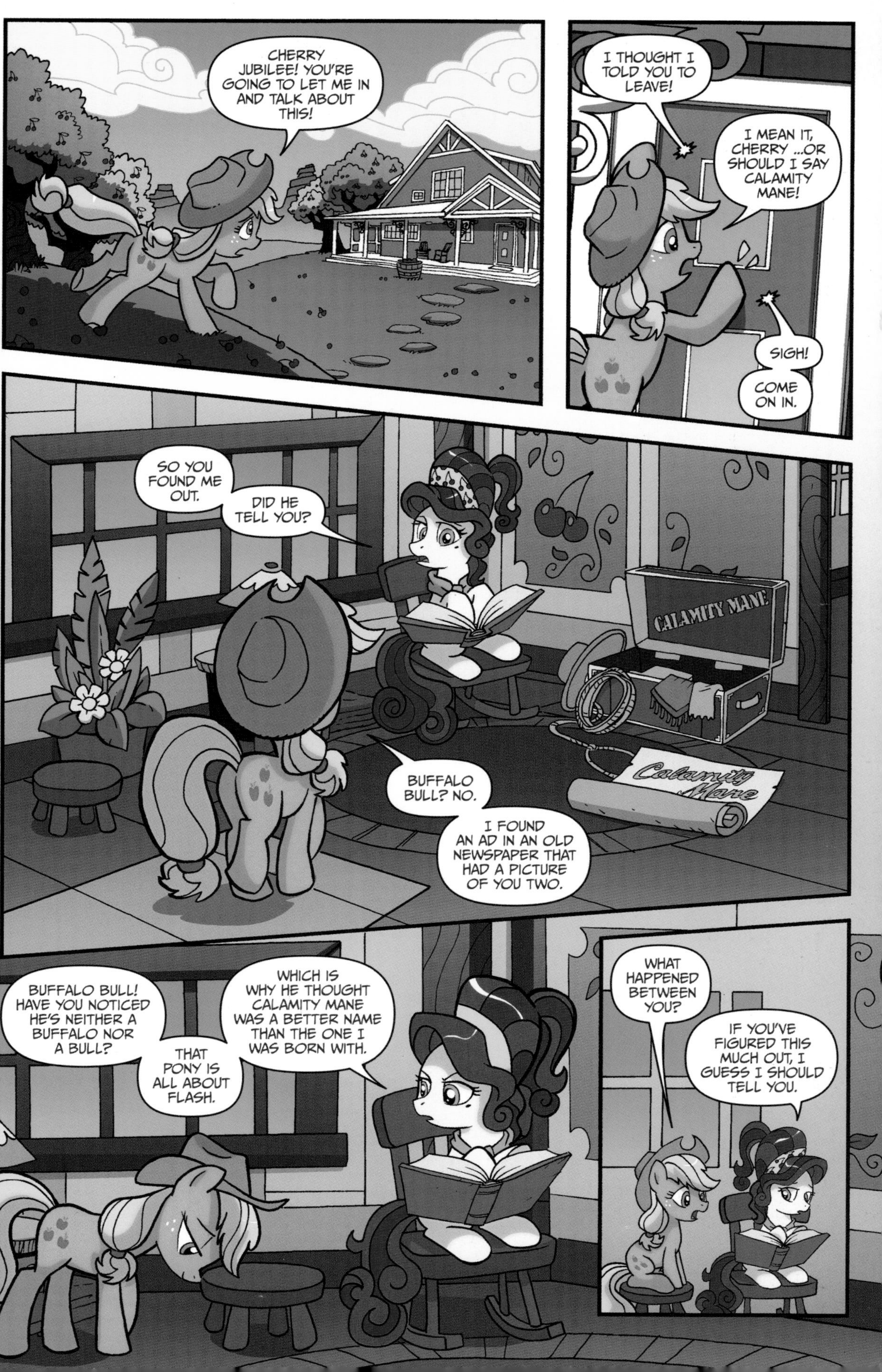
CHERRY JUBILEE! YOU'RE GOING TO LET ME IN AND TALK ABOUT THIS!
I THOUGHT I TOLD YOU TO LEAVE!
I MEAN IT, CHERRY ...OR SHOULD I SAY CALAMITY MANE!
SIGH!
COME ON IN.
SO YOU FOUND ME OUT.
DID HE TELL YOU?
CALAMITY MANE
Calamity Mane
BUFFALO BULL? NO.
I FOUND AN AD IN AN OLD NEWSPAPER THAT HAD A PICTURE OF YOU TWO.
BUFFALO BULL! HAVE YOU NOTICED HE'S NEITHER A BUFFALO NOR A BULL?
THAT PONY IS ALL ABOUT FLASH.
WHICH IS WHY HE THOUGHT CALAMITY MANE WAS A BETTER NAME THAN THE ONE I WAS BORN WITH.
WHAT HAPPENED BETWEEN YOU?
IF YOU'VE FIGURED THIS MUCH OUT, I GUESS I SHOULD TELL YOU.

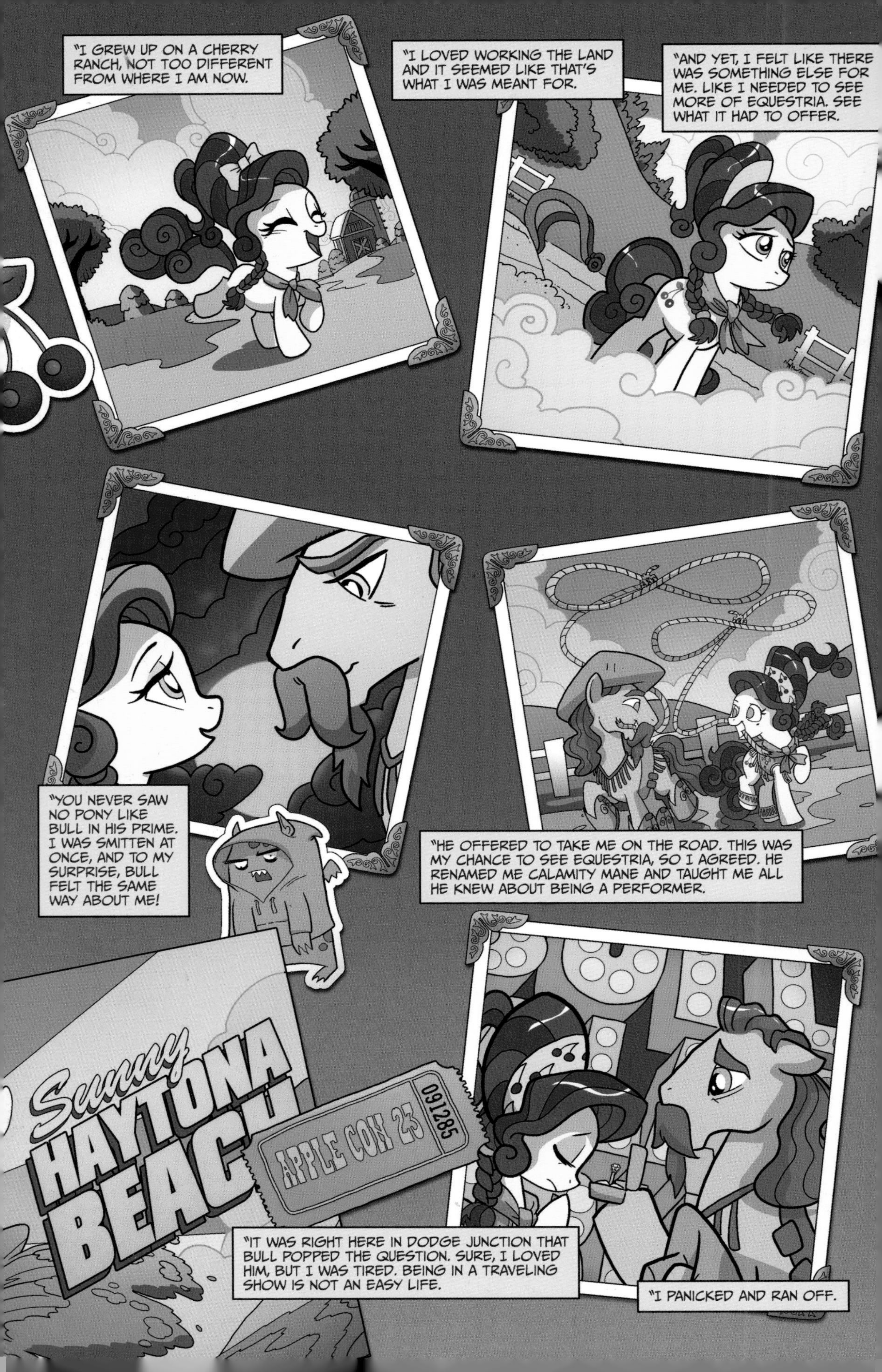
"I GREW UP ON A CHERRY RANCH, NOT TOO DIFFERENT FROM WHERE I AM NOW.
"I LOVED WORKING THE LAND AND IT SEEMED LIKE THAT'S WHAT I WAS MEANT FOR.
"AND YET, I FELT LIKE THERE WAS SOMETHING ELSE FOR ME. LIKE I NEEDED TO SEE MORE OF EQUESTRIA. SEE WHAT IT HAD TO OFFER.
"YOU NEVER SAW NO PONY LIKE BULL IN HIS PRIME. I WAS SMITTEN AT ONCE, AND TO MY SURPRISE, BULL FELT THE SAME WAY ABOUT ME!
"HE OFFERED TO TAKE ME ON THE ROAD. THIS WAS MY CHANCE TO SEE EQUESTRIA, SO I AGREED. HE RENAMED ME CALAMITY MANE AND TAUGHT ME ALL HE KNEW ABOUT BEING A PERFORMER.
Sunny HAYTONA BEACH
APPLE CON 23
091285
"IT WAS RIGHT HERE IN DODGE JUNCTION THAT BULL POPPED THE QUESTION. SURE, I LOVED HIM, BUT I WAS TIRED. BEING IN A TRAVELING SHOW IS NOT AN EASY LIFE.
"I PANICKED AND RAN OFF.

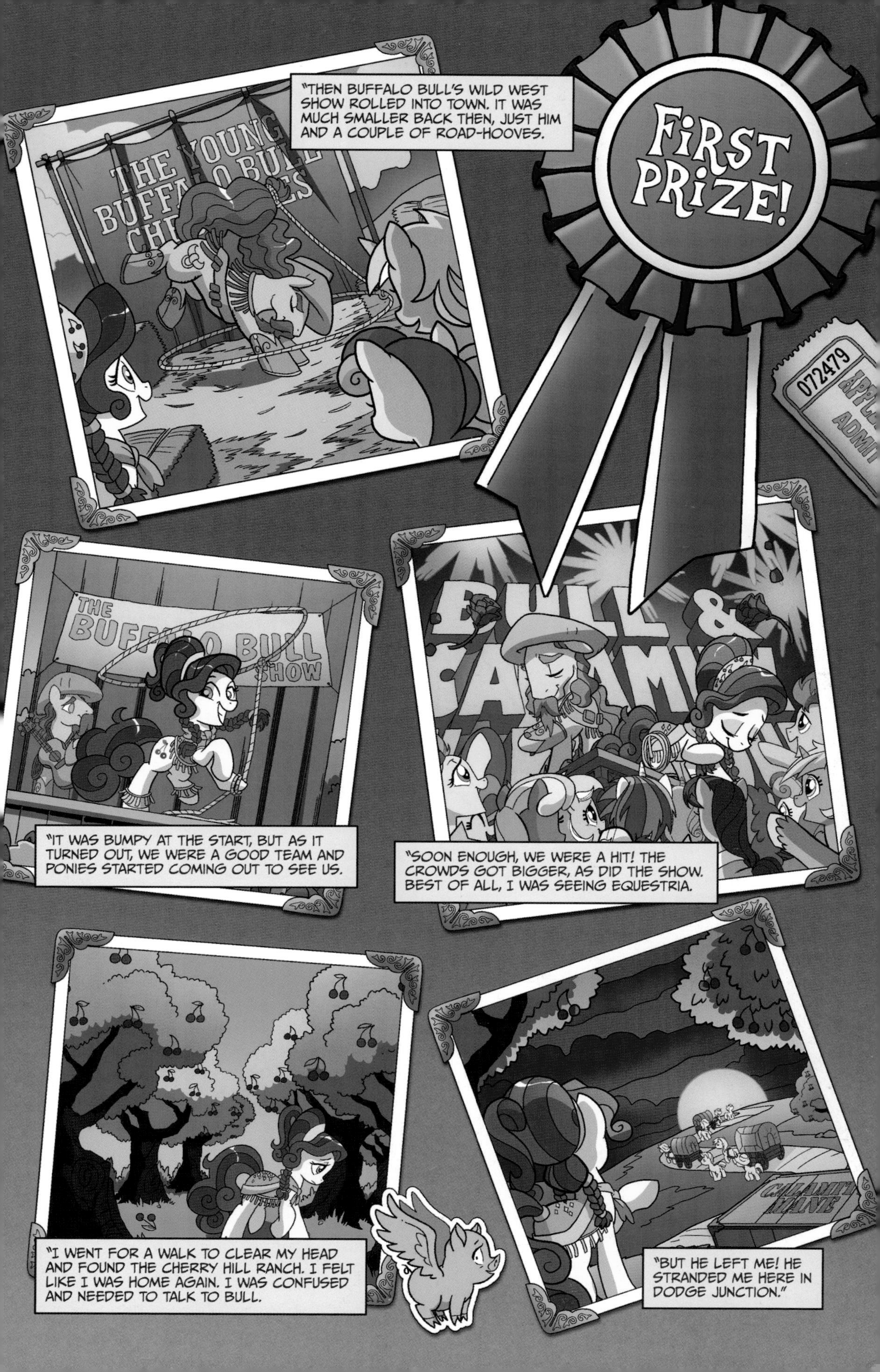
"THEN BUFFALO BULL'S WILD WEST SHOW ROLLED INTO TOWN. IT WAS MUCH SMALLER BACK THEN, JUST HIM AND A COUPLE OF ROAD-HOOVES.
FIRST PRIZE!
072479
"IT WAS BUMPY AT THE START, BUT AS IT TURNED OUT, WE WERE A GOOD TEAM AND PONIES STARTED COMING OUT TO SEE US.
"SOON ENOUGH, WE WERE A HIT! THE CROWDS GOT BIGGER, AS DID THE SHOW. BEST OF ALL, I WAS SEEING EQUESTRIA.
"I WENT FOR A WALK TO CLEAR MY HEAD AND FOUND THE CHERRY HILL RANCH. I FELT LIKE I WAS HOME AGAIN. I WAS CONFUSED AND NEEDED TO TALK TO BULL.
"BUT HE LEFT ME! HE STRANDED ME HERE IN DODGE JUNCTION."

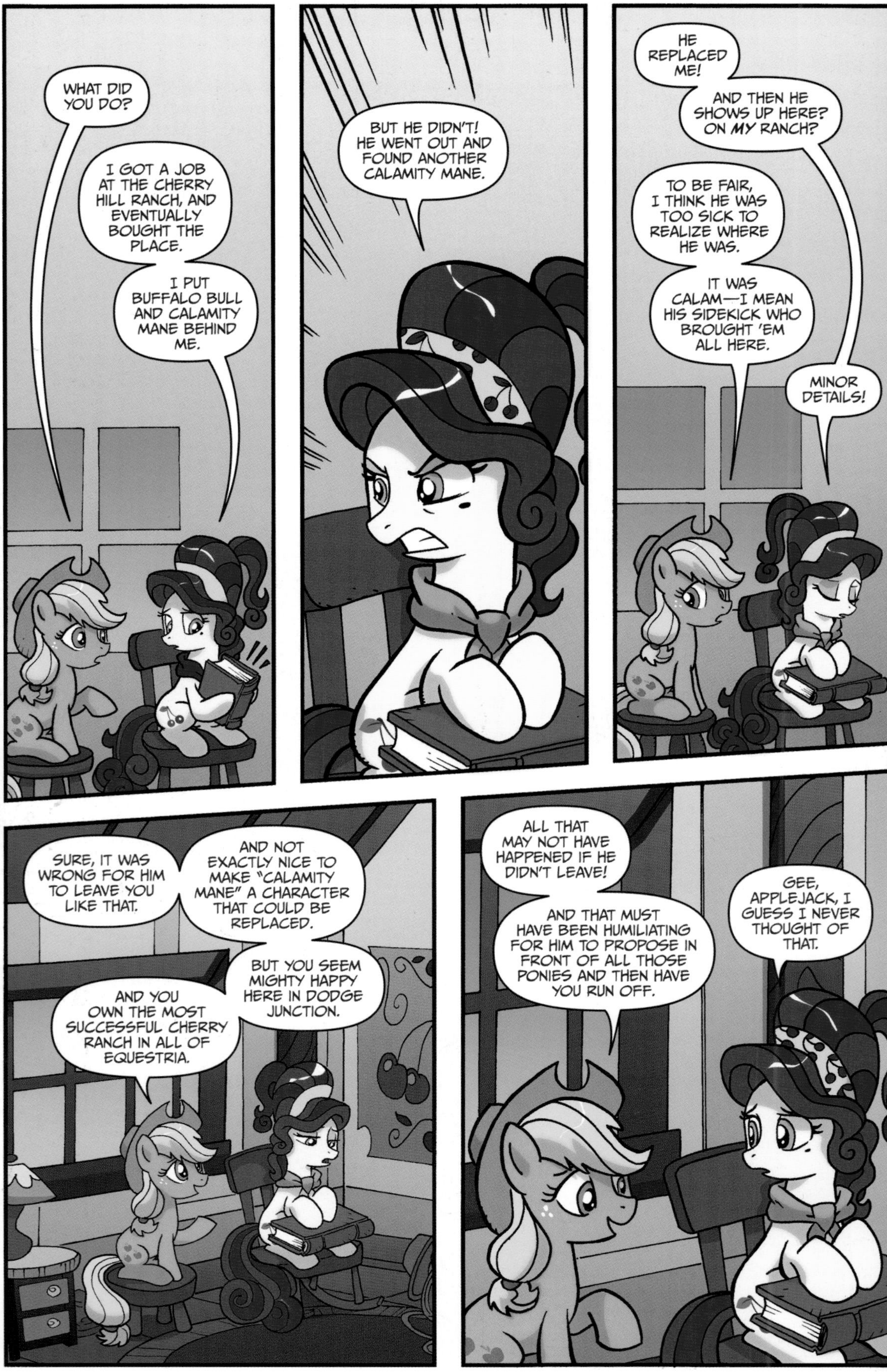
WHAT DID YOU DO?
I GOT A JOB AT THE CHERRY HILL RANCH, AND EVENTUALLY BOUGHT THE PLACE.
I PUT BUFFALO BULL AND CALAMITY MANE BEHIND ME.
BUT HE DIDN'T! HE WENT OUT AND FOUND ANOTHER CALAMITY MANE.
HE REPLACED ME!
AND THEN HE SHOWS UP HERE? ON MY RANCH?
TO BE FAIR, I THINK HE WAS TOO SICK TO REALIZE WHERE HE WAS.
IT WAS CALAM—I MEAN HIS SIDEKICK WHO BROUGHT 'EM ALL HERE.
MINOR DETAILS!
SURE, IT WAS WRONG FOR HIM TO LEAVE YOU LIKE THAT.
AND NOT EXACTLY NICE TO MAKE "CALAMITY MANE" A CHARACTER THAT COULD BE REPLACED.
BUT YOU SEEM MIGHTY HAPPY HERE IN DODGE JUNCTION.
AND YOU OWN THE MOST SUCCESSFUL CHERRY RANCH IN ALL OF EQUESTRIA.
ALL THAT MAY NOT HAVE HAPPENED IF HE DIDN'T LEAVE!
AND THAT MUST HAVE BEEN HUMILIATING FOR HIM TO PROPOSE IN FRONT OF ALL THOSE PONIES AND THEN HAVE YOU RUN OFF.
GEE, APPLEJACK, I GUESS I NEVER THOUGHT OF THAT.

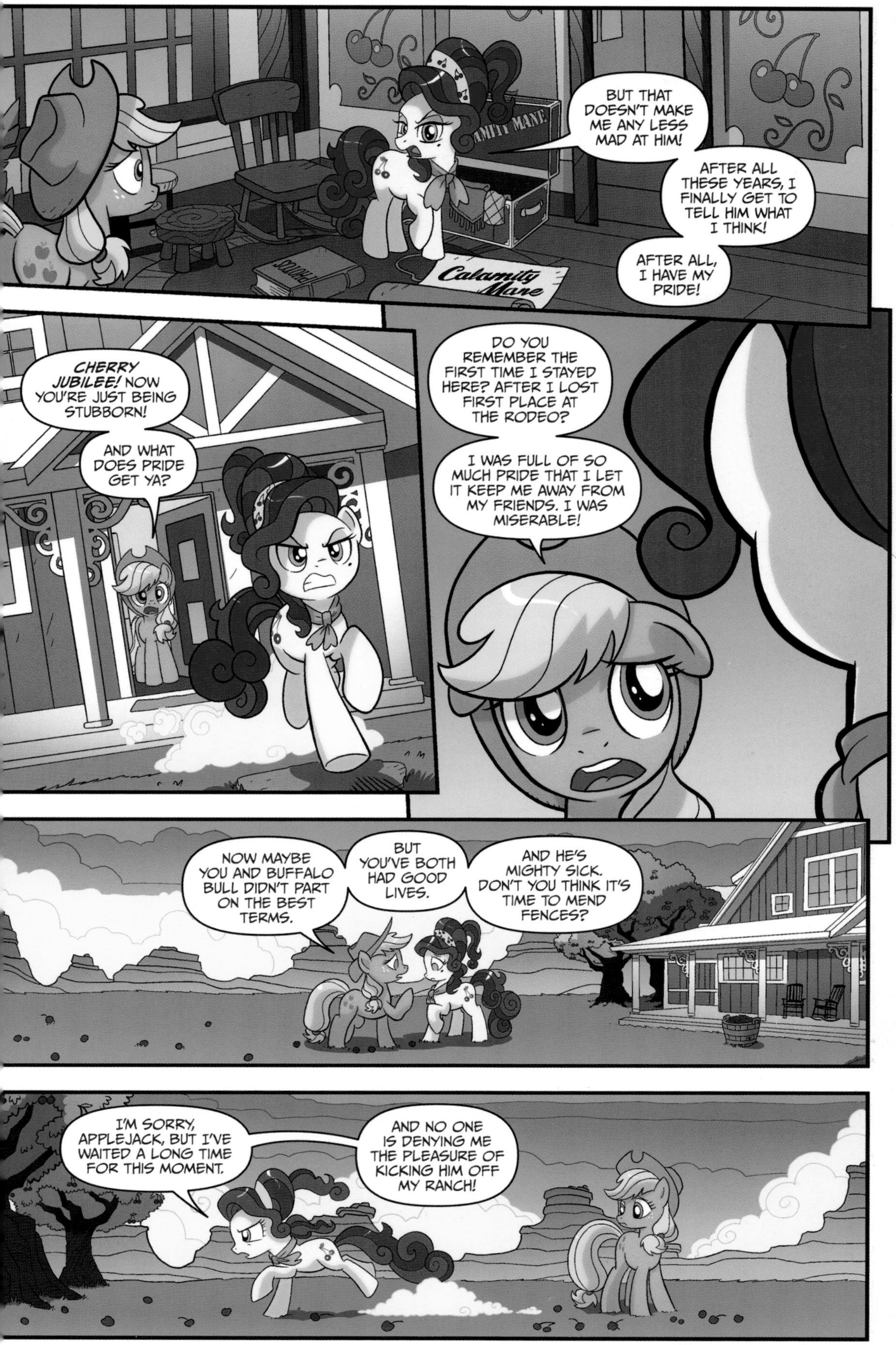
AMITY MANE
HOOVES
Calamity Mane
BUT THAT DOESN'T MAKE ME ANY LESS MAD AT HIM!
AFTER ALL THESE YEARS, I FINALLY GET TO TELL HIM WHAT I THINK!
AFTER ALL, I HAVE MY PRIDE!
CHERRY JUBILEE! NOW YOU'RE JUST BEING STUBBORN!
AND WHAT DOES PRIDE GET YA?
DO YOU REMEMBER THE FIRST TIME I STAYED HERE? AFTER I LOST FIRST PLACE AT THE RODEO?
I WAS FULL OF SO MUCH PRIDE THAT I LET IT KEEP ME AWAY FROM MY FRIENDS. I WAS MISERABLE!
NOW MAYBE YOU AND BUFFALO BULL DIDN'T PART ON THE BEST TERMS.
BUT YOU'VE BOTH HAD GOOD LIVES.
AND HE'S MIGHTY SICK. DON'T YOU THINK IT'S TIME TO MEND FENCES?
I'M SORRY, APPLEJACK, BUT I'VE WAITED A LONG TIME FOR THIS MOMENT.
AND NO ONE IS DENYING ME THE PLEASURE OF KICKING HIM OFF MY RANCH!

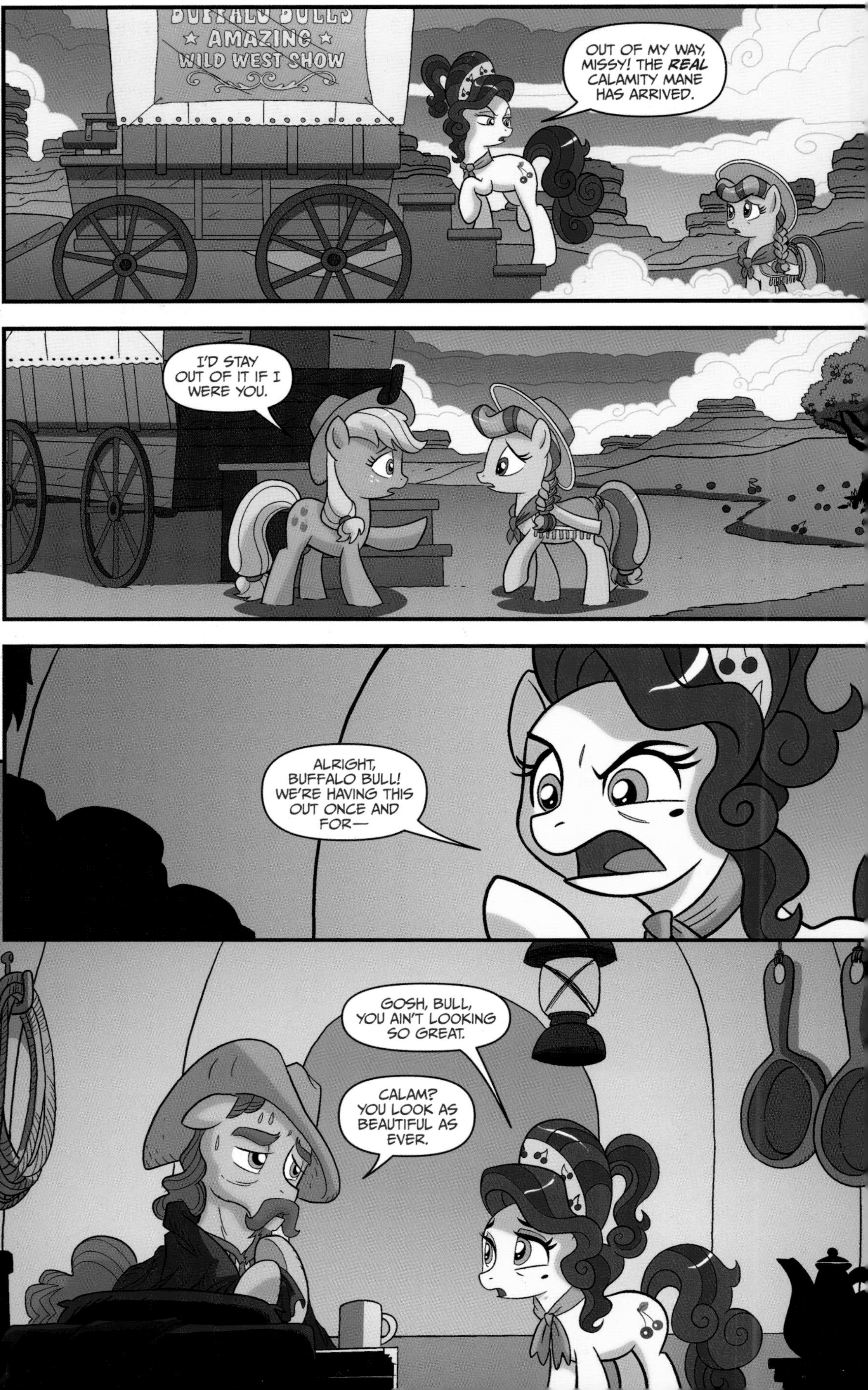
BUFFALO BULL'S
AMAZING
WILD WEST SHOW
OUT OF MY WAY, MISSY! THE *REAL* CALAMITY MANE HAS ARRIVED.
I'D STAY OUT OF IT IF I WERE YOU.
ALRIGHT, BUFFALO BULL! WE'RE HAVING THIS OUT ONCE AND FOR—
GOSH, BULL, YOU AIN'T LOOKING SO GREAT.
CALAM? YOU LOOK AS BEAUTIFUL AS EVER.

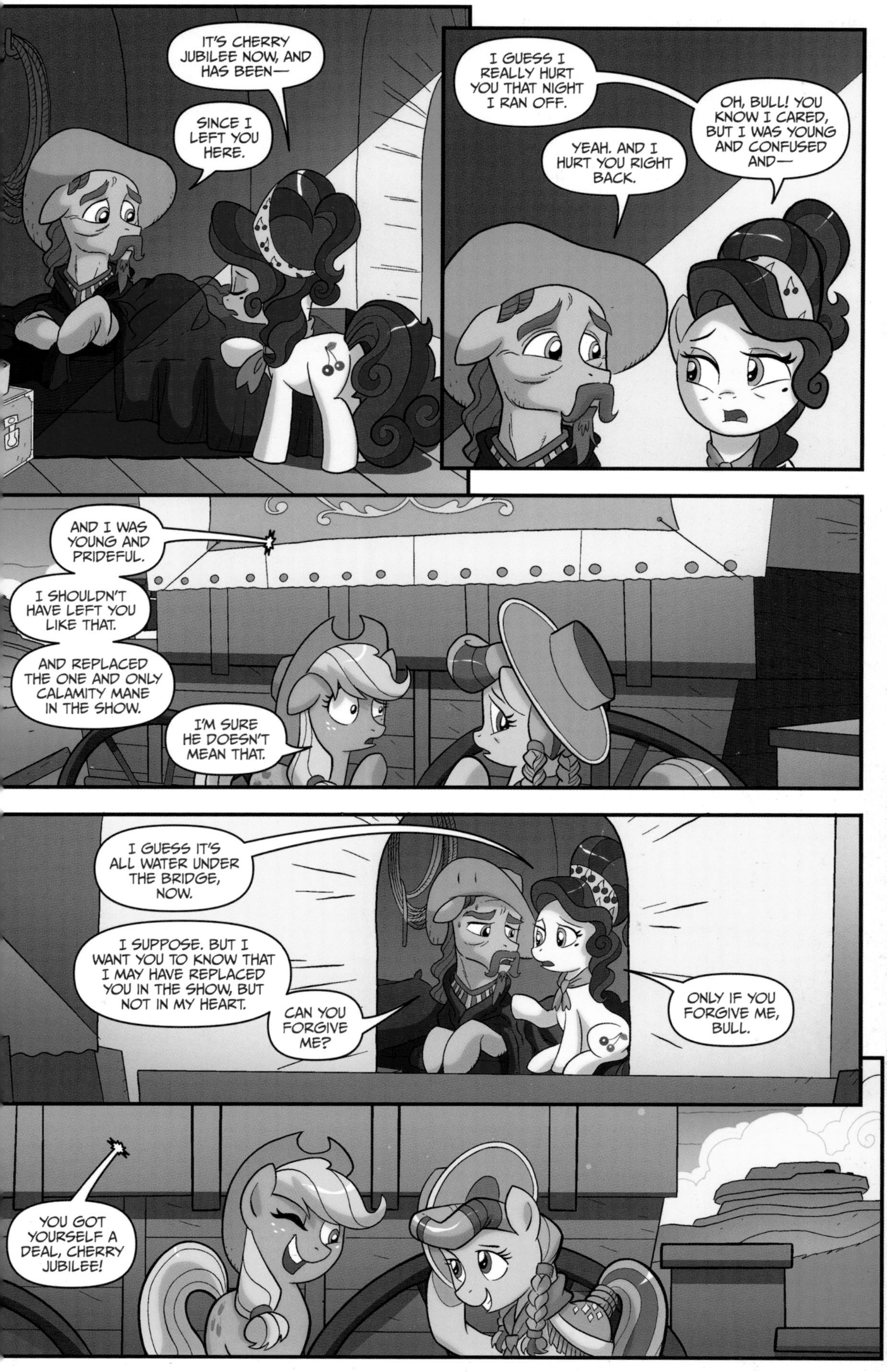
IT'S CHERRY JUBILEE NOW, AND HAS BEEN—
SINCE I LEFT YOU HERE.
I GUESS I REALLY HURT YOU THAT NIGHT I RAN OFF.
OH, BULL! YOU KNOW I CARED, BUT I WAS YOUNG AND CONFUSED AND—
YEAH. AND I HURT YOU RIGHT BACK.
AND I WAS YOUNG AND PRIDEFUL.
I SHOULDN'T HAVE LEFT YOU LIKE THAT.
AND REPLACED THE ONE AND ONLY CALAMITY MANE IN THE SHOW.
I'M SURE HE DOESN'T MEAN THAT.
I GUESS IT'S ALL WATER UNDER THE BRIDGE, NOW.
I SUPPOSE. BUT I WANT YOU TO KNOW THAT I MAY HAVE REPLACED YOU IN THE SHOW, BUT NOT IN MY HEART.
CAN YOU FORGIVE ME?
ONLY IF YOU FORGIVE ME, BULL.
YOU GOT YOURSELF A DEAL, CHERRY JUBILEE!

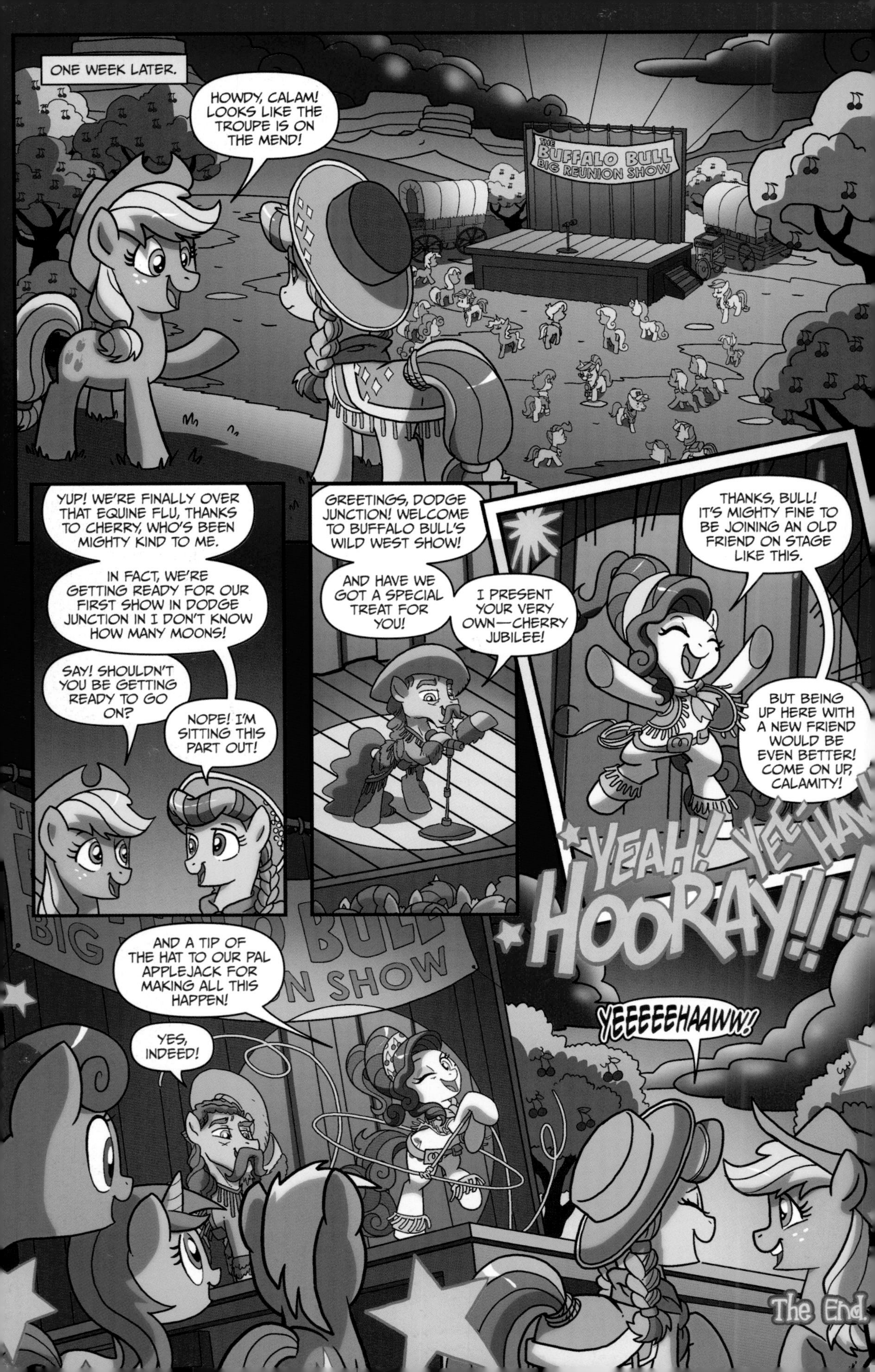
ONE WEEK LATER.
HOWDY, CALAM! LOOKS LIKE THE TROUPE IS ON THE MEND!
THE BUFFALO BULL BIG REUNION SHOW
YUP! WE'RE FINALLY OVER THAT EQUINE FLU, THANKS TO CHERRY, WHO'S BEEN MIGHTY KIND TO ME.
IN FACT, WE'RE GETTING READY FOR OUR FIRST SHOW IN DODGE JUNCTION IN I DON'T KNOW HOW MANY MOONS!
SAY! SHOULDN'T YOU BE GETTING READY TO GO ON?
NOPE! I'M SITTING THIS PART OUT!
GREETINGS, DODGE JUNCTION! WELCOME TO BUFFALO BULL'S WILD WEST SHOW!
AND HAVE WE GOT A SPECIAL TREAT FOR YOU!
I PRESENT YOUR VERY OWN—CHERRY JUBILEE!
THANKS, BULL! IT'S MIGHTY FINE TO BE JOINING AN OLD FRIEND ON STAGE LIKE THIS.
BUT BEING UP HERE WITH A NEW FRIEND WOULD BE EVEN BETTER! COME ON UP, CALAMITY!
YEAH! YEE-HAW! HOORAY!!!
AND A TIP OF THE HAT TO OUR PAL APPLEJACK FOR MAKING ALL THIS HAPPEN!
YES, INDEED!
YEEEEEHAAWW!
The End.

my LITTLE PONY

FRIENDS FOREVER

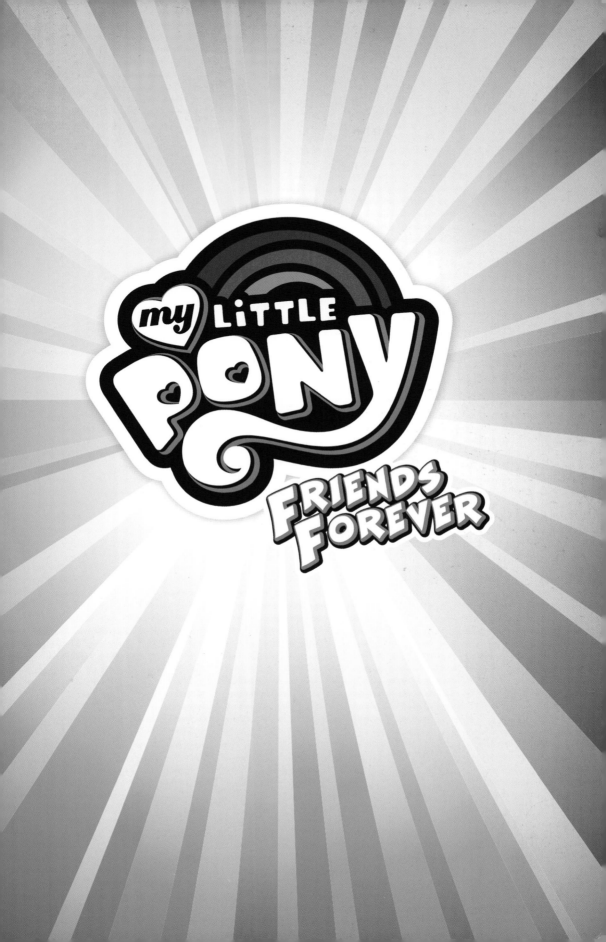

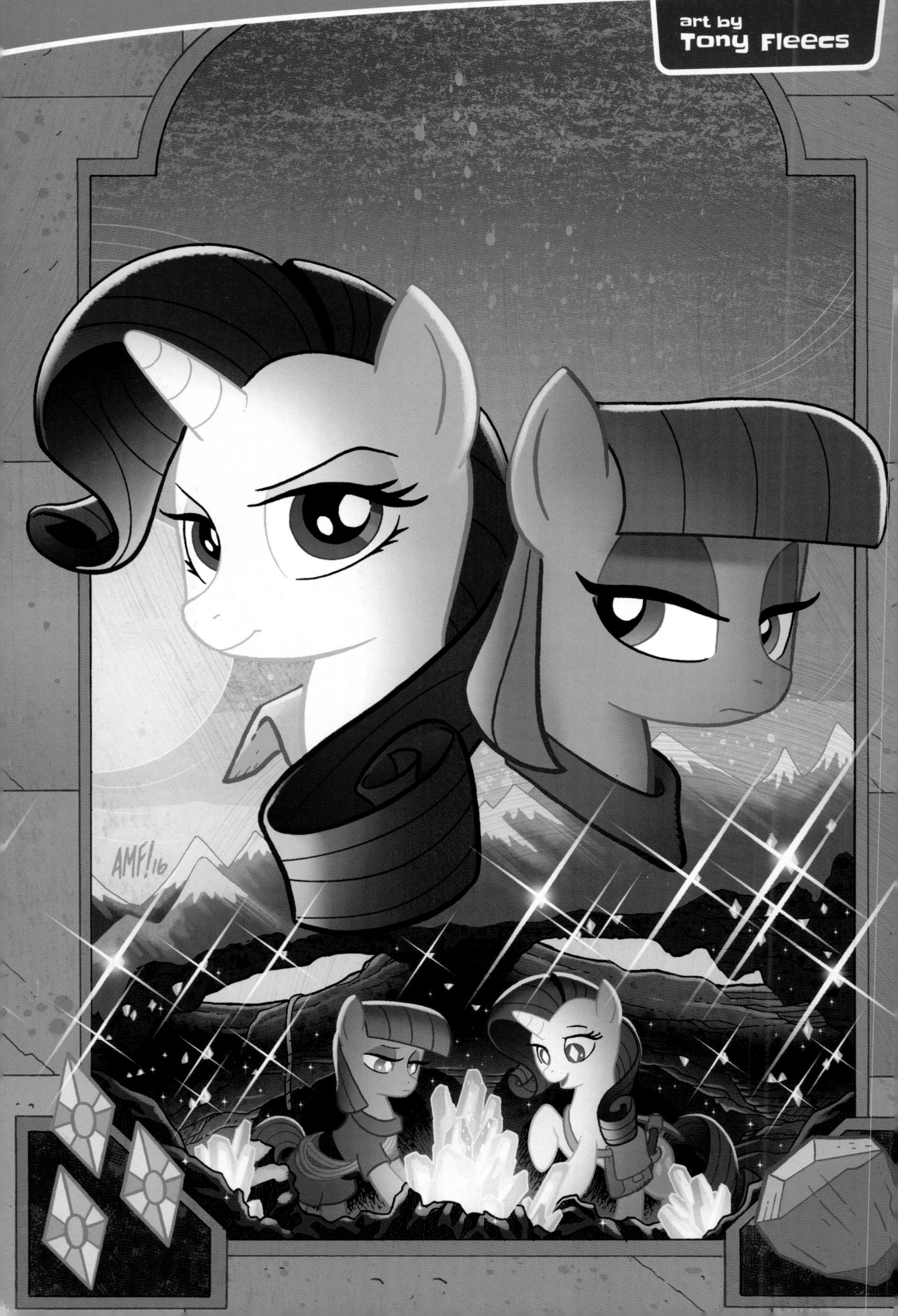

art by Tony Fleecs

art by
Tony Fleecs

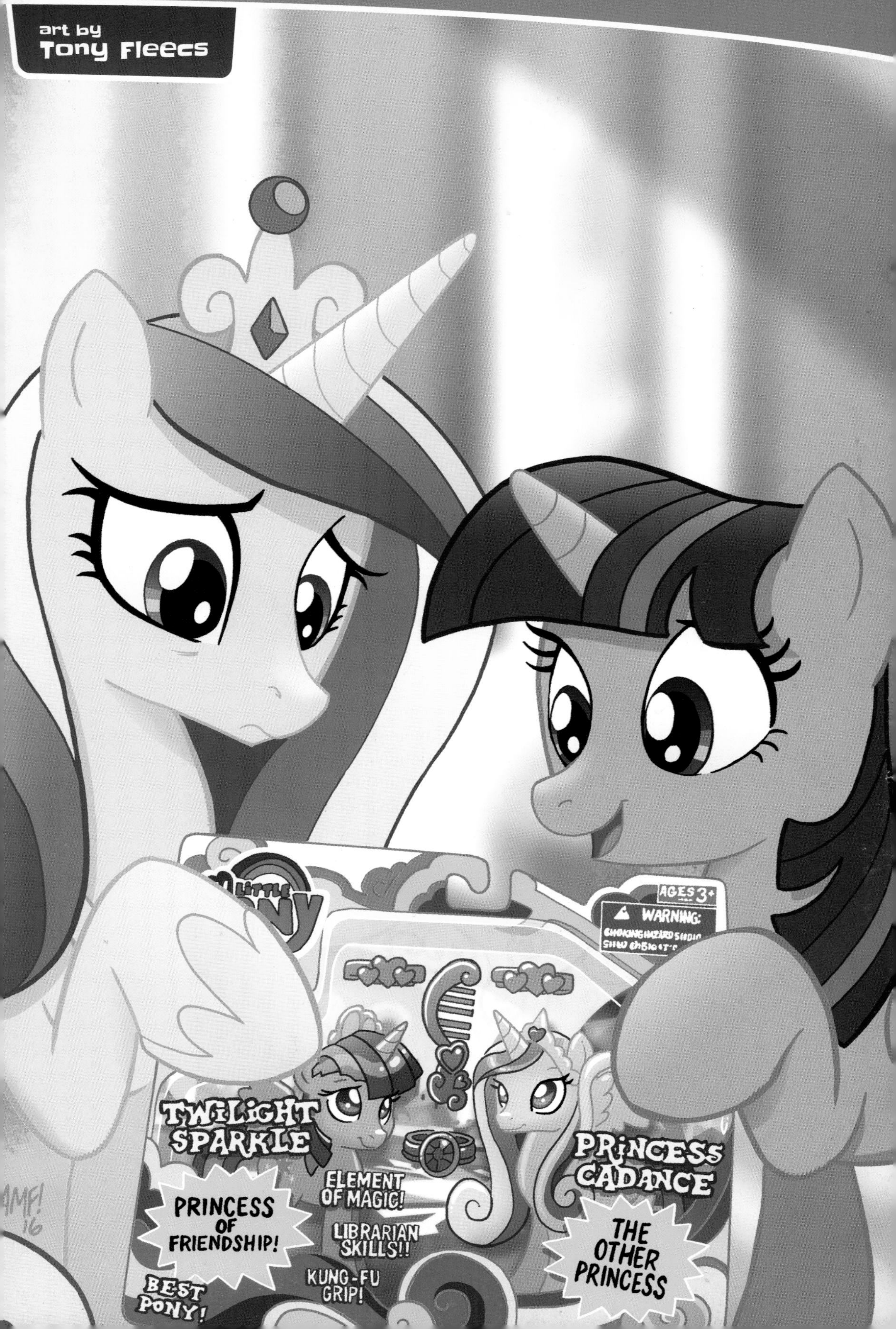
AGES 3+
WARNING:
TWILIGHT SPARKLE
PRINCESS OF FRIENDSHIP!
ELEMENT OF MAGIC!
LIBRARIAN SKILLS!!
KUNG-FU GRIP!
BEST PONY!
PRINCESS CADANCE
THE OTHER PRINCESS
AMF! 16

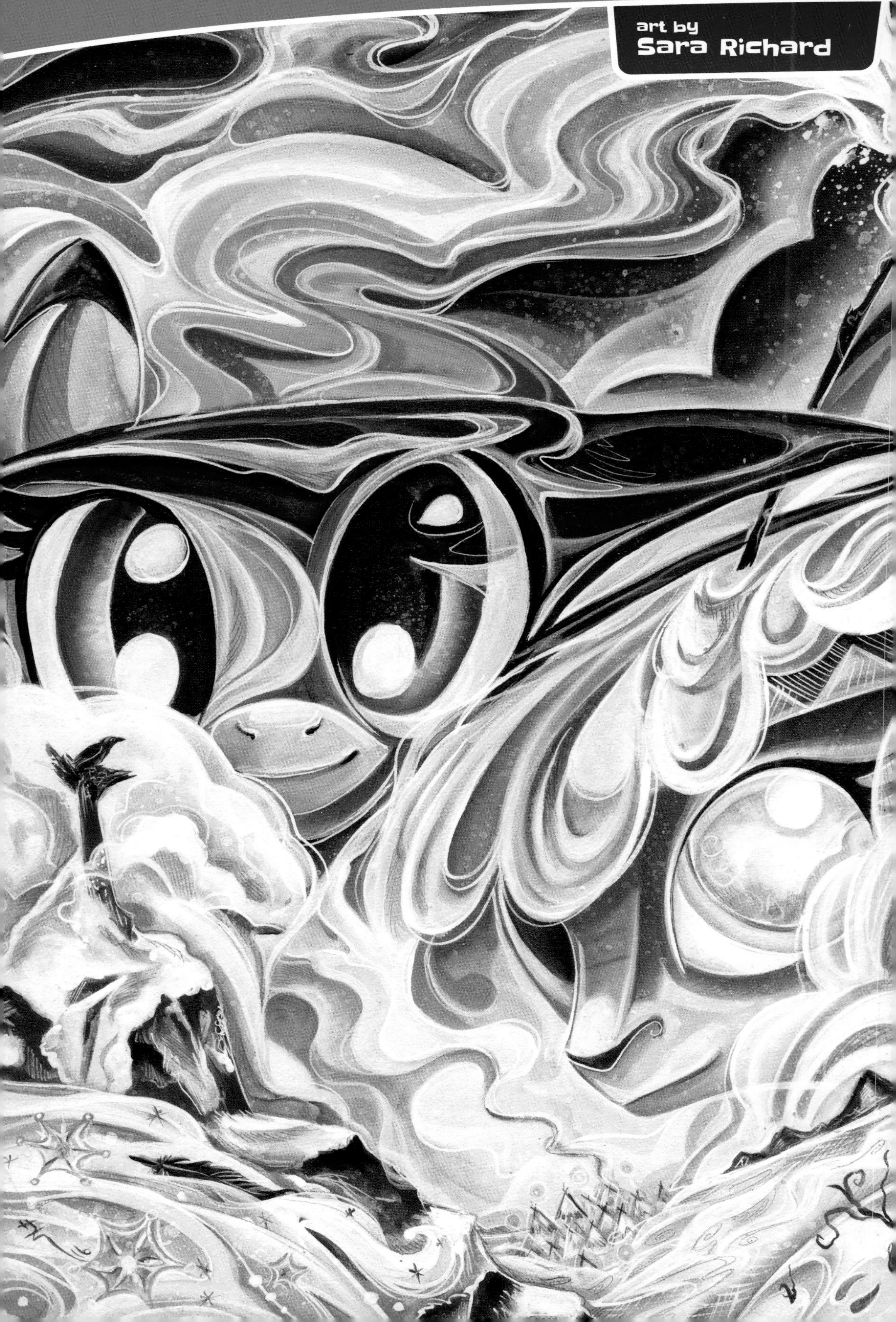
art by
Sara Richard

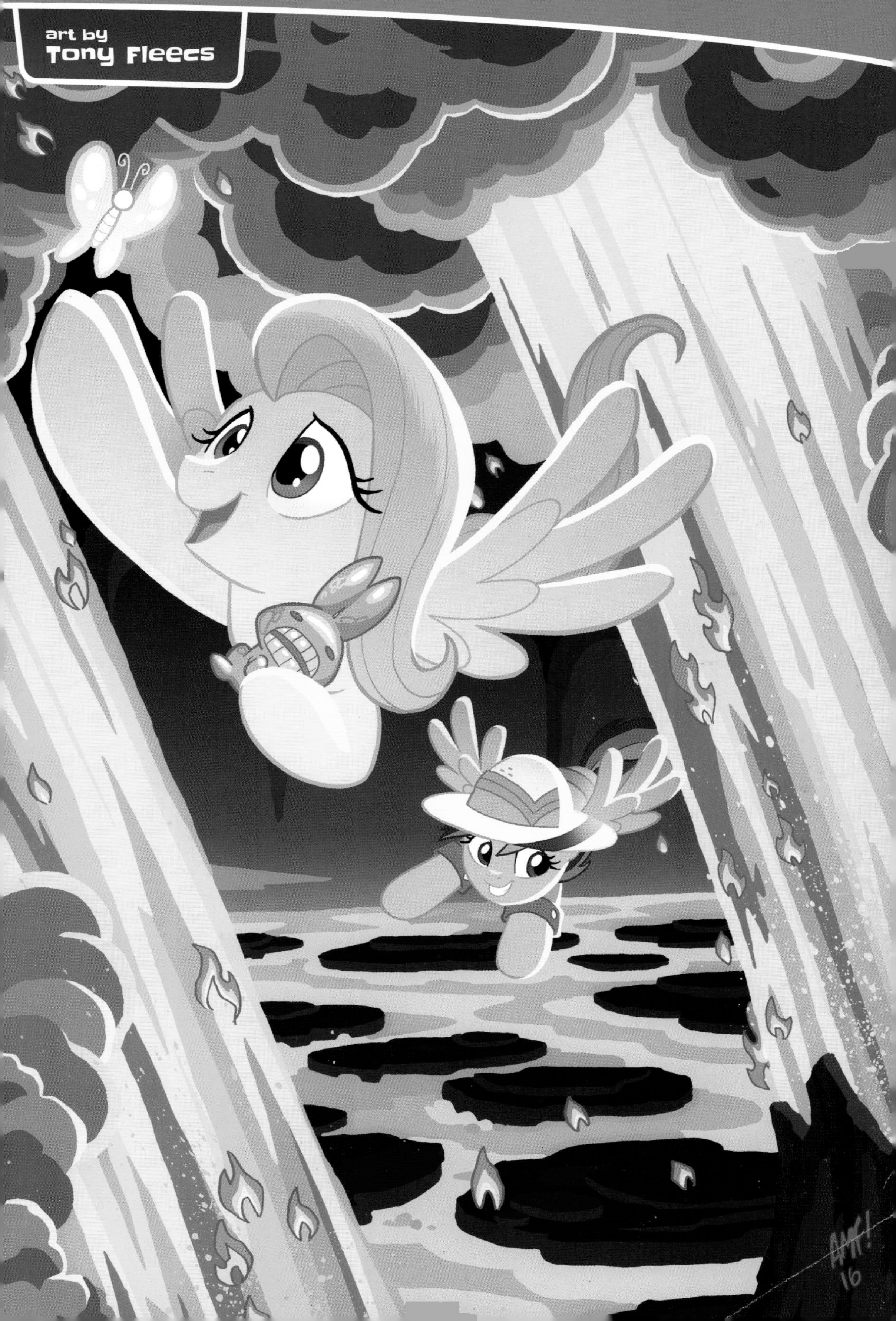
art by
Tony Fleecs

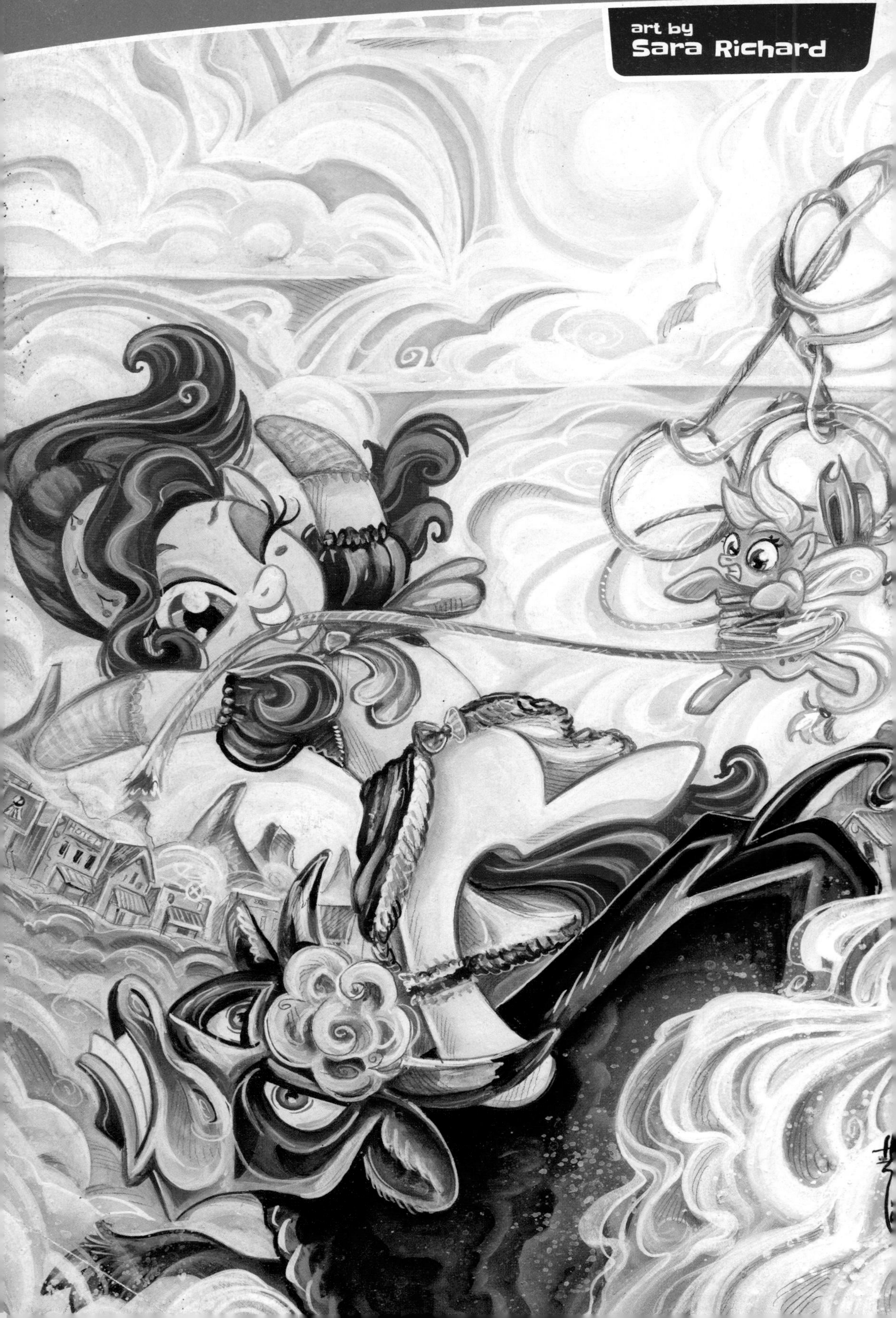

art by
Sara Richard